HIDDEN IN THE SHADOWS

Enjoy the read Jean Walker

JEAN WALKER

1

Previous titles by this author:

Shattered Web of Lies
Echoes of Tragedy
Fortunes of Fate
Devious Dream Weaver
Red Kite Valley
Secrets of the Past
Missing Presumed Dead

Web site: www.jeanwalkerauthor.com

All are available for purchase, either in paperback or Kindle format at www.amazon.co.uk

Cover photograph by courtesy of
LYNDA WILSON

Taken in the beautiful lanes of North
Wales around her home

Not only a seriously good photographer
but a very talented artist as well

Thank you for giving me permission to use
your photograph

CHAPTER 1

Hector Bannerman opened his eyes and looked up into the dazzlingly blue sky above him.

There wasn't a cloud to be seen and the sun was shining brightly – but it was cold – oh so cold! He couldn't understand why that should be when the sun seemed so strong. The sun meant warmth – so why did he feel so cold?

Now the sun was dimming. There was a haze coming over everything and it was beginning to go dark, but the darkness wasn't black. There seemed to be a red mist blurring everything. He blinked his eyes to clear them, and a glimmer of light began to filter through once more. He could see the sky again. It was still brilliantly blue!

He tried to raise his arm and clear away what was blurring them, but his arm wouldn't move – try as he might. He seemed to have no sort of control over it.

He blinked again, and this time he managed to gain a bit more vision, but once more the film came back to blur them, and he was powerless to clear it properly.

Then he seemed to be drifting – out of his body and onto another plane. He was looking down on himself, but it wasn't his normal self he was looking at, it was another being – another man – no, not a man – some sort of being – but definitely not of human form: it was just a mere memory of the man he once had been.

Then his eyes opened again and he found himself looking up at the clear blue sky once more, but this time he started shivering

4

and he couldn't stop. He was cold – oh, so cold – unbearably cold. It was like being in a 'fridge for hours on end and with no way of warming himself up. He had to get out of the 'fridge and get warm again; but no matter how hard he tried, he couldn't manage to move.

Something was running over his face and his vision cleared. He was looking up into the face of a man – a man holding a handkerchief and wiping his face – but the handkerchief wasn't white, it was red!

He tried to speak, but his mouth wouldn't form the words, and his brain wasn't functioning properly – he couldn't manage to make any sounds.

'You all right, mate?' the face above him said.

He looked up at it. It was the face of a middle aged man with a well tanned face; swimming in and out of focus as he spoke.

He tried to say 'no, he wasn't. Something was wrong,' but the words, although they formed in his mind, just wouldn't come out of his mouth, and all he could do was stare up into that face.

'He's not all right, can't you see that?' It was the panicked voice of a woman and it came from somewhere behind the man. 'I've rung for an ambulance, but heaven knows how long that'll take to come – we're so far from anywhere. Is there anything we can do for him?'

'Not unless you've got a magic wand!' the man answered. 'Neither of us has any medical knowledge, and I daren't try and remove his helmet. He's bleeding from somewhere underneath it. I might do more damage by trying to take it off. Best leave it until they arrive.'

Hector looked up at him as he wiped the liquid from his face once more and tried to say he was cold, but the sounds still wouldn't come out. All he could do was lie still and look up at him, hoping he'd guess what was wrong.

'He's shivering,' the woman finally said. 'Do we have a blanket in the car?'

'Don't think so, I've never noticed one.'

5

Hector heard the sound of her footsteps going away, but he didn't hear her return until he heard her voice again.

'No, we haven't got anything – not even a coat.'

His vision was becoming blurred once more, and the man leaned over to wipe his face again.

'Never mind,' the man said, 'I don't suppose the ambulance will be long. They'll take him inside and wrap him up when they get here.'

Hector looked pleadingly up at him, and a kind of lethargy began to creep over him. The cold had gone away. He couldn't feel himself shivering any more, and a strange serenity was stealing over him. The liquid had stopped running into his eyes, and he just felt the need for sleep. He was tired – oh so tired! He'd just close his eyes and sleep for a while; then when he woke up, everything would be all right again.

Darkness was stealing over him. He'd be all right after he'd had some sleep, and perhaps this odd feeling would have gone away by then. After that he'd be refreshed and ready to get back to life as it had been before, when he'd been cruising along on his motorbike in the last of the autumn sunshine and at peace with the world. Just a little bit of sleep was all he needed.

'I think I can hear the ambulance,' the woman's voice said, as she stood up and listened.

They were on a quiet country road, with open moorland all around and a large lake on the far side of the road, with more moorland and open hillsides beyond.

The man stood up and listened. He could hear the sound too but it was still some way off. Sound carried a long way in open countryside. It could still be a while before they got here.

He bent down to look at the man again, but this time his eyes were closed and he seemed to be completely unconscious. He felt helpless, but without any medical knowledge he was powerless to do anything. At least the bleeding from under his crash helmet seemed to have stopped. It was no longer running down into his eyes.

6

It was almost another five minutes before the ambulance reached them, and the two paramedics came over immediately, carrying all their equipment with them.

They bent over the man and shortly began to remove his helmet; one holding his head whilst the other bent to the task, kneeling on the grass behind him and easing it carefully away.

'Is he all right?' the car driver asked as the helmet came away.

The first paramedic was now holding the broken helmet in his hand and looked at his companion; a look of grave concern on his face, before he stood up.

'Would you like to take your wife back to the car and wait there for us – we'll come over and see you when we've finished,' was all he said.

Seeing the looks on their faces, and those that passed between them, he knew nothing was ever going to be right again for the man lying on the ground. He'd reached the end of the road!

'Is he dead?' he asked, looking from one to the other, but already knowing the question was superfluous.

'I'm afraid so,' the older man said. 'His head injuries are far too extensive for him to ever have had any chance of recovery! It looks like he hit the stone wall head on! Did you see what happened?'

The man nodded.

'The police will be here shortly so we'll wait for them and you can tell us all what happened,' the other paramedic said, beginning to pick up their kit and take it back to the ambulance.

His wife was already sitting in the passenger seat, the door open and her feet out on the ground alongside.

'He's dead, isn't he?' she said, her pale face looking up into his. Even as she asked the question, he could see that she already knew the answer.

All he could do was nod, before he turned away and was violently sick onto the verge. He'd caught a glimpse of the man's head when the helmet had been removed! It was a wonder he'd still been alive at all when they went over to him. It looked as if it was only his helmet that had been holding his skull together.

It was another ten minutes before a police car arrived, and the man's body had been covered over to hide it from passing eyes – of which there'd been only a few – but all slowing down to look at the smashed and mangled motorbike lying in the middle of the road. Luckily, his own car was partially hiding the covered body at the side of the road.

After a consultation with the ambulance crew, carried out in the back of the ambulance, one of the traffic officers came over to see the man and the woman, who were still sitting in the car, casting a casual glance at the body as they passed. Both were officers of many years standing, but both still found accidents as bad as this could sometimes leave them traumatised for weeks or even months afterwards. Even then, they haunted their thoughts for ever afterwards, often being called to mind at the least little provocation.

'Did you see what happened sir?'

Ralph Carlton nodded, his wife Theresa still sitting in the passenger seat and holding a handkerchief to her face.

'Can you tell us exactly what did happen?'

Ralph climbed out of the driver's seat and went towards the front of his vehicle where he indicated the crumpled right hand wing pushed in against the wheel, now seeing that the wheel was out of alignment and at an odd angle; something he hadn't noticed before.

'We'd been down to the lake at Trawsfynydd for the day, and we'd had a picnic there, as well as a walk around the lake. It was on the way home from there that this happened.

I spotted the bike coming towards us from some distance away, and he pulled to the centre of the road waiting to turn right. He did everything correctly, and his indicator was flashing. I wasn't quite sure whether he'd go across in front of us so I slowed down just in case – but he didn't, he was waiting for us to pass first.

My window was open, and I was only a short distance from him when I heard a car coming up from behind. I looked in my mirror and it didn't look as if it was going to stop. I was worried he was going to run into the back of me. Both of us were wearing seat belts, so I gritted my teeth and took my foot off the brake.

He suddenly seemed to realise that I'd slowed down and he was heading straight for me. At the last minute, he speeded up, pulling out to the centre of the road to try and pass on the opposite side. I don't think he'd noticed the motorbike waiting to turn right.

When he did see it, it was far too late. He hit it side on and the bike skittered across the road towards me. I couldn't stop in time and it hit my front wing. The driver was thrown up in the air and landed on my bonnet before he cartwheeled across the grass verge and went head on into the drystone wall. The rest is as you see it now. He's lying just where the paramedics found him, but he was still alive when I went over to him. Even then, it was obvious he was going to die. He was bleeding badly and his eyes weren't focusing.'

The second officer had joined his companion and was listening to what was being said before looking up and down the road.

'Can you give us any details of the vehicle? Make – model – registration number?'

Ralph looked at him for a moment or two, a look of concentration on his face before saying, 'Silver or grey – two lads in it. It all happened so fast. I didn't get the number. The car braked hard and slowed down further on. They seemed to be having some sort of argument between them, and then it suddenly drove off. All I could think of then was to get to the man and see what had happened to him.

He seemed to be trying to say something, but he couldn't get the words out. I wiped the blood out of his eyes, but I think it was only a few seconds after that that he died. His whole body went limp and his eyes just looked vacant.'

The officers noticed that Ralph looked as if he was about to collapse himself, and helped him back into the car, where he sat down heavily in the driver's seat once more; feet still resting on the ground, elbows on his knees as he put his head in his hands. He sat still and very quietly, contemplating what had just happened and feeling himself beginning to shake.

'Keep an eye on him while I go and speak to the ambulance crew,' the older officer said. 'I don't want him freaking out on us.'

The paramedics were sitting on the tailgate of the ambulance and waiting for further instructions when he reached them.

'I've radioed for scenes of crime to attend. Once they've photographed everything he'll be taken away and you'll be able to leave. Hopefully, it won't be too long. We don't want too many rubberneckers coming along and causing another accident. Luckily the road's been quiet so far.'

One of the crew moved over so that he could sit alongside, handing him a spare cup and pouring out some coffee for him.

'Bad business this,' one of them said, 'and a hit and run as well. Hope you manage to get the buggers soon.'

'We may get them on CCTV in the next village they come to, and if we're lucky, we'll get a registration number as well. The bike has a red stripe along the tank and it's been scraped off where it's been hit a glancing blow, so it'll probably still be there when we manage to find the car. That should tie them into the accident nicely.'

He wasn't hopeful of getting anything from one of the small villages around, but there may just be a pub or a garage with CCTV if they were lucky.

It was over an hour before a SOCO, or scenes of crime officers' team arrived – by which time the two officers had radioed for back up and the road had been closed to allow for forensic examination of the scene.

They found part of a front skirting from the hit and run vehicle in the centre of the road, and a good sized chunk of plastic alongside the motorbike, which seemed to have come from the front wing, as well as a broken off wing mirror.

It was while they were examining the wing of Ralph's own vehicle that one of them noticed he had a dash cam.

'Is that working?' he asked Ralph, indicating the camera.

Until then, Ralph had forgotten all about it!

'It should be,' he answered, 'but I haven't checked it just recently.'

Turning on the ignition, they both looked at the little camera, and sure enough, it was picking up activity from other officers moving around the scene.

'Good,' the SOCO officer said, 'we'll take that with us. That should tell us exactly what make and model the car is; and it might possibly give us a registration as well.'

'When can we go home?' Theresa piped up in a small and inconsequential voice.

'We'll let you know,' the man said, moving off to continue on with his work.

Ralph had almost forgotten her presence, so quiet had she been throughout the whole operation, and he suddenly noticed she was looking pale and distressed.

He left the car and went over to the Sergeant who'd arrived on the scene some time ago. He seemed to be taking charge of the whole operation and organising people around him.

With nothing to do but watch the comings and goings around him for the time being, the Sergeant was sympathetic as he glanced towards Theresa, still sitting and looking lost in the front of the car.

'Shouldn't be too long now,' he said. 'How long have you been here already?'

'Over two hours now,' Ralph answered.

'I'll check up with the SOCO's for you. Once they've finished, the body can be removed, and if they've finished with you and your car, you can be on your way too – but I'm afraid you're not going anywhere in that car,' he finished up, indicating the displaced wheel and the smashed bodywork. 'It's not driveable like that. Are you a member of a motoring organisation?'

Ralph nodded.

'Then I'm afraid you're going to have to rely on them to get you home, but I wouldn't ring them yet until you're told when you can go. They might be here very quickly if there's somebody in the area – but then again, if they're busy, you could wait hours.'

Depressed now, Ralph returned to the car, wondering just how much longer they were going to be here.

'Any food left over?' he quizzed his wife. 'They've no idea how much longer we're going to be here. It could be a long time and I'm already hungry.'

'Only that half a bar of fruit and nut chocolate – that's all that's left – you'll have to make do with that.'

It wasn't much, but it was better than nothing. If they'd been in their own car, they could have stopped for a bite to eat on the way home, but if they were being taken home, they'd have to wait until they got there – and who knew how long that might be!

Another hour later and the SOCO team began to pack up.

'We've got all we can,' their leader told the Sergeant. 'I don't think there's anything left to find. You can get everything cleared up now and reopen the road.   We're just going to have the body taken to the morgue for post mortem, and by the way, we've removed all this stuff from the dead man. I think this is yours to follow up on.'

The Sergeant took the bag he was handed and looked at the small amount of possessions they'd removed.

It didn't look very much to show for a man's life, as he glanced inside – noticing the driving licence sitting on top of everything. He whistled when he saw it.

I know you, he thought! I've seen you often enough during my time on the police force.

It wasn't just the name he recognised, but the photograph as well. It was the face of a Crown Court judge – Judge Hector Bannerman! A man he'd appeared in front of many times before to give evidence: usually a just and fair man who could be relied upon to hand down the right sentence for the severity of the crime.

He'd be sorely missed by those who'd appeared as Counsel in his Court!

That morning, Hector Bannerman had woken at his usual time of 7.30 and gone down to make himself a cup of tea, before taking it back to bed with the morning paper which always arrived shortly before he awoke.

He'd always breakfasted with his wife, Felicia, during all the years they'd been married, but sadly she'd died a few years previously, and he was now all alone in the house except for the staff, some of whom lived in.

Gavin Davis and his son, Morgan attended to the garden and the grounds, including the extensive area of woodland behind the cottage they rented from Hector; Cyril Swaine to all the odd jobs that needed doing, seeming able to turn his hand to anything, bringing in local contractors if something more qualified needed attention; and last, but not least was his housekeeper cum cook, Isabelle, ably aided by her cousin Sandra, who came in from the village on a daily basis.

The staff had been with them for many years, even when his wife was still alive, although she was the one who'd mainly seen to the cooking in those days, relying on Isabelle for her help in the preparation, ordering of groceries, serving food at table, and seeing to the dishes afterwards.

Since she'd died, Isabelle had taken over the kitchen duties and preparation of the meals entirely by herself; the rest of house being kept clean and tidy by her cousin Sandra, together with another young girl who came in from the village two or three times a week to help out. She'd even cajoled him into buying a dishwasher to make her job easier, and seeing as she was managing in the kitchen all by herself now, he'd acceded to her wishes, but he had no idea how the thing worked. That was solely her domain.

Isabelle lived in and was always down in the kitchen by 8.00a.m., her arrival heralded by the loud and joyous barking of Henry, his Springer Spaniel. She'd let him out into the garden for his morning constitutional, and when he arrived back, there was always a tasty morsel of bacon or sausage awaiting his return.

Hector would then haul himself out of bed, wash and dress, before going down to the dining room where his breakfast was always ready for him at 9a.m.

The day was his after that.

Having retired shortly before his wife passed on, most of the morning ritual was taken up with finishing his paper before he and Henry took a long tramp through the woods, or over the surrounding moorland, arriving back just in time for lunch. Afterwards he enjoyed a short nap, followed by another late, and much shorter, afternoon walk with the dog. It was an ordered existence, and one which he'd become familiar with since his retirement; and one which he enjoyed immensely.

Felicia herself had led her own life, together with their daughter Jayne, and the couple often took themselves off into town on shopping trips. Both of them had their own friends as well, and all the household seemed to revolve around each others' comings and goings harmoniously enough.

His eldest son, David, had also shown an interest in the law, and was now an up and coming young barrister in his own right, or so he'd heard He was beginning to make a name for himself, as had Hector in his younger days.

The year before Felicia's death, David and his father had had a terrible row, the sounds of which could be heard all over the house, and for sometime afterwards the staff had stepped on eggshells when in the main part of the house as they tried to keep out of his way. David had packed up all his belongings and left the day after.

Felicia knew nothing of the reason behind it, and even though Jayne seemed to know what it might have been about, she denied any knowledge. Hector never made any attempt to contact him again, and nor had David been in touch with any of them since, as far as he was aware. He had no idea whether David was even aware of his mother's death or not. If he was, he never returned to his childhood home, not even for the funeral.

Hector had always been very protective of his young daughter Jayne, almost to the point of obsession, and after her mothers' death, things got even worse. He always vetted her friends, and always controlled where she went, and what time she had to be home after an outing.

Shortly after that, Hector had informed the staff that he was having extensive alterations done, and gave the whole staff some time off while it was carried out. When they arrived back, Jayne was gone and there was no explanation forthcoming from Hector concerning her sudden departure. They though she might have gone to live with David, but Hector never spoke to any of them about her sudden disappearance.

It was just after this that Hector had purchased the motorbike, having enjoyed riding around the countryside on one when he was younger. He'd bought it on a whim, and had to get used to riding it once again, but found that once he did, he enjoyed it immensely.

Today, with the slight nip of autumn in the air, he'd decided to take a trip out on it. It would make a nice change, and then it could be mothballed until the following spring, when he could enjoy the delights of the open road and the wind whipping into his face once more.

He had no idea when he left the house that morning that he would never be returning to it again!

15

CHAPTER 2

'Anyone seen Richards and Pryce?' Sergeant Jack Horner said, opening the canteen door and looking around, finding they weren't anywhere in sight.

'Out on patrol, Sarge,' one or two voices called back to him.

'Thanks,' he said, as he closed the door and strode back to his office. They'd only just come on duty and he already had a full schedule for them to complete: one that would probably fill up their entire shift.

Radioing from the confines of his small office, he finally managed to contact Robbie Richards.

'Is Pryce with you?' he asked.

'Yes, Sarge, just been answering a call of nature.'

'Are you doing anything at the moment?' he asked, trying to hide his distaste.

'No, it's been quiet out on the streets today. There's nothing come in for us at the moment. We're just cruising round and waiting for something to happen.'

'Yes; well I have something for you now. We have some next of kin for that hit and run near Llyn Celyn. I need you to see as many of them as you can, and give them the news before you clock off. Where are you now?'

'We're just outside Denbigh at the moment; on the A543.'

'Good; then you can make a start on it straight away. The first two live not far from Bodfari,' and he rattled off the addresses. 'They're his daughters, and when you've finished those, there's another five immediate relatives that have to be told as well.

Seems he's been a busy boy, has our judge. He had seven offspring that we've managed to find so far, but his wife died several years ago, so you don't have to face telling her as well. It'll probably take you all shift to get through that lot. Radio in when you've finished and I'll give you the rest of the names and addresses.'

Robbie shuddered. Bodfari wasn't that far away from where they were now, even though they weren't exactly where he'd said they were, but he didn't relish the task in front of them. Having to impart the news to one person was bad enough; but having to do it seven times over was even more distasteful, and he realised they probably wouldn't be able to complete the task in just the one shift either. Hopefully, some of it would be passed on to the next patrol coming on duty – otherwise it would be handed back to them the following day.

It all depended on whether something more urgent came in in the meantime.

Just at that moment, his colleague, Steve Pryce, arrived back at the car and opened the passenger door, the aroma of hot pies wafting in with him. They were parked in a bus stop, and although he knew nobody would question their parking there, they weren't on any official business, and they weren't that far away from the police station either. It would be just his luck for an Inspector, or one of the higher ups, to see them parked there and stop to question why.

'Let's get out of here,' he said, as soon as Steve shut the door, 'we've got a job to go to.'

Steve looked suitably unimpressed.

'Does that mean we don't get to eat these?' he said anxiously, sniffing in the delicious aroma.'

'Na! We'll get out of town and eat them on the way. It's only near Bodfari, so we'll find a quiet little lay-by or a pull-in and eat them there. It's not that urgent!'

Within a short time, they'd found somewhere quiet and off the beaten track to demolish the pies, arriving at their destination within another quarter of an hour afterwards.

'This is the place,' Robbie said, as the slowed in the quiet country road and looked for somewhere to park. It was only a narrow road, with grass verges bordering unclipped hawthorn hedges on either side, leaving just enough room for two vehicles to pass each other safely.

The white rendered cottage they were looking for was sideways on to the road, its gable end in line with the drystone walls bordering its roadside boundaries. L-shaped, it contained a rough patch of grass out front in the angle of the L, and the front door, standing near the centre, was accessed by a paved path right across its middle.

'Where we gonna' park?' Steve asked his companion. 'Even if we pull onto the verge, we'll still be in the way if a tractor or any other big vehicle comes along. It's too narrow to get right off the road.'

Robbie looked further down the road, where there seemed to be an opening in the wall.

'Looks like there might be a driveway further down,' he answered, as he drove slowly towards it.

Sure enough, the driveway did seem to belong to the house, but when they reached it, there was no room for them to pull fully inside. It was just hard-packed earth; at the far end of which was a fairly new looking four wheel drive, and behind it sat a battered old Toyota pick-up with a trailer attached. The trailer was piled high with chunks of wood, as was the rear of the pick-up, and alongside the driveway was a long storage shed, open-fronted and piled high with more pre-cut logs. From inside an enclosed area at the far end could be heard the incessant buzz of a heavy table saw.

On the back of the trailer was an advertisement for a 'TREE SURGEON', giving both home and mobile numbers.

'Best of both worlds, eh?' Robbie commented.

Steve looked at him, unsure of what he meant.

'Charge 'em for cutting down their trees – and then charge others to flog them the logs afterwards,' Robbie explained; a grin on his face.

Steve returned his grin when he realised what Robbie meant, and quipped back, 'Waste not, want not!'

'Anyway, he sounds like a busy boy for the moment,' Robbie continued, 'so we'll just pull in behind the trailer and hope he doesn't want to go out before we've finished carrying out our first unpleasant duty. I presume he won't want to anyway after we've given his wife the news. He'll probably want to stay with her for the rest of the day. She'll most likely be upset.'

Remembering the task they now had to perform sobered their thoughts and brought them back to earth again. Neither of them relished the task they were about to perform, as Robbie parked behind the trailer and they made their way to the front door, trying to look suitably sober as they rang the bell.

Paula Lewis was just about to mop her kitchen floor when the front door bell jangled loudly, followed immediately afterwards by the wild barking of her eighteen month old Labrador, Rooney.

She'd shut him out in the garden while she washed the floor, using their old baby gate to stop him coming in from outside. It had always been effective in the past when she needed to leave the door open on warm summer days. Today wasn't quite so warm, but the floor always dried quicker if the door was left open.

Running wildly round the garden and barking frantically at the sound of the bell, he suddenly took a run at the gate and knocked it flat, slipping on the tiled floor as he jumped over it and careering on into the bucket. It tilted for a moment, slopping water over the edge, and then, as he charged on past, it tipped over onto its side, emptying its entire contents of hot soapy water right across the kitchen floor.

Paula jumped back out of the way – but she wasn't quick enough – and found herself standing in a pool of water, which had splashed against her legs as well. Her slippers were soaked and so was the bottom part of her jeans – almost up to her knees.

Annoyed at the unwarranted intrusion, which had caused so much mayhem, she slopped her way to the door, her feet squelching in the sodden slippers, and gripped Fergus's collar tightly as she opened it. Although all he wanted to do was greet the newcomers enthusiastically, she knew, once the greeting was over, he'd be off up the lane and it would take hours to find him again.

He'd never shown any predilection to chase sheep, but there were all too many of them around the area, and who knows what he'd do once out on his own and with no authoritative voice to guide him if the frightened sheep started running from him.

She was astonished when she saw two police officers standing on her doorstep.

'Mrs. Paula Lewis?' the older one queried.

'Yes,' she said, nodding, while the other officer bent down to fondle the dog. It wasn't so much that he liked dogs, but as more of an attempt to stop him jumping up at him when he saw how wet the animal was.

'Can we come in for a moment?' the first one was now saying.

All Paula could think of was her son, Aaran. Had he been up to something? He'd been caught once before for taking a car without the owner's permission, but as it was somebody local who'd decided not to press charges, he'd been let off with a caution – and it **was** after 2a.m. this morning before he'd come home! Worried about his safety, she hadn't managed any sleep until she heard him come in and go straight up to his room.

'Let me put the dog away first,' she answered, leading Rooney firmly from the house and over to a sturdy pen alongside the wood store, where she pushed him roughly inside and shot the bolt home on the door. As she walked back to the house, his sad little face peered through the bars at them, his tail slowing now as he realised he wasn't going to be let out again before the visitors had gone.

'Come inside,' Paula instructed the two officers as she kicked off her slippers and preceded them towards the living room – her wet feet leaving footprints on the slate floor.

They glanced at each other as they followed, wondering how the slippers had become so wet; but they weren't about to ask.

She stopped by the fireplace and waited for them to drop the bombshell of Aaran having been arrested, but instead she was surprised at the news they began to impart.

'It's about your father, Hector Bannerman,' Robbie began. 'I'm afraid we have some rather bad news for you. Your father was involved in a motorbike accident earlier today, and was badly injured. I'm afraid he has since died from the injuries he received.'

She looked from one to the other without saying a word.

'Would you like to sit down for a moment?' Robbie asked, thinking she was suffering from shock, as Steve asked, 'Would you like me to make you some tea?'

She did look to be in shock, but her next words weren't what either of them had expected to hear.

'My father?' she said. 'I think you've made some sort of mistake. My father isn't Hector Bannerman. My father was called Roger Baines, and he died years ago, when I was only 12. I was in the car with my parents when we were in a crash. A fence post broke off and went right through my fathers' chest. Mum and I were okay, but my father died instantly. I've never even heard of this Hector person you mention.'

This time it was the turn of the two police officers to look shocked.

Robbie was the first to recover his senses.

'I'm so sorry,' he apologised. 'There seems to have been some sort of mistake. We'll get out of your way and let you get on. I'm so sorry for the mix-up.'

This time she smiled, the shock seeming to wear off – but it wasn't really shock – it was relief on hearing that her son hadn't been involved in any sort of trouble.

She showed them to the door and watched as they climbed back into their car, her husband appearing from the woodshed just as they were about to drive off.

'Not Aaran again?' he said, a mixture of anger and disbelief registering on his face.

'No, not this time,' she answered. 'I'll tell you about it when you come inside for lunch.'

'I'm already in,' he answered. 'I've got those two lots of logs to deliver this afternoon – both of them the other side of Denbigh, so I want to make an early start. If you've not got anything made, I'll make do with a sandwich for the time being.'

It was then that she remembered the kitchen floor. It would still be swimming in water, and she'd need to clean all that up before she could even make a start on lunch.

'Oh dear,' she sighed, and told him all that had happened.

'Never mind,' he said. 'You clean it up and I'll go down to the garage and pick up some sandwiches. Should only take me a short while, and you can put the kettle on while you're clearing up – then we'll have a brew to go with them.'

His old motorbike was propped up just the other side of the wood store, and not being able to take either vehicle, he used that instead. As Paula heard it start up, it brought to mind what the two police officers had told her, and she shuddered when she thought of her husband. Even though he was only going to the garage less than half a mile away, he hadn't bothered to don his leathers or his motorcycle boots, and the thought of that poor man who'd been killed on his own motorbike brought to mind how quickly life could come to such a sudden and tragic end.

Robbie and Steve drove well away from the house, before they stopped and reviewed the situation.

'Well, that was embarrassing,' Steve commented. 'How come they've got it so wrong?'

22

Robbie thought for a moment.

'I've no idea,' he said, 'but let's carry on to the next one. It's at the far end of the village, and there should be no problem with parking. I know the place. I attended a burglary there about three months ago, and it's a fairly new bungalow with plenty of parking space at the front.

They reached the house within ten minutes, just in time to find the couple returning from a shopping trip.

As the woman had just gone inside the house, Robbie decided to speak to her husband first and ask him to continue unloading the car while they spoke to his wife.

'We have to impart some rather delicate news, so perhaps you'd finish unloading the shopping and lock the car before you come and join us,' turning on his heel and indicating for Steve to follow him inside.

Perhaps it was his rather quiet and sombre tone that made the husband continue without further question, but he did as he was asked and unloaded the rest of the bags before following them.

His wife was just coming back out of the kitchen as the two officers stepped into the hallway, and she stopped and stared at them.

'What's this about?' she asked, as she saw her husband following them in.

'Go into the living room, Fliss,' her husband said, 'and I'll finish seeing to this lot, then I'll join you.'

'Please sit down,' Robbie said as she went into the room and stood watching them warily. He seemed to be falling into the all too familiar routine of imparting bad news, and it never sat well on his shoulders. He'd had to repeat these words so many times before, but it never got any easier.

'I'll stand if you don't mind,' she said, her face registering surprise and something akin to fear.

Suddenly she seemed to come out of her lethargy and spoke rapidly, wanting to know the news without waiting any longer.

'Is it one of the boys? Has one of them had an accident?'

'No, it's not a boy. Are you Felicity Bryant, and is your father Hector Bannerman?'

'Yes, I'm Felicity Bryant,' she said, 'but I've never heard of a Hector Bannerman. He's not my father.'

She looked firstly at them, and secondly at her husband, who'd now entered the room and was standing immediately behind them

'I'm sorry,' he said, taking the matter out of her hands, 'but I think you've definitely got the wrong person here. Fliss's father is Peter Danson, and he's in a nursing home suffering from dementia. We've been to visit him this afternoon and it's only just over an hour ago that we left him to do some shopping on the way home.'

Robbie turned back to Fliss, where she'd sat down in a chair by the fireside.

'I thought it was one of the boys!' was all she could gasp out. 'You gave me such a fright when I saw two policemen standing in front of me! I thought something had happened to one of them!'

Robbie and Steve looked at each other, not knowing quite what to say. This was another duff piece of information they'd been handed down.

Apologies over, they returned to the car, and Robbie was really annoyed.

'I'm not going to any more of these addresses before we've spoken to control. I don't know where they've got their information from, but it all seems to be an almighty cock-up, and I've no intention of upsetting anyone else until we've got this all cleared up.'

Steve, in the meantime, had picked up the piece of paper with the addresses they'd just been given and now pointed to the next two names on the list.

'I don't think they've got it all wrong,' he said. 'This next one seems to be right. His name is David Bannerman, and he's got the same surname as the dead man. It's not a very common name, so this one's probably correct, and so's the next one. Her name is Jayne Bannerman and her address is the same as the dead man's.'

24

Robbie took the paper from him and looked carefully at it.

'Maybe those two might be correct, but the one after that is another male; and his surname is Cockcroft. A woman changing her name after marriage I can understand . . . but a man? That looks like another wrong 'un to me.'

'Okay, I accept that, but I think we should go and visit the two named Bannerman. I think they're probably cosher.'

'Okay, let's give those two a go, but I'm not going to the last one until it's been checked out properly. I'm not upsetting anybody else today just because somebody hasn't checked out their information properly.'

David Bannerman's address wasn't close, and it took them a good half hour to locate it; situated as it was on the other side of Denbigh, and off a quiet country road. It was reached up a small track, the nameplate LITTLE BANNERMAN displayed on either side of the opening and facing traffic whichever way it was approached. It was an unassuming two storey house rendered in white limewash but there was plenty of parking space outside the front entrance, occupied by just two other vehicles at present.

Their ring on the ancient bell pull was answered by a woman somewhere in her mid to late thirties, whom they took to be his wife.

'Is Mr. Bannerman in?' Robbie asked politely, taking off his cap.

If he was the son of a judge, which seemed highly likely, he did feel that a more deferential attitude might be in order, indicating with a nod of the head for Steve to do the same.

'Wait here,' she said, closing the door to as they heard her footsteps receding.

After a few minutes, the woman returned and ushered them inside.

'Mr. Bannerman is in his study. He can spare you a few minutes, but not much longer. He has to leave for Court very soon. Please come this way.'

Definitely not his wife then – more like some sort of servant!

David Bannerman was sitting behind his desk when they entered, in a very plush and well padded brown leather chair, papers strewn across the desk in front of him. There were two ordinary straight backed chairs on the opposite side of the desk, but he didn't offer them a seat.

'What can I do for you gentlemen?' he asked, not getting up and leaving them standing.

Steve had decided to play it carefully this time, just in case they'd got it wrong again, and he started the conversation by saying, 'Do you know a Hector Bannerman, sir?'

This time the man had begun to take more notice, putting down his pen and looking upwards with more interest now.

'Yes, I do. He's my father. Has something happened to him?'

'Is he **Judge** Hector Bannerman, and does he own a motorcycle?'

'He is a judge, yes,' he answered, 'but as for the motorcycle, I've no idea about that. My father and I don't see eye to eye and I haven't seen him for some years now. I know he used to ride a motorcycle when he was younger, but I've no idea if he has one now.'

Robbie looked across at Steve. At least this contact was genuine.

'Then I'm sorry to have to inform you sir that your father has been involved in a motorcycle accident, and I'm afraid he's passed away as a result of it. I'm so sorry for your loss.'

David Bannerman stared at him in silence for a moment without a flicker of emotion, before standing up.

'Thank you for letting me know,' he said, 'my housekeeper will see you out,' and with that he walked across to the door and opened it, calling out into the passageway, 'Anna, will you see these gentlemen out please.'

'Just one more thing, sir,' Steve said, as the woman materialised as if from nowhere, 'we believe you have a sister named Jayne, and she is still living with your father at Bannerman's. Is that correct, sir?'

The man's face showed some sort of change – a slight emotion at the mention of his sister.

'She was the last time I saw her, but I don't think she knows where I am. I'll make the effort to contact her now though.'

'And are there just the two of you? Your father doesn't have any more descendents, or close relatives, does he?'

'I did have three brothers, but they all died in childhood many years ago. My father had two brothers, but we've never been a close family and I haven't seen either of them in years. I don't think I'd even recognise either of them if I saw them again. One went abroad – Australia I think, but I can't swear to that. I don't remember him mentioning them for years, and there were certainly few visits or get-togethers with the other brother that I'm aware of. I'm afraid I can't be of any more help there.'

As he spoke, he began to withdraw into the room with a nod towards Anna.

'This way, gentlemen,' she said, taking over from her employer, as she ushered them to the front door, shutting it immediately behind them. She hadn't been able to hear any of the conversation but was anxious to know what they'd wanted. It must have been something serious to bring them all the way out here, but when she turned back, David had gone back into his study and the door was firmly closed.

'Well, he's a cold fish,' Steve said, whistling between his teeth as they walked back to the car. 'I don't think he could have cared less about his father being dead.'

Robbie merely shrugged his shoulders.

'It takes all sorts,' he said. 'Now we have to inform his sister. I wonder if we'll get the same reception there! By the way, did you notice he's a barrister as well? There's a brass plate alongside the bell pull with his name, and the words 'Barrister at Law' beneath.'

'Can't say I did,' his companion replied as they climbed into the car. 'It runs in the family then. Bet the old man was only too glad to finance that if his son showed some interest in following in his footsteps.'

'Maybe – maybe not – but the son certainly doesn't seem too grateful towards him with the attitude he's displayed at the news of his fathers' death.'

With that they turned the car around and drove away, ready now to find his sister and impart the news to her. This time their journey wouldn't take too long, but the return journey back to their home patch would. The judge's home, where they'd been told they'd find his daughter, was way out on the wild and windswept Denbigh Moors!

'Wow, this place is bleak!' Steve said as they drove out onto the moors. It was the first time he'd been out here, and it baffled him why anybody should want to live so far away from civilisation.

'It looks quite colourful here at the end of the summer, but I bet it's a bleak place to live in the middle of winter! I remember coming out here for a picnic on the shores of Llyn Brenig with my mum and dad when my brothers and I were little, and that was on a beautiful hot summers' day, but I've never been here since,' Robbie commented.

It took them some time to reach the small hamlet of houses and farms that constituted all that there was of a settlement on the edge of the moors – its one and only shop, situated right in the centre and acting as both shop and home, had once been a small barn connected to the main house.

Driving into the yard, Robbie stopped alongside the door.

'Let's get some directions from here,' he said, as they climbed out and looked around. 'It's supposed to be not too far from here, and we can get something to eat as well. I'm starving!'

There were no customers when they entered the shop, and only a young girl sitting behind the counter, her eyes glued to a mobile 'phone.

She seemed astonished to see a police officer enter the shop. Perhaps there weren't many crimes committed in such a rural area and seeing anyone appear in police uniform was quite a rarity.

'Mam,' she called loudly, seeming to appear unnerved by their presence.

A few seconds later a woman appeared from the back, wiping her hands on a tea towel, a smile spreading across her face as she saw them.

Okay, cariad, (sweetheart)' she said, and stepped to one side so that the young girl could go through to the back.

'Pnawn da, (good afternoon),' she greeted as she replaced her daughter at the counter.

'Sorry, we don't speak Welsh,' Robbie said, seeming mildly embarrassed. 'Neither of us is Welsh by birth, and neither of us speaks anything but a smattering of your language, so could we continue in English please, but prynhawn da i chi, (good afternoon to you) and that's about my limit.'

She smiled, pleased with the effort he'd tried to make, even though it wasn't well pronounced.

'Wha' can I do for yew today?' she asked, as Steve made directly for the chiller cabinet.

'We're here for some food and directions to Bannerman's if you know where it is.'

'Oh yes,' she answered, 'follow down ye're until you come to the next turnoff on yew're left. Yew'll find Bannerman's right at the end – yew can't miss it – it's the only place down there and road stops at its gate.'

'Thanks,' he said, just as Steve returned to the counter, carrying a couple of pies, together with some jam tarts.

'This do?' he asked, waving them in front of Robbie.

'That'll do me fine,' he observed, turning back to the woman who was entering their purchases into the till, as he handed over a £10 note.

'Diolch yn fawr, (thanks very much)' he said, as she passed back the change, what little there was of it, another smile spreading over her face on hearing his efforts once again.

'Are you sure this is the right place?' Steve asked, as Robbie drove down the lane. 'It doesn't look right to me. There's nothing here, and I don't see a house.'

To their left, empty farmers' fields stretched up a hillside, which was topped with stunted trees, but on their right, and also stretching out straight ahead of them, was open barren moorland for as far as the eye could see.

To their right, it sloped steeply down into a valley; another hillside rising steeply upwards on the opposite side, giving them no view beyond its summit, except of burgeoning rain filled clouds, rapidly taking the place of the blue skies that had surrounded them all day so far.

Robbie stopped right at the end of the road and they both looked around, in awe of the enormity of the barren moorland surrounding them, and stretching away towards the hazy blue and purple hills in the far distance.

'That must be it,' Robbie said, pointing to a pair of stone gateposts on their left, almost completely covered in ivy. Leaning drunkenly at an angle was a small wooden sign, less than a metre high, bearing the name 'Bannerman's', and almost completely hidden by the uncut hawthorn branches growing around it.

'Don't seem to want to encourage visitors, do they?' Steve commented as they drove in. 'It'd be a surprise if anybody ever found this place.'

The compacted earth track eventually rounded the side of the hill, and there stood Bannerman's; a circular rose bed set in the middle of a gravelled parking area – a large stone edifice in the shape of a shell standing right in the middle.

The house itself was built of stone and rose three storeys high, weathered ancient trees standing to its rear, and its other sides all facing out across the wild landscape. It looked very imposing standing all alone and dominating the view.

'Heathcliffe, Heathcliffe, wherefore art thou Heathcliffe?' Robbie quipped as Steve sat staring in awe.

'Who? What are you talking about?' he said, coming back to earth and turning to look at him.

'Never read Wuthering Heights?' Robbie commented.

Steve sat looking at him, before shaking his head.

'It's a classic, written by Emily Bronte. Didn't you even see the film?'

Steve, not wanting to appear ignorant, climbed out of the car, trying to break the invisible barrier which had suddenly grown between them. He'd never been one for book learning; playing truant from school with his mates more often than he'd spent time attending his lessons. His parents had never seemed to care very much where he was. He was one of seven children; his father out drinking with his mates down at the pub most nights, rather than spending time at home, where he gave his wife no help with the children; expecting her to attend to them all by herself. In his mind, the care of the home was down to her. His job was to bring in enough money to feed and clothe them – and then the rest was his to spend down the pub.

Steve had been a bit of a thief in those days, trying to make himself some pocket money, something they were all kept very short of, and had narrowly avoided being caught by the police on several occasions. He'd joined the army when he was old enough, wanting to get away from his home life, and it was then that he'd turned the corner, finding his calling in that sort of world – and he'd applied to join the police force when he came out.

'Come on then. Are we doing this or what?' he called back to Robbie, who was just stepping out of the car, trying to evade the issue of his lack of knowledge.

They climbed the three wide stone steps, and Robbie pressed the bell set at the side of the thick oak front door recessed back from the outer walls.

It jangled loudly from somewhere deep in the heart of the house, and after a short wait, they heard shuffling footsteps coming towards them. The door was opened by a small middle aged woman, and she looked scared when she saw police on the doorstep.

Before they had time to speak, she said, 'I'll get Isabelle for you,' and closed the door to without shutting it properly.

Robbie pushed it open and they both stepped into the stone flagged hallway, with ornately carved stairs rising to one side. There was now no sign of the woman who'd first opened the door, but they could hear voices from the back of the house, shortly followed by the appearance of another more elderly woman from that same location.

'Can I help you with something?' she asked, annoyed that they'd stepped inside without permission.

'Yes, we're looking for Miss Jayne Bannerman. Is she around?'

'Miss Jayne? No, she isn't, she hasn't lived here for a long time now, and I've no idea where you might find her; but Judge Bannerman should be home soon. He said he'd be back for dinner tonight.'

They exchanged glances.

'I'm afraid he won't be. He had a motorcycle accident earlier today,' Robbie said.

'Oh dear, is he in hospital then?' consternation written all over her face. 'Will he be home at all then tonight, or will he be spending the night there?'

'We really need to see Miss Bannerman first before we speak to anybody else. Is there anyone around here who might have her address – a friend or a relative?'

'Miss Jayne was always very quiet, and stayed home most of the time. She brought very few friends to the house, and she very rarely went out either. Judge Bannerman was always very protective of her. She does have a brother, David, but I don't have an address for him either. He left home shortly before Miss Jayne did.'

'Yes, that's all right, we've already seen his son,' Robbie said.

'You've seen Mr. David? How is he? Is he all right? Does he live far away?'

'No, he's not too far away, and he is well, but I can't give you his address I'm afraid. I'm sure he'll be back soon to clear up his fathers' affairs.'

She looked aghast.

'Are you saying Judge Bannerman's dead?'

Robbie looked down at the floor. He'd already said too much.

'I'm afraid I can't give you any information until Jayne Bannerman has been informed.'

She knew for sure now that her employer was dead; the policeman would have denied it if he wasn't.

'Oh my God,' she said, leaning back against the wall. 'I've been here for years now and I've nowhere else to go, unless Mr. David comes back here to live.'

'I don't think that's likely,' Robbie answered her. 'He has a house of his own, and a very nice one too; but he'll probably be back soon to see to things here.'

There was no more that could be said or done for the time being, so there was no alternative but to head back towards their home turf. They should arrive back just before it was time to finish their shift.

'Where to now?' Steve asked as they climbed back into the car.

'Back home now; just in time to clock off,' his companion replied.

'But what about this other contact we've still got to see?'

'We'll check up with that one first thing tomorrow before we head out. This time it's a man, what was his surname again?'

'Cockcroft,' Steve said, looking down at the list.

'I can see a woman changing her name when she marries, but a man . . .? That one doesn't look at all right to me, and it's a long way to go haring off to Colwyn Bay so near the end of our shift. If we go there now, we'll be late back, and I doubt we'll get any overtime pay out of it. Let's go straight back to the station and ask them to re-check their information. I don't know where they got it from, but it sure needs checking out,' Robbie replied as they turned around and drove back towards Denbigh.

'Are you sure this is right Sarge?' Robbie asked, when the same desk sergeant was still on duty.

He put the list of names and addresses down in front of him and pointed to the ones they'd scored through.

'These two have never even heard of Judge Bannerman, and one of them still has a living father. The other is dead, but the woman was in the car crash when he was killed, years ago. And as for the last name . . . how does a man have a different name to his father?'

'Could have changed it by Deed Poll,' the Sergeant replied jokingly. 'Or his mother might have re-married and the new husband adopted the child. They'd probably have changed his name then. Things like that do happen you know.'

Robbie looked at him with a wry expression on his face.

'Okay, I'll accept that,' he answered, 'but could you check out the information before we go off to Colwyn Bay tomorrow. It's a long way to have to go if the information's as duff as we've had today.'

'Okay, I'll pass it back up the line and ask them to re-check it,' taking the sheet off Robbie and putting it to one side without giving it a further glance.

Next day, Robbie and Steve were paired up again, and once again, the same desk sergeant was on duty when they arrived. They didn't want to have to go all the way to Colwyn Bay, but if the information did turn out to be correct, they knew they'd have to.

'Yeh, it's been checked and apparently it is correct. All show paternal matches through DNA to the judge, and they've also found another one as well.'

Robbie sighed.

'Go on – where's this one then? Don't tell me it's at the far end of our patch and miles away from Colwyn Bay!'

'I'm afraid it is,' the sergeant looked balefully at him over the top of his glasses, but seeing Robbie's agonised look, he continued, 'but you won't have this one to deal with as well.'

'Why not? Is somebody else handling it?'

'Probably, but this time it's not even on our patch. The man lives in Hertfordshire, with a flat in London – and he's an MP.'

'My, my! Seems Judge Bannerman liked to spread himself around a bit, didn't he? He must have been a very naughty boy in his miss-spent youth. All the people we've visited so far have been in their thirties or forties – so what age was he when he died?'

'Not sure; but he'd already retired several years ago, so he must have been pretty elderly by now.'

'So thirty or forty years ago he'd probably already have been married and with a young family of his own.'

'Seems like it. You should be able to find out more about him on the internet if you're really that interested, but for now you've still got that visit to Colwyn Bay. I suggest you get on with it straight away and don't waste time talking. That should take you the best part of the morning.'

Once again their visit to the next contact on their list was definitely a waste of time.

The address was in a street of terraced Victorian houses, and set back from the road was an empty plot of land where a house had been bombed during the last war and never been replaced.

The address they'd been given was next to this once empty lot, where there was now a metal building erected on it furthest away from the road, the front doors standing open.

They knocked first at the house, getting no reply, and at the second knock, a voice hailed them from the plot next door.

'Whadda' ye want?'

35

A definite Liverpool twang that!

'We're looking for Dennis Cockcroft. Do you know where we might find him?'

'Yer've found him – so whadda' ya want? I 'aven't gorr' all day to waste.'

'Can we speak to you for a few moments in private please?'

'Yer' are doin'. Like I said – whadda' ya want?'

It wasn't a very private place, even though there weren't many people around, but he wasn't going to hold the conversation across a boundary fence, so they walked back to the pavement and round to join the man.

'We may have some bad news for you. Do you know Judge Hector Bannerman?'

'Never 'eard of 'im! What's 'e gorra' do with me?'

'Our information tells us that he's your father.'

Robbie's back was up by now as he stood in front of this rather belligerent individual, and he couldn't help regarding him with distaste.

'You gorra' be joking!' the man now laughed. 'Me! The son of a judge – that's a bit rich! I've stood in front of a few in me time, but never owned one as a father!'

Then he turned away from them and looked towards the open-fronted building.

'Did yer' 'ear that dad. They think me dad was a judge!'

A scruffy looking older man in overalls came out from behind a car he'd been working on; spanner still in hand, and walked out into the open.

'There's me dad,' Dennis Cockcroft laughed. 'Does 'e look like a judge to yew?'

'What wanker give yer' thar' idea?' the older man said as he laughed out loud – a raucous phlegmy sound that ended in a bout of coughing. Hawking up, he spit a gob of phlegm into some car parts alongside and prepared to walk back to his job.

'Ay dad, 'ave an 'eart! I'm just gonna' use them in this job I'm on,' Dennis said, none too happily, his expression showing disgust.

'Oh well, I won't tell 'im if you don't – and a little bit of spit never 'urt no one,' he older man said, already walking away from them.

Steve stepped forward as if to explain, but stopped when he saw Robbie shake his head.

'Sorry for your trouble,' he said, trying to stay polite and steering Steve back to the car, pushing him into the passenger seat before returning to his own side.

'Leave it,' he said. 'No use wasting your time on him. He obviously knows nothing about what Judge Bannerman was up to with his mother. Better to leave him ignorant; or he'll probably want to make some sort of claim against the estate before you know it. Let's go and find somewhere for coffee. That was only a short trip, we can spare half an hour for coffee and doughnuts before we're missed.'

CHAPTER 3

David Bannerman sat for some time after the police had left, thinking over what they'd just told him.

So his father was dead!

Nothing he could do about that now. They'd never spoken since that last bitter row they'd had. It had been brewing for a long time before he'd spoken out in a fit of anger provoked by his fathers' behaviour towards his mother and his sister, and now increasingly towards other members of the household. His treatment towards both had been churlish in the least, controlling at the worst, and at the very end it had provoked his angry outburst, unable to control himself any longer.

He'd barged into his fathers' study unannounced after seeing his sister mounting the stairs, crying bitterly. It was the second time in two days that had happened, and being quite a shy and unassuming girl, she never spoke up for herself. Perhaps that was what allowed his father to get away with so much!

His mother, too, was becoming downtrodden since his retirement. They'd all known how bad tempered he could be when he was at home, but luckily his work as a judge had kept him away for several days most weeks, staying in hotels when he needed to, and sometimes they only saw him at weekends. That had been bearable for all of them, especially when he'd been away at University, where he lived amongst his fellow students, but on his return home during the holidays he'd noticed his fathers' bullying attitude getting worse. Once he'd got himself

38

settled in a job, he vowed to look round for a place of his own as soon as he could, and try and persuade his sister to come and live with him.

When he'd left University, he didn't have a job to go to and had spent some time at home before finding one. It had been peaceful and relaxing in the company of his mother and sister, but everything changed when his father arrived home. It seemed as if the whole household were treading on eggshells, watching every word they said, and trying not to arouse or annoy him in any way.

David had a little money from an allowance left to him by his mothers' parents, which had kept him during his days at University, but it wasn't enough to pay for the upkeep of a home as well, so he had to stay at Bannerman's until he was able to afford a place of his own.

After the row, he'd decided enough was enough. He and his father just couldn't get along living side by side.

He spent the rest of the day in his room, and when his father took the dog out for his usual afternoon walk, he sought out his sister and they had a long talk together in her room, where she'd been ever since she'd fled there in tears. She'd had no lunch either, and he himself had eaten in the kitchen with the household staff, so he asked Isabelle to prepare her a plate of cold food that he took up with him.

She was sitting in a chair by the window when he knocked and called to say who it was. She invited him in straight away, pleased to have his company.

'I've brought you some lunch,' he said, setting the tray down on the small table in the window and sitting in the adjacent chair. 'There's a full pot of tea, so we can both have a cup, but the food's only cold and you can eat that now or later, whichever you prefer.'

Her face was still red and blotchy from the tears she'd shed, and she looked none too happy; but she did manage to give him a wan little smile.

'What just happened?' he asked, thinking she might feel better after telling him.

She turned her head away and looked out of the window; staring out at the moorland landscape as a small sigh escaped her.

'I'd rather not talk about it if you don't mind,' she finally answered. 'Let's forget about it. It's over and done with now.'

'Not as far as I'm concerned,' he said forcefully. 'I've had enough! I, for one, will not stand for any more of his bullying behaviour. I'm leaving tomorrow. I have a friend whose parents have a small flat over their garage, and they've said I can use it for the time being. Will you come with me? You have an allowance from our grandparents, the same as I had, and I've just got a job. Together we can pool our resources and live there until you're old enough to find a job yourself.'

'But what will I do?' she said, turning towards him. 'I've done nothing since I left school. I'm not trained for anything, unlike you, and I wouldn't know what to do with myself.'

'Don't worry about that,' he answered. 'I'm quite willing to help keep you until you find something you're interested in. In the meantime, you can keep house for us both and do the cooking and cleaning. That'll do very nicely for me.'

She seemed to think about his suggestion for a while before she spoke.

'But what about mother? We can't leave her here with father the way he is now. He bullies her as well and she's not in the best of health these days.'

'I'll speak to mother later and tell her what we plan to do if you'll come with me. I'm sure she wouldn't object, and she's managed to put up with him through all the years so far.'

She wasn't sure. There were other factors governing her thinking at the moment – something that she didn't dare speak to anyone about; least of all David.

'Leave it for now and let me think about it,' she answered.

'Dad will be home soon. Couldn't you make up your mind now and I'll go down and speak to mum straight away before he gets back. After what happened before, I'm sure she wouldn't be averse to our going away. We're both adults now, and both well able to take care of ourselves.'

She still looked unsure of her decision as he looked into her face.

'When are you going?' she asked finally.

'First thing after breakfast tomorrow. I'll be using my own car, so if you pack this evening, I'll take your things down and put them in the boot when dad goes to bed.'

'Let me think about it first. Then I'll see mum and tell her myself if I do decide to go. I'd like to tell her in person, but I'm still worried about leaving her alone with him. I want her reassurance that she'll be okay. I'll come to your room last thing and let you know after they've gone to bed.'

He left her then.

She looked worn out and was eyeing up the cold food as if she were very hungry. He wasn't hopeful that she would go with him. She'd always been a timid little thing, and being the last of the five children born to the family, she'd always been treated as the baby.

He'd been born the eldest; his three younger brothers all having perished without growing past childhood, and the family had always been protective of her, particularly he and his mother. His father had never really cared about anyone but himself, but as the only girl child, he'd always seemed particularly fond of her. Now that fondness seemed to be turning to possessiveness as time went by.

She didn't come to his room that night, and when he saw her in the morning, he asked her if she was packed and ready.

'I'm not going with you,' she said. 'I've decided I can't leave mother alone with him, and there'll be nobody for her to turn to if I'm not here. Besides, I've never lived anywhere else, and I'm a bit scared of making that move when I'm still so young.'

'You're old enough,' he said. 'Lots of young girls leave home at your age, and besides, you'll have me with you, I'll look after you.'

But there was no changing her mind, as she shook her head.

'I just can't,' she said. 'I'm not ready to leave here yet, in spite of father. Please, don't ask me again. I've made up my mind. I'm staying here. Let me have your address when you get settled in and I'll come and visit you.'

He knew there was no changing her mind. It was already made up, and when it came down to it, he knew she was as stubborn as he was.

He'd parked his car in the small yard just outside the kitchen door, and packed all his things into it while his father was reading his paper in the study. Before leaving, he went to say goodbye to his mother, where he found her in the kitchen helping Isabelle clear away the breakfast things.

He'd told his mother the previous evening that he was leaving, and she'd totally agreed with his decision. She knew it was obvious that he and his father couldn't live together harmoniously any more, and it was probably the best thing for him now. As long as he had somewhere to go, she was happy with his decision, knowing that he seemed fairly settled in the job he'd found.

His new job kept him fairly busy, and he'd now made some new friends, so he'd only found time for the odd 'phone call to his mother and sister after that, but he'd never made the time to visit. Both said that his father had mellowed a bit since his departure, and he thought that was probably the reason why. It had been many years since they'd seen eye to eye, and his leaving had been just what was needed.

Now his father was gone, and, without anyone informing him, so was his mother. He couldn't understand why Jayne hadn't rung to let him know, but his 'phone call to her the following morning went unanswered; and she didn't call him back. She was now left all alone with that big house to run – something he was sure she wouldn't be able to manage on her own – but what more could he do if he couldn't reach her?

He knew he had to find the time to go back and see her.

'Anna' he called down the passage, 'please come into my office for a minute.'

Her own little domain, the housekeepers' room was next door to his study, and she always left the door ajar in case he called her.

'Yes, David, what can I do for you? Coffee?' as she came into the room.

'No, not at the moment, thanks. It seems that my father's been killed in a motorcycle accident, and I've just found out my mother died some time ago as well. I can't get hold of my sister either. I need to go back to my home and find out what's happening. She won't know what to do now that there's none of the family still left, and nor will the staff.'

She looked surprised. She knew the police presence had been something serious for them to come to the house, but all of this came as a complete surprise to her. He hadn't talked very much about his home life. She knew that his father was a judge, and the family had been fairly wealthy, but that was about all she did know.

'I can hold the fort here,' she said. 'You go; and take as much time as you need.'

'No, I don't want you to stay here. I want you to come with me. I may need your help to get things straight, and I know you're very capable of doing just that.'

Not only had Anna been employed as a housekeeper by David, but once she'd shown her hidden talents with the computer, and her efficiency around office duties, she often helped him out with the paperwork as well.

She'd worked in a busy office previously, but found it far too strenuous, and when she'd seen this job offered, she'd decided to apply. It was a live-in post, and as the rent was just about to go up on her pokey little rented flat, it seemed far too good to refuse.

He'd offered her the job immediately after seeing her c.v., and shown her where she would have her own quarters.

The housekeepers' room wasn't very big, but was large enough to contain two armchairs, a small table, and facilities for making drinks when she was alone, as well as a cupboard unit to keep her things in. The kitchen, just along the hallway from his study, was where she would prepare all their meals, and although there was a good sized dining room, David usually ate in the kitchen with her right from the time she first started work. He said the dining room was far too cold, and the table far too big for one person to be eating there on their own. Besides, the kitchen was far warmer and cosier, with the large range along one wall, and he also found her company refreshing – not that he ever told her that. As he didn't entertain very often, the dining room had now been shut off, as had the three other bedrooms not in use at present, and only when he was expecting guests did she go in and spruce it up, spending only a couple of hours doing that, as it only got slightly dusty during its time of disuse.

Her bedroom was in the attic space, reached by a narrow set of stairs from the upstairs landing. It had a dormer window on either side which let in plenty of light, and a double bed with a comfortable mattress; its bedding also provided. It even had its own small bathroom; big enough to contain a bath as well as a shower unit above. Occupying half of the available attic space, it was of a good size and even had a fairly new looking fitted carpet.

Although she didn't know it, there had been only two applicants for the job he'd advertised in the local paper – the other David hadn't liked from the moment they first met. Her own previous background seemed to be just what he was looking for, and besides that, he liked her at first sight. After just a brief interview, he knew they'd be able to get on together, and offered her the job immediately.

Anna had previously been married for a brief period of time. After she left technical college at the age of 18, her parents had persuaded her to go on a short holiday with them to Cornwall, and as she had no plans for the future at that moment in time, she allowed them to persuade her. They booked into a small hotel near Crantock Beach, where she'd met her future husband, Andrew Tremayne.

He was the son of the owners, and was 5 years older than her. She was in awe of his handsome good looks right from the first moment she saw him arriving back from a walk with their German Shepherd dog, Simba. He was a big black animal who looked very striking; leaving her feeling a little nervous of him. However, once she got to know him, she found him a great big softy and very gentle considering his size. He also took to her immediately, as did Andrew, and she started accompanying him on his afternoon walks with the dog. He took her to all the local beauty spots, and they were sometimes out for two or three hours at a time.

By the time they went home, she and Andrew were smitten with each other, and thinking it might just be a fleeting holiday romance, she made up her mind to treat it as just that and put it from her mind – but that wasn't about to happen. He called her several times during the following weeks, and he eventually asked her to go down to Cornwall and take a job looking after the rooms. One of their staff had just left, and if she wanted it, there was a vacancy for her to join them.

She was a little nervous of how her parents would take the news after sending her on the secretarial course for almost 2 years, but she needn't have worried. They were pleased that it would give her a new outlook on life and provide her with some much needed job experience.

Six months later, she and Andrew were engaged, followed 12 months later by a wedding catered for at the hotel.

Andrew owned a small cottage just half a mile down the road, which had been left to him by his grandparents, and which he'd rented out as a holiday home ever since. It was close to the beach with a lovely view out over the bay, and they moved into that straight afterwards, but both kept on working at the hotel together;

she now having moved on to an office job keeping the hotel records and bookings up to date, and included keeping the financial side in order as well.

It was just over 5 years later that Andrew dropped the bombshell. He'd met somebody else and wanted out of their marriage.

In a pique of anger, and after several rows, she'd left the cottage and given in her notice. She moved back into her parents' home in Wales, and after the divorce had gone through, she'd never heard from him again.

The job with her previous employer had come along just over a month later, and as it was in Corwen, far away from their home in Conwy, she'd found a small flat to live in.

She found her present job with David far pleasanter and the surroundings more peaceful than the flat above a take-away overlooking the busy A5. She got on well with him, and sometimes they seemed more like friends than employer and employee, but after her unpleasant experience with Andrew, she tried to keep her distance and never appear too familiar; so this request from him to accompany him to his former home came as a complete surprise to her.

'That's fine with me,' she answered. 'I'd like to see where you grew up. I hope I can be of some help to you, but I'm so sorry to hear of your parents' deaths. I'll do what I can to help smooth the way for you until you can get everything organised.'

He smiled wanly.

'I'm really sorry to hear about my mothers' death, but I can't say I'm very cut up about my fathers'. We never saw eye to eye, and truth to tell, he was a bit of a bully to everybody living there. We're all well rid, and life should be a bit easier without him for all concerned!'

Although he'd never voiced these opinions about his father, she'd learned that they weren't very close from the little things he'd said over the time she'd been with him.

'When do you want to leave?' she asked. 'I'll get everything sorted and I'll be ready when you are.'

'I have to be in Court on Monday with a new case. It's only something minor so it shouldn't take more than a few days. After that I've nothing to keep me here for the time being, so we could possibly go next weekend and spend 10 days or a fortnight there getting things sorted out. I'm sure my father must have left a Will, so it's probably in his safe. He wasn't very good at remembering numbers and he always left a piece of paper with the combination written on it taped to the underside of a drawer alongside his bed. I found it one day when I was about 14. I was hunting for Christmas presents while they were out and I pulled the drawer too far out. It fell on the floor and turned upside down. I saw the paper and didn't at first know what it was, but I noticed after that that my father always went up to his bedroom before he opened the safe, and I realised what that number must be.'

She laughed.

'Kids eh! Nothing's ever safe from them, is it? I remember my sisters doing the same thing to me. They were both a few years younger than me, and they were always rooting through my things. I was very tidy, and I knew just when they'd been rooting through. They never put things back where they found them.'

It was his turn to laugh now as he took up his pen once more.

'I'll get on with what I'm doing. I should be finished in about half an hour, so that coffee would be very welcome then. I'll come down to the kitchen and we'll have it together – with some of your delicious cake if there's any left.'

'Fine by me,' she answered. 'I've a casserole for tonight, so I'll go and put it in the oven while you're finishing up here,' and she shut the door behind her as she left the room.

CHAPTER 4

'Morning,' Jim Shannon called as he saw his day worker arriving at the farm gate. 'Sorry it's such a cold day, and it's threatening rain as well, but we really must bring those sheep in off the moors and get them nearer to home for the winter. There's plenty of pasture ready for them, and the tups are due to be separated out now as well. We can do the two jobs at the same time.'

'Fine by me,' Dafydd replied. 'Due to clear up soon accordin' to forecast, and it'll take us a while to round them all up anyways. Pasture should be dried up a bit when we get back, innit!'

Jim smiled inwardly to himself. Nobody was surer than the old shepherd of the weather, forecasting or not. He could tell what the weather was about to do just from looking up at the sky, and he was invariably right most of the time.

Jim went over and unlocked the barn doors. Time was when they never had to be locked many years ago, but these days, with so much technology and expensive machinery finding its way onto the farms, they were experiencing a lot more theft than they ever had in the past. When he was young, his fathers' old tractor had always stood just inside the doorway, with the doors wide open and ready for action at any moment. The keys had always been left in the ignition, night or day.

'Tad Taylor's meeting us up there near the old quarry this morning with his quad bike and his dogs, so I reckon we can get most of them in by the end of the morning, if we don't have to go hunting round for too many,' Jim said, 'and wife's putting a big steak and tattie pie in the oven for dinner, so we'll all have a good feed when we get back.'

'Nice one,' Dafyydd said, 'one o' her pies would put a lining on any man's stomach, and I have to tek the wife shopping when I get back. I'll need a good feed inside me afore I has to endure that as well.'

Laughing, Jim made his way over to the dog pen just inside the barn and let the three sheepdogs out, excited barking accompanying his approach. They milled around them both, wildly wagging their tails in excitement as he opened the door.

'Tha'll do! Tha'll do!' he called, as he tried to calm their excitement, and went over to the quad bikes he was going to use. Dafydd had one at his own place, but as they'd be coming back here afterwards, they'd decided to use Jim's two instead. Dafydd had come over in his battered old Land Rover instead; his two sheepdogs already waiting anxiously in the rear compartment. They were eager to get out and join in the excitement.

It took them fifteen minutes to reach the first of the sheep, all looking nervously round as they heard the bikes arriving, and saw the first of the dogs approaching, a lot of them taking flight immediately. But flight was useless. The dogs, well trained, and used to rounding up all the stragglers, were quicker than them and had them all heading for the lower pastures quite quickly.

Safely penned in the nearest pasture, the two men headed back out to the moorland once again, where they saw Tad already on the side of the nearest hillside, his two dogs running upwards and herding the sheep down from the higher ground.

Soon they were heading towards Jim and Dafydd, who called in their dogs until it was too late for the sheep to change course, and then they commenced the roundup once again, driving them into the pasture along with the others.

This went on for the best part of the morning, until there was only the old quarry workings left to check.

It was further away than the rest of the flock had been, but there were always some stragglers who were intent on doing their own thing, and they'd found sheep there before.

'I reckon there's about fifty to a hundred outstanding,' Jim said, 'let's have some snappin and then we'll work our way over there.'

Taking out the flask of hot coffee and some homemade scones, they sat on the quad bikes while they enjoyed the rest and ate the food; the dogs still frisking around and drinking loudly from a nearby rill of water. They knew there was still more for them to do and were anxious to get going once they'd finished. They also knew that when it was over they'd be heading for home, a good feed, and some welcome rest.

The weather, just as Dafydd had forecast, had improved. The threat of rain had gone and a watery sun had begun to shine, even though it still wasn't very warm – but their exertions over the last few hours, together with their extra layers of warm clothing, had warmed them up and they weren't feeling the cold any more.

'Right! I reckon we'd better get started again,' Jim said, putting the box and the flask back on the quad bike; the dogs already jumping up behind once they saw the men were ready to move again.

Tad had noticed a few sheep up on the higher slopes of the hills while they were eating, and he and his dogs went after them, whilst Jim and Dafydd made their way further on, to where the moorland bordered the road.

The ground was flatter here and there were no signs of any other sheep, but they still needed to check the quarry itself. It was well sheltered from the elements, and they often found a good quantity of sheep inside if the weather turned bad.

To access it, they had to find the opening that wound its way down to the bottom, and they couldn't see all of the quarry floor until they were right at the bottom. There were many little nooks and crannies down there where the sheep would be hidden from sight.

On first reaching the bottom there were no sheep to be seen and at the far side they could see right into the furthest reaches, also empty; but on either side of them, there were several openings which couldn't be seen from their present position and needed closer inspection.

'You take the left, and I'll take the right,' Jim called to his companion, as they both roared off to complete the task.

Jim found nothing, but when he returned to the place where he'd left Dafydd, there was no sign of him, and everything was quiet.

'Dafydd,' he called several times.

There was still no reply!

Thinking the man might have had an accident, he followed to where he'd last seen him disappearing, and was relieved to find him inside the last of the openings.

His quad was silent; the engine switched off, and the dogs were sitting patiently in the back, while Dafydd was examining something tucked out of Jim's sight.

'What is it?' he called as he drove towards him – but as he rounded a corner of the rock, the object of his attentions came into view.

There was a car tucked well out of sight behind some rather stunted and blackened gorse outcrops, and as Jim drove up to join him, he could see that the car had been on fire. It was blackened almost beyond recognition, and had obviously been there for some time, as there wasn't a whisp of smoke still to be seen.

Dafydd turned towards him as he heard the quad arrive, and Jim cut the engine so's they could speak.

'Not another one!' he said, approaching and standing at his side.

Dafydd nodded.

'Afraid so!' he added, 'Probably been stolen and another poor bugger's lost his pride and joy – but they didn't get away with it scot free this time. Look, all the passenger door's been caved in, and there's a lot of blood on the floor just the other side of it.'

Jim walked towards it and checked. The front wing was dished right in nearest the door; and the door itself was also crumpled right back to the door pillar; right next to where the top of the leg or the passenger's arm would have been, with a lot of scuff marks and more dents and scrapes extending towards the rear door.

'Looks like they've hit something sideways on,' Jim qualified as he examined the marks, 'and these on the rear door look like the patterning from a tyre. We'd better call the police. It might have been involved in an accident.'

So saying, and knowing there was nothing more they could do here, they jumped back on their bikes and drove towards the road.

Mobile 'phone signals were often non-existent in this remote part of the countryside, and Jim knew that if they did get one, it wouldn't be from inside the quarry; but up on the flatter ground, there was probably more of a chance.

Standing on the roadside, and by moving around for some distance, he did manage to get a signal and called them straight away. He had a GPS app on his 'phone, something that was invariably crucial in this terrain, and managed to give them an exact location.

'Can you wait there so that we know exactly where you are, and we'll have somebody with you shortly,' the voice on the other end intoned, and Jim agreed that they would – but almost an hour later they were still waiting.

'Well, I'm not waiting any longer,' Dafydd complained. 'Me belly's feeling as if me throat's been cut, and that meat and tattie pie seems good to me right now. Why don't we leave them some sort of signal and head back to yours?'

'Shouldn't really need a signal,' Jim replied. 'I gave them an exact GPS location, and I told them it's in a disused quarry, so there shouldn't be any problem, should there?'

They both laughed.

'No, there shouldn't be!' Dafydd agreed, 'but you know how dim some folk can be!'

More than two hours from when the call was made, and well after the men had returned to the farm and eaten their fill of the pie, a traffic patrol car appeared on the scene.

'This looks like the place,' the passenger said to his driver. 'I remember this old quarry from years ago. Me and me mates used to bring our scrambles bikes up here and use it as a race track. As far as I remember, you can drive right in,' which is exactly what they did, and after a short drive round, they found the object of their visit.

'Mm-m-m! Well burnt out, and by the looks of it, it's been here for a good while, but it does bear the signs of having been in an accident. We'll bring in the investigations team just in case there's any evidence to be found, but I doubt it!' the driver intoned, not giving much significance to their find.

His mate, who'd been looking round while he'd been talking, had walked round to the side nearest the quarry wall, the rear part of the car hidden from view by the open passenger door.

'There is some evidence,' he called back. 'There's blood here – and quite a lot. If he's known to us, we'll probably be able to trace him through that.'

Meanwhile, the driver had walked further away and was examining the ground a few feet further on.

'There's more tyre tracks here,' he called back. 'Looks like motor bikes. The tread isn't very wide, but quite chunky, so probably scrambles bikes. Do you think they originally came here on them, and used them for a quick getaway afterwards.'

His passenger came across.

'I doubt if they'll hold any clues. This place has always been used by motorbikes – look at the tyre tracks all around. The land is still owned by the quarry company, but I doubt they've bothered with it for years. We've always known about the bikers using it, but we've never ever bothered with them. Better charging round here on their bikes than out on the public roads – and it's so remote they're not causing a nuisance to anybody else.'

CHAPTER 5

'Anna. ... Anna,' she heard David calling from the front door, as she emerged from her little room.

She'd already heard his car arrive, and having put down her book, she was ready to greet him

'I didn't know what time you'd be home, so I haven't prepared anything hot for lunch, but I can have something ready by the time you've washed and changed. I was just going to have a sandwich, but I have some nice local ham and some free range eggs if you'd prefer that,' she said, pleased that he'd returned so early in the day.

'A sandwich will do me nicely, but I would prefer the ham and eggs if you don't mind cooking them,' he answered, a sly grin spreading over his face.

'Coming up,' she smiled back.

She knew he was always hungry when he returned at the end of the day, but she hadn't expected him to be quite so early today. When he had a day in Court, he never usually arrived home until after five o'clock most days.

As he made for the stairs, discarding his coat on the end of the banister, he stopped and called back down to her as she passed him on her way to the kitchen.

She'd already picked up his coat and was taking it to hang in the understairs cupboard as she stopped and looked up at him.

'That trial I was attending today – it finished early. The plaintiff changed his plea to guilty, so the judge stopped proceedings while he considers his verdict. It should all be over by the end of the week, so I'll probably be free for the entire following week.   Are you ready if we make tracks for Bannerman's on Friday afternoon?   We can probably get there within an hour.'

She was surprised, but delighted.   A week of peace and solitude without the 'phone ringing and no callers was just the thing she needed – and a week of David all to herself was something to look forward to as well.

She'd worked for him for several years now, and during that time they'd formed a real bond of companionship, and she knew that her feelings for him were now becoming more than just that. If he'd noticed, he never said anything, and seemed to still be treating her as an employer first and a friend second.

He always watched television or went out on his own in the evenings, leaving her to her own company, and many evenings, when he was working on a difficult case, he often burned the midnight oil in his study without speaking.

On these occasions, she left him well alone; only taking in the odd cup of coffee and some biscuits or a slice of cake without taking up more than a few minutes of his time.   He was always grateful for them, and always thanked her, but he showed no inclination to stop and chat on these occasions.

She knew many people wouldn't have liked this sort of life, but she enjoyed it.   There were always jobs that needed doing around the house and meals to be prepared, and she loved looking after him and seeing to his needs.

Besides that, she'd made some good friends amongst the local community, where she visited the local farms and bought free range eggs, vegetables, and ham, cheese, and fresh yogurt from one farm supplier during the often long days on her own.

When the weather was fine, she often walked there along the quiet country lanes; enjoying the sound of birdsong and the fresh countryside smells of hawthorn flowers in spring and elder flowers in summer, together with new mown hay when it was time for cutting.   Once she arrived, they all had time for a friendly chat and a cuppa, and she was often out for a lot longer than intended. Together with little trips into Denbigh for shopping, her days seemed to slip by quite quickly.

The ham and eggs ready, she called up the stairs to him, where he was just about to come down to join her in the kitchen.

Today he was dressed in jeans and a sweatshirt, something she didn't often see, except at weekends when he didn't have to go out again.

When she looked at him in surprise, he laughed out loud.

'Yes, I do intend to dress more casually when we go to Bannerman's,' he said. 'My father always dressed formally in a suit and tie, even when he was at home, but I intend to change all that. Start as you mean to go on, and the staff will just have to get used to it. I spend enough of my working life in a suit!'

She smiled. This was a new David Bannerman to the one she normally saw, and this attire suited him well. It made him look even more handsome than she already thought him, with his wavy blonde hair and aquiline nose.

Thinking about it while she washed the dishes and put them away, a thought struck her. If his father was dead, and his sister a lot younger than him, there was every chance that he was now the new owner of Bannerman's.

What would he do with it? Would he sell it, or did his cryptic remark, "start as you mean to go on", indicate that he intended to keep it on and perhaps go back and live there?

It was on Friday afternoon, hearing his footsteps descending the stairs, that she dried the last of the dishes and put them away.

'I'm going to put my bags in the car now. How long will you be?'

She closed the cupboard door and looked round – there was only the bin to be emptied and left at the bottom of the track ready for collection during the week. It could remain there until they returned next week. She'd already packed what she'd need the previous day, so all she needed were the few last minute items and then she was ready.

Coming through to the hall and carrying the almost full bin bag, he opened the front door for her.

'Just got some last minute things to bring down and then I'm ready,' she said, depositing the rubbish outside. 'We can drop the bin at the end of the lane when we leave.'

'I'd forgotten that,' he said. 'I'll do that now before we forget. You go and finish off while I do it.'

Within ten minutes, and after a last minute check around, making sure all the doors and windows were locked, they were off, and she felt excited at the prospect of seeing Bannerman's for the first time.

'Are you sure we're in the right place?' she asked, looking around her, aghast at the empty open wilderness all around. Although rather beautiful, it was also very wild and there weren't any signs of other habitation around.

He'd said it stood alone and surrounded by its own land, but just how remote it was she'd had no idea.

The road had come to a dead end, where there was nothing but wild open hillsides going far out into the distance. She couldn't see any sign of a house, and she was becoming worried about its remote location – if it was here at all! She couldn't see any sign of a road leading to one, let alone any sort of dwelling! Maybe David was having a joke at her expense!

He gave a soft chuckle at her bewilderment, and she was taken by surprise as he suddenly turned the wheel to the left into what looked like a dirt track. There was still no sign of a house as they progressed further on round a hillside, until suddenly the house appeared in front of her – seeming even more incongruous in this wild landscape surrounding them than she could ever have imagined.

'Wow!' she let out a gasp without realising it. 'I wasn't expecting to find a house out here!'

'I thought you'd say that,' he laughed as he continued onward.

Finally, the dirt track gave way to a gravelled parking area, showing no sign of demarcation between the two, with a circular raised rose bed right in its centre. Surmounting this was a large ornamental stone shell rearing up above it.

David seemed perplexed as they got out of the car.

'What's up?' she asked as she came round to join him. 'Is something wrong?'

He was looking out over the rose bed, before looking round the rest of the flower beds surrounding the edges of a well clipped lawn.

'Dad's had the fish pond filled in,' he exclaimed. 'That's always been here since I was a kid. My sister and I used to climb up on the edges of it and dangle our feet into the water, and the fish used to come up and nibble our toes. There were some really huge ones in there when I was younger, and that stone shell in the middle used to be a fountain as well. You could see the sun shining off the water as it shot up into the air. It sometimes turned into a complete rainbow when the sun hit it at the right angle. This was always the feature I loved most about the house. I wonder why he had it filled in.'

She didn't know what to say, but she had a picture in her minds' eye of what it must have looked like in its heyday. It must have looked really magical to a young child.

Just at that moment, the front door opened and a woman came out, standing on the top step and looking flustered.

'Mr. David. I didn't know you were coming. Why didn't you ring? We'd have had everything ready for you.'

He turned to look at her – his attention diverted for the time being.

'Sorry Isabelle, I forgot. We weren't intending to arrive today, but circumstances changed and I was able to get away earlier than I expected. I had intended to ring in the morning before we left, but ....' the rest of the sentence unfinished as he gave her a sheepish grin. 'Anyway, it's good to see you're still here,' he finally finished up.'

The woman still looked flustered as she stood back to let them enter; her eyes scrutinising Anna as she looked her up and down wondering if Mr. David had been married without letting anyone know.

'Will you be staying?' she asked.

'For the time being,' he answered. 'I suppose you've already heard my father's been killed in a motorcycle accident?'

It was more a question than a statement.

She nodded.

'The police were here a few days ago, and they wouldn't tell us anything until Miss Jayne had been informed, but from their whole attitude, we realised he must have been.'

'I see,' he answered. 'And has she been told now?'

'I don't know, Mr. David, she left home a few years ago, and nobody here knows where she went. Your father never told us nothing and I don't think he's been in contact with her since – or not that we've heard anyway.'

He looked stunned.

'You've never heard from her? And she's never been back?'

'No, Mr. David, if he did, your father never said nothing. He give us a week off while he was having some work done on the house, but she'd already gone before that – probably about a week or more if I remember rightly.'

David glanced at Anna before looking back at Isabelle.

'So she probably doesn't even know my fathers' dead?'

'Not to my knowledge,' she added, seeing how agitated he was becoming. 'She hasn't called, and we don't have any address for her neither.'

Then a sudden thought struck her.

'We haven't seen or heard from you either. You do know your mother died as well, don't you?'

He nodded.

'I'm surprised you didn't come back for the funeral. We all thought you'd be back for that.'

Looking rueful he said, 'I didn't hear anything about her death 'til well after the funeral. I'm a barrister now, and I was working on a big case in London for some weeks. When I got back, there was a message from my friend, a solicitor, asking me to call him, and it was him who told me the news. As it was well after the funeral had taken place, I decided not to come back. My father and I have never been on good terms, as you know, so I decided it wasn't worth the aggro.'

'I see,' she said, realising that there was really nothing more that needed to be said on the subject, but then, more brightly, she continued, 'will you and your lady wife be wanting your old room? Sandra's still working here, so I'll get her to make the bed up for you. It's big enough for you both – but I'm afraid I don't even know Mrs. Bannerman's' name yet.'

David and Anna looked at each other and burst out laughing, but it was Anna who spoke first.

'David and I aren't married,' she explained. 'David has his own home now, and I'm his housekeeper. As I help out with the financial side of things and a lot of the paperwork, he decided to bring me with him to help sort things out here. There's nothing for me to do at home while he's away anyway. I can be of much more use here.'

'Oh, I do beg your pardon!' Isabelle replied, smiling herself. 'My mistake! Then I suppose you'll be wanting a room of your own as well. I'll get Sandra to make one up for you. You can use Miss Jayne's room, and you can have your old room Mr. David. We haven't heard from her, so I don't suppose she'll be back yet, if ever.'

'No, not Jayne's room,' David was quick to add. 'I want to check her room out for myself while I'm here. There may be something in there that will lead us to where she's gone. Make up the room at the far end of the corridor,' and turning to look at

Anna he continued, 'It's not quite such a big room, but it does get the morning sun.'

'Fine by me,' she answered. 'Provided I have somewhere comfortable to lay my head, I'll be quite happy.'

'Good, I'll see to that,' Isabelle crowed, 'and in the meantime, you can leave your things in the hall and I'll get Cyril, the odd job man, to take them up to your rooms, while Sandra makes up the beds. I'll put the kettle on for us all. I'm sure you won't say no to a cuppa and some homemade cake, will you?'

'Thank you very much, that would be lovely,' Anna smiled at her, 'but first thing, where's the loo? I can't go much longer without.'

'Upstairs, fir . . . .,' David began to say, when Isabelle interrupted him.

'No need,' she said. 'That was another of the Judge's alterations. He had the old butler's pantry turned into a downstairs bathroom. It's right at the end of the hallway if you'll just follow me. When you're ready, just continue further on down the corridor and you'll find the kitchen. Tea should be ready by then.'

'Thank you so much,' Anna said, as they both followed her, indicating the bathroom on the way; her and David continuing into the kitchen.

When he sat down at the table, he asked Isabelle, 'What else did he have done?'

'The fish pond was filled in, as you've probably already noticed,' she said, 'and he had a shower fitted in the upstairs bathroom, as well as a new boiler for the central heating. He said the old one wasn't as efficient as the newer ones nowadays, and it would probably cost less to run.'

'True, I can understand all that, but why did he find it necessary to give you all a long weekend off for that? There were only you and Cyril living in the house, surely it wouldn't have caused too much inconvenience to you both.'

61

'No idea,' she answered, 'but it was very welcome. I spent the weekend with my sister in Anglesey. Her husband died five years ago and she's all alone now. I've only seen her once since the funeral, but she does want me to go and live with her when I retire,' and with a sigh she sat down in the armchair she always used alongside the range. 'I suppose that's on the cards now, isn't it? If you have a home of your own, I don't suppose you'll want to keep Bannerman's on, will you? Are you thinking of selling it?'

It wasn't something David had really had time to think about so far.

'I don't know yet. I haven't given it much thought. I need to find my fathers' Will first and see how much money he's left. I don't know what he decided to do after the row we had. I may have a new beneficiary to find, and that may very well be my sister. I need to find her as well – find out what's happened to her and where she is. You wouldn't have any idea would you?'

Isabelle looked sad.

'No, I haven't seen her either. I had no idea that she'd be gone for so long. The judge never said nothing to none of us about her leaving. It was only when she didn't come back after a few weeks that we began to realise she'd gone for good; not just for a holiday as we all thought..'

Just at that same moment, the kettle began to boil, and Anna arrived in the kitchen, both at the same time.

'Sit yourself down,' Isabelle said to her graciously, 'and I'll make that cuppa,' standing up and lifting the kettle off the range, at the same time as the back door opened and a man appeared in the doorway.

He was dressed in corduroy trousers and a plaid shirt covered by a waistcoat streaked with soil. On his feet were a pair of filthy and very muddy brown boots.

Isabelle turned in his direction immediately.

'Don't you come into my kitchen with those filthy boots!' she admonished.

'Don't worry, I know the rules,' he answered. 'I jus' wondered if there was a brew going.'

Turning in the direction of David and Anna, she said, 'I swear that man can hear the kettle boiling from a hundred yards away!'

It was only then that the man noticed the other two figures sitting at the table, and looked wide eyed at David.

'David!' he said. 'Ain't seen you in such a long time. Good to see yew back.'

'Thank you, Gavin,' David answered.

Then turning to Anna he said, 'This is our gardener, Gavin Hammond. He's been here for as long as I can remember. Gavin, this is my housekeeper and friend, Anna.'

'Nice to meet yew, miss,' Gavin replied, nodding his head and smiling in recognition before turning back to Isabelle.

'If yew could manage two cups, I'd be grateful. Morgan's just outside. I'll tek 'im one as well.'

'Morgan's his son. He helps out with the garden,' David explained to Anna before turning back to Gavin once more.

'How is Morgan?' he asked. 'Haven't seen him in years. We spent a lot of time together when we were both younger.'

'Not so young now!' Gavin explained. 'If I remember rightly, 'e's a few years younger than yew, but he's doin' fine. 'oping to get married next year to a farmer's daughter from rownd about. Lovely girl, she is. I'm very pleased for 'im. Gwen's doin' fine too – she'll be right pleased to see yew if yew'll be 'ere long enough to call in for a cuppa and some of 'er 'ome-made cake.'

David was pleased to hear that everything was still as it was when he left – and Gwen's cooking had always been legendary. Even if they didn't have much time, it would be a good opportunity to introduce them all to Anna, as, if he had inherited the house, he hoped to bring her to live here as well.

'I'll make sure we find time,' he said, as Isabelle came over and put the cups down in front of them before opening a cupboard door and taking out a tin of homemade cake of her own.

'Aye, well, I thank you,' Gavin added, taking the two mugs that Isabelle handed to him by the door. 'We were all sorry to 'ear of yewr fathers' death. Will yew be coming back to live 'ere now?'

'I don't know yet – there's a lot to be sorted out first, and I don't know where I stand until I find my fathers' Will. We're here for a whole week, so I'll let everybody know when I find out what he had planned for us all.'

Gavin took the two mugs and left them then, Isabelle waiting patiently to shut the door after him, before putting the cake out on a plate and handing out side plates, cake forks and napkins.

David smiled across at Anna.

'A bit formal, aren't we?' grinning at Anna whilst addressing Isabelle. 'What's wrong with fingers? They were always good enough in the past!'

'Well, you're a barrister now. I thought you'd expect more formality these days!' she said in mock severity.

'Being a barrister doesn't change a person, you know. I'm still the same person I always was. I hope I don't seem to have changed that much to you, do I? Sit down with us and have your tea and cake. I've no objections, and I'm sure Anna hasn't either.'

'Thank you, Mr. David. It's nice to hear that, but if you don't mind, I'd rather sit in my own chair. It's comfortable, and it's already shaped to my bottom,' and with that she plonked herself down in the chair and put her cup on top of the covered range, 'keeps my tea warm as well on top of there.'

She'd put three different kinds of cake out onto the plate, and David and Anna both helped themselves to a slice of each. They were both beginning to feel very hungry by now.

Seeing them eat so much, Isabelle said when they'd finished, 'You go up to your rooms now and get yourselves settled in. I'll get some lunch ready for about an hour's time. Will that suit?'

Glancing at Anna, who nodded her head, David answered, 'that'll be fine – but we'll eat in here. Don't bother opening the dining room up, this'll suit us both just fine.'

64

Next morning Anna awoke to the sound of a quiet knock on her door.

Turning over, she looked at the small clock she'd brought with her. It showed 9a.m.

'What the hell! . . .' she murmured. She hadn't slept this late in years.

The knock sounded again, accompanied by a quiet voice saying, 'Are you awake, miss?' and followed by the door beginning to open.

'Yes, come in,' she called back.

The woman who appeared was middle aged and was carrying a cup of tea.

'I'm Sandra,' she announced, as she put the cup down on the little table alongside the bed. 'I'm Isabelle's cousin and I help with the jobs around the house. I brought you a cup of tea – but I'll change it for coffee if you prefer.'

'Tea's fine,' Anna answered, making no attempt to sit up.

She always slept naked, and realised now that she'd have to wear a tee shirt to bed if Sandra was going to bring her a cup of tea every morning while she was here. She felt embarrassed by her nakedness. When they were at home, it never caused a problem because she had the whole of the attic floor to herself, and her own bathroom, so there was no need for David to ever venture up there.

Sandra was already turning back to the door, but before she went out, she turned back.

'Isabelle says breakfast will be in half an hour; and she'll serve it in the kitchen if that suits you.'

'Yes, that'll do me fine,' she answered, and then, as an afterthought, 'have you woken David yet?'

'Mr. David's been up for a good hour now,' she answered. 'He took his father's dog out for a run on the moors. The poor thing hasn't been out for a few days now. He'll be glad of the exercise.'

Once Sandra was gone, Anna got out of bed and pulled on her dressing gown, opening the curtains and sitting on the window seat in the bay window while she drank her tea.

As David had told her, this room got the morning light, and, although it was late in the autumn, the sun was already above the horizon and shining in.

Looking out, she could see a steep hillside descending into a valley in front of her, and ascending once more to a higher hilltop beyond. Further out behind that were yet more hilltops, finally giving way to mountain peaks rising even higher above them. From what little knowledge she already had of the area, she knew that she must be looking towards the mountainous regions of Snowdonia.

As she looked out over the view, her eyes strayed to the left hand side of the window. Just coming into view from over the rough moorland towards her was the figure of David; his father's Springer Spaniel scampering in and out of the already dying bracken; his tail almost going round in circles with his efforts to put up some game. Dressed in waterproof trousers, with a tweed jacket and cap, David looked every inch the country gentleman he could once have been if it hadn't been for the row with his father.

Heavens! He'd be back soon and breakfast would be ready too! She'd have to get a move on, gulping down the last of her tea as she made for the bathroom and washed quickly.

From the way David was dressed it looked like informality was going to be the order of the day, and to that end she dressed in jeans and a polo neck sweater, together with socks and trainers before running downstairs to the kitchen, finding David already seated at the table.

'Morning Anna. Did you sleep well?' he asked as she entered.

'Brilliantly!' she answered, before turning to Isabelle. 'I'm sorry if I'm late for breakfast – I had no idea I'd slept so long.'

The woman was standing by the range and didn't look at all put out by her late appearance.

'Doesn't matter,' she said, opening the oven door and producing two plates from its interior. 'Wrap yourselves around that. I'm sure Mr. David's ready for it after his walk this morning.'

'Sure am,' David replied, eyeing up the ham, sausage, tomatoes and mushrooms on the plate. 'I'm sure I can do this justice! I usually only have toast and marmalade at home.'

Anna looked a little put out.

'I'd be only too happy to do that for you at home if you wanted it. You only have to ask.'

'I never have the time,' he answered, looking at her sheepishly and realising he'd put his foot in it. He'd meant no criticism of the way she looked after him, 'I wasn't criticising you – honestly I wasn't! It's just nice to have the time to sit and enjoy something like this for once in a while.'

Breakfast over, David and Anna went straight to his father's study, where they began to search through the paperwork for anything of significance.

'His Will is the main thing I'm looking for,' was David's first comment. 'Let me know if you find anything looking remotely like one – and look through his files as well – he could have hidden it away in one of those. I'll nip up to his room and get the combination for the safe – I know where he kept it, and he used to change it every month to make sure it was kept secure.'

Entering the bedroom was like entering a blast from the past. Nothing much had changed since he was last here.

The big old four poster bed that his grandfather had bought when he and his wife first brought their young family to live here still stood against the opposite wall to the window, where his mother had always looked out and enjoyed the view whilst she drank her morning cup of tea. She'd spent so much time working out what each mountain peak was that she'd become quite expert at it, and it was with regret that he realised he'd never see her again. For the first time the full impact of that knowledge hit him, and he began to feel the emotion welling up inside him.

Too late for recrimination! She was gone for good and he'd never ever see her again. It was time to stop dwelling on the past before self-pity overwhelmed him – time to get on with the job in hand and find the combination to his fathers' safe. They had a lot of work to do within the short space of a week and he couldn't waste time thinking about the past.

The paper bearing the combination was exactly where he expected to find it – taped underneath the drawer in the bedside cupboard. Quickly extracting it, he took it downstairs without allowing himself to look back.

Anna hadn't yet found anything of significance, save for a notebook with login details for all his online accounts, which he'd kept in his desk.

'Thanks,' David said, as she pointed it out to him. 'That'll probably be very useful, but I need to find his Will first. Without that, and knowing who is to inherit, nothing else is of any use for the time being.'

The safe yielded exactly what he was looking for!

Sitting on the top shelf was a copy of his fathers' Will, and alongside it, a well-thumbed copy of his mothers as well.

'Anna, go and ask Isabelle for some coffee would you, and then we'll take these into the lounge and go through them there. It looks pretty thick and may need a lot of going through. I know he always made a lot of investments, so there's probably a section assigning them as well.'

After a quick stop for some cold lunch, followed by a full afternoon of going through everything, David was fairly confident that he was getting to grips with it all.

As he'd thought, his father had cut him out of his Will almost entirely, save for a yearly stipend of £50,000 a year for the first 10 years following his death, as well as a few lesser value stocks and shares – the rest was left entirely to his wife, and if she predeceased him, everything was to go to Jayne – including the house. If she decided to sell it, David was to receive just one eighth of its value.

It wasn't entirely unexpected, but it still came as quite a shock!

Noticing him sitting there staring into space, Anna stopped what she'd been doing.

'Have you found it?' she asked, coming over to him.

He nodded.

'And . . . ?'

'He's left me a very minor share, as I expected,' he replied, ruefully. 'He's left the house entirely to Jayne, and I only get an eighth share if she ever decides to sell it.'

She sat down alongside him, knowing how much of a shock this must be to him, and seeing, from the look on his face, how much it was affecting him.

'That must have been some row!' she finally said. 'Care to tell me about it?'

'No, I can't!' was his almost abrupt reply; then, as if realising just how abrupt he had been, he dropped his head, saying, 'It was far too personal. I don't think I'll ever be able to tell anybody!'

His tone was adamant, leaving her in no doubt how much bad feeling the row must have caused between them. If, and when, he was ready, he might feel able to tell somebody, but for the time being it was far too raw.

'Can you contest it?' was her next thought.

'I can try, but I don't deal with inheritance law – I'm a criminal barrister. I'll need to get proper advice from someone who does know before I can decide what's best to do. If he'd left me absolutely nothing, I might have had a better chance, but seeing as he has left me something – and it is quite a lot when it boils down to it – I probably wouldn't have a chance of contesting the Will. These were his wishes, after all. They were what he wanted, and what he intended, so who am I to try and change those wishes.'

She could see how sad he seemed about the situation, she nodded towards the other Will sitting on the small table alongside.

'What about your mother's Will? Does that leave you anything?'

'No. They left everything to each other if one died before the other. The only thing I get from my mother's Will are her personal bequests to me, and I don't know where they are at present. I presume we're going to find them somewhere amongst my father's things when we have a proper look, but it's not that much. I've already had the money my grandparents left. All her jewellery and clothes have been left to Jayne, but she's probably already had those if she was still here when mother died.'

She felt sorry for David, but when it all boiled down to it, £50,000 a year for the next 10 years seemed a princely sum to her, but compared to the value of all his fathers' assets, and the house as well, it was poor pickings for his son. When they did eventually find Jayne, she'd be a very wealthy woman!

After a few more minutes of rummaging around, David finally put everything down and stretched.

'Come on – let's go and have another yomp across the moors with the dog. It's far too nice an afternoon to spend indoors, and it starts getting dark around 6 o'clock these days.'

'Good idea. My backs starting to ache as well and my concentration's flagging; I could do with stretching my legs out in the fresh air for a bit,' she answered, pushing the papers aside and rising to her feet. 'This lot'll still be here tomorrow.

CHAPTER 6

All the rest of the week they spent their days after leisurely lie-ins and enormous breakfasts going through the rest of the Judge's papers and making the funeral arrangements. In the late afternoons, they laid everything to one side and took the dog for a walk, spending a couple of hours in the invigorating fresh air before returning for dinner.

One afternoon they even went into Denbigh and spent their time browsing round the shops – something that David had never ever considered doing before; and just for the fun of it. He'd always gone to a shop with a purpose in mind, and with a need for something to buy, but never just for the fun of it. He couldn't say he found it particularly invigorating either, but he did enjoy spending time in Anna's company, and without the constant need to work their way through paperwork for hours on end. They found a nice little teashop for coffee and cake before their return, spending their time chatting while they ate.

The entire following day after that was taken up with the funeral, which took place on Friday. They'd decided to make it just a small private affair for family and close friends only, even though he knew his father had had many acquaintances who would have wanted to attend. With only a stay of such short duration, it was totally impractical to open up all the rooms for those who needed to stay over, and it eventually ended up with being just what they'd intended – a small private affair with only about a dozen close friends, including himself, and the staff.

Anna, who'd never even known his father, stayed behind to put out the prepared food, and Irene, the young girl from the village who helped on a daily basis when needed, was brought in to dust, polish and tidy everything in the rooms where the guests were likely to visit.

A notice was booked for one of the national newspapers for the following day to inform the rest of the legal fraternity, and anyone else who might be interested. He knew a lot of them would be put out at not knowing beforehand so that they could have been present at the funeral, but it was exactly what David intended.

The funeral took place at 11.00a.m. His father had never been religious, and he never remembered him going to church; nor had he ever voiced his wishes as to how he wanted his send-off, so David arranged for a cremation.

It was shorter and necessitated less time and fuss, and besides which, it cost less. Not that David couldn't afford it, just that he didn't intend to spend any more than he had to on the old bastard.

Their row had been acrimonious – and the reason for it was still stark in his memory. It was something for which he would never ever forgive his father, and something that he doubted he could ever speak to anybody about ever again.

During the service, it brought it all back to him in a very vivid way, and he found himself hoping that the old man would never be able to rest in peace for what he'd done in his lifetime. The burning of his body seemed to be a fitting end for him!

The next day, while the staff were re-arranging the furniture, putting away crockery and left over food, David and Anna slept late and shut themselves away in the study after breakfast once again; this time trying to tie up all the loose ends. The rest of the paperwork could be taken back to Little Bannerman and gone through there at their leisure.

As a result of all the tidying up, lunch wasn't served until late, and Anna announced she needed to take a trip into Denbigh before their return home.

'Sorry, but I need some shopping to take home with me. I haven't got my car with me, so I'm afraid I'll have to prevail on you to take me – unless you lend me yours?'

'Sorry, but it's only insured for me, so if looks like I'll have to take you after all,' he said, smiling ruefully, but deep down feeling glad of the welcome break and being able to enjoy some more personal time with her.

When they arrived back, it was nearly 4 o'clock, and Anna declared that she was going to take a long hot soak in the bath before dinner.

'Like me to join you?' he quipped, half joking, but knowing that if she'd said 'yes', he'd have joined her in a flash.

'Not today,' she quipped back and laughed, but deep down inside feeling a little embarrassed. He'd never said anything like that before, and there'd never been any allusion to any sort of sexuality between them before either.

'Shame!' he said, laughing too. 'Looks like I'm stuck with taking the dog out then!'

He was out for a lot longer than he'd expected, enjoying the fresh air and the last of the autumn sunshine, when he decided to look round the gardens before going indoors.

They'd be going home the next afternoon, and he hadn't yet had a chance to look round them properly, so wrapped up had they been in looking though his fathers' affairs that he'd only seen them fleetingly through the windows.

There was a terrace at the side of the house with three steps leading down to a lawn, which was open to the vagaries of the winter winds, and which only held the hardiest of ornamental shrubs and trees. It had been the place where he and his brothers always played when they were younger, but now they were all gone, and the garden was taking on its autumn colours yet again as winter drew nearer – the lawn beginning to cover over with yellow and orange leaves.

Matthew, only 2 years younger than him, had been killed at the age of 15 when he'd had some mates over on a hot summer's afternoon, and they'd gone into the woods to play.

Years previously, Gavin had fixed up a rope swing on one of the tree branches, with an old car tyre for a seat. It was an old oak, and had always been considered solid and strong, but, unknown to them, it had been struck by lightning at some time in the not too distant past, and the branch had been damaged at its junction with the trunk.

After only a few swings, it was Matthew's turn again; and he was always a bit of a daredevil! He tried to go higher than the others, and as he came down towards the ground, with an enormous crack, the branch parted from the trunk, falling straight down; but he wasn't killed by the branch. He was catapulted a good distance by the velocity of his downward swinging arc, and hit another sturdy oak standing right in front – head on!

One of the other boys, traumatised by what he'd seen, told David sometime afterwards that he'd seen Matthew's brains "splattered all over the trunk". A rather insensitive thing to say to his brother, but then, at the age of 14, lads that age never thought about things like that, or considered the feelings of other people. Some never even gained that sensitivity all through their lives. Although David hadn't seen it for himself, it was an image he'd never forget throughout his entire life, and was one that came to him sometimes at the most inappropriate moments during the rest of that lifetime.

Karl was the next in line, just 18 months younger than Matthew. He'd always been prone to chest infections throughout his short life. At the age of 13, he'd had a particularly bad one and developed pneumonia, from which he never managed to recover.

Raymond was the next child, born 3 years after Karl. He was born with a heart defect, and even though his father took him to an eminent heart surgeon to try and save him, there was eventually nothing they could do for him and he died at the age of 6 months.

There followed quite a gap after that before Jayne was born – she was a curly, blonde headed child, and always up to mischief, causing his mother endless worry when she kept wandering off.

One day, when Jayne was only 4 years old, his father came home from work and caught her sitting on the edge of the fish pond, and he was furious with his mother for not keeping a closer eye on her. Jayne was the apple of his eye, and he treated her much better than he ever had any of the boys, with whom he'd always been very strict.

From then on, everybody in the family, even the staff, kept a closer eye on her, but David was already away at University by then, and he'd seen little of her while she was growing up.

Turning his thoughts away from their morbid side, David's attentions were drawn to the walled garden, which stood alongside the lawned area.

They hadn't been allowed in there when they were younger, except under supervision, and a high wrought iron gate barred the way. It was never locked, and had a gravelled path leading from the driveway straight to it, but it had always acted as a barrier to them. They knew they weren't allowed through it without prior permission or without another grown up being present. Its produce was used to feed the household, and whatever was left was sold to the local shops.

Today, he stopped as he reached it. The gate was shut, and some primeval instinct was telling him that he wasn't allowed through it.

Smiling to himself, he opened it and went through. There was nobody to stop him, or to tell him off now. He was free as a bird to do as he liked.

The walled garden wasn't very big, but it was still very well kept as he looked around. The soil beds flanking the sides had always been filled with the various vegetables the gardeners grew – most of them empty now that the summer produce had finished. They'd already been dug and manured in preparation for the following year – sheep dung always readily available off the surrounding moorland. The retaining walls behind the beds were surmounted with espaliered fruit trees growing up and across. They were tied up on wooden frameworks – mostly apple and pear, but he now noticed there were plums as well.

The small central area was gravelled, with a square brick plinth raising two large water butts up off the ground. Rainfall was high here, and they rarely ran out of water, taps at the bottom allowing watering cans to be filled during dry or hot weather.

There was a man sitting on the edge of the brick plinth today, and he was filling a pipe with tobacco from a pouch.

He was sideways on to David, and he couldn't be quite sure who he was, but he did seem vaguely familiar.

As he walked over, the dog shot ahead of him and began to show signs of greeting towards the man, jumping up and then down to the ground again as he got a whiff of the disagreeable tobacco.

'Hello, boy, what you doin' 'ere? 'ave you got out again?' the man said, putting down his pipe and reaching down to fondle the dog, turning as he heard the sound of David's footsteps coming towards him over the gravel.

His look turned to one of recognition as he got to his feet.

'David, I 'eard yew were back. Long time no see! Dad sed yew were back. Ow are yew?'

'I'm fine, Morgan,' he answered, 'and it does seem an age since we last met. How are you?'

'I'm fine. Yew' bin' takin' this little tyke for a walk then? I done it a few times since the Judge died, but 'e really should ge' out more.'

'Mind if I sit alongside for a while? I could do with a rest before I go in to wash for dinner,' David replied, pleased to see his childhood friend again.

'It'ud be my pleasure,' Morgan said. ''Eard yew're a fancy barrister now. I's a wonder yew've go' time for us poor country bumpkins these days,' as they both sat down side by side.

'I had to come home to see to my father's affairs and get everything straight. You don't know where Jayne's gone, do you?'

Morgan dropped his head.

'No idea. Been a few years since I las' saw 'er. Jus' up and left one day and nobody's seen 'er since. Judge never give us no explanation.'

'I need to find her. She's a beneficiary of the Will.'

This time Morgan just shrugged his shoulders without saying anything, and they chatted on for a while without mentioning Jayne again – but Morgan did seem to have something on his mind.

Finally, David was about to stand up and leave when Morgan put a restraining hand on his arm.

'David, I need to tell yew' somethin' – but I want it to stay just between yew' and me. Will yew' promise me tha'?'

'Of course I will,' he said, sitting back down again.

Morgan seemed a little abashed as he began to speak – as if a little ashamed of what he was about to tell David.

'Me an' Miss Jayne got quite close at one time – in fac' we was very close, if yew' take my meaning.'

David looked at him, surprised. Morgan was only a couple of years younger than him, and a great deal older than Jayne.

'Go ahead, it's all water under the bridge now. There's nobody left I could tell that'd be interested – and you certainly don't have to worry about my father any more. I won't say anything to your father either if that's what you're worried about. I presume he doesn't know?'

Morgan hung his head again, his voice almost imperceptible as he spoke this time.

'No, he doesn' know, bu' it's yew' I'm more worried about. I don' know what yew're goin' to think of me when I tell yew.'

'Go ahead,' David sighed. 'You've gone too far to stop now. If you don't finish it, I'll be conjuring up all sorts of things in my head. Nothing could be worse than that.'

77

Morgan hesitated again before continuing.

'As I sed, we go' very close. She come to see me one day. Sed' she thought she was pregnant,' then with a sheepish sideways look at David, 'she were on'y 17 at the time, an' it on'y 'appened the once. I knew yew're father would be furious. Couldn' 'ave 'is daughter marrying the 'ired 'ands, could 'e?'

'But that was years ago!' David said. 'Did she have the baby?'

'I never found owt. It was just after tha' tha' she disappeared. I never saw 'er again. I don't know where she went, or whether she 'ad the baby. I wanted to find owt, but I couldn' ask yew're father, could I? An' there was nobody else to ask.'

'You could have found me on the internet,' David rebuked. 'I don't know where she's gone either, but if I'd known sooner, I could at least have tried to find her and help her. I've more resources for finding people than you have, but the trail's probably well cold by now.'

Morgan looked shamefaced.

'David, it's been 'ard enough telling yew now, and face to face, without 'aving to tell yew over the 'phone, or worse still, in an e-mail.'

David had to agree that that was the least favourable way of telling him, but there must have been some way round it, even if it meant giving Morgan his address, or meeting him somewhere in an out of the way place; but even though it was so much later, he was still glad he knew now.

How could Jayne have managed anywhere else with no assets and an illegitimate baby? Her mother was already gone, and even though he knew she'd have helped her daughter through it, there was no way Jayne could have turned to his father. He was sure he'd have turned her out, or at least made her have an abortion. There was no other help he'd have given her.

Was that just what had happened? And if not, where could she be now? Possibly the only person who had any idea where she might be was his father – and it was too late to find out anything from him now.

The next afternoon, whilst they were looking through the last few things in his father's study, Anna came across an insignificant looking notebook tucked away in a small, and at first, overlooked little drawer in his desk.

'Any idea what this is?' she asked, holding it up in front of David.

He took it from her and looked at it.

'No idea,' he said, 'never seen it before.'

The notebook was only A5 size, bound in black leather and with an attached red tassel for marking the place.

He put it down in front of him and opened it at the first page.

The sheets inside were lined in black, and three precise vertical lines had been drawn down the page; the first column on the left quite wide, and the other two on the right hand side much narrower.

The top line had only a date written on it – that of 1972, and the left hand column consisted of a list of names, all looking to be the surnames of people. In the column to the right of each one was written an amount, and the far right hand side contained a tick or a cross.

The lines read:-

Spencer	£25	√
Davies	£25	√
Ranson	£25	√
Stansfield		x
Williams	£25	√
Shenfield	£25	√

There were a total of 6 names on the page, but the name of Stansfield hadn't been marked with an amount.

79

Turning over, the second page was again laid out the same, with the same series of ticks and crosses, although the date on this page was now 1974, and there were only 4 names written on it.

Again the name Stansfield was inserted, once again with no amount, and a cross alongside.

On the third page, marked 1975, there were another 4 names. Amongst them was the name Stansfield yet again, and this time with a tick alongside it and an amount of £50.

The rest of the book continued in the same vein, sometimes missing several years altogether, but as they progressed through it, the amounts began to grow larger, until the final year in the book, 1999, showed the amounts to be £300 each time, although the crosses or blanks remained the same.

'Any idea what it means?' Anna said, as he showed it to her.

'I've no idea,' he answered, turning to the next page, equally as baffled as her.

After another look through it, an idea began to form in his head.

'I wonder if my father could have been lending out money to people. It certainly could account for the ticks and crosses alongside each amount, and maybe the blank spaces indicate that he hadn't been repaid,' as he handed it to her for her opinion.

With this notion in mind, she went through it once again, paying much more attention to the statistics, while he continued with the other papers he'd been looking through. Finally she turned to him and said, 'I don't think that can be right. Over the last few years until 1999 when it stops altogether, he's lent out far more money than he's had in returns. Surely he wouldn't have gone on lending out so much money if it wasn't being repaid.'

'Doesn't sound like my father,' he answered, taking it from her and looking through it again, 'but I don't suppose we'll ever find out what it means now he's gone. For the time being, there's other things need looking at, and that's all in the past now. There've been no entries since 1999.'

CHAPTER 7

Marnie Peters' mother died just 3 months before her own 50th birthday.

Her death was as sudden as it was unexpected!

They'd only spoken on the 'phone at lunchtime, and by 8 o'clock that night she was on her way to the hospital – but she arrived just too late! A kindly doctor who'd been awaiting her arrival told her that her mother had passed away just minutes beforehand.

She sat at the bedside holding her mothers' hand and weeping copiously for 20 minutes before she pulled herself together and decided to let them take the body down to the mortuary. There was nothing more she could do for her here, and common sense told her that a much needed bed was being held up from someone else who was probably in more need of it.

She didn't believe in an afterlife. Her mother was gone! What now lay before her in the bed was just an empty shell that had once held her mothers' spirit. Now that was gone, the body before her no longer represented her mother; who would go on living only in her memory, and that of others who'd once known her: that memory itself only fleeting as the years rolled inexorably by and they themselves passed on, leaving nobody behind who still remembered them.

The doctor asked if she was all right to drive home, but luckily her husband Warren had had the good sense to drive her there, fearing that she might speed recklessly in her need to get to her mothers' side. He'd come in with her to see the dead woman, but after a few minutes, she asked if he'd wait outside. She wanted to spend some time on her own and gather her thoughts together, but instead she cried like a baby for most of the time without really thinking about anything else.

When she did finally emerge, he said nothing, seeing the red and swollen face emerging, and they drove all the way home in silence; he, realising that she wasn't in need of conversation at that moment in time, wisely kept his counsel.

Together they ran a successful jewellery shop in the centre of Chester, and they'd just finished eating dinner when that fateful call came through.

Once they pulled up in front of the house, she was too distraught to focus on anything else that evening, and went straight upstairs for a shower and an early night, leaving Warren to clear the dishes away and run the dishwasher.

When he went up to join her, just over an hour later, it was obvious that she'd been crying again, but she was now fast asleep.

Next morning, she got up for work as usual, but Warren stopped her.

'Take today off,' he persuaded, 'It's Wednesday, and it's always a quiet day. Diane and I can manage in the shop for one day, and then we'll see how you feel tomorrow. Besides, you've 'phone calls to make – her sister for one!'

She'd forgotten all about Carolyn, her mother's sister. She must ring her first thing. They'd lived only half a mile apart on the outskirts of Mold in North Wales, and, having lost both their husbands some 5 years ago, and within a few months of each other, they'd spent a lot of time in each other's company ever since.

Carolyn was upset when she heard, but didn't seem unduly surprised.

'Was it another stroke?' she asked, wearily.

'Another stroke?' Marnie asked. 'Had she had one before?'

82

'Yes,' Carolyn answered, 'two previous ones – but only very minor. I told her she ought to tell you, but she didn't want to. She recovered very quickly from both and said you had a busy enough life without her heaping more worries on your shoulders.'

'I would have wanted to know,' Marnie said in a small voice. 'How could she have kept it from me!'

'What could you have done if you'd known? Nothing! And I was always here to see her through it,' Carolyn replied.

She knew both statements were true. Their jeweller's shop was always busy, and the sisters had always been close, particularly since they'd both been widowed. Warren had a flair for the designing of gold and silver jewellery, and a lot of his pieces adorned the necks and fingers of some of the top families in the country.

With the money they'd earned over the years, they'd bought a beautiful old sandstone house on the outskirts of Chester, situated in the Cheshire countryside overlooking the River Dee, and not far from the Duke of Westminster's home.

They'd never had any children – but then, neither of them had ever felt the need to have children cluttering up their lives. They'd been quite content with each other and their work in the shop, which they both enjoyed – Warren's creative side spilling over into their home life as well. He often spent whole evenings in his small room at the back of the house, which had become his workshop, when he was working on something new, and she was happy with her own pursuits. She went for her habitual evening run round the quiet lanes, or, if the weather was too bad, or if it was too dark in the winter, she had her own gym within the house itself.

'Look Carolyn,' she said, 'I'm not at work today. Do you fancy meeting me at mum's house and we'll go through her things together?'

'Yes, that would suit me just grand. Your mum and I were going to go shopping today, but now I'm at a loose end. How long will you be?'

Now the die was cast, and she met Carolyn at her mother's home just over an hour later, noticing that her face too was rather red and blotchy. She'd obviously been crying since she'd heard the news. Both of them had a key to the house, and the kettle was already on when she arrived.

After a quick coffee, they started rummaging round the cupboards and drawers and soon amassed a pile of things to go through.

Some were immediately relegated to the bin – one house insurance policy even dating back to before her father's death, and a miscellany of oddments in the bottom of various drawers also found their way there. Surprising how much clutter one collected over the years without taking the time to go through it every so often!

She noticed Carolyn take out a green folder from the bureau that had once been her father's, but instead of opening it, she put it to one side.

'What's that?' she asked.

'That?' Carolyn sounded as if she were trying to put her off, feigning not to know what it was, but she was obviously well aware of what it contained. 'Oh, nothing that need bother you for the time being. You can look at it later after we've finished.'

The petulant and spoilt side of Marnie came out at once. She herself had been an only child, and to a mother and father who adored and, although they tried hard not to, had sometimes overindulged her.

'No secrets, Carolyn,' she said, facing her aunt full on. 'You're not keeping anything from me! What is it? I want to know now!'

Knowing her niece wasn't going to be put off, Carolyn sighed reluctantly.

'Ok,' she said, 'but let's do it over some lunch. I'm hungry and I noticed some slices of leftover chicken in the 'fridge. Let's make a sandwich with it – your mother won't need it now, and it needs eating up. I don't know just how long it might already have been there, but it smells fresh enough.'

84

Marnie followed her into the kitchen, picking up the folder as she went. Her aunt had either forgotten it, or deliberately left it where it was. Maybe it was a delaying tactic, or in the hope that she'd forget it, but she wasn't about to find out, and made sure she took it with her.

With their sandwich eaten and a pot of tea emptied, Marnie leaned over and picked up the folder once more.

'Let's open this now, shall we?' she said, looking her aunt straight in the eye. 'What is it you don't want me to see?'

Carolyn looked down at the table before lifting her eyes and looking back at her.

'I suppose you've got to open it sometime, and now's probably as good a time as any. Go ahead and open it!'

The first thing she found inside was a rather yellowed envelope, addressed on the front: *To my dearest daughter.*

Her mother had written her a letter, but what it held she had no idea, and it didn't seem to be in her mothers' handwriting. Perhaps it was something she hadn't been able to tell her face to face during her lifetime.

'Look at the next piece of paper first,' Carolyn's voice interjected, 'then the letter will make more sense to you'.

She lifted out the next sheet of slightly more authoritative looking paper, again a little creased and discoloured.

It was a Birth Certificate, outlining the birth of a girl child, but with no name given, and the mother's name as Celia West. The space where the father's name should have been was blank.

'Look at the date of birth,' Carolyn's voice intoned, 'and then open the letter.'

Her eyes roved across the page until she found the right place – it was exactly the same birth date as hers.'

She lifted her eyes questioningly towards Carolyn, who merely reached over, and, picking up the envelope, handed it to her.

'Read this now,' was all she said.

Anxiously, Marnie ripped open the envelope. There was no address given, and the letter started straight off from the top of the page.

The hand was easy to read, and the person who'd written it was obviously well educated, judging by the spelling and the punctuation, but she was beginning to feel a sense of dread as she skimmed quickly through the sheet of yellowed paper in front of her.

'Read it properly,' Carolyn's voice urged, knowing they'd gone too far to turn back now. 'I'll put the kettle on while you try to take it all in.'

Smoothing the paper out on the table, she began to read:

My dearest daughter,

When you read this, the dear woman who brought you up will be long gone, and so probably will I. I asked her to keep this letter for you to read after her death.

When I was at University, I went to a student party that got out of hand, and we all became very drunk, with the result that I became pregnant – but sad to say, I don't remember who your father was.

When my family found out, my own father insisted I get rid of the child, and I really had no choice or he said he would put me out on the streets. I had no money of my own, and without anywhere to live, I wouldn't be able to bring you up. Believe me, I really had no alternative but to find someone to take you from me and keep you safe. We were together for the first few weeks of your life, and I found our parting almost unbearable.

Please believe that I have always loved you dearly, and I left this letter for you in the hope that you wouldn't think too harshly of me.

Your loving mother forever, Celia West

Hardly able to believe what she was reading, Marine looked up at Carolyn when she'd finished.

'Did you know about this?'

Carolyn nodded; a guilty look on her face.

'I've always known – right from the day they picked you up. I always said you should have been told, but they refused. They said it would be time enough when they were gone. Your adoptive father had just found out he was infertile, so there'd never be any children of their own, but they wanted to go on pretending that you were their very own.'

Marnie looked down and re-read the letter, before opening the folder again.

'Where's the adoption papers?' she asked. 'Why aren't they here?'

'There weren't any. Your grandparents were friends of Celia's parents, and it was arranged between them. When Celia became pregnant, it coincided with the time your adoptive parents found out they'd never be able to have children, so the solution seemed obvious to both parties. Your mother was only 10 years older than Celia herself, so it was just an arrangement made between them. hey took you from her at just 6 weeks old, and Celia never knew who'd taken her baby.'

'That was very cruel,' Marnie said in a small voice.

'Cruel to be kind,' Carolyn replied, shrugging her shoulders. 'Morals were different in those days, and an illegitimate child in a family was a very shameful thing. Celia couldn't look after you by herself, and her father was adamant he wasn't having an illegitimate child under his roof. Your adoptive parents sold their former home and moved here soon after. They didn't want you and Celia meeting up at any time in the future.'

'My mother was 79 when she died. If Celia was 10 years younger she'd only be in her late 60's now. She could still be alive.'

'Possibly,' Carolyn said, 'but I've no idea where she is now.'

The trail seemed to be going cold, as Marnie turned back to the folder, but it was empty and contained nothing else. No little mementoes or information had been left for her to find.

What about my father?' she asked. 'Have you any idea who he might have been?'

'Absolutely none! I didn't go to University, and Jim and I have lived around here since we first married. We never knew Celia or her family, and your parents lived in Cheshire when they took you. They moved here to get away from Celia to stop you meeting up in the future. I don't think Celia ever knew who your father was herself.'

Even as she spoke, Marnie was trying to think of ways to find her mother. There was a possibility of her still being alive, and she wanted very much to meet up with her before it was too late – if it wasn't already!

When Marnie's 50th birthday arrived, she received the most surprising birthday present she'd ever had from her husband.

Instead of jewellery or a foreign holiday, he'd presented her with just a small cardboard box and a birthday card. Inside the card was a password and login details for a web site – and inside the box was a DNA kit.

She gaped at him in bewilderment.

'What's this?' she asked.

'Why don't you use the login details and find out,' he laughed, registering the surprised look on her face.

When she switched on the computer, she found that the login took her into a genealogy website, and the details to begin her family tree had already been entered.

There were her and Warren's parents' names, with their dates of birth, and also dates of death filled in, as his parents too were both dead.

'It's up to you to start building it up from there,' he stated, looking at her.

'And just how am I going to do that when I don't know who my father was?' she asked.

'That's what the DNA kit's for, dumbo! There may be a chance that your father's DNA may be on record somewhere, and it may throw some light on just who he is!'

The penny dropped!

'What a wonderful present,' she gasped. 'I'd never even thought about doing anything like that.'

'Well, now's your chance! All you have to do is drop some saliva into the little test tube and send it off. It shouldn't take very long to come back.'

'I'll do that straight away,' she said gleefully, pulling out the instructions.

'Yes, but read them first,' he said. 'It wasn't cheap so make sure you get it right first time. I don't want to have to pay for it all over again.

She'd completed the task within the next few minutes, and posted it on the outskirts of Chester on their way to work the next day.

CHAPTER 8

David and Anna had arrived back at Little Bannerman, and since then, their association seemed to be on more level ground than before. There were a lot of steps to be taken after Hector's death, not least of all the finding of the two lads in the car responsible for his death.

The car turned out to be stolen, and it looked as if they'd just been joyriding in it – turning a boring afternoon into a spin in a high performance car, which they were eventually to find too powerful for them to handle.

The owner, a businessman returning home to Corwen from a trip to Conwy, had stopped in a layby to 'take a leak', as he put it, and had unwisely left the door unlocked and the engine running. He told the police that the road was very quiet and that there were no other vehicles in the small parking area when he arrived. It was surmised that the lads had been hanging around nearby and spotted a likely opportunity. As soon as he'd gone out of sight of the road, they'd seized the chance, leaving him stranded in the middle of nowhere.

Unfortunately, the police weren't very sympathetic, knowing how stupid he'd been, but due to the seriousness of the collision, causing the death of such a prominent figure as Judge Hector Bannerman, the search went on for the lads who'd stolen it.

It wasn't the first time this had happened on a quiet country road, and it wouldn't be the last!

The police realised there was every chance that they lived nearby, but finding out who they were, and just where they lived, was another matter entirely. Their main chance was through the blood that was found at the scene – that's if it could be definitively identified. If they were new at this game, or hadn't come to the attention of the police before, their job would be all that much harder.

Once David and Anna arrived back, he had become embroiled in another case that needed his full attention, and had left a list of people for Anna to contact on his behalf. She was asked to inform them of his fathers' death, and to give his apologies for not being able to speak to them himself, due to the pressure of work. She also gave them the assurance that he'd be in touch once he was able.

They both knew he probably wouldn't, and this was all the contact they'd get, but it seemed to appease everyone for the time being.

Things like insurance companies, Inland Revenue, and pension companies she was able to inform, having been given the papers with all the relevant details, but David had put all the details relating to his stocks and shares, investments, etc., into the hands of a professional accountancy firm specialising in that sort of thing.

Once all that was done, they'd be able to settle down to a normal life once again.

Although David was very busy, and shut away in his small study most days for nearly the whole day, Anna felt their relationship had moved up a notch, and he was no longer looking on her as just the hired help. They seemed to be much more than that these days!

Their evenings, once they'd eaten dinner, were often spent together, when she informed him of what progress she'd made. Then she'd make them a hot drink and they'd talk about more general things, or watch television together, before they retired to their separate rooms.

He always seemed to be so busy, and she began to realise that he didn't have room for anyone else in his life at present, only someone to talk to when he needed to, and someone to look after his needs – but then, that's just what she'd been employed to do!

'David,' she said, broaching the subject for the first time one evening, 'have you decided what you're going to do with Bannerman's yet? You've not mentioned it since we got back.'

'I haven't really had much time,' he sighed resignedly. 'I just don't know what to do with it. The staff have all been looking after the place for years, so I'm confident they'll go on doing that until I make up my mind. If I sell it, I don't know what'll happen to them, and I can't just put them out after all the year's service they've given. Isabelle has lived in her own room on the top floor since I was in my early teens, and so has Cyril, the odd job man. Sandra also lived there too until she married a farmer's son from the local area.

The two gardeners, Gavin, and his son Morgan, have always lived in a rented cottage father owned on the edge of the woods, together with his wife Gwen. I can't ever remember a time before Gavin and Gwen lived there. Morgan and I spent a lot of time together when we were younger, and we were great mates!

They've nowhere else to go – and I'm still not sure whether I want to go back and live there myself. It's rather a large place for one man living on his own, and very remote to say the least – not that that would really bother me. I spent all my life living there when I was younger, and it didn't bother me then, so I doubt it would now.'

She felt rather crestfallen. If he did go back to live at Bannerman's, he wouldn't have need of her any more, then she'd have no job, and no place to live either. She'd have to start looking round for both all over again, and she had little money saved to keep her going until then.

Over the next month, they went back to spend a couple of weekends at his fathers' house. The staff seemed to be running the place efficiently enough; but then, there was little for them to do without a family to look after.

The house itself was being kept clean and tidy, and everything was in its place. Cyril had managed to get some odd jobs done that he'd been unable to manage previously; ones that needed to be done before the winter arrived, and Gavin and Morgan were busy getting the rose bed and the rest of the garden pruned and cleared of dead and dying foliage.

With the new boiler that Hector had had installed, and some new and larger radiators fitted, the house was much warmer than it ever had been in his youth, but he dreaded to think what the heating bills would be like at the end of the winter. At least Cyril had thought to fit draught excluders all around the house, which would ease the situation somewhat.

On their last visit in November, he instructed Isabelle to have all the family rooms closed off and the radiators shut down in them for the rest of the winter. That would alleviate the burden – but he did instruct Cyril to make sure they were turned on for a short period each day when the weather was particularly cold – to make sure there were no burst pipes. Those in the rooms of the staff, together with all the hallways and landings were to be left on, together with those in the servants' common room. This opened off the kitchen, which itself was heated by a large range, on which most of the cooking was carried out, and was always warm.

Their last visit before Christmas was a festive one, as Isabelle prepared them a Christmas meal and served up a turkey with all the trimmings, which they ate in the kitchen with the staff. He'd told her they probably wouldn't be returning before March, so he was leaving everything in her capable hands, and insisted that they all have a fortnight off over the Christmas period, asking only that Gavin pop in every few days to make sure there were no burst pipes or anything else. Living in the small cottage only a few hundred yards from the main house, he was the most obvious choice to keep an eye on things during that period.

He knew they'd keep things on an even keel, and they had his 'phone number in case anything should go wrong.

Later that day, he was putting their things back into the car ready to leave when Isabelle accosted him in the hall.

'Mr David,' she said. 'Could you spare me and the staff a few minutes of your time before you leave? There's something we'd like to get cleared up with you.'

'Of course,' he answered. 'We're not in any rush. I'll come down to the kitchen and meet you all there in half an hour. Does that give you enough time to get everyone together?'

She nodded.

Sandra, now treated as a general dogsbody, since there were few duties for a maid to carry out now, was already in the kitchen preparing vegetables for the evening meal, and Cyril, the handyman, was putting up some new shelving in the larder just to one side of the kitchen, so they were easy enough to find.

Gavin and Morgan she knew were in the small yard at the back of the kitchen, where the bins were kept at the far side and she hung out the washing. They were re-roofing the small store in the far corner, bringing in more logs to fill it for the winter after having cleared up a lot of dead wood from around the property and in the woodland.

'That'll be fine,' she answered. 'Everybody's already in or around the house, so that's no problem,' and turned back down the hallway to rally them all together.

David followed her in, and found Anna standing on the bottom stair, her own small suitcase in her hand.

'Problem?' she queried, having overheard the exchange.

He sighed.

'The staff want to speak to me. I think I know what it's about. They're going to ask the same question as you did – what am I going to do with Bannerman's?'

She nodded.

'I thought that wouldn't be long in coming. Have you made up your mind yet?'

He shook his head.

94

'No, I'm afraid not – but it looks as if I'm going to have to very shortly, for everybody's sakes.'

He was right in his assumption!

The small delegation of staff was clustered around the kitchen table when he joined them, taking Anna with him for moral support.

'Cup of tea, Mr. David?' Isabelle asked, lifting the large pot off the hotplate.

'No thanks,' he replied.

'You Anna?' as she turned in her direction.

She didn't bother to call her 'Miss', now knowing she was just an employee the same as they were.

'Thank you, yes,' she replied, smiling, trying to break any tension there was in the room.

'Right,' David said straight away. 'I think you're all wondering what's going to happen to Bannerman's now that my father's dead, aren't you?'

They all looked at each other and nodded.

'Yes, Mr. David,' Isabelle said. She seemed to have appointed herself as spokesperson. 'As you know, we've all been here many years, and most of us have seen you grow up. We'd just like to know where we all stand, and whether you intend to sell Bannerman's. We'll all need to make other arrangements if you do decide to sell, and we'd like plenty of notice if you're going to.'

David glanced at Anna before speaking. It was exactly what he'd been expecting, and he already knew what he was going to say to them, but it wasn't going to be an easy thing to have to tell them.

'I understand how you all must feel, but I'm afraid I'm not in a position to make that decision yet. All I can assure you of is that once I am, I'll give you all plenty of notice, I promise. I can't say fairer than that!'

They glanced at each other, before Isabelle spoke once more.

95

'I see,' she said, 'so there is every chance that we may have to look for new homes in the future! That won't cause me a problem, as I can always go and live with my sister in Anglesey. It's a good time for me to retire anyway, but some of us don't have that luxury. Cyril doesn't have anywhere to go, and what about Gavin and his family? They've lived in that cottage since just after Morgan was born.'

Gavin was looking crestfallen and Morgan was looking expectant, hoping that David would do something about the situation. They'd always been mates, and he didn't expect David to let his parents down at so late a stage in their lives.

'Gavin and Gwen will be safe in their cottage – **that** I have made up my mind about. It's right on the fringes of fathers' land, and as such, it can be annexed off easily enough. The cottage will be yours for the rest of your lives, Gavin,' he said, turning to the pair watching him with eager eyes. 'The cottage was left to me, so there'll be no more rent to pay from now on. I reckon you've paid more in rent over the years than the cottage is actually worth anyway. The deeds of the cottage, together with one acre of land will be made over to you, and you'll own it completely. I'll have no more say in it, but you'll still keep your jobs here until a decision is made about the future. The woodland also belongs to me under the terms of the Will, so that will be made over to you as well. If the house does have to be sold, you should be able to earn a good income from the sale of the timber until you manage to find other jobs.'

The others looked dumbstruck as he turned towards them.

'As for the rest of you, whatever happens to Bannerman's isn't mine to decide. My father didn't leave the house and the grounds to me, but the cottage and the woodland was the one concession he did make to me. He left his entire estate and most of his assets to my sister Jayne. I'm only administering things until she can be found.'

They looked even more concerned now. The row between Mr. David and his father had been no secret, as they'd all heard heated voices raised in anger, but they didn't realise the Judge had gone to such lengths as to cut him off completely.

It was several years now since Jayne had last been seen, and nobody had any idea where she might have gone, so they still had no idea what their futures might hold.

'As for the rest of you, if Isabelle is intent on retiring to her sisters' in Anglesey, then so be it. Cyril, you can come and work for me at Little Bannerman if you'd like to,' turning to look at him. 'I could do with some more general help around the place. And Sandra, you're already married and living on the farm – I'm sure you'll find work there, or around the local area.'

Then, as if adding a codicil, he continued.

'Of course, if my sister does return, she may decide to live here again. She has a sizeable inheritance from my father, and then I'm sure all your jobs will be safe for the foreseeable future.'

The delighted looks on their faces said it all, now that the future looked a little rosier for them. They knew David would keep his word to them, and if Jayne decided to return at some point in the future, they knew that the pair had always been close, and she'd probably adhere to the promises he'd made. Unfortunately, knowing how long she'd already been gone for, who knew if, or when, she would ever return.

David assured them all that every effort was being made to find her whereabouts, but so far they'd all been unsuccessful, despite the hiring of a detective agency and newspaper advertising.

She was either no longer in a position to reply – or, for some reason, she just didn't want to be found.

Once they arrived back at Little Bannerman, Anna made them something to eat – just some boiled eggs with toast, as Isabelle had provided a tasty beef stew and dumplings at lunchtime, followed by damson crumble and thick creamy custard. Neither of them felt they needed very much to eat after that.

It was afterwards, when Anna joined David in the lounge, bringing coffee for them both, that she found him in a thoughtful mood. Trying to cheer him up, she said, 'I thought you handled that very well today.'

'Yes, I suppose I did, but I'm not feeling all that happy about it myself,' he said, smiling wearily.

'Why so? You did the right thing by everybody.'

He grinned, and then his expression changed to one of worry all over again.

'The cottage and the woodland were the one asset my father left me, apart from a few stocks and shares, which aren't very high earners. I've committed myself to paying the staff wages until my sister returns and I can't touch any of the money my father left. I'm sure she'll reimburse me when she does, but seeing as she's been missing for years now, it could cost me a pretty penny until then – that's if she ever does return. If it becomes too much of a burden, I may be forced to break my promise.'

In an attempt to find her, David had taken a quarter of a page advert in one of the prominent national newspapers, showing a picture of his father in full judge's robes and announcing his death.

Alongside had been printed a picture of his sister, taken when she was just 17. He'd been unable to find any later ones. Photographs weren't something his family ever seemed to bother with – but he had found one of his youngest brother, the child who'd been born with the heart defect, and who'd died when he was only a baby. It showed a smiling, curly haired baby, who looked far too thin for his age.

The pictures of Jayne and his father had brought in many letters of sympathy, all addressed via the newspaper, but there was still no word from Jayne, and not one of the letters mentioned ever having seen her or knowing of her whereabouts.

CHAPTER 9

Having sent off her DNA for analysis, Marnie Peters waited anxiously for its return, eager to find out something about her past, and what connections it might throw up.

According to Warren, it had been her aunt Carolyn's idea to buy it for her it as a birthday present, knowing Marnie had shown an interest in the past and she herself having already started a family tree of her own some years ago. She was a little nervous about what it might bring to light, but as Marnie was now aware she'd been adopted, if not legally, then very happily, and as her adoptive mother was now dead, it couldn't possibly cause any upset or harm to anyone – except perhaps her father if she ever did manage to find him. That would probably be a great surprise to him if she did.

Finally, arriving home from work one evening, the expected results were awaiting her, and she opened them eagerly, surprised at what the results actually were.

'I'm 45% Scottish,' she said in amazement. 'I've never been to Scotland in my life!'

Warren laughed.

'You don't need to have been. It just means you have that amount of Scottish genes in your ethnicity. It could be going back hundreds of years. What else does it show? You must have another 55% from elsewhere.'

'Yes, I do,' she answered, scanning through them before answering, 'the rest is 32% North West England stroke Isle of

Man, 15% Scandinavian and only 8% Wales. I lived all my life in Wales until I married you. That seems very strange to me.'

He laughed again.

'I've already told you! You only play a very minor part in the makeup of your DNA – it's what's gone before over the centuries that makes up who we are and what genes we're carrying.'

'I suppose you're right,' she answered, seeing the sense in what he was saying. 'I'm too excited to think about getting anything to eat. Can you go and get us a takeaway while I ring Carolyn. I want to tell her the news.'

'A takeaway?' he said, looking at her incredulously. 'You do remember where we live now don't you? I'd have to go miles to get us a takeaway.'

'Oh, sorry, I forgot,' she said offhandedly. 'There must be some ready meals in the freezer, one of those would do.'

Shaking his head and smiling to himself, he went to the freezer, putting two lamb curries into the oven, as he went back to see how she was getting on.

'I'm going over to Carolyn's after we've eaten. She's not doing anything tonight, so we're going to make a start on my family tree. You don't mind do you?'

'Of course not,' he answered. 'I'd rather enjoy an evening all on my own.'

Carolyn had already fired up the computer when she arrived, and put in the necessary details for them to get started.

Celia West's name hadn't brought up too many alternatives with the same name, but two of them appeared to live near to the area where the birth had been registered.

'I'd bet a pound to a penny that she'll live somewhere in either of those areas, so let's try and narrow it down, shall we? Let's see if either of them have had a child registered at the same time you were born.'

Neither of them had!

'We'll have to try slightly further afield then. There's one here in Liverpool, but it could turn out to be a possibility. It's not really that far away.'

It was a good possibility!

The child's birth was registered only a couple of weeks after Celia had been born, and the year of birth was about right.

'That looks like a good possibility,' Carolyn said. 'Now let's see who her parents were, and where they lived.'

Both parents turned out to have been born in Liverpool, her father being named as Frederick West, a businessman, and her mother as Janice Cole, who'd been a secretary at the time of the marriage. They were living in the Crosby district of Livrpool when Celia was born.

'What about my father? How can we find anything out about him? That's the information I want most,' Marnie said. 'I want to know who he is, or was. There could be just a slight possibility of him still being alive!'

Carolyn ruminated on this for the moment.

'Your mother's age is given as just 20 when you were born, so that would place her around 70 now. There is a chance that they could both still be alive. Although the letter says she became pregnant at a drunken party at university, it doesn't necessarily follow that your father was also a student. He could be somebody who just joined the party and was brought along by another student, or even a gatecrasher. He could even be years older, but it's more likely he was a fellow student.'

They continued with Celia West's line and found the birth of a girl child registered in her name when she was just 20 years old, but no marriage seemed to have been registered for her, even though they spent some time looking.

'I think we've probably found your mother,' Carolyn said. 'Now, let's look at the Birth Certificate and see what it says.'

The birth had been registered just two weeks after Marnie's own birth date, which was also shown as that of the child's, but here any further information petered out. The child's name had been left blank, as had that of the father.

That took a little bit of the shine off their findings, but she still felt a little frisson of excitement that she'd more than likely found her mother.

'You could send for the Birth Certificate if you want,' Carolyn said, 'but you'll have to pay for it, and it won't contain any more information than you see here.'

'Let's do that – and also my mother's Birth Certificate as well. I'd love to try and find out more about her.'

'There, that's all done,' Carolyn said when they'd completed the procedure. 'All you have to do now is wait for them to arrive, but it can take a couple of weeks or more.'

The money had been paid through her aunt's account, so she scrambled through her purse, finding the correct amount in cash to pay her, while Carolyn went out to make them some supper.

Marnie was excited to tell Warren what she'd already found out when she arrived back. He'd been watching television, and he'd sunk a couple of large whiskies while he was doing so.

'I'll make some coffee,' she volunteered; anxious to impart the news that she'd probably found her mother.

He was impressed but far too tired to really take on board what she was saying, so as he went off to bed, she logged into her laptop and continued her research. Finally, finding no more information on Celia, she knew she'd reached a dead end and switched off the laptop. As she looked at the clock, she realised it was well past midnight and she was really tired.

CHAPTER 10

Winter came early to the Denbigh Moors that year!

At the beginning of December, Jim Shannon returned from his nightly round of checking the stock before eating some supper and making for his bed.

There was a biting cold wind blowing, and he was glad the sheep were already down in the lower pasture. Most of them were huddled in the lea of the dry stone walls and well sheltered from the wind, and yet others were huddled under the gorse bushes on the far side nearest the woodland.

As he let himself into the farmyard, he closed the metal gate with a clang, making sure the catch had fastened securely before walking over to the henhouse huddled against the side of the cattle barn. Taking a quick peek inside, most of them already seemed to be sleeping, and he shut the door once again. He knew the foxes would be on the prowl if the weather was bad, but they were secure in there. He'd never had a problem with it before.

There were only a few stirks in the cattle barn that year as he peered in whilst passing. They seemed to have a good amount of bedding and most of them were already lying down. They were well sheltered from the worst of the weather by the farmhouse opposite, and the waist high metal panelling at the front, as well as the overhanging roof.

Crossing the yard, he opened the door into the barn alongside the house. The dogs were in their pen and only looked at him with bleary eyes, tails giving a half-hearted wag. They'd been fed earlier and had plenty of bedding. They'd be fine until the morning.

Just as he made his way to the kitchen door, he saw the first flakes of snow beginning to fall. Looking up, he saw the sky was leaden, and not a chink of light could be seen – it was going to be a bad one tonight!

'Branwen,' he called, as he entered the kitchen door.

'Be there in a minute,' her voice came back from somewhere inside the house, appearing in person a few minutes later.

'Snow's beginning to fall,' he said, as he took his outdoor clothes off and peered through the window, where he could see it was already much heavier and was swirling around in the wind.

'Ah well, as long as beasts are all right, so are we. Cocoa's on and once we've had that, we'll be away to our beds.

He smiled, sitting down at the big oak table and helping himself to the oat cakes cooked liberally in butter and still warm, while she made the cocoa – something they drank a couple of mugs of every night before going up.

'I feel at peace with the world when the weather's bad and we're snuggled up safe and warm in our beds,' she said, as she put a large mug of the hot liquid down in front of him.

He smiled ruefully.

It was all very well for her. She could stay warm and safe in the house. It would be him who'd have to make his way out and check the beasts in the early morning, making sure they'd weathered the worst the weather could throw at them during the night and make sure they were all well fed.

As he closed the curtains in the bedroom, he peered out. The snow was coming down thicker now and beginning to pile up against the less sheltered places as the wind still picked up. It was turning into a real blizzard now. He could no longer see the bottom bars of the gate onto the track towards the lane. That would probably be well covered by the morning, and he'd have to dig it out before he could see to the sheep.

He woke shortly before 6a.m., his normal time to awake, and cancelled the alarm before it went off. Luckily, the kitchen range, although turned down, was left running all night, and the room was still passably warm, as he got out of bed and padded across to the window. Every year when the weather turned cold, he blessed the time they'd had central heating installed, and the house was always warm to come back to after a cold day on the moors.

Parting the curtains, he saw that it was a world of white outside, although the snow had stopped and the wind had died down. Luckily the yard was reasonably clear, being sheltered between the barn and the house, but as he turned towards the gate, things were totally different. The snow was up to the middle bar, and the track beyond looked to be full of snow where it had blown across the fields and piled up against the hedge on the opposite side, covering almost the whole track.

It would take him some time to get to the sheep, but he'd have to do it in order to take them some food – and it would have to be on foot! The drifts would be too deep for the quad bike.

'Whaa's it like out there?' Branwen's sleepy voice cut in on his thoughts.

'I's stopped snowin', bur' is' pretty deep out there. Yard's not too bad, but the track's deep.'

She was out of bed by now and joined him at the window, shrugging on her dressing gown, saying nothing, but peering all around.

'Ow yew goin' to get t'the sheep?' she asked. 'Yew'll not get quad bike through.'

He looked down at his legs, at the same time quoting the old song "these legs were made for walking".

They both laughed.

'Le's get dressed,' she said, making for the bathroom. 'Yew go and see to t'sheep and I'll make us a good fry up – then I'll clear the yard for yew while yew see to cattle.'

It may have seemed to be a simple enough suggestion, but as things turned out, it definitely wasn't going to be that simple.

Letting the dogs out into the yard, he hefted a bag of sheep nuts onto his shoulder and prepared to make his way out to the field, also carrying a spade in the other hand to clear the gate.

Propping the bag against the stone gatepost alongside, he set to and cleared the gate, before stepping out onto the track.

Wearing sturdy wellingtons, he was prepared for the snow, but several times it came over the tops, and before he reached the sheep, his feet were wet and cold from the melting snow inside.

Most of them came plodding across when they saw him arrive with the food, which allowed him to make sure they were all accounted for, but he did a recount when he saw there were at least half a dozen missing. Now he'd have to go further over and make sure they weren't caught up somewhere.

Reaching the far side, he still hadn't seen any sign of them, when he suddenly noticed a gap in the drystone wall right up alongside the woods. There must have been a weak point, and the wind, combined with the weight of snow against it, must have toppled the wall! He'd have to get the sheep back in and rebuild the wall before he could go back for his breakfast, and he hadn't brought a dog to help him – what more could this farming life throw at him?

He trudged back across the field, and found there was still some food left in the bottom of the bag. Once they heard the rattle of the sheep nuts, they'd probably follow him back into the field – that's if they'd all stayed together.

Trudging back to the far side once again, he climbed over what was left of the wall, and made his way into the woods, finding four of them almost immediately only a short distance in – but there were still two missing. Enticing those four back over the wall, he dropped some food for them further from the collapse, and finding a stout couple of logs, be breached the gap with them until he could rebuild. Then he went in search of the other two, finding they'd made their way towards the road, and were feeding in the bottom of a hollow. The sides were almost sheer on his side and there was only one way out, on the side nearest the road.

Making his way round through the undergrowth, he rattled the bag and their heads came up immediately. As he neared the top of the incline, they were already making their way towards him, when he stumbled and almost fell over something lying hidden in the thick vegetation and covered by a thin layer of snow. He thought at first it was a broken branch, or a rock, but the stench now reaching his nostrils told him it was neither of those. A dead animal then?

Parting the grasses and weeds, he looked down.

In the undergrowth were a pair of legs, the discoloured and emaciated flesh beginning to peel from the bone – and they were definitely human!

On the feet were a pair of black trainers with a white stripe down the side and adorned by the unmistakable tick of the Nike logo. Higher up, he could just see the frayed bottoms of a pair of cut-off jeans; the rest was hidden from his view.

For a moment he was stupefied, staring down and not knowing what to do. Eventually, taking out his 'phone, he tried to call the police, but he found the battery was dead. It was debatable anyway whether he'd have got a signal around here. It had always been a bit hit and miss in this extremely rural area.

Finally, realising whoever it was wasn't going anywhere, he took the sheep, who'd already arrived to join him, and put them back in the field, before rebuilding the wall in a very temporary manner and leaving the logs in position for the time being.

All he could do now was to go back to the house and call the police on the landline, then he'd eat his breakfast – if he was able – and await their arrival.

He knew he'd have to go back with them to show them where the body was, but it was so near the road, he'd be able to go that way and by Land Rover this time.

CHAPTER 11

'Robbie, got a job for you,' were the words every police officer dreads to hear so near to the end of his shift.

'What is it, sarge?' he asked.

'Dead body's been found up on the moors. Apparently been dead for some time according to the farmer who found it – seems to be nothing more than a skeleton from what he says,' as he handed him a piece of paper containing the details.

'Okay,' resignedly. 'I'll get Steve and we'll take a look. He has made sure it's not just an animal – a deer perhaps?'

'Does a deer wear Nike trainers and cut-off jeans?' the sergeant replied in a somewhat sarcastic tone.

Robbie grinned.

'Okay, we'll go take a look.'

They'd just arrived back from their last job twenty minutes ago, and hoped to spend the last hour of their shift drinking coffee and getting something to eat in the canteen, where Steve was already waiting for him. This early in the morning, there wasn't usually much happening. Their last job had been to a domestic which had already been cleared up before they arrived, and there was nothing left for them to do except calm the crying woman. Her husband had already left for work, and it seemed that it was the neighbours who called them after hearing raised voices and crockery being smashed.

It wasn't the first time they'd been to that address, and it probably wouldn't be the last!

'Steve,' he said, going over to the table where his partner was already sipping coffee and devouring an Eccles cake. 'We've gotta' job. Hop to it.'

'At this time?' Steve asked.

'Afraid so!'

'What is it this time? A moggy not come home all night?'

Robbie grinned, knowing how boring some of their jobs could be.

'A bit more serious this time,' he answered. 'Some farmer's found a dead body up on the moors. We've been asked to go and check it out.'

'Up on the moors? Can't the next shift go? We've nearly finished ours. It'll take us a ages to get there, and we'll be there even longer if he does turn out to be right.'

Robbie shrugged.

'That's the name of the game,' he said, 'and I'm afraid the sergeant's assigned it to us.'

Steve grimaced.

'Okay, let me finish this and go for a wazz, and then I'll join you down at the car.'

The roads out of Denbigh weren't too bad, but they began to encounter far worse the further out and the higher up they got. Thank goodness for their X5 being a reliable four wheel drive.

Reaching the entrance to the small copse of trees, they found Jim's Land Rover parked in the entrance awaiting their arrival.

'Are you sure it's a human body?' were Steve's first words, earning him a quick grimace from Robbie. He knew the man would probably be traumatised by what he'd just seen. So would he have been coming across something like that when he'd least expected it.

'Oh yes, I'm dead certain,' Jim replied, as both policemen donned high viz jackets and began to follow him, their stout police issue boots shielding them from what little snow had penetrated through the trees, a lot of them being conifers.

From this side, the well worn footpath leading into the woods led straight to the depression in the ground, and he indicated for them to follow him round the edge to where he'd found the body previously.

Even before they reached it, their noses indicated that he was right! The smell of rotten flesh was unmistakable!

Robbie had seen this sort of thing a few times before, but Steve hadn't. The smell was forcing its way into his throat and making him gag even before they reached the exact location.

Robbie asked the farmer to stay back and wait while they investigated. If there was any chance of foul play, forensics wouldn't need too many people muddying the scene and fouling up any evidence there may be.

Seeing Steve beginning to go green around the gills himself, he asked him to stay back as well. It only needed one to check if the man was right, and then they'd vacate the scene immediately and wait by the car for the whole kit and caboodle to descend.

Hunkering down where indicated, he parted the vegetation and looked down, realising that the man was undoubtedly right.

'Okay,' he said, standing up, feeling a little queasy himself. 'Let's get back to the car and radio it in. Nothing more we can do for the poor soul here. Whoever it is has been dead for some time now.'

Within the next couple of hours, the pathologist had arrived and checked out the body, declaring it to be that of a juvenile male somewhere in his late teens or early twenties. There seemed to be no sign of foul play, but the earth and vegetation around showed signs of a great deal of blood having been shed, and the left femur, the large bone at the top of the leg, had been traumatically broken; the bones poking through the flesh. The large amount of blood around indicated that an artery may have been severed as

110

well, and if it was the femoral artery, as he thought it probably was, the person may well have bled to death within a very short space of time.

The ankle on the same side was also broken, although this was only a minor break.

The forensics team started an investigation, almost immediately finding a scrambles motorbike hidden in some bushes not far from the road, but nothing else of any significant value.

Robbie and Steve were told they could stand down, and their relief shift took over from them, but they were still very late home and spent most of the day sleeping before going on duty again. Robbie's wife wasn't happy about it, but she accepted that was the life she'd married into and she now had to put up with it.

Steve, however, had no such problem, as he was living with his girlfriend in a flat near the town centre. She, being a nurse at Glan Clwyd hospital, led a life of irregular hours herself, and never queried the irregularities of his shifts.

That evening, when they arrived for duty, the sergeant collared them as they walked through the door, having arrived together at exactly the same moment.

'Mac wants to see you both as soon as you arrive,' he said.

Mac referred to their Inspector, Angus McDonald. Despite his name, he was an Englishman, born and bred in the Lancashire town of Ormskirk, and who'd been living in Denbigh, North Wales, for over 30 years now. He was a fair man, but could be a little strict if they got out of line, and he always seemed to know straight away if someone were lying to him.

They decided it would be best to see him before they did anything else. Robbie knew he'd be annoyed if they didn't go straight there.

'Ah yes, Richards and Pryce,' he said, as they knocked and entered when told. 'It's you in particular I want to see, Richards.

I believe you've lived around Denbigh for all your life, haven't you?'

Robbie agreed that he had.

'I believe you were the two called to the scene of the body found yesterday on the moors.'

Robbie agreed once again, wishing the man would get on with it. He often went the long way around everything, but he was a stickler for wheedling out the facts and getting everything straight.

'Do you know a family called Muir, living at Muirhead Farm?'

'Yes, I know them fairly well. I was at school with Frank Muir.'

His heart sank. He already knew that the body was that of a teenage boy, and also that Frank had 3 boys. All of them were born very close together. The body could be any one of them as all of them must now be in their mid to late teens.

'Is it one of Frank's boys?' he asked.

The Inspector nodded.

'We think it could be. The age of the body is too young to be Frank himself, but we found a motorbike not far from the body and it was hidden in some bushes. It's registered to Frank. I'd like you to go and see him and find out if any of them are missing from home before we can narrow down which one it is.'

Robbie didn't like the idea of having to face Frank with the news, but surely he must be aware if one of the boys had been missing for all this time. He hadn't reported one of them missing from home as far as he was aware.

As Robbie and Steve pulled into the yard, Frank was just emerging from the barn driving a tractor. He stopped and switched the engine off when he saw them drive in.

'Hello Robbie,' he greeted, climbing down when he saw who it was. 'Anything wrong, or is this just a social call? Called in for a cuppa, have you?'

Robbie's face was sombre, and Frank immediately deduced there was something very wrong.

112

'What is it, Robbie?' he asked as he joined them.

'Can we go inside for a moment,' Robbie said. 'We need to speak to you for a few minutes.'

Frank looked worried, but led the way into the kitchen.

'Okay, spit it out,' he said, immediately they entered. 'One of my lads in trouble?'

'No, Frank – not in trouble,' Robbie replied, 'but could we sit down for a minute?'

Frank indicated the kitchen table and they all sat down, Robbie not relishing the news he had to impart.

'Do you own a scrambles bike?' he asked without preamble.

'Yes, there's one in the barn. It's an old thing and it's been there for years. The lads all use it, but they're only allowed to ride it on our own land or in the old quarry. It's not road legal – it's not taxed or insured, but they only have to cross the road from our own land to get to the quarry, and that's the only time it leaves our own property. They haven't been using it on the roads have they?'

'We think one of them has, and I'm afraid to say that whoever that was has been involved in some sort of accident. Have any of your lads been missing from home for some time?'

'No, I don't think so. James is working on a quad at the back of the shed, or at least he was when I saw him a few minutes ago, and Sean has gone into town with the wife. She's going to do some shopping while he drops in an order with the feed merchants.'

'What about Nathan?'

'Oh him! Haven't seen him in weeks. He hangs around with Kevin Williams – him from Moorside Farm. Kevin's turned one of their old barns into a den for hisself, and even sleeps there during the summer months. Our Nathan spends most of his time over there now. Don't know what he's doing for money. He certainly doesn't get any from me. You'll probably find him there.'

Then the proverbial penny seemed to drop.

113

'Do you think it's Nathan that's been in the accident? Is he badly hurt? I knew his hanging around with that Kevin would end in no good, but you know what they're like at that age – won't listen to no-one!'

His expression was one of anger, but Robbie could see it was tinged with worry as well.

'It certainly looks as if it could be him, but we'll check at the Williams's before we can be sure. The bike we've found is registered to you.'

Frank's whole attitude changed as he looked towards the window.

'I dunno' what to do. His mother'll go spare. Is he in hospital then? Can we visit him?'

'I'm sorry,' Robbie said, glancing across at Steve who didn't seem to know what to do or say. 'I'm afraid the lad we've found is dead, and has been for some time.'

Frank seemed to shrink in on himself.

'How am I going to tell his mother? She'll be devastated!'

'Don't say anything to her for the time being. Try to act your normal self. Give me your 'phone number and I'll ring you when we've been to the Williams place. Meanwhile, I need to take a DNA sample from you so that we can make sure.'

'You already know, don't you?' Frank said, turning tear filled eyes on him.

'Yes,' said Robbie, 'I think you're going to have to prepare yourself for the worst.'

An hour later they drove away from Moorside Farm with heavy hearts. They now had the unpleasant task of returning to Muirhead Farm and telling Frank Muir that Nathan hadn't been around there for some time, and that Kevin hadn't seen him either, from which they must draw their own conclusions, however unpleasant.

Kevin had told them the last time he'd seen Nathan was when they'd taken the bike up to the old quarry and spent the whole afternoon taking turns riding around on it. When asked about the

114

stolen car and the accident, he'd told them he knew nothing whatsoever about it, and when pressed, he'd clammed up, claiming he knew nothing whatsoever about it.

They'd drawn their own conclusions from that – but where was the proof that he'd been involved?

Save for the blood having been positively identified as belonging to Nathan Muir, there was nothing more to connect Kevin Williams to any of it.

CHAPTER 12

Seeing bad weather setting in so early in the year, David was worried about leaving Bannerman's empty right throughout the Christmas period, and he didn't know which of the staff had chosen to go right away during that time. He knew Gavin and Morgan were close at hand in the cottage, but somehow it didn't seem fair to ask them to check on the place all the time when he'd given them a full fortnight off.

The first fall of snow wasn't very thick, and after a few days it had all gone, but the forecasters were still giving out warnings of more to come, and he found he couldn't rest easy in that knowledge.

He'd been asked to join some friends over the Christmas period at their rather grand old 16th century manor house set in rolling Cheshire countryside near Tarporley, but after some thought, he declined.

Anna had already offered to cook a Christmas dinner for them both, and for any friends he wished to invite, from which he deduced she'd made no plans of her own. He couldn't ask his friends in Cheshire to play host to his housekeeper as well as himself. They had staff themselves, and it would probably have seemed odd to them that he'd wanted to bring his housekeeper along – besides which, she would have been expected to remain with their own staff, and it probably wouldn't be much of a Christmas for her amongst people she didn't really know.

Even if they had accepted her presence at their table, which was highly unlikely, they'd probably have written more into their relationship than there actually was.

It was one morning at the end of the second week in December that he made up his mind.

He'd heard on the weather forecast that more snow was expected at the end of the following week, and when it was time for his normal morning cup of coffee, he told her he'd join her in the kitchen to drink it. She was a little surprised, as he usually liked to keep working until lunch was ready, but she knew he enjoyed sitting in the kitchen where it was always warmer in cold weather, and today really was a cold day.

It was dry and a thin watery sun had shown its face in the early morning. Having changed his bed, she'd washed the bedding and decided to hang it out on the line, as a brisk breeze was blowing. However, when she'd looked out of the window just before eleven, it wasn't blowing as freely as it was before, and after she'd gone out to check on it, she'd found it was beginning to freeze. No recourse but to relegate it to the tumble drier now, but at least it had had a blow in the fresh air, even if it was only for a short time.

She was just pouring the coffee into the cups when he arrived, and they both sat down at the kitchen table to drink it, but she saw at once there was something on his mind.

After a few sips, he seemed to make up his mind as to what he wanted to say.

'Anna, I know you offered to cook us Christmas dinner here, but how would you feel about going to Bannerman's for the Christmas period? I'm worried about the place being empty with all the staff away and more snow forecast. I'll quite understand if you want to make other arrangements, but I feel I really ought to go and make sure it'll be secure.'

She knew there'd been something on his mind!

'I haven't made any arrangements to go anywhere else,' she said. 'My mother and father are going to friends in Lincolnshire

117

for the whole of Christmas and New Year. It's a bit late to arrange anything now, but if you want me to, I'll be quite happy to go with you. I don't mind at all.'

There still seemed to be something else bothering him.

'Is there something else?' she asked.

'Yes, it's my sister Jayne. You know I've been advertising and hiring people to try and find her, but so far without success; I don't want her to suddenly turn up at Christmas and find there's nobody around. She doesn't know yet that it now belongs to her.'

'Why do you think she might do that?' She was surprised at his train of thought!

'She loved Christmas when she was younger. The house was always full of people, and she was always spoiled rotten. Christmas, as far as I was concerned, just revolved around her and I was sometimes left feeling very jealous at the amount of attention that went her way, although I always loved her too.'

The speech he'd just made seemed to have upset him, so she stood up and went to the cupboard.

'I've made some Yorkshire Parkin if you'd like a piece,' she said.

It was a delicacy she knew he always enjoyed.

'I'd love some,' he answered, his spirits seeming to lift once again. 'You know I always love your Parkin.'

He returned to his study ten minutes later and she spent the next hour planning what they'd need to take to Bannerman's with them before making some lunch.

Bedding wasn't an issue, as there was plenty already there, but food was the main item on the agenda, and she'd have to get used to cooking on the old range first if she were to manage a full Christmas dinner on it.

While they ate their lunch, he told her they'd leave in the middle of the following week. He should have finished all he needed to do by then, and they should just be able to beat the coming snowfall.

118

They arrived on Thursday afternoon to find Gavin sweeping up handfuls of leaves from the entranceway and burning them on a bonfire to one side of the garden. The smell of burning leaves, mingled with that of wood smoke, was evocative of her childhood, when her father had burned the leaves falling from the beech trees along one side of their garden.

'Hello, Mr. David,' he said in surprise. 'We weren't expecting yew before Christmas.'

Gavin still gave David the respect his father always insisted on, even if his son Morgan didn't, merely calling him David. They'd known each other for far too long, and played together in such familiar circumstances throughout their childhood, to keep to any such formalities.

'Nobody knew. I thought there'd be nobody here when we arrived, so I didn't ring ahead. We'll be okay. I have Anna with me and we'll cope between us.'

'I'm afraid yew'll 'ave to – unless you want my Gwen to come and do some cooking for yew: after what yew've done for us, she'd be only too willing to give an 'and.'

'No, that won't be necessary. When you've finished here, you go off and enjoy your Christmas. We'll be fine. Has Cyril left the heating on?'

'Cyril's still 'ere, Mr. David, 'e 'asn't said where or when 'e's going yet; or if at all. 'e 'asn't shown any signs of packing up. 'e'll sort it all out for yew, but I'm afraid Isabelle's already gone. Gone to Anglesey to spend the 'oliday with her sister, and Sandra's been told she won't be needed 'til after New Year. I can get her back if yew need me to.'

'No, Gavin, I've told you. My promise of a Christmas fortnight off still stands for all of you. Pretend we're not even here.'

Gavin smiled.

'Well, if yew're sure . . .?'

'I am – and have a good Christmas. I don't want to see you here again until you've enjoyed your full fortnight off.'

119

'I will that, Mr. David. Gwen's already bought in all t' necessaries. Seeing as we 'ave no rent to pay from now on, she's used the money she put aside for it to buy us a real good feast, and Morgan's bringing along his young lady as well.'

'I'll look forward to meeting her while she's here,' he said, genuinely meaning it. 'We'll probably go for a walk on Christmas afternoon to help our dinner go down, and we'll call in to see you, if it won't be too much of an imposition.'

'O'course not,' Gavin said. 'Yew've always been welcome at our 'ome, yew know that. Yew spent enough time in our kitchen when you and Morgan were kids. I know 'ow much yew used to enjoy my Gwen's baking,' and they both laughed – David knowing how wonderful her baking had always tasted, especially after spending whole days playing on the moors or in the surrounding woodland.

Just as he was about to go inside, Gavin's voice stopped him.

'By the way, yew'r father's dog in't there anymore. Morgan brought 'im down to ours after you left last time, so if yew want to take 'im with you at any time, 'e'll be there and waitin' for yew. 'e's always ready to go for a walk.'

David smiled ruefully. He hadn't made any plans for the animal over the period, but he hadn't worried about him, he knew somebody would look after him – and that somebody would more than likely be Gavin or Morgan.

Cyril must have heard them bringing in their luggage and going up and down the stairs to their respective rooms. He was waiting in the hallway as David descended from his second trip upstairs, making his way outside for the last time to lock the car.

'Mr. David,' he said, 'what a surprise to see you back. I thought you wouldn't be back until March!'

David smiled.

'Neither did I at the time, but there's a forecast of snow, and I didn't want to leave the house completely empty while you were all away. Anything could happen if it's very bad.'

Cyril smiled back at him, looking rather sad.

'I'm not going anywhere,' he said, looking sheepish, 'I've nowhere else to go now.'

'You mean you were going to spend Christmas here all alone?'

Cyril nodded.

Just then, Anna was preparing to descend the stairs and heard their conversation.

'You mean you have no family to go home to?' she interjected.

'No, I've no-one now. My mother died when I was very young and I never knew who my father was. I was brought up in care, and my wife died from breast cancer many years ago. We never had any children.'

David and Anna glanced at each other.

Cyril had always kept himself to himself when he'd joined the staff, and David had never heard any of this before, in fact, he'd never ever heard anything about his personal circumstances before.

'Then you must join us for Christmas lunch,' David said, glancing at Anna and seeing her nod of approval. 'We can't have you sitting alone in your room on Christmas day.'

'Oh, I can't possibly, Mr. David. I'm only staff, and I can't possibly sit down at table with you.'

'So am I,' Anna piped up. 'I'm only staff too, so you won't be at all out of place. You can help me in the kitchen too if you like. You can peel the vegetables, and lay the table. It'll make my job a lot easier.'

He seemed to accept this solution, saying, 'I'll give the dining room a bit of a dust too. Sandra hasn't been here for a few days so it probably needs doing by now.'

'Oh, sod the dining room!' David burst out uncharacteristically. 'Let's all eat in the kitchen. It's much more homely there, and much warmer too. I remember the dining room as somewhere cold and draughty when I was a kid. My mother always used to wrap a rug round her legs when we ate in there.'

'The kitchen it is,' Anna said, 'and it'll make my job of serving everything piping hot much easier too.'

121

The following day, when she was in the kitchen and preparing them lunch, Cyril came in through the door leading to the pantry and boiler room.

'I want to thank you for helping me out yesterday,' he said sheepishly when he saw her.

She was surprised.

'What did I do?' she asked.

'I could never have felt comfortable, and would never have accepted Mr. David's invitation to eat Christmas lunch with him if it hadn't been for you. Once you said that you were staff too, it made it much easier for me. I'd always thought when you'd been here previously that you an' him were an item.'

She laughed before saying, 'Of course not. I'm the hired help the same as you. I'm only his housekeeper, but as he's living on his own at present, we tend to eat together, and I do help out with his paperwork and any other little jobs I can turn my hand to. I was once an office worker.'

'Thank you, all the same,' he said. 'Christmas has never been an easy time for me, being all alone. My wife died on a Christmas Eve, so it's always been a sad time of year for me.'

'Sit down and I'll make us some coffee,' she said, turning away so that he didn't see the unbidden tears spring to her eyes.

Poor man! He'd worked here for years, and she was sure she was the first person he'd ever told about this. David didn't seem to have had any idea.

Lunch could wait for the time being as she made their coffee and sat down to drink hers with him.

'Didn't you eat Christmas dinner here with the staff?' she asked.

'Yes, I did – but the memory of my wife has always haunted me at that time of year, and I spent most of the rest of the day in my room thinking about her. I just didn't feel like joining in the festivities.'

Suddenly a thought occurred to her.

'What about a home? Did you never have one of your own?'

'Oh yes,' he answered straight away. 'We had a nice little house on the outskirts of Wrexham – a three bedroom semi, and I had a good job too.'

'What did you do?' she asked, intrigued.

'I worked in a factory. I'm a multi-skilled electrical and mechanical engineer by trade.'

She felt her jaw beginning to drop open.

'Then what are you doing working in this job?' she finally asked, trying not to show her surprise. 'You can't be earning anywhere near as much as you could be doing. It's rather a comedown for you, isn't it?'

He smiled weakly this time.

'Yes, it is, but after my wife died, I went completely off the rails. I started drinking and got behind with the mortgage. My boss noticed that I smelled of drink when I went into work, and he warned me about it, but I just couldn't stop myself. Then when he smelled drink on my breath once again, he sacked me straight away. That gave me the impetus to pull myself together, and I finally managed to wean myself off the drink, but with no job, and already behind with the mortgage, I had to sell the house. I ended up living in hostels. When I finally saw this job advertised in the paper, I decided to apply. It was really the only way to find myself somewhere else to live, and to get another job. My boss had refused to give me a reference.

I think the Judge was impressed by my qualifications, but he never asked why I wanted a job so much below my standards. He hired me immediately.'

Suddenly, David's voice interjected from the doorway.

'Perhaps he'd seen so many cases of people appearing in front of him that had fallen on hard times that he decided to give you a chance for a new start. I probably would have done the same thing.'

They both looked round, startled by his sudden appearance.

'I'm sorry if I was ear wigging – comes with the job,' he laughed, 'but I'm glad I know that now, and I certainly feel we've gained an asset to the family. Any water left in the kettle? I wouldn't mind a coffee myself.'

Anna stood up to make him one as he sat down opposite Cyril.

'I've never smelled any alcohol on you since you came here. Did you manage to kick the habit entirely?'

Cyril nodded.

'Never touched a drop since, and I don't intend to.'

'Good for you! And what do you intend to do with yourself now my father's dead?'

'You did offer a job at your place . . .' hesitant now that he thought David may have changed his mind.

'And the offer still stands if you want it, but it's way below your pay grade. I can't afford to pay you any more than my father did. You could do so much better for yourself.'

'I don't want to go back to my old way of living – shift work, odd hours, and no wife to go back to any more. I'm happy surrounded by beautiful countryside and a ready-made family, even if they're not my own. At least I have company and somebody to talk to if I need it, and there's plenty of work here for me. I've never regretted coming here.'

After that, he seemed to come alive, and the three of them enjoyed a happy and enjoyable Christmas, which they all helped with the cooking of.

The one thing that did mar it for David was the fact that his sister never put in an appearance. He thought she would have seen the announcement of his father's death in the papers and realised he might have come back to sort out the finances, without even realising that everything had been left to her. She would obviously have thought it would all go to him, but surely she must have thought there'd be something for her as well.

The promised snow was only a few heavy flurries which fell overnight, but during the following day, all melted away – until the day after Boxing Day!

When they awoke on that morning, it was overcast but it didn't feel too cold.

Finishing off in the study, David decided to lock the door and leave the key where his father had always left the combination number for the safe, taped to the underside of the bedside drawer, just in case anybody decided to have a nosey round. If anybody needed access to the room, he could always tell them where the key was, or else go down and get it himself.

After a good lunch of fried left over potatoes and a cheese omelette, David suggested a long walk over the moors, and then back through the woodland; somewhere she hadn't yet visited.

She was only too happy to agree, especially as a weak sun had peeped its head through the clouds and the day didn't appear to be too cold now.

They picked up Henry from Gavin's home and took him with them. Morgan was spending the day with his new girlfriend at her parents' home, and the job of walking the dog would have fallen to Gavin. He was only too glad not to have to go out again and was only too happy to sit with his feet up in front of the television for the rest of the afternoon.

David set off at a good pace, striding out through the dead and dying bracken which rustled and rattled against their legs as they walked. A couple of red grouse flew up from the undergrowth almost alongside, disturbed by Henry charging through the undergrowth, their wings making a loud whirring sound as they took off, and their chattering cries of alarm startling them both.

Anna jumped back, letting out a startled cry and making David laugh.

'They're only red grouse,' he said. 'There used to be loads of them up here when I was a boy – black grouse as well – but their numbers have dwindled over the years. My father used to shoot them sometimes, and they make good eating, but there are too few of them now to indulge in their eating anymore.'

Shortly afterwards, a flight of large birds flew over their heads, their mournful, chirring cries echoing across the valley.

'Curlew,' David explained. 'There's some wet boggy ground down by the stream. That's where they nest. Another bird that's dwindled in numbers since I was a boy! It wasn't unusual to see 30 or 40 at a time fly over our heads then; now we're lucky if there's just a handful at most.'

They'd reached a point where there were some rocks sticking out on a promontory overlooking the valley, and the gurgling stream could distinctly be seen and heard down below.

David climbed up on top of them, and helped her up.

'It's a wonderful place for views from up here. I used to bring Jayne here when she was old enough, and she was always delighted to learn the names of the places and enjoy the views.'

'I think I like the sound of your sister,' she said. 'I'd like to have got to know her.'

'Hopefully you might one day if she ever does come back. Maybe she's married and has a family of her own by now. Maybe she doesn't want to come back here again. Wherever she is, I hope she's happy and nothing bad has happened to her.'

She let the subject drop. She didn't want to spoil his enjoyment of the afternoon.

'What's that peak I can see over there?' she asked, trying to break up his thoughts.

'That's Carnedd Llewellyn,' he said, 'and over to the left is 'Glyder Fawr. You should be able to see Snowdon itself behind it, but it's shrouded in mist today. On a clear day, especially when it's been snowing and the sun hits it, it gleams white, and all the shadows show up as blue and purple. It looks spectacular then, and even though we're miles away, it looks so very close on a day like that.'

She stood and adjusted her eyes, taking in the wonderful array of peaks comprising the mountain range of Snowdonia, before casting her eyes down into the valley bottom.

Without saying a word, she touched his arm.

'What's that down there?' she whispered.

His head turned to follow her gaze.

126

Not far below them and sitting on another protruding rock was a large bird, the sun shining off its nut brown plumage. Even though they had been quiet, the bird turned its head, a wary eye looking in their direction, and she could see the side of its beak was a gleaming yellow colour; its large glaring eyes also bright yellow.

'It's a red kite,' he whispered, 'and look, it's caught a rabbit!'

She looked again.

Sitting beneath its scaly yellow legs, and held by its huge talons, was a rabbit, its head dangling from the edge of the rock.

Even as they watched, the bird curved its talons around the rabbit and took to the air, the dead animal dangling beneath it, and disappeared from their sight round the curve of the hillside.

'It's huge,' she said, as they watched it flap lazily away.

He smiled – his eyes no longer on the bird, but now focused on the horizon.

'I think it's time we turned back. Look at the horizon, you can't see any of the mountains now, and the sun's just about to go in. I think there's more snow coming – the air's already turning colder.'

She shivered even as he spoke. He was right! The weather was definitely changing and they needed to hurry back.

'The quickest way is over the hill behind us, and then up into the woods. We should be fairly sheltered if the snow does hit before we manage to get back, and hopefully it won't come down too thickly – but he spoke too soon!

The hillside behind them was steep, and even before they reached the tree line, the snow had started – small flurries at first, but soon thick fat flakes were swirling around them, and beginning to lie on the cold, hard ground beneath their feet.

Once inside the shelter of the trees, they entered a silent world: no sound of any animal or bird, and only the thick white snow already beginning to coat the almost bare overhanging branches.

'This way,' David said, taking her hand and guiding her along what could still be seen of the pathway made by the numerous animals who passed that way.

Further on, a couple of muntjac deer crossed their path. The smallest of the native species of deer, they gave their ubiquitous coughing sound of alarm as they spotted the intruders, and quickly disappeared from view into the high ferns and scrubby vegetation on the opposite side of the path.

Stopping to look along one of the fire breaks through the trees, David saw how quickly the snow was beginning to lie on the open hillside beyond, and taking her hand, he urged her off the path and into the trees.

'Where are we going?' she asked through rapid breathing.

'Not far now,' was his only answer as he urged her on.

A few moments later, the trees gave way to a relatively open space, to one side of which was a small stone building with a corrugated iron roof; large logs of wood piled in small stacks around the edges of the clearing.

Hurrying on towards the front of the building, he left her standing by the door while he went round to the side and came back with a key to the rough wooden door.

'Thank goodness it hasn't been moved in all these years,' he said, as he inserted the key in the lock and opened the door.

Stepping inside was like stepping into another world once they were out of the whirling snow.

The floor was just hard-packed earth, but against the far wall was a small stove, a basket of logs standing alongside. Only the tiniest of windows set in one wall gave any light into the interior.

'Gavin built this place many years ago when Morgan and I were just kids,' David explained. 'He had the help of another old woodsman in those days, but once he died, father never replaced him. Morgan was old enough to give his father a hand by then, and he seemed quite keen to take the job on.'

'It's cold in here,' she said, looking around. 'Can we light the stove?'

'Don't see why not?' he answered, looking around for matches, and finding a half full box balanced on top of the basket of logs.

There was no paper to get it going, but there were some small twigs in the basket as well as logs, and with the help of some sheets from a small pocketbook he always carried, a few twists of the paper soon produced flames. Once they were able to add some bigger logs, there was soon a good blaze warming the small room as they sat on the floor waiting for the snow to stop – Henry happily curled up in front of the stove and snoring quietly.

CHAPTER 13

Marnie Peters had been getting on quite well with the research into her family, with some help from her aunt Carolyn. She had now traced her birth mother's family right back to the early 1800's, where she learned her many times grandparents had been a blacksmith and a kitchen maid when first married, and that they'd had 7 children, but beyond there the trail ran cold.

Records in those days were at most sketchy, and proving lineage was often doubtful where so many children were given the same name as their mother or father. Parish or church records were often the only records kept, recording mainly births, marriages and deaths, and some with christenings, if they were still decipherable.

In those days, a lot of the poorer people, or those less well educated, were unable to read and write, and records were only kept by them speaking their names and other people writing them down for them, often causing the misspelling of names, as Carolyn explained to her.

The last person recorded was a Martha Dyer, or Diyer, Dyre, Dye, as it was also recorded, and born in 1805, but when her mother's given name and details were inserted, it brought up surprising results.

They were taken to a prestigious and well-documented website showing the woman to have been of Plantaganet lineage, and her husband, a Knight of the Realm, whose family could be traced back to William the Conqueror. It also showed that she would only have been 10 years old herself when her daughter was born.

'I think somebody's taken a leap too far here,' Carolyn said. 'They've picked up the wrong information. Apart from being too young to bear a child, do you think somebody with such a distinctive background would have allowed their daughter to become a kitchen maid, and marry a blacksmith? I don't think there's a hope in hell of that having happened!'

Marnie had to agree with her.

'You probably never will find anything more about her parentage until more records are found and made available – but there may not be any more. Whoever Martha's parents were, they'd have been born in the 1700's, and records weren't very well kept around that era, especially amongst the poorer and less important people of this world. Let's have a look at Martha's husband and see what we can find out about him.'

Bringing her family tree back up again, Marnie opened up the information on Martha's husband, William Bright.

'Now that's another problem I've found,' Marnie said. 'He's named on the marriage certificate as Bright, but in other places he's named as Brightly, Brighty, and Brighton, but they all seem to point to the same person – same date of marriage, same place of birth and same parents' names.

Carolyn took a look through the information she'd gathered.

'I'd agree with that,' she said. 'Despite the different name, I'd say that is the same person – everything else seems to tie in.'

There was a lot more information relating to him, however, and it led them to a churchyard in Norfolk, where he seemed to have been buried as Brighty in the late 1800's, and there still seemed to be plenty of people researching the line. Other graves, relating to the same family line, and of much later origin, were also pictured in the same churchyard.

After a few minutes looking through, Marnie began to get fed up.

Closing down the family tree she said, 'What I'm really interested in is my father – all this is long gone and just water under the bridge. I really need to research him and see if I can find someone who might know him – a near relative perhaps!'

'Well, you've had your DNA taken, so why don't we look there?' Carolyn interjected.

Lifting the cursor to the top of the page, she clicked on the link marked DNA, bringing up Marnie's own DNA information.

It replicated that she'd already received in the post, and they then went on to look for likely familial matches amongst those already researching their own family trees on the site.

'Look,' Carolyn said. 'You have a match denoted as a first cousin. Her name's Gaye Smith.'

Luckily, the tree had been made public, so they were able to open it up, finding that the person in question was the daughter of a Randolph Bannerman, and a Kathryn Tudor, and was also their only child.

'Okay,' Carolyn said. 'Let's have a look through her family tree.'

With that she clicked on the section to open up the woman's family tree, both studying it for familiar names.

'Nobody there that I know,' Marnie said after they'd both browsed through it.

'No, me neither,' Carolyn agreed. 'Gaye's mother, Kathryn, only had one sister, and she died aged 17 according to this. Let's look at her father's side of things, see if that may be a bit more enlightening.'

After a quick look through, Carolyn brought up details that showed Gaye's father to be Randolph Bannerman, and that he had two brothers; Hector and Jacob.

Jacob had gone to live in New Zealand in 1972, where it appeared he was running a large cattle station until his death in 1999, and which was now in the hands of his only son, again not named, denoting that he was probably still alive. He was born in

New Zealand, as was his mother, who seemed to have died giving birth to him.

'The other brother, Hector, still seems to be alive. Let's have a look at his profile page.'

'Oh!' Carolyn said in surprise as it opened up. 'There's a picture here of Hector in a wig and gown. It seems he's a judge.'

The page hadn't yet been updated, and didn't show that Hector had died just recently.

'I think Hector's the only possibility of being your father, unless Jacob fathered you before he went to Australia. There is just a possibility of that having happened, as you'd have already been 3 when he left. We both know your mother didn't marry your father, so how about we try looking her up and see if there's any association.'

They found a birth online for her mother, but it seemed she'd died in 1975 without ever marrying, and there didn't appear to be any records of her ever having had another child. The Death Certificate only recorded her passing as 'myocardial infarction'.

'I was born in 1969, so I wonder if she already knew she was dying when she gave me up,' Marnie pondered.

'Possible, but unlikely,' her aunt replied immediately. 'It was another 6 years later, unless she was already suffering from a heart condition when you were born.'

'I'm hungry,' Marnie announced. 'Let's have a coffee and something to eat before we carry on.'

They felt much better after the coffee and a couple of slices of rich fruit cake when they returned to the keyboard.

'Okay,' Carolyn said as they sat down. 'As far as I can see, the best possibility, and the best candidate for being your father is Hector. Let's see if there's anybody else researching his family tree.'

Trawling through, they were out of luck, so they returned to the page of Gaye Smith.

'Hector seems to have married, and still lives in the family home near Denbigh where he was brought up,' Marnie said. 'It seems he had 4 sons, only one still living, and a very much younger daughter. It's a good distance away, but not too far to take a look see. Fancy coming with me one day?'

Carolyn wasn't averse to the idea, but she didn't know what Marnie hoped to achieve from it, or what she intended to do when she got there. They couldn't just burst in on them unannounced and declare that she was Hector's illegitimate daughter. She'd probably be thrown out straight away, and they wouldn't gain anything by it.

'We don't even know exactly where the place is,' she answered warily.

'I'll soon find out,' Marnie said. 'He's a judge and a well known figure. There must be some information about him online.'

She wasn't mistaken!

Soon she knew quite a bit about the man, the part of Wales where he lived, delineated simply as Denbighshire, his wife's name, and all his children's names; particularly that of the man she suspected was also her brother, or as Carolyn corrected, her step-brother. There was also a step-sister, who seemed to have been born many years after her other three brothers had died, and was consequently a lot younger than Marnie.

Her brother seemed to be following in father's footsteps, as he had become a barrister.

'A shame we don't have an address for him,' she commented. 'It might be best to approach him first before trying to approach my father, but he may still live at home.'

Carolyn wasn't at all happy with her idea of contacting any of them.

It might not really be prudent to approach David, who probably didn't know anything about an illegitimate child that his father had sired before he married – and probably wouldn't want to know either. He'd probably be very wary of any approach she made to him, wondering what she was hoping to gain from it.

134

And if she did approach the person she thought to be her father, he definitely wouldn't want to know about an illegitimate child he'd unknowingly fathered years ago. He was probably as drunk as Celia at the party, and wouldn't remember anything about it anyway.

And as for the girl she thought to be her sister, there was almost thirty years between them. She definitely wouldn't be prepared to accept a sister born so many years before her. Marnie was old enough to be her mother.

To both of them, it would seem a betrayal by their father. An indiscretion committed years ago in his youth, and possibly even before he knew their mother. They'd both think she wanted more from them – possibly money in order to keep quiet – and if their father found out about it, he'd probably do everything in his power to keep her quiet.

No! What Marnie was considering doing in contacting them was definitely not a good idea – but how could she talk her out of it? She seemed set on the idea!

CHAPTER 14

Worried about David and Anna, Cyril kept glancing out of the window. He'd seen the ominous clouds gathering overhead, and knew they heralded either heavy rain or snow – and after he'd seen the weather forecast on the television in his room that morning, he knew it was more likely to be snow.

He waited and hoped for their imminent arrival, but as the snow began to fall, and soon began to grow thicker, with still no sign of them, he grew more and more concerned.

He tried to think of some way of finding them, but he didn't know exactly where they'd gone, and where they might be now. All he could do was wait and hope they were safe. David knew this place like the back of his hand, having spent all his young life here, and he knew that if he could, he would find a way back.

He looked out of all the windows regularly, unable to settle to anything, wandering around the house from room to room, and hoping he'd hear them enter the house at any moment; but it just didn't happen, and the snow was growing ever deeper as time went on.

Going to the front door, he looked out for the umpteenth time. There was no sign of them, but he did notice that the central rose bed, which had once been the ornamental fish pond, was almost completely covered over. Nothing could be seen of the stone wall surrounding the bed, and the large carved shell in the middle was fast disappearing. Nothing could now be seen of the roses that Gavin and Morgan had so recently pruned – the only features in

136

the barren landscape being the bare and weighed down branches of the trees. He hoped they'd be a guide that David could follow.

Winter had come early and with a vengeance! He was all alone in the house, and even though the larder was well stocked, he didn't know how long they were likely to be cut off for.

He could remember times, many years ago, when it had lasted for several weeks and they'd been almost completely out of food before anybody was able to get through. He only hoped that wasn't going to happen now, especially with master David and Anna still missing. He kept hoping there'd be some sign of them soon and they wouldn't perish in the deep drifts that were now beginning to form all around – but there was nothing he could do except wait and pray it would stop soon, or he'd see them plodding towards the house!

Anna and David were, however, safe and well in the little stone hut, and comparatively warm.

The earthen floor had been cold to sit on, but luckily they'd found some old hessian sacks stuffed in a corner, and, although they were dirty and dusty, they afforded relief from the cold.

David had been going to the small window every so often to check on the snowfall outside, but each time it was still as heavy as before, and there was no sign of a let-up. It was so thick, he couldn't even see across the clearing any more.

After they'd talked about all the topics they could think of, Anna said something that stirred his thoughts.

She'd never really spoken about her former life before she'd worked for him, and he'd never asked, fearing she might think he was prying. All he knew about her was that she'd worked in a busy office, and lived alone in a rented flat – and that was his full knowledge of her former life.

Now, out of the blue, she'd mentioned living in Cornwall, leaving the way open for him to question it.

'How did you come to live in Cornwall,' he asked. 'I thought your parents lived in Conwy.'

She smiled.

'Yes, they did, but we went on holiday to Cornwall after I finished Commercial College, and I met my husband there. I was only just 18 and he was the son of the owner. He was quite a few years older than me and I fell for him while we were there. That turned out to be the biggest mistake of my life!'

'Want to tell me about it?' he asked.

He'd heard so many sad tales during his short career as a barrister, and he'd always found himself intrigued by other peoples' problems.

'Nothing much to tell,' she sighed. 'We were happy for a few short years, or at least I was, but it seems he still had a roving eye, and it was only 5 years later that he met someone else and was asking for a divorce. After that, I moved back in with my parents until I found my previous job in Corwen and moved into the little flat.'

'I'm sorry,' he said, feeling genuinely sorry for her. 'It must have been awful for you.'

'It was rather. I still loved Andrew, even though he'd fallen out of love with me. It took me a long time to get over him, but that's all behind me now. I'm happy working for you, and I hope you feel the same. I'm happier than I have been for a long time, and we get on well together. I hope you feel the same way?'

The final part of her speech was framed as a question, and he agreed immediately, not quite knowing how to carry the conversation on.

Shortly after that, she curled up on the sacking and fell asleep. Henry was still occupying his place in front of the stove and sleeping deeply. They'd folded a sack in half for him as well and he'd snuggled down happily on it, but David couldn't sleep. He was thinking about what she'd just told him, beginning to realise that he enjoyed being and working with her more than he'd realised so far.

This Andrew she'd mentioned must have been a real cretin not to have seen what a treasure he'd found in Anna. She'd always been more than willing to cook and clean for him, and to be there

138

when he needed her; but then he began to brood. Was that just because it was her job to look after him, or did she genuinely care about his welfare? Now it was his turn to keep her safe. He'd brought her here at this time of year when he knew there was a likelihood of snow, and he needed to get her back safely.

He'd already noticed that the light was beginning to fail. With the heavy snow clouds above, night was coming early, and even though it was barely 3.30 in the afternoon, it was already going dark.

In this alien environment, would they be able to find their way back to the house if the snow stopped? Everything looked so different after a heavy snowfall, and the old familiar landmarks seemed to disappear from sight.

He only hoped that they wouldn't have to spend the night here. The wood for the stove was dwindling, and that outside would be too wet now to use. To say he was worried was putting it mildly!

Going back to the stove, it had burned itself down to ash, and he put on just two pieces of wood. Better to have just a little heat now than to run out altogether before the snow stopped.

Lying down and curling up on his own sacks, he fell asleep after a few minutes, awaking some time later to the sound of Henry scuffling at the door. He must want to go out.

David was loath to open the door, as it opened inwards and the snow would fall in, making it impossible to shut it again until it was all cleared, and he had nothing to do that with besides his hands. They'd lose all the heat as well, and there wasn't enough wood left to warm the place up properly again.

Henry turned and looked at him and whined.

The fire was almost out. If he put logs on it, it would be a waste of the heat as it would escape through the open door, but if he didn't, it might go out altogether, and he had no more matches to start if off again.

Going to the window, he peered through the small pane of glass.

The snow had stopped, and even though everywhere was covered in a deep layer, there was enough moonlight shining down to help them find their way home.

Glancing at his watch, he saw it was already 7p.m.

'What time is it?' Anna's sleepy voice murmured through his thoughts.

'Time to go home,' he said. 'That's if I can find the way. The snow's stopped and we have some moonlight to see by. It's time to make a move. It may cloud over again and we may get more snow – then we'll be completely stuck.'

'I'm cold,' she said.

'That's okay. Climbing through all that snow will warm you up, but it'll probably take a while. I reckon its knee deep in places. Think you can manage it?'

'I'll have to, won't I?' she answered, smiling up at him as she got to her feet.

Opening the door, he let Henry out, who immediately shot past him and disappeared into the trees opposite, doing a bouncing act through the drifts, and almost disappearing from sight in some places.

As he'd anticipated, a mound of snow fell in, and he couldn't close the door after they left. He'd have to leave it open for the time being and try to either get word to Gavin about it, or come back himself to shut it when the snow had gone. His main priority now was to get Anna back to the house, get them both warmed up, and get some food inside them. He was extremely hungry, and he thought Anna must be too.

'I need to pee too,' Anna said once outside and seeing Henry bounding off, 'but I'm not going to expose my nether regions in this environment. How far do you reckon it is back to the house?'

'In normal circumstances – about 15 minutes, but who knows in this snow – it could take double that time or even more!'

'Then it'll just have to wait until I'm desperate! Let's go!'

140

It wasn't easy going as they found themselves struggling through the deep drifts – but they weren't cold at least. Their exertions were keeping them warm, but their feet were becoming extremely cold after only a short time.

Even though they'd both been wearing stout walking boots, thick socks and waterproof trousers, it wasn't long before the snow had made its way inside the boots; the warmth of their feet melting it almost immediately.

The gap in the trees made the pathway easy enough to follow, even though they did trip and fall several times over protruding tree roots and fallen debris, but once away from the trees, the going got tougher. They were now walking in open moorland, and all the hazards that presented.

The dead bracken and ferns had been flattened by the snow and could no longer be seen, causing them to catch their feet in the bent fronds, or stub their feet against rocks that littered the uneven ground. Several times they both sprawled or fell to their knees, but they did manage to make some progress, if only slowly, and they were both beginning to tire.

David's guide to the way they were heading were the hills on the opposite side of the valley – if they kept them on their left, they should soon come in sight of the house. The land to their right was just open moorland: a featureless expanse of nothing but whiteness, stretching as far as the eye could see into the darkness and with no distinguishing landmarks of any sort. If they managed to wander off in that direction, they would soon become hopelessly lost.

He kept glancing up at the sky – hoping each time he looked up that it wasn't beginning to cloud over again, but they were in luck, as it was still blue black and there were a myriad of glittering stars above them still. The moon still lit the way, but on his last look, he could see a whitish, purplish cloud moving over the hills and towards the moon. It was only moving slowly, so slowly as to make its movement almost imperceptible, but if it did cover the moon before they reached the house, they could be completely lost.

With one final look, he bent to the task in hand and tried to make more progress with each stride he took, hampered by Anna who was finding the going much tougher. She'd never had to cope with anything like this before, and she wasn't coping well.

Suddenly, Henry, who'd also been finding the going tough as well, gave a joyous bark and bounded off ahead of them, finding renewed energy in his legs as he bounced off over the snow.

David looked up and felt a pounding of his heart in his chest.

'We've made it! Anna, there's Bannerman's just ahead of us,' he cried, pointing to several lights shining from the windows, the vague outline of the house just coming into view.

It was much further to their right than he'd anticipated, but at least they'd be able to make their way across to it. He didn't say anything to Anna, but he knew that if they'd kept on the way they were going, there was an area of boggy wet ground ahead of them, and before long they'd have found themselves in a very marshy bog.

He remembered his father losing a dog in that marshy ground many years ago. The poor animal must have floundered about in the morass for ages before it finally drowned, and they found its almost submerged body the next day.

He heaved a sigh of relief and they both found a renewed sense of energy as they made their way towards the house, which seemed to grow nearer with each few steps they took, and before long they felt the gravel of the driveway crunching under their feet beneath the snow.

Henry was already standing on the doorstep when they arrived, whining and pawing the door, which shot open as they approached.

'Am I glad to see you!' Cyril gasped. 'Come inside – you must be frozen!'

Henry had already shot past him and disappeared into the kitchen, making straight for his bowl. It was well past his mealtime, and food was high on his list of expectations.

Cyril helped them out of their wet clothes. She'd hurt her arm on one occasion when she'd fallen, but she'd said nothing to David, thinking it might hold them up.

'There's hot water if you'd like a bath to warm you up, and I've put clean towels on your beds,' Cyril said. 'There's one of Isabelle's casseroles in the oven as well, and I've put some jacket potatoes in to go with it – you must both be very hungry!

'That's putting it mildly,' David said, 'but there probably won't be enough hot water for two baths, so I'll have a nice hot shower. Which would you prefer, Anna?'

'Oh, I'll take the bath,' she answered, 'but I won't be in it very long, I'm ravenous too!'

But she was longer than she'd expected! Once in the water, she lay there, up to her neck in hot suds, and savouring its warmth before finally making her way downstairs. David was already seated at the table in dressing gown and pyjamas, and eating his.

'Sorry, but I just couldn't wait,' he said. 'I hope you don't mind!'

'Not at all,' she answered, as Cyril took her plate from the oven and set it in front of her.

As befitted her status, he'd set her place opposite and not alongside their employer. She realised their easy familiarity while in the hut was now over. They had returned to their status of employer and employee once again.

Henry, having found his own bowl full when he returned to the kitchen, had eaten his fill, and was curled up in his bed next to the range and fast asleep.

'I think I'll take a leaf out of Henry's book and go to bed myself,' David announced when he'd finished.

'Me too,' she returned. 'I'm tired as well!'

CHAPTER 15

'Robbie,' the voice boomed out across the canteen. 'Robbie Richards!'

It was the voice of his Inspector, Angus McDonald.

The imperious voice sounded as if it was calling him back to duty again. Oh well! He had at least managed to eat his dinner before he'd been called away, even if he hadn't managed to drink all his coffee.

'Sir,' he answered, standing up so that the man could see where he was and walking towards him.

'I have a job for you. Where's Pryce?'

'I think he's gone to the bo . . ., loo,' he ended, changing the word he'd been going to use, for something more befitting to the person standing before him.

'If you mean bog, say it. I have heard if before you know,' McDonald said, a twinkle in his eye.

Robbie said nothing, his embarrassment covered by his partner entering through the same door the Inspector had just used.

'Ah, Pryce! I'm glad you're both back. Come to my office for a moment, would you.'

They followed behind him at a discreet distance.

'Take a seat,' he said, perching on the edge of his desk as they did as he'd told them. 'It's about the Bannerman case!'

They both nodded. The case he was talking about was still fresh in both their minds.

'You know we found that body in the trees some time ago!'

144

They both nodded in unison.

'Well, it's been positively identified as Nathan Muir, but as we're already aware from the dash cam footage, there was definitely another lad involved. It clearly shows them having some sort of altercation when it stopped after the accident, but we only see the back of their heads and a partial side view as they look at each other. It's too far away to identify either of them with any accuracy. Any idea who the other lad could be?'

Oh yes, Robbie had a very good idea who it could be!

'He always hung about with a lad called Kevin Williams from Moorside Farm. Kevin had turned one of their barns into his own den, and Nathan, as his parents previously told me, often stayed there with him. They said he's been spending a lot of time there in recent months and they haven't seen much of him.'

'Yes, I see your report mentions this Kevin Williams. Are you sure he's the other lad involved?'

'As sure as I can be, but as far as I can see, there's no proof of that, although he may crack if we interview him. He's only 20, the same age as Nathan is . . . was,' Robbie corrected himself.

Although they'd both been young tearaways, as lads of that age often were, he'd always thought it was just their youth and they'd both grow out of it.

'Bring him in for questioning,' McDonald said, standing up and walking back behind the desk.

As he noticed them both still sitting there, he barked, 'Well, what are you waiting for?'

'Do you think he'll crack?' Steve said, once they'd climbed into their patrol car.

'I'd bet on it. He's not a bad lad, and he's never been in any serious trouble before. He may well crack under a bit of pressure,' was Robbie's reply.

It had snowed heavily a few days ago, and they thought the going might be treacherous up on the moors, but a sudden thaw had set in on the previous evening, and by the time they reached Moorside Farm that afternoon, the winding track up to it was just passable, with a bit of slipping and sliding.

Both the senior Williams's were at home when they arrived. Frank was reading the paper and sipping a strong cup of tea at one end of the table, and Megan, his wife, was kneading dough at the far end.

Frank opened the door to them, but Megan continued kneading, without glancing up at them.

Usually, any knock at the door was for Frank, and any farm business wasn't usually anything to do with her.

He glanced over at his wife when he saw it was the police, and she stopped kneading.

'Now what is it?' she said. 'We've already told you all we know. What more do you want with us?'

'We'd like to speak to Kevin again. Is he at home?'

'No, he's not here,' she said emphatically.

Her husband gave her a warning glance.

'I think you'll find him in the barn,' he said. 'I saw him there not half an hour ago,' and taking them outside, he pointed out the place at the far end of the other barns.

When he went back inside, his wife had stopped her bread making and was glaring furiously at him.

'What did you want to tell them that for?' was her angry retort.

'There's no use in lying to them. They'll only be back again. They won't give up until they've spoken to him. If he did take a car and he's been riding around the roads with it and caused an accident, then that's up to him. They're gonna' find out if it was him in the end, and it might just teach him a lesson.'

'But he's never been in trouble before. What will they do to him?' She was near to tears now.

'I don't know,' he answered, 'but he'll probably have to pay for the damage, and he might even have to pay compensation as well, but that's up to him. I'm not gonna' fork out to get him out of trouble. He'll have to face up to this on his own. If he did it, he's gonna' have to take the punishment. He's old enough to know right from wrong.'

They knew there'd been an accident, but what they weren't aware of was that it wasn't only vehicles that had been involved, but that a human life had been lost as well.

Their son would probably be charged with much more serious offences, and could possibly find himself with a prison sentence if he was found guilty.

What they'd thought of as only a minor misdemeanour had turned into something far more serious, and seeing as it involved a well known and prestigious judge, one of his compatriot judges probably wouldn't show any inclination to be lenient.

As Frank had already told them, Kevin was in the barn, and it was with horror that he opened the door to two coppers standing in front of him.

Trying to show bravado he said, 'What do you want? I was just going out.'

'Not until we've spoken to you, you're not. Mind if we come in?' and Robbie walked in past the lad without waiting for an answer.

'Hey, you can't come in without my say so,' Kevin blurted out.

'I thought you'd just invited us in,' Robbie said, looking at his partner with a smile on his face. 'Didn't you think he'd just invited us in?'

'Yes, I'm sure he said come in,' Steve agreed.

'Well, now that we're in, perhaps you'd spare us a few minutes to answer some more questions,' Robbie continued.

'I ain't answerin' nuthin,' Kevin said, his feet firmly planted on the ground with his legs apart.

'Okay, if that's the case, I'm arresting you on a charge of the taking and driving away of a motor vehicle. Let's go!'

'Hey, you can't do this,' Kevin howled as they took an arm each and roughly manhandled him to their car, where he was handcuffed and pushed into the back seat.

Two hours later, after leaving him to cool off in a cell for a while, Robbie and Steve went back to interview him, and after reading him his rights, the interview began.

At first he refused to say anything, but under the constant pressure of an hours' solid questioning, he began to crack.

'We did take the car,' he finally admitted. 'It was a beauty, and I'd never driven a car like that before. I'd never driven any car at all, only my dad's old tractor and I hadn't passed my bike test either.'

'When you say we, who were you with?' Robbie was quick to add.

'It was Nathan Muir,' he admitted.

'Did you know Nathan died that day?'

'Not then, no, but I did hear later. It nearly cracked me up. I called for an ambulance for him and I thought he'd have been alright once they got him to hospital. He was with me while we took it in turns riding the bike round the quarry. We was just on our way back to my pad, when we saw the car parked in the lay-by near the entrance.

We saw the driver go into the bushes, so we dumped the bike and decided to take the car for a spin. We never meant no harm by it.'

'You've just told us you didn't have a licence. Didn't you think you could have come to grief when you took such a powerful car?' Steve cut in.

'Never thought about it – it just seemed like a bit of fun at the time. We didn't intend to hurt no one.'

Robbie glanced at Steve. He didn't need any sort of intervention at this stage. He wanted the lad to go on talking and for them to hear the whole story before plying him with questions. There'd probably be plenty that needed answering when they'd finished.

'Go on, where did you go with the car?' he prodded.

'I dunno' really. We drove round all over the place. I remember we passed a lake – could have been Llyn Brenig.

There's a few lakes round there. Can I have a drink of water please?'

This was a very different lad to the one they'd first arrested. He was trying to dig himself out of the mess he'd gotten into, and he wasn't making a very good job of it. It now looked as if he was trying to stall for time – trying to give himself time to get his story straight.

Robbie paused the tape while Steve went to fetch the water, but when it arrived, Kevin only took one or two sips out of it.

Switching the tape back on, Robbie urged him to carry on.

'What about the accident? Was it you who was driving when it happened?'

Kevin nodded.

'And where was it?' Robbie pressed.

'I dunno',' he answered again. 'I was too busy driving. It was a fast car and it took me all me time to keep it on the road. I remember passing the Sportsmans Arms though. That's all I do remember.'

'You were going fast then?'

Kevin hung his head before nodding.

'How fast?'

'Dunno,' the same reply again.

'Was it near the Sportsmans where the accident happened?'

'No, not there. It was further on. Dunno' where it was.'

It was no use pressing any further with that line of questioning. He already knew where the accident had happened, but Kevin obviously had no idea. If he did know the area, he'd obviously been too busy trying to keep the car on the road to take any notice of where he was going.

'Tell us what happened with the accident,' Robbie urged, giving the lad no time to think or make up a story.

'I come round this bend, and Kevin was going on at me to slow down. I took me eyes off the road for a minute to shout at him to shut up, but when I looked back, there was this car in front of me. It was slowing down, and I knew I couldn't stop in time. There

149

was nothing coming the other way, so I swerved round it, but there was this motorbike in the middle of the road waiting to turn right. It was stopped, but I couldn't see it 'cause the other car was hiding it from me. I tried to miss it, but the car wasn't doing what I wanted. I think it was skidding a bit. I remember the bang as I hit it, and I saw bits of the bike flying up in the air, but I didn't see what happened to the rider. Kevin was screaming at me to stop, and the car wasn't behaving right, so I slowed down and stopped. I didn't know what to do. I'd almost run off the road meself when I managed to stop. I looked in the mirror and the driver of the other car was climbing out. There was no sign of the biker. I didn't know what to do. I panicked. I didn't wanna' get caught, so I drove off.'

He'd said all this in one wild rush, before he stopped and took a big gulp of water this time, obviously reliving that wild moment of panic.

'And what did you do then?' Steve intervened.

There was obviously more to tell concerning Nathan's death.

'We managed to find our way back to the quarry. Nathan seemed to know where it was. We knew there'd be evidence in the car, forensic evidence I mean, so we looked in the boot. There was a small can of petrol there, and the driver was a smoker. The ashtray was almost full, so we looked for some matches. We found a lighter in the central console panel, and I poured petrol on the seats and on the rubber mats. I set it alight with a yellow duster I found in the boot.

Nathan couldn't help 'cause his leg was hurting and it was bleeding too. The passenger door had been dished in and something had been pushed against his leg, but I managed to get it open and pulled him out. He was bleeding badly.'

Once he'd started talking, the full story was coming out, and most of it tied in with the account given by the other car driver, who they already knew was in no way to blame.

'What happened then? How did you get Nathan to where he died?' Robbie pressed again.

150

'We used his underpants to tie round his leg to try and stop the bleeding, then I brought the 'bike back to where he was, and got him on the pillion seat. I told him to hold on tight, but after only a short way, it ran out of petrol.

I wasn't far from home, so I told him to stay where he was and I'd go home across the fields and call for an ambulance from there.'

'Why didn't you use your mobile?' Steve cut in this time.

'There was no signal,' came the quick reply, prompting an even quicker one back from Steve. 'Don't you know that emergency calls work on any network? Any emergency calls you make will be picked up by any provider, even though it's not your own?'

'No, I didn't know that,' head hanging again.

Robbie glanced warningly at Steve. He didn't want the lad sidetracked in any way now that he was talking freely.

'And did you call them when you got home?'

'Yes, I did, but me dad wanted me to do a job, so I couldn't go back. I thought he'd be okay, and I heard the ambulance from across the fields, so I knew they'd probably find him.'

They'd already heard the ambulance crew's statement, and knew that they'd been unable to find Nathan, even though they'd spent nearly half an hour searching. The voice on the 'phone had said he was in some woods and he'd be waiting by the side of the road. When they arrived there was no sign of anyone, and the woods stretched some way along the road. They'd searched, calling to the person they were looking for, but all to no avail. Finally, they concluded that it must have been a hoax call and returned to base.

Robbie had already realised it wasn't a hoax call at all, but that Nathan must have been deeply unconscious from loss of blood even before they arrived, and totally unaware of their presence.

Sadly, here was a 20 year old lad, sitting across the table from them, tears glistening in his eyes. In a moment of reckless stupidity, something anyone could have been capable of at that young age, he'd stolen a powerful car for a bit of a joy ride. As a result of that moment of madness, he'd caused the death of two people, neither of whom had deserved to die – a prominent and well-known judge, and his own friend, Nathan Muir.

As a result of that, he now faced a long prison sentence ahead of him, taking away his own youth as well, and possibly his chances of finding a wife and fathering a family of his own.

The charges he now faced were at the very least the taking away of a motor vehicle without the owner's consent, and the second, a charge of causing death by dangerous or reckless driving. The first may have earned him a prison sentence, but the second definitely would.

CHAPTER 16

Anna and David relaxed for most of the following day, neither emerging from their bedrooms before 10 o'clock.

David was already eating a breakfast of bacon, mushrooms and fried tomatoes, together with plenty of toast and marmalade, cooked generously for him by Cyril, when Anna entered the kitchen.

'Morning, Anna,' Cyril said, a smile radiating his face as she entered the soothingly warm kitchen. He hadn't, until now, realised how much he needed the company of others when he found himself all alone in the house, as he would have been all over the Christmas period. 'What would you like for breakfast? I'll cook some for you too.'

'Thank you. I'll have the same as David if you don't mind,' she said, seating herself opposite. 'Have you had yours?'

He nodded.

'Long ago! I've been clearing the areas around the house so we could get out, but it's pretty deep, so I doubt anybody's going too far away today.'

David shrugged.

'That suits me. I've a few more of my father's papers to root through, so that'll probably keep me busy for a good part of the day, then I reckon some daytime telly with my feet up would be in order – that's if there's anything worth watching! I reckon we had our fill of exercise yesterday to last us a good while.'

Anna laughed.

'Don't forget Henry will need a walk as well!'

'Do you think that's really necessary today? Doesn't look as if he needs it,' as they all looked over at Henry, already curled up in his bed next to the stove and sleeping soundly once again.

As if aware that they were talking about him, Henry opened his eyes and looked at them without lifting his head, his tail giving a couple of listless wags, before he tucked his nose back under his front paw and went back to sleep again.

Cyril laughed.

'He was out with me when I was clearing the snow before, and he's had a good breakfast, so I reckon he'll be content to fall in with whatever plans you have for today.'

Anna found David's plans to her liking as well. The fall she'd taken yesterday while they were struggling home had hurt her shoulder more than she'd realised, and this morning it was aching quite badly. Checking in the mirror, she'd noticed a large bruise coming up, and she doubted she'd be able to do very much with that arm for the rest of the day.

When she'd fallen, she'd fallen sideways and hit it on a rock that was sticking out of the ground; hidden as it was by the lying snow.

Cyril noticed her awkwardness while she was eating, and asked if anything was wrong; David too looking over at her.

'I fell yesterday and caught it on a rock. It's only bruised. I'll be all right in a day or so,' she said, trying to make light of it.

'I'll take a look at it when you've finished eating,' Cyril said. 'Better to be safe than sorry, and I **was** a trained first aider while I was in my previous job.'

'I'll be fine,' she protested, 'there's no need to bother.'

'What's the harm in letting him look,' David said with a concerned expression on his face.

'Okay,' she replied, shrugging her shoulders and wincing as she did so, 'but it's all a big fuss about nothing. It's not that bad!'

But it was!

As soon as Cyril started feeling around her shoulder, a sharp pain shot through it and she cried out.

'It doesn't sound like nothing to me,' David said, sipping his third cup of tea before going to his father's study.

Pulling the shoulder of her sweater back up again, Cyril said, 'I think you'd better rest that for a while. I can feel a slight grating in the bone. I think you may have a small hairline fracture there, but I don't think it's any more than that, and there's no way we can get you to a doctor today. Best rest it for a while, and then if the snow is still here, and it doesn't get any better in a couple of days, we'll find some way of getting you there. I don't think we have any sort of medical kit, but I'm sure we have a bandage at least. I'll wrap it round your wrist and make a small sling with it to go round your neck. That should ease the pressure on it, and it'll remind you not to try and use it.'

Now that they'd all finished eating, she offered to help with the dishes, but Cyril wouldn't hear of it.

'I can manage on my own,' he said. 'You go and put your feet up. Watch of bit of daytime telly yourself. It won't harm for one day, and when I've finished here, I'll go and find that bandage.'

As she wandered out of the kitchen, the idea of daytime television really didn't appeal to her, so she went to find David.

'Anything I can do to help?' she asked, opening the door and peering in.

He was surprised to see her there, but he wasn't averse to a bit of company.

'You can go through those papers if you like,' pointing to a small pile on a table in the window where his father's computer sat. 'You should be able to manage that with just one hand. See if there's anything relevant or interesting in them, and if not, I'll consign them to the recycling. I've already found some old receipts going back years. I've no idea what they refer to, but there's even a receipt for a microwave that blew up just before I left. I remember being in the kitchen when it gave a loud pop, and the flash lit up the whole room, then it didn't work again. I

155

remember it being here for years before that, so we'd got our money's worth out of it.'

Laughing, she started on the pile, and found exactly the same problem with the ones she was looking through.

There was even a receipt from a builder for work carried out on the roof in 1996, and was consigned immediately to the recycling pile.

'Well, that looks like it!' she said after going through them twice to make sure. 'I haven't found anything remotely relevant to this day and age. What about you?'

'Me neither – most of these can go for recycle too. Whatever we may have missed, I don't think Jayne's going to be too bothered about it when she finally gets back.'

As he held out the open carrier bag to her, she forgot about her shoulder and tried to pick up the papers from the desk with her left hand, giving a shriek as the pain from her shoulder shot through her whole body. The papers fluttered from her fingers and spread out all over the floor between them.

Cradling it with her other hand, she tried to bend to pick them up, but David's voice stopped her.

'Hey, I'll do that. You take care of that arm!'

Reaching down to pick them up, he noticed some of them had fluttered under the desk, and he had to go down on his knees to reach them. Anna moved her chair back and out of his way.

It was as he was crawling back out of the opening that his hair caught on something which made a jangling sound. Looking back into the opening, he saw three keys hanging from a brass hook just to one side of the foot well, the hook screwed in just below the desk top and on the left.

'This is something we've missed,' unhooking them and holding them up.

'Where are they from?' she asked.

'I've no idea. Maybe Cyril will know. I've never seen them before.'

Unexpectedly, just at that moment, Cyril appeared in the doorway carrying the bandage he'd been looking for.

'What is it I'll know?' he asked, surprised to find David down on his knees.

David laughed.

'And they talk about eavesdroppers not hearing any good of themselves . . . ! You couldn't have picked a better moment to arrive!' as he got to his feet.

Cyril looked embarrassed.

'Sorry, I wasn't eavesdropping. I've just brought this bandage for Anna.'

'Don't worry about it! It was only meant as a joke! It's these keys I've just found on a hook under the desk – any idea what they fit?' as he held them up.

Cyril put the bandage down next to Anna and took them from him.

'I've no idea – I've never seen them before. Where did you find them?'

David pointed out the small hook in the desk foot well, and Cyril looked at them again, before shaking his head.

'I've no idea. The judge always kept his study locked, and Sandra was only allowed in once a week to clean it; and that was always under his supervision. I haven't been in here for years.'

David took them from him and examined them again.

'Well, wherever they're from, it looks as if they're both from the same lock. The two larger ones mirror each other exactly, and the smaller one looks as if it belongs to a small cupboard or drawer of some sort. Anyway, you'd better get Anna's arm strapped up before she does herself any more damage.'

Cyril concurred, and David slipped the keys into his pocket while Cyril applied the makeshift sling.

He'd have to keep his eye open around the house, and see if he could find a locked door to which they didn't seem to have a key. Maybe they'd fit that door, but it seemed a strange and secretive place to keep a set of keys, especially as his father always kept the door to his study locked.

The one place they hadn't really searched was the top floor where Isabelle and Cyril had their rooms. He hadn't thought there'd be anything up there of any significance, as he'd never known his father go up there; but then again, it was years since he'd last lived here, and he could have been up there during that time for reasons of his own.

A quick glance round that floor whilst Cyril was making them some coffee and urging Anna to rest more brought nothing of any interest to light. Apart from the two occupied rooms, there were several small maids' rooms which hadn't been occupied in years and were completely bereft of any furniture, save for iron bed frames with no mattresses, and the attic space, which in itself revealed nothing of interest either. Everywhere was covered in a layer of dust and didn't look as if it'd been disturbed in many years.

He'd drawn another blank there.

Two days later the snow began to thaw, as a weak sun peeped through the grey clouds that had covered everything for days.

What was left of the virgin snow glittered and shone in the sunlight as David and Anna peered through the front window after breakfast.

Anna's arm was beginning to improve and the swelling was going down, although the bruising was still clearly visible.

'Fancy trying to get out for a walk today?' David asked. 'I'm getting bored sitting around here.'

'Sounds like a plan to me, but you'll have to help me with my coat. I don't think I should try and get my arm into the sleeve,' Anna replied. 'It still hurts to move it too much.'

'No problem,' he said, 'but let's have an early lunch and go out straight afterwards. It gets dark just after 4 o'clock, and it may freeze again tonight.'

'Good thinking! Where do you want to go?'

'Not too far. Perhaps into the woods and we can shut the door to the hut. I had to leave it open when we left. The snow had fallen inwards and I had nothing to shovel it out with.'

'That's a good idea. Perhaps we should call on Gavin on the way back and tell him what happened. He may have already been there and wondered why the door was open.'

'Okay, let's do that. They may be glad of some company as well. I don't suppose they've seen anybody for days either.'

They struggled a little at first with the soft slushy snow, but Henry, whom they'd decided to take with them, loved every minute of being released from his enforced incarceration, and bounded around exploring everywhere.

Once they entered the trees the pathway was almost completely clear due to the overhanging branches, and they made good progress to the hut, where they found Gavin already there. He was surprised at their appearance, but seemed delighted to see them.

''Ullo,' he greeted. 'I suppose yew're glad to get owt of the 'ouse too. We been cooped up for days with no sign of a soul. I wuz just about to go stir crazy by today, so I thought I'd come up 'ere and 'ave a look if there's any damage to the trees. Morgan's round 'ere somewheres as well.'

Turning back to the hut he continued, 'Someone's been up 'ere too. I found the door open and there wuz snow all inside. I must 'ave left the key in the lock when I was last 'ere. I've just finished clearing the snow owt of it.'

David gave a light little cough and offered a rather sheepish smile.

'I'm afraid that was us,' he said, apologetically, and went on to explain what had happened.

'I noticed yew didn' 'ave your arm in the sleeve,' Gavin smiled at Anna, 'is it feeling better now?'

She nodded.

'It's getting better, but not completely yet. Cyril's strapped it up for me to avoid any more injury. He wants me to see a doctor, but I don't think that's necessary. I'll make an appointment with my own doctor if it's no better when we get back.'

'Tell yew what – why don' yew come back down to t' cottage with me? I'm sure Megan would be on'y too glad of a bit of company, an' I know she did some baking yesterday. We 'ad some delicious sponge cake for owr tea last night, but there was no cream to go with it. We had to have it spread with jam only.'

'Won't do your waistline any harm, but that sounds good to me; even without the cream,' David said. 'What about you, Anna?'

'Me too,' she agreed. 'We had an early lunch and it was only sandwiches. I could do justice to some home baked cake with a cuppa.'

'Right, I'll just lock up 'ere and leave a message for Morgan,' and taking out a piece of slate from inside the door, he scrawled a brief message on it in chalk, locked the door, and left the slate propped against it.

'Now we know what we did before mobile 'phones!' David quipped.

'Very effective too,' Gavin replied, smiling, 'specially when the 'phone signal isn't always reliable round 'ere!'

Megan was delighted to see them and welcomed them profusely, Morgan following them in just ten minutes after they arrived.

'Lovely to see you both,' she cooed, moving the ironing she'd just finished off the chair and onto the staircase ready to go up.

The kettle was soon on, and slices of ginger parkin and some Welsh cakes fried in butter and drizzled with sugar were set in front of them as the conversation flowed.

One topic of conversation eventually stopped the flow.

'Yew left t' key to the hut still in the lock,' Morgan chided his father. 'I put it back where it belongs.'

That brought to mind the keys that David had found in his fathers' study, as he told them about finding them hidden under the desk.

'I haven't found anywhere they fit yet, and as far as I know, there aren't any more doors in the house to try.'

''ave yew tried the shed up behind the 'ouse?' Gavin asked.

'What – that old place!! I never remember it being locked, and I doubt if it would need locking!! Last time I saw it, it wouldn't have taken more than a good puff of wind to blow it down. I think it was there even before I was born.'

Both Gavin and Morgan laughed.

'Things do change yew know – it's quite some time since yew wuz 'ere last. Thar' old place wuz beginning to fall to pieces, as yew say, and a winter gale blew part of the roof off just a short while after yew left, so yewr father 'ad a new one installed.

We thought it would be for us to keep the gardening tools in, bur 'e never offered it for that purpose, and we never knew wha'r he kept inside it. The window was covered with a piece of net curtain that yewr sister pur up for 'im, so it was impossible to see anything inside.'

'I'll give it a try and see if the keys fit it before we leave. If he never let anyone else inside, it may contain something important – or at least – something important to him! That's got me intrigued now!

When they left, the light was beginning to fade, the sun had already disappeared, and there was no moon that night. The sky was filling with ominous looking clouds once again – they too aiding the onset of early darkness.

'We'll have to hurry,' David urged. 'It'll get dark very soon now, and without a moon we'll have a job finding our way back. We shouldn't have stayed so long.'

'Yes,' she replied, 'but I'm glad we did. I really enjoyed this afternoon. It was nice to have somebody else to chat with for a change.'

When they neared the house, lights were showing from many of the windows, and they both realised Cyril had put them on deliberately in order to guide their way back.

'Thank you Cyril,' David said under his breath as they hurried towards the house and its welcoming warmth. It was already turning very cold as darkness began to descend.

The house greeted them with a welcoming smell of something tasty cooking as they entered by the back door; David wanting to return that way to see if he could see the new shed before they went inside.

It was only a short distance from the house, but since the last time he'd been here, nature had taken its course, and much more foliage had grown between the house and the shed since then. He could see the very top of the roof, but nothing more, although the gravel path leading towards it was still there.

'Glad you're back,' Cyril greeted as they came through the back door, accompanied by a blast of cold air. 'Get your coats off and get warm by the stove. You've just time for a quick wash and brush up before this steak pie's ready for your dinner. Isabelle left the freezer well stocked, but I'm afraid she wasn't counting on you being here as well. We'll need a big shop soon – the fresh food is coming to an end.'

'Don't worry,' David said. 'Just get her to put an order through to me online and I'll see to the ordering and the payment from now on. I'll get it delivered straight to the door.'

'She'll be pleased with that,' Cyril replied. 'She's been trying to persuade your father to do that for years, but he wouldn't agree. He always said he preferred Isabelle to choose what she was buying herself. He always thought we'd get the leftovers if we ordered from the supermarkets for delivery.'

'Well, I've been doing it for some time now, and I've never found a problem,' Anna joined in. 'It saves a lot of leg work.'

162

The next morning, the idea of exploring the shed hadn't left David's mind, and he was anxious to go and try the keys to see what might be inside.

The old shed had never been locked when he was younger, but had always been well filled with junk.

He and his mates had often shut themselves inside when they were younger, taking with them a packet of cigarettes with a few left in it, or a crafty bottle of beer swiped from a mates' home.

His own father only drank good wines, or the very best whisky and brandy. None of them had ever fancied anything like that, and besides that, his father would have noticed if any of those went missing. He was always meticulously careful about keeping them catalogued, and always knew how much of the spirits were left in a bottle at any one time. David had often thought that his father must have measured them to make sure nobody was taking a crafty swig.

There'd been a forecast on the news that morning of heavier and more prolonged snow within the next few days, and, having discussed this with both Anna and Cyril, he'd decided to cut short their stay and leave sooner than expected.

Anna had been sorry to leave Cyril alone over the rest of the holiday, but he'd said he'd be fine. There were usually plenty of old films to watch, and he didn't mind being at home alone for a few days. Isabelle and Sandra were due back on January 2nd, but he was privately dreading the rest of the time he'd have to spend alone in this great mausoleum of a house – even if it was only for another few days.

After breakfast, David wandered up to the shed alone, leaving Anna behind to do their packing, and he was surprised to find that the new one was almost a complete replica of the old one. That had always been so full of junk, or as his father put it, "things not needed at present, but too good to be thrown away", that he presumed he would have bought a bigger one.

Both keys fitted the lock perfectly, and the door opened on well oiled hinges as he let himself inside, shutting the door behind him as there was still a bitter wind blowing.

He stood for a moment just looking around. The cluttered junk had all gone, and the interior looked more like a rest room than a shed.

The window was covered with a fairly new looking piece of net curtain, and under it stood a table, covered by a piece of blue oilcloth. There was nothing standing on the oilcloth but a packet of antibacterial wet wipes, and beneath the table was a black plastic bucket – clean and empty when he looked inside it. It looked almost brand new, and didn't look as if it had yet been used.

On the opposite wall was a wooden bench covered entirely by a dark blue plastic looking cushion; the base of which was completely enclosed by wooden sides.

David wondered if there might be storage underneath it, and lifted up the cushion to see if the base might be hinged, but he was disappointed. It was completely solid and screwed to the frame, as were the sides.

The only other addition seemed to be on the end wall where there was a wide shelf – the only thing on it a washing up bowl, a plastic jug containing some water, now covered in scum and dust, and a bottle of liquid soap.

His attention turned to the other small key he held in his hand. Where did that fit into things? It obviously fitted some sort of cupboard, but there was no sign of one in here.

It must have something to do with the shed and its use, otherwise why would it have been attached to the door keys?

Unfortunately, it looked as if that was going to have to wait for his next visit, when he could have a good look round the house and try to find the illusive cupboard or drawer it fitted. They were leaving for home straight after lunch.

CHAPTER 17

Marnie, ably aided by her aunt Carolyn, was beginning to build her family tree up well, and had decided to ignore the mysterious lineage of Martha Dyer, her ancestor with the baffling past, for the time being, and try to find her father.

It would have been nice to have been able to say she was descended from William the Conqueror, but all the evidence they'd uncovered so far pointed to the fact that it just wasn't right.

They'd hosted a small house party over Christmas, inviting Carolyn to stay with them for a couple of days, and having a few friends over to join them for Christmas day.

Realising she was going to have to cook for eleven people, and knowing how busy their trade would be, right up to, and including Christmas Eve, she'd persuaded Warren to bring in a small catering firm to do the cooking. They'd been advised by others that this husband and wife team were good and that the food and service were excellent, although they weren't cheap by any means.

Her insistence on bringing them in was somehow mollified for Warren when he sold the diamond and sapphire necklace and earring set he'd been working on to a local businessman on Christmas Eve for £15,000. That would well and truly cover the cost of bringing in the couple and their helpers, as well as provide him with a handsome profit.

Besides that, he knew the meal would definitely turn out to be a success, as Marnie's interests had never been in the kitchen, and her culinary efforts could sometimes be a bit hit and miss.

Their guests, seeming to be enjoying themselves, had stayed until late evening, and Warren had booked a small mini-bus in advance to drop them back home. All living only a short distance away, they could make their own arrangements to pick up their cars within the next few days, and the parking area at the front and side of the house was large enough to accommodate them easily.

Boxing Day morning was spent mainly in clearing up and returning everything to its proper place, but the afternoon was free for just mooching around, and the couple, together with aunt Carolyn, went for a short walk around the lanes to clear their heads, walking off some of the excess food still weighing heavily in their stomachs from the previous day.

There'd been some snow recently, although here in Cheshire it was only a light smattering and hadn't caused any inconvenience to anyone; but there was a stiff breeze blowing that day and it was very cold. Their fingers and their feet were beginning to feel icy cold as they decided to call it a day and return back to the house. They were all glad to feel the welcome warmth once inside, imbibing in a large glass of the heated mulled wine left in a pan on the stove from yesterday.

It was yet only 3.30 in the afternoon, and Warren had switched on the television while he put his feet up in front of the brightly blazing logs in the stove.

There was only horse racing on, so Marnie and Carolyn went into the study and switched on the computer to do some more research into their respective family trees, although it did turn out to be more about Marnie's research on her father in the end.

'I'm going to contact this cousin who's been researching the family,' she finally said.

Carolyn already knew Marnie was hot-headed, and had never liked anybody saying no to her. As her mother had always said, it was better to try and divert her attention elsewhere than try to stop her doing something she'd set her mind to. That always seemed to make her more determined to go ahead with whatever she had in mind.

'Do you think that's wise,' she asked. 'She may not be too pleased to hear what you have to say, and it will already have come up in her DNA as a match, so why hasn't she contacted you?'

'Look,' Marnie pointed out. 'It says she hasn't logged in for three months, so she probably hasn't spotted the match yet. It's only a month or so since I had it done.'

Point number one to Marnie. She had to find another way round it.

'Then if she hasn't logged in for three months, it may be ages before she does so again.'

'Possibly, but don't you get some sort of communication from the website showing you have a message waiting?'

Carolyn had to agree that was correct. There seemed no way of stopping her doing what she'd set her mind to.

'How about we go and get something to eat while you think about it. We didn't have any lunch and I'm getting hungry now. She probably won't be on the computer on Boxing Day anyway.'

Before Marnie could raise any argument, Warren's head appeared round the door.

'Did I hear somebody mention food? I'm starving! What are we having?'

Marnie roused herself and looked at the clock. It was almost five o'clock and they'd last eaten at 10a.m. None of them had wanted very much after the previous days' amount of food they'd all gorged themselves on, but they'd all managed a few croissants each with some of Carolyn's home-made marmalade and a glass of fresh orange juice. It had seemed to be a sufficiency then, but now they all seemed to be very hungry again.

'I've some salmon en croute with some fresh salad and some coleslaw. I'll just put it in the oven and lay the table while it's cooking.'

'And I'll make us some coffee. I could do with a cup myself. Does anyone else want one?' Carolyn asked; glad of his timely interruption.

Thank you Warren, she thought. You've broken her train of thought. I only hope she doesn't pick it up again after the food.

That evening there was a film on the television that Marnie wanted to see, so the computer was switched off and no more mention of her intention to contact the woman whose name had appeared on the screen was made – Carolyn hoping that she would have been distracted enough to forget about it for the foreseeable future, but she couldn't have been more wrong.

Now that the train of thought had entered into her head, Marnie worried at it like a sore tooth, and when she went to bed, it was still strong within her.

Carolyn went home the following day, and Marnie went back with her to make sure everything was okay, stopping to buy some milk at a local farm on the way. It was the only thing they were both short of.

The farmer had installed a chiller cabinet just inside one of his barns near the road, and by putting the money into the slot, the cabinet could be opened and the milk retrieved, locking itself again once the door was closed.

Things were very much on a trust basis, as once the cabinet was opened there was nothing to stop anyone taking as many cartons as they wanted, but apparently, according to what he'd once told Marnie, it wasn't usually abused. Selling in this way, and also to local shops, paid him more than selling to the supermarkets, and he only had a small herd of cows anyway. All his milk was usually sold by mid afternoon, so very little was ever wasted, and, although unpasteurised, the milk was from a regularly tested herd, and was always fresh and delicious, with a creamy flavour all of its own.

When they reached Carolyn's home; a three bedroom bungalow set in a small development with only four others around her, and surrounded by farmland, she went in with her and they had coffee and some shortbread before she decided to head home.

Warren was working on a piece of jewellery that he was repairing for a customer and he wanted to open up the shop next day, when he'd told the woman she could collect it. Marnie had also decided to go into work herself, not intending to bring any staff in over the Christmas holiday. They'd all had a busy time beforehand, and all been kept very busy, so they'd be glad of the extra time off.

She needed the rest of the time that day to give the house a bit of a clean before she did so. It had been rather neglected during the run-up to Christmas as well as the festive period itself, and there were pine needles from the real tree they'd decided to have that year beginning to shed all over the living room floor.

In the hallway and dining room she'd placed holly wreaths and intertwined them with some of the beautiful russet and red leaves she'd picked from the trees around the house, together with some evergreen branches wound through the spindles of the banister rail. These too were shedding from the heat inside the house, and she'd noticed some holly berries had been squashed into the hall carpet. They needed cleaning up before they stained it too much and it became impossible to get out.

Warren was still in his room when she arrived back, so she started on the hall carpet straight away; removing the offending displays and consigning them to the area around the outdoor trees. They'd rot down there as well as the trees own fallen leaves and provide more nutrients for their growth, as Warren had already told her.

It seemed to take ages to get the berry stains out of the carpet, not being able to get them out completely, but as it began to dry out during the day, the stains began to fade. They'd never go completely, but probably wouldn't be noticeable to anyone but her in the future.

Just as she finished, Warren emerged.

'Dinner?' he queried.

'Just going to put it on,' she answered, realising that it was almost one o'clock, and her own stomach was rumbling too.

'What we having?' he asked, following her into the kitchen.

'There's plenty of leftovers, so I'll concoct something from them. What's left of the turkey needs eating up too – unless I freeze it?'

'No, don't do that,' he answered. 'Weren't there some veggies left over? Some sprouts and red cabbage would be nice fried up in some butter and you could dice the rest of the turkey and mix it in with that.'

She agreed. There was enough to make a substantial meal with that if she mixed in some herbs and spices and served it with rice.

It was a quick meal and tasted good, but the rice could have done with a bit more cooking – it **was** a bit chewy in the middle.

After they'd eaten, Warren went back to his studio, and after a quick dust around and a really necessary use of the vacuum cleaner, she decided to have another look at her family tree.

Taking a coffee in to Warren, he told her he'd finished the item he'd been repairing and was working on another idea for a new piece. The sale of the expensive piece just before Christmas had stirred his imagination to create another.

'You don't mind me getting on with it, do you?' he asked. 'I won't have much time when we get back to work.'

'I don't mind at all,' she answered. 'I'm going to have another look into my family tree.'

Warren frowned as she left the room.

Carolyn had already told him that Marnie had had the idea of going looking for her family, and he had to admit, he wasn't keen at all keen on the idea. At best, she might be very upset by the experience if they rejected her and wanted nothing whatsoever to do with her, which seemed highly likely, but at worst they might threaten her with legal action and things could become very unpleasant. If either happened, it might, and probably would, upset her badly.

He knew, in his own youth, and before he'd met Marnie, he and his then girlfriend had had a serious scare when she thought she'd become pregnant after a very careless night of passion.

The whole night was something he'd always remember with pleasure; when her parents were away for a weekend and they'd had the whole of the Saturday night to spend together in her large bed. They'd indulged themselves with a reckless abandon to the possible consequences – followed by several weeks of fear and trepidation when she thought she'd become pregnant.

Luckily, nature took its course and she finally realised she wasn't; but the whole scare soured their relationship, and several weeks later they split up, never to see each other again since then.

He'd met Marnie just three months later and they'd been together ever since.

He didn't at the moment know how he'd go about dissuading her from her disastrous notion of finding her family, but for the moment, he went back to his work. At least she was safe in the study for the time being, and researching them on the computer couldn't bring about any harm, so he continued with working on his own interests.

Marnie, for her part, had taken her own coffee back to the computer with her and fired it up, staring out of the window at the grey clouds scudding about above her, heralding rain, or possibly more snow, to come, whilst she waited for it to load up.

It was while she was staring idly out of the window that the idea struck her – this woman, whose DNA profile she shared, and who was definitely a first cousin, might be the best one to approach for more information about the family. The woman, named as Gaye Smith, would already have been made aware that Marnie was a first cousin, so perhaps wouldn't be too surprised if she contacted her.

She hesitated for a while longer, thinking what she wanted to say, before hitting the 'contact' button, and then hesitated a while longer wondering what exactly to say in her first message.

The words she eventually wrote weren't too probing, and left it up to the woman whether she replied or not:

'I've just had the results of a DNA test that I took, and it's brought your name up as a first cousin. I recognise none of the family names shown on your tree, so can you please let me know how we are related; if you or your family know.   I understand my father was also named Bannerman, although my mother's name was Alicia West and she died in 1975, just 6 years after I was born. Hoping you can be of help to me, Marnie Peters, Cheshire.'

She re-read it several times before pressing the 'send' button – now all she could do was to wait. As the web site showed, the woman hadn't logged in for the last 3 months, so it could possibly be some time before she received a reply, but she had no intention of letting her impending visit drop.

She was sure it was Hector that was her father, and although she knew he probably wouldn't want to know her, she needed to know what the place looked like that he lived in, and possibly her approach to Gaye Smith might bring about a favourable reply. For the time being, all she could do was wait and hope.

Gaye might even contact David if she was in touch with him and tell him of the possible existence of a new sister, and the name of her mother. He may even be aware of Celia's existence – even know who she was. He may even be intrigued enough to want to know more and get in touch himself.

According to Gaye's family tree, Hector would have been 19 when he fathered her, and 25 when he fathered his son David, so there were only 6 years between them – just enough time for Hector to have met someone else and married. There could even be a chance that Alicia had been a friend of the family, or possibly another relative, and David might already know her name and whether she fitted into the family's history. He could

172

never have known her personally as she was dead before he was born.

A favourable reply from either of them was something she hoped and anticipated, even if her father didn't want to know her!

For two days she kept checking on the computer, hoping for a reply, but there was still nothing. She knew her message had been sent, as the message board on the website showed it had been.

Soon she began to feel disappointed. Maybe Gaye Smith felt it was too much of an intrusion, or she might feel it was someone trying to perpetrate a scam – but all she'd have to do was to check her own DNA results and matches to see that it wasn't.

On the third day and with still no reply, she decided to take matters into her own hands.

The last couple of days had turned out quite mild, and it would be pleasant to take a trip down to see where father lived, and perhaps hope to catch a glimpse of him.

Warren was still busy with the new piece of jewellery he was designing, so she told him she was going on a shopping trip to Manchester with a girlfriend and would be away all day. Obsessed as he was with his new piece, he paid little heed to her going, and she'd left a pie for him to heat up for lunch, so he probably wouldn't even notice her absence.

Checking her route, she keyed it into her sat nav and set out just after breakfast the next morning – her shouted goodbye receiving only a peremptory 'bye', and he didn't even come out of his workroom to see her off. Her journey would take about an hour and a half according to the sat nav; but it did take a little longer, allowing for traffic hold-ups on the way.

When the machine told her 'you have reached your destination', she drew to a halt and looked around her, totally bewildered. Surely this couldn't be right!

She was at the end of a small lane – nothing in front or at the side of her but snow covered open moorland, and beyond that, bare hillsides leading into the Snowdonia mountain ranges, their tops standing out white in the far distance.

She looked around. There was no sign of a house here – not even a chimney pot poking up from below a hillside. The landscape was completely devoid of any sort of human occupation! The sat nav must have brought her to the wrong place!

It was while she was sitting there, wondering what to do next, that she heard a sound behind her and, looking in the rear view mirror, she saw a quad bike coming up behind her. The rider was a man and he looked at her strangely as he slowed down alongside her, then increased his speed and turned in through two stone gateposts to her left.

They were almost completely hidden by the overgrown and snow-covered hawthorn hedges alongside together with the ivy which had grown up and over them. Getting out, she went to take a look, and by parting the ivy, she could see the name BANNERMAN'S carved into the stonework.

So she was in the right place, but she couldn't see any sign of the house itself.

The quad bike had now reached a slight rise in the land and was disappearing from view over the top. That must be where the house was and completely hidden from the road.

Warily, she turned the car in and followed the quad, stopping slightly before the rise so that she could walk the rest of the way. Her figure would be far less visible than that of a car if anybody was watching.

Using the cover of a large holly bush off to one side of the path, she peered over the rise, and saw the house straight in front of her, surprising her with its size and its age – built in an era long gone.

The quad bike was parked just at the right front corner of the house and a man was lifting a box of wrapped packages from the back and disappearing round the side with them. She assumed

174

he'd been out buying food, but it didn't seem very much for the size of family that must inhabit such a large house. Perhaps this was just to tide them over until a delivery was made; after all, it was just after Christmas.

The man had now finished unloading and was climbing back on the quad once more, but to her horror, he was turning it back in her direction again. She could hide herself by moving around the bush, but her car was still parked on the path where he couldn't fail to miss it. It was directly in line between him and the gateway! The only thing left for her to do was keep hidden and hope he didn't come looking for the driver. He'd wonder why she'd stopped here and not come right down to the house if she was on a visit of any sort.

Her heart was pounding as she watched him coming directly towards her, but then he suddenly veered off down another rough track to his left and kept going towards a stand of trees, where she could just see the roof of another dwelling with smoke rising from the chimney.

Thank goodness for that! She'd very nearly been caught out spying on the house! What explanation could she have given for her behaviour? Absolutely none!

She needed to get her car back to the road she'd turned off and find a parking place there; then continue her exploration on foot. Stupid not to have thought of that before!

She drove back to where she'd seen a small shop and decided to find out if they sold sandwiches. That would do for her lunch, and then she could ask if they minded her leaving her car outside in their little parking area for an hour or so. The only places she'd found for parking on the way there were farm gateways, and she knew, if she parked there, somebody was bound to want to use the gate.

The woman who was serving was quite happy for her to do so, but she'd decided to say she was here to see someone on business. If she'd said she was visiting a friend, everybody always knew everybody else in such a small community. The woman would be bound to want to know who she was visiting, and she didn't even know anybody in this whole area.

Eating her sandwich in the car and taking the bottled water back with her, she went back to Bannerman's and walked up to the rise, where she sat on a fallen log and watched the house for a while. Apart from the quad bike returning some time later, nothing else moved during the whole time, and once he'd gone round the back, nothing stirred. The whole area was silent and still, and it was then that she realised she was feeling very cold and the weak sun that had been shining all day had gone.

She looked up at the sky. Ominous grey clouds were rolling towards her, and it was beginning to turn very cold. It looked like they were in for a heavy downpour – or even more snow.

Time to go back to her car and make tracks for home!

CHAPTER 18

Cyril had been down to the local farm shop and brought back with him two large joints of pork, and three big bags of stewing meat.

Once meat had been jointed, the butcher was left with lots of little bits of offcuts which he threw into weighed bags and sold as stewing meat, consisting of a little bit of everything – lamb, chicken, pork and sometimes beef. These they sold much more cheaply than the normal prices for those cuts, and Isabelle always said they made very satisfying and tasty stews and pies. Everyone else, even the old judge, had agreed, so they were always on their order.

He would put them into the bottom of the large 'fridge and Isabelle would joint and freeze them when she arrived back in two days time.

He was surprised to find a woman sitting in a car by the gates of Bannerman's when he arrived back. He'd never seen either her or the car before, but concluded that she'd taken the wrong turning. It wasn't hard to do in these meandering country lanes, and people were always getting lost.

After he'd put the meat into the 'fridge, he took another bag down to Gavin and Megan for their use, staying for a chat, together with some well-buttered scones and several cups of tea.

Returning to the house, he'd intended to check whether the car was still there, but in the end he forgot about it until he'd put the quad away and was back inside the house, where put his feet up in front of the television.

It was some time later that he remembered, and then decided not to bother. It would have meant trudging outside in the cold again and getting the quad back out, but then, he was already warm and comfortable and enjoying an old film.

It was nice to have the big television in the judge's living room to himself while there was nobody else around, and he'd lit the log burner as well before he went out, so the room was warm on his return. Going out to the kitchen, he returned with a bottle of beer and some more scones that Megan had sent him home with and he watched it for a while, but soon he started breathing deeply, beginning to snore shortly afterwards.

He didn't know how long he'd been asleep when the bell jangled in the hallway. He looked at the clock on the high mantelpiece above the fire. It was nearly six o'clock!

Rousing himself, he tucked his feet back into the slippers he'd donned when he arrived back, and went to answer it, as he heard a second peal from the bell.

Outside was a woman, standing wrapped up in a black hooded parka and black jeans. It looked like the woman he'd seen sitting outside the gateway previously, but he couldn't be sure, as her hood was now pulled up.

'Can I help you?' he asked, as he realised she was huddling inside her coat and looked very cold. It was only then that he realised it was very dark and there were snowflakes whirling all around.

'I'm so sorry to bother you,' she said in a timid voice, 'but my car won't start and I can't manage to get a signal on my mobile 'phone. Could I trouble you to use your landline if you have one so that I can call for assistance?'

'Of course,' he answered. 'Come in. The 'phone's here in the hall.'

She thanked him and stepped inside, going straight to the 'phone as Cyril peered out of the door before closing it.

Night had already closed in and the snow was already beginning to form a layer on the ground as it seemed to be getting thicker.

'Oh dear,' she said, as she came off the 'phone. 'They've said they're very busy and it could be a couple of hours or more. Would you mind if I make another call to my husband and tell him what's happened, then I'll go back to my car and wait there.'

'Where is it?' he asked.

Outside the village shop – they said I could leave it there for a while, but they'll probably be annoyed when they find it's still there. I tried knocking to use their 'phone but they seem to be out.'

'You call your husband, and then go and sit by the fire. You look as if you need warming up. I'll go and leave a message on the windscreen to say where you are then they can come and pick you up here. The quad bike's only under the log shelter at the back and it won't take me long.'

He didn't relish going out again, but he couldn't let her walk back to the car in this weather, and besides, she'd be frozen to death if she had any length of time to wait.

When he'd gone, she called Warren.

'Where are you? I was expecting you back ages ago. You've been gone for hours.'

He sounded very worried, and as she glanced at her watch she realised how late it was, hurrying on to explain that the car had broken down.

'Leave it there and I'll come and fetch you. There's a forecast of snow arriving any time now, so let's get you safe home before it does.'

She suddenly remembered she'd told him she was going shopping to Manchester, now she'd have to own up and tell him the truth.

'Warren, I'm sorry, I told you a lie. I'm not in Manchester, I'm in Wales, and the snow's already falling heavily here. By the time you get here, it'll probably be too deep to get through.'

She'd already heard his sharp intake of breath at what she was telling him, but he seemed too concerned for her safety at the moment and wasn't thinking about the lie she'd told.

'Are you all right? I see you're ringing from a landline and not a mobile. Where are you?'

'Yes, I'm fine,' she answered, feeling it necessary to explain where she was and why she was there.

There was silence on the other end when she'd finished speaking, and she knew he was trying to contain his anger at her stupidity.

'Will you be able to get home after they've fixed the car?'

'I very much doubt it,' she said, peering through one of the small windows alongside the front door.

'Then what are you going to do for the night?'

She hadn't thought about that, but now she had to.

'I'm in the house, so I'll try and beg a sofa for the night. The man here is nice, and I don't think he'll turn me out. He's already gone out in the snow to leave a message on my car for the rescue service telling them where to find me.'

'Okay,' Warren answered. 'I don't suppose there's anything I can do to help anyway. Stay safe and ring me in the morning.'

When she put the 'phone down, she went into the living room and sat by the fire; the stove still glowing brightly with the burning logs and throwing out a welcoming heat, as she waited for Cyril to return.

When he did return, he put the quad bike away and entered by the back door, finding her in the kitchen, where she'd made a big pot of tea.

'I hope you don't mind. I took the liberty of making us both a drink. I thought you'd be cold when you got back.'

He smiled and went over to sit at the table while she poured the tea and sat down opposite him to drink her own.

'I saw you earlier, sitting outside the gates. What brings you out here in the middle of winter? Have you been visiting someone? I haven't seen you around here before,' he probed.

Ever since she'd found out her car wouldn't start, and there'd been nobody at home when she'd knocked at the shop, she'd been wondering what she'd say when she came back to the house, but there was no other dwelling in sight where she could have asked for help.

She blushed.

'It was so nice this morning that I decided to go for a run, and I just happened to find myself here.'

'Nobody just finds themselves here!' he said, looking at her strangely. 'Where've you come from?'

'I live near the village of Eccleston – in Cheshire,' she explained, colouring up.

'That's miles away!' he exclaimed. 'I lived not far from there myself once! You came here deliberately, didn't you? Care to explain why?'

Again she blushed. She'd never thought this moment would come when she set out from home this morning.

'Yes,' she said in a small voice. 'I did come here to see this house.'

'Why?' The voice was direct and probing.

'I think Judge Bannerman might be my father.'

Now she'd said it, she found it wasn't so hard to say after all. The man sitting opposite her didn't look like a judge, and he certainly didn't sound like one, but then, it took all sorts these days. He may possibly be her step-brother, but she didn't think so. A member of the staff was her more likely guess.

'Your father?' he queried, his tone softening. 'I've worked here for years now, and as far as I know the judge only has one daughter, Miss Jayne – and you're not her! Begging your pardon, but she's years younger than you!'

So, she'd been right – he was staff.

'If I tell you something, can you keep it quiet for the time being?'

181

Why not? The judge wasn't here to tell any more, and master David might not be back for some time to come, so it wouldn't hurt to keep it to himself for the time being.

'I think my father, the judge, had a fling in his student days at university, and, without his knowing, my mother became pregnant. Her family wouldn't let her keep me, and so I was adopted. I only found out recently through having a DNA sample taken, which pinpointed him as my father.'

She didn't go into detail as to how she'd found him, but Cyril was grinning now.

'The old dog!' he breathed. 'Who'd have thought it, eh? Seems he was sowing his wild oats even before he married!' he chuckled, thinking of the pompous and controlling old devil he'd become.

Then, more seriously, 'What do you hope to find out by hanging around here?'

'Nothing,' she answered. 'I don't want anything from him or his family. All I wanted was to try and see what he looked like, and to see if I could see my step-brother and sister as well. I thought they might have been out and about – I had no idea the house was so remote and so far from the road!'

His manner turned rueful.

'I'm afraid you won't find any of those things possible now! Master David left home years ago after an argument with his father, and the judge was killed in a motorcycle accident some months ago. It's a wonder you didn't see it in the papers. Miss Jayne also left home a few years ago and nobody's seen her since.'

After a few moments silence while she took the knowledge in, she suddenly volunteered another thought.

'So is there a chance that my brother will be coming back here to live if he's inherited the house?'

Cyril was loathe to give her too much information – after all, he'd only known her for a short while, and he didn't really know if her story were true or not.

'I don't think so,' he answered warily, 'he has a home of his own now. None of us know what's going to happen to the house yet.'

She looked sad.

'So I'll never know what my father looked like, or find out anything about him, or my family.'

She seemed wistful.

'Hold on – there are some photos around. I'll go and find them,' Cyril said, easing himself away from the table, realising that showing her photographs could do no harm.

He returned several minutes later bearing some framed photos, as well as a leather bound album.

Most of those showed her father in judges' robes, but some were of family photos, and some showed other young boys, whom Cyril explained were also the judges' children, but who'd died young. There was a particularly nice one of Jayne as a toddler, with curly blonde hair and a cheeky grin, and a good one of David alongside her in graduation robes.

'Is that David and Jayne,' she inquired, looking intently at the picture.

He nodded.

'There's a big gap in their ages,' she said, inspecting the framed photo.

'Fifteen years, I think, or thereabouts,' Cyril replied. 'The three boys that died all came in between them.'

She looked at it again. David certainly was a handsome lad with his shock of curly blonde hair, and strong features, and Jayne, although so much younger than him, was certainly turning into a very pretty girl, although she looked a little sad and wistful in this picture.

Suddenly her stomach gave a loud grumble.

'Sorry,' she gasped, as they both laughed.

'I take it you haven't eaten for a while,' he said, standing up from the table. 'I'll see what I can find for a meal in the larder.'

Coming back to the kitchen once again he was carrying a wire bowl containing some eggs and some slices of bread he'd taken from the freezer.

'I'm sorry, but we're a bit short of food at the moment. The cook, Isabelle, is away until the 2nd January, and I'm coming to the last of what food we have left. Luckily, I got these eggs from our neighbour this afternoon. How would you like them?'

'However you want them will suit me fine. Having made such an impromptu call on you, I'm only too happy to take whatever there is.'

'Boiled is easiest,' he smiled, pouring water from the kettle simmering on the range into a pan, and slipping the bread into the toaster.

Seeing plates on a dresser against the wall, she asked if she should use those, and he replied in the affirmative, telling her the cutlery was in the drawer below, buttering the toast while she laid the table.

After they'd eaten he produced some fruit cake from the larder, but they only had one thin slice each, as Cyril told her that was the last of what was left.

Just after they'd finished eating, the 'phone in the hall started to ring, and Cyril got up to go and answer it.

'That was your rescue service,' he said. 'Apparently there's a big wagon turned over on the main road. It's spilled its entire contents everywhere and it's completely blocking both carriageways, including the road leading down to here. The police have told them that it probably won't be cleared before tomorrow morning at the earliest.'

She felt the tears welling in her eyes, and seeing her distressed state, he tried to cheer her up.

'I guess you're going to have to stay here tonight,' he said, 'then we'll see what happens tomorrow.'

'I'm sorry to be such a nuisance,' she said. 'That sofa in the living room looks comfortable enough if you have a spare blanket.'

184

'No need for that,' he said brightly, as he cleared away the dishes. 'There are six bedrooms up on the top floor – servants' rooms as you might guess. Isabelle and I occupy two of them, and the third has been turned into a bathroom, but the others are unoccupied now. We don't have live-in maids any more. You're welcome to use one of those. I'm afraid they only contain two single beds in each one, but I've bedding and warm duvets for them, and I'll go and turn the radiators on in there when I've finished, then they'll be warm when you go up.'

'Can I trouble you for another call to my husband?' she asked.

'Of course! You need to let him know what's happening. If it was me, I'd be worried sick about you, and just between you and me, I don't pay the bills anyway. Master David pays all that.'

They talked for a short while afterwards, but she found herself yawning shortly after nine o'clock. It had been an eventful day, and she was feeling very tired.

'I think you could do with an early night,' Cyril said, smiling down at her as he got up to make them some cocoa. 'You can take a cup up to bed with you.'

It was years since she'd had cocoa – probably not since she was a child, as she climbed the stairs with mug in hand, looking forward to its bitter sweet taste.

The door he opened was at the far end of a long narrow landing, and opened into a very small room, with extremely dirty windows – the dirt seeming to be on the outside and not on the inside. He apologised for their grimy appearance, indicating that it was caused by the house martins that nested under the eaves, and explaining that everybody welcomed their presence and wouldn't have dreamed of getting rid of them.

There was barely room for the two beds in the room, which both stood on varnished floorboards; with just a small rug on the outer side of each, with another in the central space between them.

The wall flanking the small window on either side contained hooks for hanging things up, with two long shelves on the side walls for whatever other possessions they may have.

Under the tiny window was a newly fitted radiator, and in front of that, a small table painted in pale blue. Judging by the circular stains on the top, it had once been used for holding a washbasin and jug.

'I've deliberately left the sheet and pillowcases, together with the duvet, in the airing cupboard,' he explained as they reached the top of the stairs, indicating its presence next to the bathroom. 'Make the bed up as soon as you're ready and they'll still be warm to get into.'

He was an extremely thoughtful man, for which she was truly grateful. Without his help, she'd have spent a cold and lonely night sitting in her car, and possibly have been suffering from hypothermia by the morning. She shivered involuntarily at the thought.

'I'll go downstairs for a bit and give you time to use the bathroom and get into bed before I come up. I've a few jobs to do anyway,' he said as he left her. 'There's a key in the lock if you feel safer locking yourself in.'

She smiled. She instinctively felt he was someone she could trust.

CHAPTER 19

Marnie was awoken by the loud jangling of a telephone from somewhere in the bowels of the house, and couldn't at first think where she was, before it all came back to her.

She was in the house where her father had lived, and even though she'd never known him, nor ever would, she felt an affinity with this place as the home she might have lived in if things had turned out differently. Even though she hadn't known him, there was still a possibility of getting to know her brother and sister in the future.

The 'phone was answered after three or four rings, and then, as she got out of bed to go to the bathroom, it rang again.

The bed had been warm and cosy, but as she hadn't any night attire with her, she'd slept in just a pair of panties, and she shivered as she left the bed. Despite the fact that the heating was on, she could have done with something warmer to slip into.

As she opened the door, ready to make sure the coast was clear before making a dash to the bathroom, something dragged along the floor and she almost tripped over it.

'What the . . . . ?' she murmured, as she looked down.

There, hanging from the doorknob, was a pink fleece dressing gown.

Quickly looking along the landing, she scooped it up and slipped into it, considering that it must have been one belonging to her sister at one time, and Cyril, realising she'd have no night clothes with her, had thoughtfully left it there for her.

187

It was clean and warm and smelled faintly of lavender.

Just to one side of the door was a pair of black fluffy mules, which she presumed had come from the same source. They were a bit girly-girly for someone of her age, but at least they kept her feet off the bare and cold floorboards.

Whilst in the bathroom, she washed quickly and went back to her room where she opened the curtains and peered out.

Outside was a whole world of white, glittering and glistening in the weak sunlight that was filtering through the still scudding clouds; the conifer trees hanging their boughs towards the ground as if paying homage to the snow pinning down their branches. She hoped there wasn't more snow to come, as it looked pretty deep already.

Cyril was in the hallway with a vacuum cleaner and a brush when she went down the stairs.

'Morning,' he called up to her. 'Did you sleep alright?'

'Fine thanks. The bed was very comfortable and the duvet was lovely and warm. I can only thank you for your hospitality. I don't know what I'd have done without it.'

'Only too glad to be of service,' he smiled, 'and it has been a bit lonely here since Master David and Anna left. Without your company I'd have been alone here for another two days before the others returned.'

Misconstruing his words, she said, 'I thought my sister was called Jayne, not Anna, and you said nobody had any idea where she was.'

He laughed.

'Anna is Master David's housekeeper – although I have my own opinion on that – and they spent Christmas here, but they left for home when they heard the snow was coming. I've left some porridge on the range for you, but I'm afraid it's been made with water. We're running a bit low on milk. There's enough to put a good swirl through it for flavour, and we've plenty of sugar or syrup to sweeten it. I'll get the quad out and go to the farm for some more as soon as I can.'

Going to the front door he opened it and stood back so that she could see out; 'but probably not just yet I think!' he laughed.

Where he'd opened the door, a wall of snow stood against it – well above knee height, and of the raised flower bed in the centre of the gravel there was no sight, save for the very topmost part of the stone shell that stood in the middle.

'I don't think anybody's going anywhere in that for the time being, do you?' shutting the door as the warmth from the hallway began to melt the snow and it started to fall inwards.

She smiled and made her way to the kitchen as he began to get on with the cleaning again.

'I'll join you when I've finished,' he called after her, and she gave a wave over her shoulder, calling back, 'I'll make some tea for you, although you'll have to have it without milk,' as his chuckle followed her.

Finishing her breakfast, she opened the back door to look out, finding that the yard at the back was comparatively clear of snow. The wind must have been blowing against the front of the building and by-passing the back, so she wondered if she might be able to get out that way and back to her car.

'Hey, you're letting the heat out!' Cyril's voice came from behind her.

'Sorry,' she said, coming back in and closing the door. 'I was just wondering whether I could make my escape that way and get back to the car to wait for the rescue.'

'Forget it,' he said, pouring water into the pot she'd left on the table. 'I've just had a call from them to say that although the main road is being cleared at the moment, they won't be clearing the side lanes for some time yet. The main roads have to take priority, and most of the side lanes are deep with snow.'

One part of her felt put out by the delay, and the other part felt glad of the time to relax and enjoy looking round the house. Wasn't this what she'd come for in the first place? To see where her father had lived, and try to find out more about him and the family she'd never ever known, and never ever been part of.

Then a thought struck her.

'I must 'phone my husband. Let him know I'm stuck here until the snow melts and not to worry about me.'

'No need,' he added. 'Didn't you hear the 'phone ring twice.'

She nodded, remembering she had.

'The second call was your husband. I told him you were safe and well, but that you wouldn't be able to get away yet. I think I put him at his ease. I told him you were welcome to stay for as long as you needed.'

'Thank you,' she answered, 'but if you don't mind, I'll give him a ring myself. He'll probably feel better if he hears my voice as well.'

'No skin off my nose,' he shrugged, 'and as I've told you, I don't pay the bills!'

'How about I make us some lunch?' she volunteered. 'That's one way I could repay you for your hospitality – if you'll just show me where you keep the food. I might be able to conjure something up for us from what's left.'

Getting up from the table he opened a door at one end of the kitchen, which opened into another room housing a long table with plain wooden chairs all around it.

'This is where the servants used to eat when there were a lot of staff many years ago – nowadays there's usually only Isabelle, her cousin Sandra, and me. We always eat in the kitchen now.'

At the far end, he opened another door into a passageway. She shuddered as the cold air hit her. Here there were just whitewashed walls and bare stone flags.

This is where the larder and the wine store are, although there's not much wine stored here now. The old judge only drank whisky or brandy, so there are only a couple of bottles left in there now. Master David may find another use for it if he comes back to live here. The house belongs to Miss Jayne now but I don't see much chance of her coming back to live in it after all this time, and nobody knows where to find her.'

She looked at him.

'It belongs to Jayne? David's the oldest – why wasn't it left to him?'

He shrugged his shoulders.

'Mine not to reason why,' he answered, 'but it could have a lot to do with the row him and his father had. That's the reason Master David left, but nobody here knows what it was about. The judge forbade anybody to contact Master David again, and refused to let anybody mention his name in or around the house.'

Realising he'd already said too much, he opened the door into the larder and showed her where everything was.

It was a long narrow room with shelving down either side, and at the far end, a solid slab of slate stretched across from wall to wall underneath a tall narrow window with frosted glass.

The top shelves contained utensils of a type used very rarely; or sometimes not at all nowadays; such as a mincer, a bain marie, an assortment of silver salvers left from a bygone era, and some metal jelly moulds.

Underneath them, the next couple of shelves held dry goods, such as rice, various types of pasta and pulses of all types. Opposite them, the shelves contained all the various baking ingredients such as flour, dried fruits and other things, together with different types of baking tins and cooking trays.

The slate slab at the end, as Cyril explained, was once used for cooling baked items and for storing cakes in the tins still sitting there.

'Can't see we've much use for this place now that the judge has gone,' Cyril said softly. 'Most days it's just the three of us for lunch, and then, when Sandra's gone home, just Isabelle and me for an evening meal. I can't see that it's going to be long before we're all looking round for new jobs, and at my age, there's not much chance of me finding another now.'

She looked at him in surprise.

'How old are you? You don't look that old? Surely you'll easily be able to find another job – you've plenty of work life left in you yet.'

'I'm 52 now,' he answered. 'I'm a trained engineer, but I haven't done that sort of work in years, and I wouldn't know where to start if I went back to it now. Technology will have advanced far beyond my capabilities, and nobody will want to take me on for re-training at my age.'

'But there must be plenty of jobs in what you're doing now. Plenty of people would be grateful of an odd job man nowadays. Couldn't you keep on doing that?'

'I could,' his voice was whimsical now, 'but the work would be piecemeal and not on any regular basis. I probably wouldn't earn enough to pay the rent on a flat, and I think I can kiss goodbye to another cosy little live-in job like this one, don't you? They're not easy to come by.'

She had to agree.

'Anyway, enough of this – it's too cold to stand around in here. Get what you need for lunch and I'll go and get on with clearing the snow at the back of the house. That shouldn't be too difficult a job, and I'd appreciate coffee and a snack when I've finished.'

When he'd gone, she rummaged around and returned to the kitchen with some rather dry remains of a Madeira cake which, together with a packet of strawberry jelly crystals, and combined with some frozen strawberries she'd already noticed in the freezer, would make them a desert of sorts. All she needed now was something more substantial for the main course.

Picking up a container of pasta, a small tin of tomatoes and a box full of different spices, she returned to the kitchen, where she looked for, and found, a small quantity of minced beef in the freezer. If she left that out to de-frost all day, she could combine them all together and make a passable dish of some sort for that evening. At least they wouldn't go hungry!

Cyril had cleared most of the area outside the back door when she went to join him.

'Got another shovel?' she asked. 'I'll give you a hand.'

He pointed to the open fronted shed at one side where the logs were stored.

'There's one in there,' he called back.

Luckily she'd been wearing waterproof walking boots the previous day and a thick padded jacket, anticipating it would be cold during the long vigil while she was hoping to catch a glimpse of her family. She'd never anticipated how useful they were going to be for a job like this, as she set to with vigour.

They'd both been shovelling the snow and throwing it into heaps either side of a pathway towards the opening in the back wall for some time, when they inadvertently bumped into each other, back to back.

They both laughed as they staggered about, and as she regained her balance, she picked up a handful of snow and threw it at him.

It hit him full in the chest, and laughingly, he picked up a handful and threw it back at her, which caused the onset of a snowball fight, each trying to outdo the other, as they cavorted about in the snow for the next few minutes.

Suddenly, running backwards away from a large amount of snow that she'd picked up on her shovel and aimed directly at him, he hit the back of the wall with his legs, upending him and sending him flying backwards over it.

All Marnie could see was a pair of legs sticking up in the air from the other side of the wall. She laughed, seeing the funny side of what had just happened, before she realised that he wasn't getting up and his legs had remained in the air without moving.

'Are you all right?' she called, as she made her way quickly towards the opening in the wall in an attempt to reach him.

When she rounded the corner, he was still lying where he'd fallen, in a deep snowdrift and making no movement. She reached him quickly, finding his eyes were closed and receiving no reply to her worried entreaties for him to wake up.

Suddenly, as she got to her knees and leaned over him, his eyes flashed open and a grin spread over his face.

'Got you there, didn't I?' he said, grabbing the front of her coat and pulling her over his body to bury her face deep in the snow alongside him.

Spluttering and gasping, she pulled herself out of the drift and spat out the wet snow, wiping away that still clinging to her face.

He was still lying alongside her, and she picked up two large handfuls as she pulled back and onto her knees, leaning over him, and rubbing both handfuls straight into his face.

He gasped and spluttered himself, as he tried to spit it out – not easy while still lying on his back.

As he tried to rise to his feet, she jumped up and ran some distance away, laughing as she tried to get the snow out of the neck of her coat before it began to melt – but he wasn't giving up so easily!

Having cleared his face of the snow, he picked up another handful and made towards her. She didn't notice his approach until she felt the cold substance squashing into the back of her neck, and she squealed as it ran down inside her jumper and trickled down her back.

Turning, she grabbed the front of his coat and pulled him towards her, intending to give him a good shove backwards and into the thick mound behind him from where the path had already been cleared, but that never happened.

As she looked up into his face, something intense flashed between them – something neither had experienced for a very long time.

For a few moments, they both stood completely still, staring into each others' faces, until he reached out, putting both arms around her and pulling her towards him. Her own arms, crushed between them, reached up and coiled around his neck, as their bodies came together and they gazed at each other for several seconds, before he crushed her against him and kissed her, long and hard.

Drawing apart, they looked at each other again, before he drew her towards him once more. This time the kiss was softer and more tender, but this time lasted a lot longer.

It was many years since either of them had been kissed like that, and they both seemed to regress to the earlier years of their

194

marriage, when love had been young and sweet, and familiarity hadn't dulled that sweetness.

It was a new and refreshing feeling for both of them, as they parted and Cyril took her hand, leading her into the house and up to his bedroom, where they both stripped off eagerly before slipping beneath the covers.

Their lovemaking was eager and passionate, and very satisfying for both parties.

Cyril was perhaps a little over-eager. It was many years since he'd indulged in any sort of sexual activity, in fact, not at all since his wife had died, but Marnie enjoyed the experience immensely, even if he was a little rough at first. It was something very different from that she indulged in with Warren, and they spent the whole afternoon in his bed, before their stomachs awoke them to an insistent hunger, making just a makeshift, and very quick meal out of the ingredients Marnie had foraged previously.

CHAPTER 20

When David and Anna returned home to Little Bannerman, things seemed to change almost immediately, and everything reverted to the way it had been before Christmas and their visit to Bannerman's.

They were now employer and employee once again, and she somehow felt hurt by this rather sudden reversion. During their stay, she'd begun to think of him more as a friend during the time they'd been there, and now she was back to earth with a bump as they settled back into the old routine.

Although New Year's Eve had arrived, he was still working in his study nearly all day, until he declared he was going out for the evening and may be back very late, telling her not to wait up for him. She had thought, up until then, that they might see the New Year in together, but obviously that same idea hadn't been in his mind.

If he'd told her previously, she might perhaps have found somewhere to go herself, but leaving it so late meant she didn't have time to arrange anything. She could have gone back to see her parents in Conwy, or visit one of the few friends she still had who lived there, but it was too late now. She faced a New Year's Eve totally alone this year, and decided not to wait up. It seemed a very sad and lonely prospect, so after watching an old film on one of the freeview channels, she decided to go to bed. She remembered enjoying the film the first time she'd seen it, but this time around it seemed a bit old hat and she hadn't really enjoyed it.

Climbing the stairs just after ten o'clock, she peered out of the bedroom window and saw the first flakes of snow beginning to fall. Perhaps David would see it too and make his way home before it became too thick, but even though she lay in bed waiting, there was no sound of his return, and she finally fell asleep just after midnight had struck on the clock in the hallway. The last thing she remembered was the distant peal of church bells from somewhere not too far distant.

Next morning when she awoke, she looked out of the window once again, anticipating his car sitting outside, but it wasn't there, and, although the snow had stopped, it was already ankle deep. Looking up into the sky, the grey scudding clouds hinted at the possibility of more snow to come.

She looked at her clock before going to the bathroom, realising that it was already past nine o'clock.

She'd grown into the habit of sleeping later while they'd been at Bannerman's, but now that they were home once again, she'd have to re-train herself back into the old habit of getting up before eight. Today, though, it didn't matter – as she remembered with a pang that it was New Year's Day and she was all alone, and possibly would be for the rest of the day.

Anticipating his possible return by lunchtime, she de-frosted some bacon, and prepared to give him a scratch meal of bacon, egg and tomatoes if he should turn up, but by two o'clock she decided she probably wasn't going to see him again before the evening. It was just as she finished her own solitary lunch that her mobile began to ring.

It was an unknown number, but when she answered, the voice was a very familiar one.

'Hi Anna. It's me, Sheena Dawes. I just rang to wish you a happy New Year, and to invite you out for dinner tonight. I lost the piece of paper you gave me when you left the office, and I didn't know how to contact you again. I've just moved into a new flat and that piece of paper suddenly fell out of a book I was putting up on a shelf. I know I didn't put it there, so it must have slipped in between the pages at some time.'

Although it was a good few years now since she'd left the office where she'd always hated working, she remembered she and Sheena had always got on well together. She was pleased to hear her voice again, even if she would have preferred it to be David's telling her he'd be home for dinner that evening.

'Nice to hear from you,' she replied, and a very happy New Year to you as well. I would have loved to come for dinner tonight, but I don't know whether my boss will be home for a meal by this evening. I can't leave him without anything.'

'Why are you preparing meals for your boss?' Sheena seemed perplexed.

'I forgot, you didn't know I'd taken up a housekeeper's job, did you? I work for a well-known barrister now, and I have a live-in post. He went out for the evening yesterday and he hasn't returned yet, so I don't know whether he'll want me to cook tonight.'

'It's New Years Day! Why should he expect you to cook for him today? Aren't you entitled to time off on a bank holiday?'

Well, why wasn't she? Sheena was right! He hadn't even had the good manners to ring her and let her know when he'd be back, so he only had himself to blame if she wasn't there when he got back.

'Alright,' she said, in a moment of pique. 'I'll come – why not? What's the address?'

'My boyfriend's just opened a new restaurant – well, not actually a restaurant, more of a glorified café really. It's not posh enough to be called a restaurant yet, and he'll make sure we have a table if I ring him.'

'I thought you were engaged when I left the office. Haven't you been married yet?'

'I'm afraid that didn't happen in the long run. We both decided we weren't right for each other, so we went our separate ways in

198

the end. I've been with Seb for about a year now, but we're not rushing into anything. He wants to make sure the business takes off first.'

Knowing how disastrous her own marriage had been, and how short lived, she could sympathise with the other girl.

'Okay,' she finally said, 'text me the address and I'll meet you there. What time?'

'I don't know yet until I've rung Seb, but I'll text you that too.'

'Fine,' she said, 'I'll look forward to it.'

Putting down her 'phone, she went to the window once more. The snow wasn't any deeper, and it hadn't snowed again as she'd anticipated it might, but there was still no sign of David.

Well, if that's the way he wanted it – two could play at that game, as she went upstairs to soak in a nice hot bath for an hour or so.

Coming down after her long soak, she found the text had already arrived from Sheena saying she'd managed to get a table for six thirty, but when she saw the address, she got a shock. It wasn't very close at all; it was in Abergele, a good few miles run from her present address.

Looking out of the window, the light was already fading, and it would soon be dark. If she'd realised how far away it was, she'd probably have cried off – but then, what else did she have to look forward to - just another lonely night in front of the television if David didn't return tonight, whilst others were out enjoying themselves? It would take her sometime to drive there, but as it was booked for an early time, she'd make it home before it got too late, and the roads would be reasonably empty.

She decided to leave around five thirty, giving her plenty of time to find her way there, and then to locate the restaurant and find somewhere to park.

Just as she'd thought, the roads were quiet and there were very few people about, until she reached the main A55 expressway, carrying heavy goods vehicles from the industrial areas of Lancashire and beyond to the port of Holyhead, where they caught the ferries for Ireland. Even on New Years' day, this road was still reasonably busy, but there were no hold ups anywhere. She reached her destination in just under forty minutes; finding a parking space on a small patch of waste land behind the shops where the restaurant was situated, but it took her a few minutes to walk back round to the street.

She was greeted at the door by a tall, swarthy man in a dark suit and white shirt. He looked to be of Mediterranean origin, but when he spoke, there was no trace of any accent.

She explained that the table had been booked for Sheena Dawes, and as soon as she said this, a grin spread across his face.

'Ah, you're Sheena's friend, are you? She hasn't arrived yet, but I'm sure she won't be long. I don't know if she's mentioned me, but my name's Seb.'

'She did,' she answered, smiling back. 'I believe you own this place, and that you and she are an item?'

'I hope we're a bit more than that – but yes – you're right. I hope we're going to be married as soon as this place is earning its keep.'

Ushering her to a small table in a quiet corner at the back of the room, he pulled out a chair for her and offered to take her coat, returning afterwards and sitting down in the chair opposite.

'I'll keep you company until she arrives,' he smiled. 'As you can see, we're not busy at the moment, but we're fully booked from 7.30 onwards. We've only been open a month, so I hope this bodes well for the future.'

She glanced around. There were only two other tables occupied, but both of them had four people seated around them, and all of them seemed to have shopping bags. These must be the end of the year shoppers looking for some possible New Years' day bargains.

Just as he spoke again, offering to get her a drink, the door opened and Sheena entered. Seb vacated his seat immediately to go over to her and took her coat. They exchanged a few intimate words, inaudible to anyone else around, before he took it from her and indicated where Anna was sitting.

A smile came over her face immediately as she made her way over, bearing two menus that Seb had handed her. Anna stood up to greet her and they exchanged hugs, just as two old friends, meeting after a long time apart, usually did.

'I've missed our daily chats,' Sheena said as they sat down opposite each other. 'You surprised me when you said you'd become a housekeeper. I didn't think that would have been up your street.'

'Neither did I, but I enjoy it very much. David's a thoughtful employer and he treats me more like a friend than an employee. He has his own study, where he spends most of his time working while he's at home, and we eat together in the kitchen every day. While he's working, or while he's out, my time is my own. All I have to do is the normal duties a wife would perform for her husband, such as keeping the house clean and tidy, and cooking his meals.'

Sheena gave her a sly little smile.

'Does that extend to bedroom duties as well?'

Slightly shocked that her friend should think such a thing, her voice was slightly acerbic as she answered.

'Of course not! We have our own separate rooms. Everything is purely on a platonic level. There's never been anything like that between us!'

Sheena laughed.

'You've certainly landed on your feet there, haven't you? I always knew you didn't like the office manager, and his overbearing attitude, but I never would've thought you'd have gone for anything like that.'

This time Anna smiled and shrugged, her annoyance somewhat mollified.

'I enjoy it, and David and I even spent Christmas together at his old family home up on the Denbigh Moors.'

'And what did his family think of that?' Sheena returned, rather surprised that he'd taken her with him. There certainly seemed more to their relationship than Anna was letting on, even if she didn't realise it herself.

Just at that moment, Seb returned to the table for their order, and conversation was suspended while they chose something to eat, handing them back to him while he took their orders to the kitchen.

'David hasn't seen his family in years, and he only went back because his father was killed in a hit and run a few months ago on the Denbigh Moors. It was a shock to find his mother had died while he was away, and nobody had let him know, but I don't think anybody had his address anyway. The police only found him through DNA records.

His sister had also left home, but nobody knows where she's gone either, and David hasn't been able to find her so far, despite having advertised for her to get in touch.'

She was beginning to realise she was perhaps being disloyal and giving too much information away about her employer, so she tried to change the subject and divert Sheena's attention away from her job. Instead she turned the conversation to her friend's own situation.

'Are you still working in the same office then?' she asked.

'Nah, I left there about six months after you did – got myself a job here in Abergele. I work as a personal assistant to the managing director of a builder's merchants. It pays a much better salary, and as you know, Seb and I are saving up to get married.'

'How did you meet?' Anna asked.

'Seb's father owns a small building firm, and Seb used to sometimes drop orders off for him when he was working in a cake shop here in the town. Seb's speciality is patisserie, as you might have guessed,' indicating the succulent pastries for sale on the counter.

'Then how did he come to own his own place?' she asked.

'It was just a café at one time, a proper greasy spoon, but the food was always good, and it was owned by his fathers' brother. When he died unexpectedly from a heart attack, Seb's father inherited it and suggested Seb take it over, and he'd help with the alterations to bring it up to a better standard. So here we are!'

'And is it doing well?'

'It's too early to tell properly yet, but it certainly seems to be. The takings are going up week by week, and it won't be long at this rate before it starts to break even. He managed to open it in time for the Christmas trade, but he's no idea what to expect for the next few months. Most businesses lapse into the doldrums just afterwards. Everybody's either spent up, or they don't want to venture from their nice warm houses and out into the cold.'

Just at that moment, their food arrived, and the conversation ended at that point. Anna was extremely hungry, having only had a bacon sandwich at lunchtime, and the delicious looking mixed grill in front of her was making her mouth water.

When they'd finished, Seb arrived with the dessert menu, and made himself scarce once again while they looked through it.

'Seb bakes a delicious lemon and vanilla cheesecake, with a swirl of whipped cream and lemon zest on top. I can recommend it,' Sheena said.

Anna was feeling full enough after the main course – but what the hell! – it was New Year's day after all. Why shouldn't she treat herself for once!

'Okay, I'll try it,' she answered, and Seb took the menus away while they sipped the delicious wine he'd brought with their meal; Anna making her one glass last throughout the entire meal as she still had a long drive home yet.

Conversation seemed to have dried up for the moment, so she excused herself to go to the ladies.

It was just as she returned that Seb set the desserts down in front of them with the ubiquitous entreaty to 'enjoy', and they both felt a cold draught of air swirl around their legs.

Anna, about to sit down, looked towards the door, where she froze in the act. Sheena, seeing her reaction, turned to look at what she was staring at.

A man and woman had entered; the man dressed in a dark blue pin-striped suit, and the woman in a long faux fur jacket; heels high enough to frighten many a woman off.

They were shown to a table near the window, and the man sat with his back to them.

'Someone you know?' Sheena's voice broke through her thoughts.

Anna nodded, sitting down and trying not to look in the direction of the couple.

She was glad the man had his back towards them, which would save embarrassment. She didn't really want him to see her here, but she couldn't for the life of her think why not.

'It's my employer,' she finally managed to say, 'David Bannerman!'

'Who's the woman?' Sheena asked with curiosity.

'I've no idea! I've never seen her before!' she answered, a sudden feeling of emotion welling up inside her.

Sheena pulled a wry face.

'In that case, I don't think he's **just** your employer, is he? Judging by your face when you saw them walk in together, there's more to it than that!'

She couldn't deny it! Her whole world seemed to collapse in front of her when she'd seen them come through the door together!

Sitting down, Anna urged her friend to finish her dessert and then she asked Seb if they could leave by the back door, where they didn't have to pass David's table.

The sweet cheesecake was delicious, but she didn't seem to enjoy it as much as she should have done. She'd never seen this woman before, and he'd never mentioned having a woman in his life either. Even though she'd never have admitted it to herself, she felt as if she and David had become closer since their

204

Christmas together, and if truth be told, she felt more than a little jealous.

Once they'd finished eating, Seb came over and asked if they wanted coffee, but Sheena declined for them both.

'I'm going to take her back to the flat and give her coffee there. She's a little upset by that man and woman sitting in the window. I'll explain later.'

Taking both cars, they drove to Sheena's flat, which was on the second floor of a large old house just outside the town. It was set back off the road in its own grounds, and the living room window afforded splendid views across fields; or so Sheena told her, although it was much too dark to see anything out there now.

They drank coffee and chatted some more, Sheena showing her round the flat, which, although it had a large living room, only had the one bedroom, a small bathroom next to it, and a long narrow galley kitchen opposite. From the possessions lying around, it was obvious she and Seb were living there together.

Sheena made them both coffee, while Anna made herself comfortable in the living room, choosing a reasonable looking armchair. None of the furniture looked very new, and when Sheena came back with the drinks, she told her that the flat was a furnished rental. It was a cheaper option than buying new furniture when they'd decided to move in together some months before. They were trying to save every penny they could to make Seb's new eatery a success.

Settling herself opposite her friend in another armchair that made a rude noise when she sat in it, she explained there was a slight hole in the stitching at the side of the leather, and it did that every time someone sat in it. They'd stopped noticing it anymore, but strangers sometimes found it disconcerting, and friends either found it embarrassing, or laughed at it.

'Well,' Sheena asked after a few moments idle chat, 'what just happened back there at Seb's place?'

Blushing, Anna explained that David hadn't told her where he was going on New Years' Eve, but that he might be back late and not to wait up for him. He hadn't come back at all that night, and this was the first time she'd seen him since.

'And the woman?' Sheen queried.

Anna hung her head and looked down into her empty mug.

'I've no idea who she is. He's never mentioned another woman, and she definitely hasn't been to the house while I've been there.'

Sheena, seeing how upset Anna was by the woman's appearance with David, changed the subject and talked about other things for some time, before Anna decided it was time to leave.

'I've a forty minute drive ahead of me, and it's already gone eleven now,' she explained, as Sheena walked her back to the car and they hugged once again before she left.

'Keep in touch,' Sheena called after her as she drove out, to which Anna nodded and gave her a wave before driving away.

When she arrived back, it was nearly midnight, and the snow, still prominent in the area where they lived, glistened for a few moments in the moonlight, before it disappeared from view once more, and the first few flakes of yet more snow began to fall. Looking up, the sky was completely covered by cloud, and it was only the security light over the front door that afforded her any light at all.

David's car was already parked in its usual spot, and luckily he hadn't bolted the front door on the inside. He must have realised she'd be coming back that night, and left it for her to do.

Taking off her shoes, she climbed the stairs as quietly as she could, leaving her coat on, as the house was already cooling down after the heating had switched itself off over an hour ago.

She heard David's deep breathing as she passed his door, but there was no other sound from within, as she made her way to her own room and climbed into bed after a rather peremptory wash. She felt tired and rather drained herself, hoping that she wouldn't find the woman with him when he came down the next morning. She didn't know if she'd be able to bear that.

CHAPTER 21

Marnie awoke hours later to the jangling of the 'phone in the hallway below, and looked around for Cyril, expecting to find him still alongside her, but the other side of the bed was empty and already cold.

The 'phone had suddenly stopped ringing and she realised he was downstairs and must have answered it. She couldn't hear his voice, or any other sounds for that matter, as she climbed out of the bed and went to the window.

The light was already fading, as she realised just how long they'd been in his bed, enjoying each others' bodies and indulging in the kind of energetic and frantic sex she hadn't enjoyed in many a year, and possibly wouldn't enjoy ever again.

She and Warren rarely made love these days. Although he was a caring and considerate lover, it really wasn't very exciting or enervating with him any more. The coupling with Cyril had been something very different, as he told her he hadn't had sex with anyone since his wife died, and had seemed to be a release of his pent-up sex drive after so many years of celibacy.

Slipping into her clothes, she went downstairs to find out who was on the 'phone, realising that it probably wasn't the rescue she'd been waiting for. The snow was still as deep as before, and was beginning to freeze over once more as the temperature dropped with the approach of the night.

He'd already finished on the 'phone when she reached the hallway and found him busy in the kitchen.

'Who was that?' she asked, as she entered the cosy warmth inside.

'It was the rescue services,' he answered, looking up from the potatoes he was just testing in the pan. 'It looks as if it's going to be tomorrow at the earliest before they can get to you, so it looks as if you'll be spending another night here.'

'Oh help,' she answered. 'Warren will be going frantic, and I should be at work as well. He'll have had to bring somebody else in to cover for me. I need to ring him.'

'No need,' he answered, as he took out a potato masher and began to kneed the potatoes with it, generously ladling a large dollop of butter in with them. 'He rang almost immediately I put the 'phone down. I told him you still weren't able to get away and that you'd probably be spending another night here. In the meantime, I've found a steak pie in the freezer and put it in the oven. The potatoes are already done. I was just going to wake you.'

'Thank you so much – I'm starving,' she answered.

'On the contrary – thank you,' he answered. 'I haven't enjoyed myself so much in many a year now. I've really enjoyed the day we've had together. I hope I didn't disappoint.'

'Far from it!' she laughed. 'When you've been married as many years as I have, sex becomes more a chore than a joy – and I really enjoyed today. It was new and very exciting.'

'Go and have a wash then, and I'll put the food out,' Cyril smiled wanly, thinking that he probably wasn't going to be indulging in such a wonderful orgy of sex ever again in his lifetime, and with such an energetic and exciting woman as Marnie Peters. Although there was no love between them as he'd experienced with his own wife, Marnie might have been the ideal woman as a companion for the rest of his days, but within a very short time he could be looking for a new place to live, and trying to find a new job as well. He was already approaching his sixties. Who'd want to take on somebody of that age?

It was as she climbed the stairs that Marnie had a sudden thought. She'd only heard the 'phone ring once, and that had only been two short rings before it was answered. Surely she would

208

have heard it if it had rung a second time! She definitely knew she hadn't heard a second ring!

The food was on the table when she returned from what had turned into a quick shower and she tucked into it with relish. Isabelle's home-made pie was delicious; the meat juicy and succulent in a rich, thick gravy.

She didn't like to question the second call that he said he'd taken, but vowed to ring Warren herself if Cyril left her alone for long enough. She was worried that he might have an ulterior motive for lying to her.

When he went out to fetch some more logs after they'd cleared away the remnants of the meal, she went quickly into the hall. She knew she didn't have time to make a call to Warren, but she did intend to try the call back facility and see if he had rung, but when she lifted the receiver, the line was completely dead. She knew she'd definitely heard it ring once, so how come it was dead now?

Glancing down under the table, she saw the end of the 'phone connection was unplugged and was lying behind one of the table legs – impossible to have been pulled out accidentally, especially with the plug being behind one of the table legs and at least a foot away from the socket. He must have unplugged it deliberately!

She heard the back door bang and hurried back to the kitchen.

'Just been to the loo,' she volunteered, as he looked at her suspiciously. 'I'll make us some coffee and we can watch a bit of telly if you fancy it!'

He nodded and carried the basket of logs to the lounge, still looking suspicious as he left the kitchen. Peering round the door he'd left partly ajar, she saw him glance down at the telephone socket before going across the hall and into the room; seeming satisfied that she hadn't noticed it was unplugged.

She was getting worried now. This seemed to be some attempt at stopping her from contacting her husband – but for what reason? Surely it wasn't in an attempt to stop her from leaving! Nobody could yet get through the thick snow anyway!

They spent the evening in front of the television, neither of them really interested in the programmes, but there was nothing else they could do for the time being.

When it came time for them both to go to bed, she feigned tiredness and declined his offer of sleeping in his double bed.

'I feel really guilty about what we did,' she reasoned, 'I can't let it happen again.'

A shadow passed over his face, but he said nothing, merely shrugged his shoulders.

As she climbed the stairs alone just after ten o'clock, she vowed to lock the door that night. It was one thing to have indulged in an afternoon of highly enjoyable sex, but it would have been quite another to have found him on top of her in the middle of the night, with her struggling to try and stop him from raping her.

She lay quietly in her bed, waiting to hear him come up, but when he did, he went straight to the bathroom, where he obviously hadn't shut the door, as she heard him peeing loudly into the bowl, accompanied several seconds later by the sound of water splashing in the sink as he washed.

Shortly after that, she heard his bedroom door close and the house was completely silent again for the rest of the night.

The next morning, there was no sign of him when she went downstairs shortly after nine o'clock and put the kettle on, but she did notice the 'phone was still unplugged.

She needed to wait for him to be out for some time before she could plug it back in and call Warren, and perhaps the police if she considered it necessary. For the time being she didn't know where he'd gone, or how much longer he was likely to be.

She found some oats in the larder and made herself some porridge with water and no milk – but with sugar added, it was palatable enough, and she didn't mind drinking her tea with no milk either. There was about a quarter of a bottle left in the 'fridge, but they'd decided to leave that for necessities, although they'd need to drink it soon, otherwise it would go off and they'd be back in the same position.

It was just as she finished the porridge that the back door opened. Expecting it to be Cyril, she was surprised to see a stranger enter. She'd thought there was nobody here but them.

The man seemed to be as confused by her presence in the kitchen as she was at his sudden appearance.

'Who are yew?' he asked, standing there with the door still open before realising he was letting out the heat and closing it behind him.

At the same time, he took off his snow covered boots and put them on the mat to one side, depositing a plastic bag alongside them, before turning back to hear her explanation.

'My name is Marnie Peters,' she answered his interrogative gaze. 'My car's broken down up the lane and the rescue can't get through to me yet.'

'An' where's Cyril?' still seeming suspicious of her.

'I've no idea,' she answered. 'I've only just got up and I haven't seen him yet. He must be out somewhere.'

The man's attitude mellowed a little and he seemed to relax.

'I see t' kettle's on. Yew making a brew?' he asked, coming forward and sitting down at the table. 'I'm Gavin Davis, and I live in the cottage over yonder with me family,' waving an expressive hand in the direction of where he'd come from. 'Me and me son see to all the outside work – gardening, wood cutting and generally seeing to the timber arownd the grounds.'

Just then, the kettle began to boil and she went over to pour water into the teapot, before setting it down on the table, together with two cups. She sat down opposite and waited for it to brew.

'Sorry, but you'll have to have it black – we've hardly any milk left, and we're trying to keep that for necessities – but I suppose it might be just as well to use it up; it won't be long before it goes sour.'

He smiled.

'Black will suit me. I like me tea good and strong anyway.'

211

Just as she was about to reach out and pour the tea, his voice cut in once again.

'What yew doing rownd 'eyre anyway in the middle o' winter? Don't get many people around 'ere 'cept in the summer – then there's strangers everywhere walking the hills and moors.'

She didn't know what to say for the moment, but her predicament was ended just at that moment as Cyril walked in through the door.

'Gavin!' he said, seeming flustered when he saw the man sitting at the table and talking to Marnie.

Then, recovering his composure, he said, 'What brings you up here? I thought you'd still be hunkered down in your cottage with the family until it all blows over.'

Gavin smiled again.

'Not likely! Can't just sit arownd the 'ouse all day – I'd go stir crazy! Me and Morgan been out shooting rabbits this morning. The snow's not so thick up in the woods, and ther're plenty of them out looking for food today, so we bagged a fair few. I brought a couple up for yew – thought you might be gettin' short of food. Morgan's skinned and gutted 'em, so all yew 'ave to do is cook 'em. We saw some Muntjac this mornin' as well. If yew've room in the freezer, we might try and get one later today and bring some up for yew. Sorry we can't oblige with milk though. We're in the same position as yew with that.'

Cyril seemed a little uneasy in Gavin's presence, but as they sat around the table drinking the tea, his mood began to lighten and he became more at ease.

'Soon as I can, I'll get up to t' farm and get us all some more milk,' Gavin said, as he prepared to leave. 'The track from my place up to the lane ain't as well covered in snow as it is 'eyre. It's bin sheltered by the trees, so unless it snows again, I should be able to ge' out quite soon. I'll take a look see this afternoon. Sun was trying to poke through when I come up, so it may melt some of it.'

212

As he left, Marnie found herself feeling more uncomfortable with Cyril. She wished she'd had more time alone with Gavin. Perhaps she could have confided her suspicions that Cyril was trying to stop her from leaving – but then she might have had to tell him what had happened between them the previous afternoon, and she definitely didn't want to admit that to him – or to anybody else for that matter.

'I'll go and make my bed,' she excused herself when Gavin had gone.

'No – stay!'

Cyril's voice was commanding.

She felt worried, but stopped halfway to the door.

'Sit down,' he said, and for fear of what he might do if she didn't, she sat down again.

Suddenly his whole attitude changed.

'Forgive me, Marnie,' he said. 'I didn't mean to scare you, but I can see that I have. I haven't really enjoyed any female company since my wife died, and it's the first time I've been to bed with a woman since then. I've missed the company of my wife so much.

I really enjoyed our little romp yesterday. It made me feel so alive and wanted again, but I can see that it didn't mean anything more to you than an exciting change in your life. I can see that you don't want to stay with me – you're anxious to get home to your husband now.

I won't try and stop you whenever you want to go, but I'll never forget the time we've spent together. It wasn't just the sex, which I enjoyed very much, but your companionship has meant so much to me, even though it's only been for such a short time.'

She suddenly realised that she'd misjudged this peaceable and lonely man. All he really wanted was the love of a woman once more in his life.

'Were you together long?' she asked.

'Almost twenty years,' he answered, as she noticed the tears glistening in his eyes. 'I'd planned to take her to a romantic island in the Caribbean for our twentieth anniversary. It was somewhere she'd always wanted to go, but we'd never been able to afford it before. I'd saved up for almost five years to make that dream come true for her, but then she died suddenly and her dreams of that holiday never came to anything.'

'What happened?' she asked, gently.

She wanted to reach across the table and take his hand, but she was mindful that he might misconstrue the gesture. It was best to keep a distance from him from now on, whilst still remaining friendly, as he seemed so needy.

He sat quietly for a moment, not saying anything, before speaking once again. When he did, it was obvious he was trying to stop the tears from falling.

'She went to bed early one evening with a headache. I didn't think anything of it, as she'd had a few just recently, but when I took up her morning tea, she wouldn't wake up. It was then I found she was cold and must have been dead for some time.'

Marnie found the tears gathering in her own eyes, as he continued.

'They had to do a post mortem, and it was then they found she had a brain tumour and it had ruptured during the night. They thought she'd probably died in her sleep.'

'Didn't she wake or make any sound in the night?' Marnie queried.

'She was asleep when I went upstairs so I decided to sleep in the spare room so's not to disturb her. I'll never know if she might have woken and been trying to get my attention to help her.'

Now Marnie felt the tears sliding down her own cheeks, and she didn't know what to say.

Poor man! How tragic must that have been to find his wife dead in bed when he brought up her morning tea! She couldn't contemplate how awful that must have been for him!

When she came down later after making her bed and having a quick tidy round, she noticed the 'phone had been plugged in again, and shortly afterwards she heard it ring.

214

It was Warren. She'd already made up her mind to ring him when Cyril wasn't around for a while.

'I've been going frantic,' he said. 'I've tried numerous times to get through. Have the lines been down?'

She was glad to hear his voice and felt really anxious to get back home now.

'Possibly – we couldn't ring out either, and there's no mobile signal here,' careful to say nothing about the unplugging of the 'phone.

'Where exactly are you?' was his next question; a question she'd been dreading him asking. She'd have to explain that she'd gone against his wishes and gone out to find Bannerman's – and her father!

'On the Denbigh Moors,' she said.

There was a dreaded silence on the other end.

'Have you been trying to find your father?' he asked; admonishment in his tone.

'Yes,' she answered; her voice barely audible.

'Why in the middle of winter?' he asked; annoyance in his own tone. 'What was so urgent it couldn't have waited for better weather? Would it have made any difference waiting a few more months?'

Defiance in her own voice now she said, 'None whatsoever – he's dead – so I'll never get to meet him now!'

There was a deathly silence at the other end.

'I'm coming to get you as soon as I can. The snow's nearly all gone here. What's it like there?'

'Still pretty deep, and it freezes over every night, so it's pretty treacherous. The rescue is on its way, so as soon as they get through, I'll be on my way back; whether it's in my own car, or by the rescue vehicle. They'll bring me and the car back home when they can get through.'

'Okay, but I hope it's not too long. I've been worried about you.'

215

'I'm fine,' she answered, hearing the worry in his voice. 'The house is warm, I have a comfy bed, and there's plenty of food in the larder. Cyril, who lives in and seems to be caretaking at the moment has been the perfect gentlemen,' feeling herself blush as she said it.

A pity she hadn't been the perfect lady herself!

Several hours later, after the temperature had warmed up a bit, and there was the sound of dripping everywhere, there was a loud knock on the door.

Cyril opened it to a man standing on the doorstep.

'I'm looking for Mrs. Peters,' he announced.

'You from the breakdown?' Cyril asked.

'Yep. Is she here?'

Just then Marnie appeared at his side.

'Yes, I'm Mrs Peters,' she answered. 'I'll just get my keys,' hurrying off to find her bag.

'No need to come with me,' he answered when she returned and handed them to him. 'You say it just won't start?'

She nodded.

'I'll see to it, and I'll come back for you when I've looked at it. In the meantime, have you got your membership card? I need a few details from it,' he asked, lifting up a clipboard and detaching a pen from under the top clip.

Formalities over, he took off down the driveway again, leaving them to stare after him, Cyril regretting that Marnie might be leaving him soon, and not wanting her to go.

'What now?' she asked.

'Well, we don't know if it's something simple, or whether it might need to be towed away,' Cyril answered, 'so I suppose all we can do is wait. How about some more coffee?'

Although Cyril sounded unhappy about her imminent departure, she couldn't wait to get away. It wasn't only Cyril's show of possessiveness that was bothering her, but her lack of clean clothes. She hadn't had a change of clothes with her, and even though she'd washed out her knickers and left them on the radiator overnight to dry, she thought her other things were beginning to whiff a bit. She'd brought nothing else with her, and she certainly hadn't thought there'd be any need for deodorant.

Within half an hour the man was back, and they offered him some coffee, but he declined.

'Got a backlog of calls to catch up on,' he said, 'so can't sit around drinking coffee.'

'Is it fixed?' she asked anxiously.

'Oh yes, it's fixed,' he said, giving her a hard stare, 'all it needed was some fuel in the tank!'

She caught Cyril's eyes swivel towards her, and under both their gazes, she blushed and wondered how she could have been so stupid as to run out of fuel. She'd been so anxious to get away and find her father she'd never thought to look at the fuel gauge.'

'How could I have been so stupid?' she stammered. 'I'm so sorry!'

'Well, you're lucky I was carrying a spare can with me. There's a gallon in your tank, and there's a petrol station just a few hundred metres away when you reach the main road, so you can fill up there. Have you far to go?'

When she told him she was heading into Cheshire, he confirmed that the main roads were pretty clear going that way, and that Cheshire itself was almost completely clear now.

Thanking him profusely on the doorstep, she pressed a £20 note into his hand.

'That's for all your trouble, and to try and atone for my stupidity,' she said as she closed the door after him.

When she returned to the kitchen, Cyril had finished washing the dishes and was standing with his back to the stove.

'That's it then – I suppose you'll be off now.'

His whole attitude showed how sorry he'd be to see her go.

'Yes. I'll just get my things and I'll be off. Thanks for the hospitality you've shown me, and for letting me stay.'

'On the contrary,' he answered, 'it was my pleasure,' making no move to come towards her or to move away from the stove.

When he heard the front door open, and her cheery call of ''Bye, and thanks for everything,' he moved from the kitchen and into the hallway, where he stood watching her figure walk away from him down the drive.

He didn't know whether he'd ever see her again. There was no reason for her ever to return. Now that she knew her father was dead, and her brother and sister no longer lived here – there was nothing to come back for!

CHAPTER 22

When Anna awoke the next morning, it was an hour later than her usual time, and she realised David would probably already be up for his breakfast.

She washed and dressed quickly. There was no sound as she passed his room, so her assumption was probably right, and she hurried down – but he wasn't in the kitchen. When she knocked on the door of his study to apologise for sleeping late, and to ask if he wanted breakfast, there was no reply. She tried the handle, but it was locked. He never locked it when he was in, but when he left, it was always locked. There was a lot of sensitive documentation hanging about, and it was for his eyes only.

A quick peek through the window in the hall showed that his car was no longer there either, so she went back to the kitchen and ate a solitary breakfast before beginning her daily household chores. She felt guilty for sleeping so late and needed to apologise when he returned.

The snow was melting fast, as she heard the drip, drip, drip of it all morning from every room she entered.

Her first task of the day was mopping the floors in the hall and the kitchen. Snow had been traipsed in ever since it had begun snowing, and together with it was a generous amount of dirt and dust from outside, together with a lot of small twigs brought down by the weight of the snow.

It was twelve thirty before she managed to sit down for a drink and a few minutes rest in her own little room, and she'd just finished when she heard a key in the front door. David must have come home for lunch.

She'd thought he must be catching up on things at work, and he'd left no word he'd be in for lunch. There was little in the 'fridge to do anything with, as she realised she needed to do a shop.

Going out to meet him, he was just hanging up his coat and taking off his shoes as she emerged from her room.

'I'm sorry, there isn't much in for your lunch. I didn't realise you'd be home today. You didn't leave a note,' she started with.

'No problem,' he answered. 'I didn't have any breakfast this morning, so I bought a bacon buttie from the café on my way in. I won't need much – a sandwich will do me.'

'I think I can manage that, and I'm sorry I slept late. I forgot to set my alarm last night.'

'Yes,' he answered, 'I noticed your car wasn't here when I got back. Did you have a good evening? The food was excellent, wasn't it?'

She looked at him in astonishment, not knowing what to say.

'I saw you there with your friend. I was going to come over and speak to you when we finished eating, but you weren't there when I looked over. I'm afraid I didn't see you leave, or I'd have spoken to you first.'

For the moment she didn't know what to say. She hadn't realised he'd seen her when he arrived, but he wasn't volunteering any information about his mysterious companion either.

'I've just got a few notes to catch up on in the study, and then I'll join you for that sandwich in the kitchen.'

As he wasn't fussed about the food, she opened a tin of salmon she kept for times like this, and defrosted four slices of wholemeal bread from the freezer, before adding some thin slices of cucumber from the bottom of the 'fridge. It would be past its best within the next couple of days, so she put what was left of it in the bin.

As she put them down on the table, he came in and sat down, not seeming inclined to be talkative as they ate.

Thinking he had something on his mind, she said nothing herself, waiting for him to speak; but for the moment, he didn't say anything more as they finished off the food.

Finally, when they'd both finished eating and she'd made them some tea she said, 'I think there's still some of those oaty biscuits you like still left in the tin. Would you like a couple to go with your tea?'

He nodded, and she went to fetch the tin, but as she passed the table, he took hold of her arm.

'Anna, forget the biscuits, I need to talk to you. Please sit down again.'

So there **was** something on his mind!

'What is it?' she asked as she sat.

'I'm so sorry I left you like that on New Year's Eve. I had meant to take you out to a nice restaurant and treat you to a meal, but life got in the way, and something urgent cropped up.'

'Anything you want to talk about?' she asked, concern creeping into her voice.

'You could say that!' he answered, his hands folded together on the table. 'I know you saw me with that woman last night, but believe me, she means nothing to me. I'd far rather have been with you.'

She felt herself blushing, and was slightly tongue tied.

'What you do with your life and who you see is none of my business, and I wouldn't dream of prying,' was all she could find to say.

'Anna . . .' he began, and then stopped. 'Sit down, please.'

She returned to the table and did as he asked.

'I have something I need to tell you,' he began, his whole attitude one of finally having made up his mind about something.

'That woman I was with last night – she's my ex-wife.'

Stunned, she couldn't think of anything to say. She never knew he'd ever been married.

'When we met, shortly after I left home, she was already divorced and had a young daughter of five years old. I don't

221

think she was ever really looking for a husband – I think what she really wanted was someone to finance her through bringing up the child. Anyway, to cut a long story short, she was several years older than me and we were only married a few years before it all came to an end. I found out she'd been seeing other men while I was acting as just a glorified baby sitter.'

Anna was feeling uncomfortable, but also fascinated to learn something of his previous life.

'You really don't need to explain anything of this to me,' she said, when he paused for breath, 'it's really none of my business.'

'It will be when you've heard me out,' he said.

'Her daughter is now 15 years old and has got herself mixed up with some unsavoury characters and has been taking drugs. To try and sort herself out, she's been lying about her age and taken out some pay-day loans. I'm sure you're aware of the interest rates on these loans, aren't you?'

She nodded, realising what he was probably about to say.

'Long story short – they're mounting up and she's had to turn to her mother for help, but she doesn't have the money to help her out either, so she's come to me.'

'Why you? You're divorced and she's not your daughter anyway. Why doesn't she go to the girl's father?'

'No chance there! He's in prison at the moment, serving an eight year stretch for fraud and theft from the company he worked for. He's still got another five years to do, and what company's going to want to take him on when he comes out if he's already been convicted of defrauding another company?'

She wanted to ask more questions but held her tongue. She had to remember her place as an employee, even though he was unburdening himself to her.

He looked at her for a few moments before continuing.

'I'm very fond of Maggie – that's her daughter – and I really want to get her out of the trouble she's in, but my hands are tied at the moment. It's taking me all my time to keep up the running of Bannerman's until my sister returns and some of my father's

222

capital can be released. I had a sleepless night last night turning it over in my mind, trying to work out what to do.'

'And have you made up your mind?' she asked, realising that her own job could be on the line.

'I think so,' he answered, looking at her. 'In fact, even without trying to sort out Maggie's problem, I think I'd already decided. I'm going to sell Little Bannerman and move back into Bannerman's. I'm sure my sister won't turn me out if she does come back, and if she doesn't, I could officially have her declared dead after 7 years and the house will become mine as the only next of kin left.'

Anna's heart fell. There was already a full complement of staff at Bannerman's. He wouldn't need her any more!

'I'm going to see an estate agent this afternoon and put the wheels in motion,' he continued.

'I see,' she said, seeing only a bleak future opening up for herself.

'Will you need me to leave straight away, or will you want me to wait until the sale goes through?'

'Leave? I don't want you to leave! I want you to come with me – as my wife if you'll have me!'

She looked at him; not quite believing what he'd just said.

'Live at Bannerman's as your wife?' she said incredulously.

'Yes,' he answered; a smile on his face. 'Will you be my wife? Will you marry me?'

She didn't know what to say. She felt as if her mouth was gaping open, and yet she knew it wasn't.

'I need a minute to think,' she said, but seeing disappointment written all over his face, she conceded, 'but only a minute! And I've already thought. The answer's – yes! There's nothing I'd like better than to live at Bannerman's with you – as your wife – provided you don't expect me to clean that huge great house, even if it is with Sandra's assistance!'

And suddenly they were laughing, hugging and crying all at the same time.

It was only the ringing of the 'phone that brought them back to reality once again, as David went into the hallway to answer it.

'Sorry to interrupt your mealtime, Mr. David. This is Cyril here from Bannerman's. Gavin's just informed me that we have a problem with the rose bed in the front driveway – the one that used to be your father's fishpond.'

'Yes, what is it?' annoyed that his and Anna's little celebration had been interrupted for something so mundane.

'Gavin's just informed me that the snow and ice has cracked the stonework around the side, and a big piece has fallen out. Unfortunately, it's next to the valve that used to top the water up when it fell too low, and there's water pis . . . running out of it. We don't know how to turn it off.'

Even further annoyed, David said, 'Don't you know where the stopcock is?'

'Yes, I do,' answered Cyril, 'but it doesn't seem to turn it off. It must have its own separate one, but I don't know where that is. We've looked around but we can't find it. I think we need to call in the water board.'

'Well, can't you do that?'

'Yes, I can Mr. David, but I need your permission first. It's you who'll have to pay for it.'

'Okay, I'll pay for it, but get them in as soon as you can.'

'I'll do that. In the meantime, we'll have to clear up the soil that's all over the driveway, together with all the rose bushes Gavin's so carefully tended, otherwise they can't get at it. The soil has mixed with the water, and it's turned to mud. It's everywhere! It'll probably mix with the gravel when we get it up, and then the drive will need more gravel put down.'

David put his hand to his head in exasperation. If it wasn't one thing, it was another! And it all cost him money – money that was fast dwindling in his bank account.

'Anna,' he called as he put down the 'phone, 'pack a bag, we're going back to Bannerman's this weekend. We've got a problem!'

224

CHAPTER 23

The next day, under David's instruction, Anna moved all her things into his room, and they began living together as a couple.

She realised that this was what she'd been wanting for a very long time. She knew now that she'd been falling for him ever since she'd first come to live here without even knowing it.

He was a kind and considerate lover, and even though she continued to look after him and the house as she had before, it was more in the role of a wife and companion rather than a housekeeper since that day. She knew now that it was something she wanted more than anything, and he seemed to feel the same way; touching her when they passed each other, giving her the odd peck on the cheek in an affectionate way, and cuddling up together on the sofa whilst watching television, instead of sitting in separate armchairs.

On Friday evening he returned from work at four o'clock and she had all their things packed ready to go straight to Bannerman's, where Isabelle, who'd finally managed to get back from her sister's in Anglesey, had a hot casserole waiting for them and some fluffy mashed potatoes to go with it.

They saw the mess around the old fish pond immediately they arrived, and David had to park the car at the end of the drive, going round to the back of the house to avoid walking through it.

Luckily, the water had at last been turned off, and, as Cyril explained when they got in, they were hoping for some better weather to dry it out before they tried to clear it up, otherwise it would be a very messy job. As it was only January, David didn't hold out much hope of that.

'Come and have a proper look,' Cyril urged after they'd finished eating. 'It's a real mess.'

Leaving Anna inside, he donned wellingtons and followed Cyril outside, where he found it was just as bad as he'd thought it would be.

Another expense to add to the ever growing list! This wasn't going to be cheap to clear up by any means! There must be several tonnes of soil covering a wide area, and it was all mud, not just soil.

Then they'd need a stone mason to repair the side wall before it could be reinstated. He had no idea what the stone was, but he remembered his father saying that it had been very expensive, and he'd had to have it shipped in from somewhere, needing a specialist firm of craftsman to carve and install it.

It was as they were sitting in the lounge that evening enjoying hot chocolate and some of Isabelle's home-made biscuits before bed, that David had a good idea.

'The fish pond,' he announced. 'Why don't we rebuild it as it was originally intended? Why don't we turn it into a fish pond again? If we're going to live here full time, it would be nice to see the fountain working again.'

'Won't it cost a lot?' Anna asked, thinking that it would be a rather nice feature if he could afford to do it. It must have looked spectacular when the fountain was working.

'No more than it will cost to repair it as a flower bed. It's the repair that's going to cost, and we might be able to sell the soil that's already in it. That should command a good price after all the nourishment Gavin's put into it. There's always a demand for good top soil.'

'Okay,' she answered, 'it's your call. Let's give it a go! It would be lovely to see it working again, and if we put some fish in it, we'll be able to enjoy them year round, instead of just having the roses in bloom through the summer, and looking at dead twigs in the winter.'

226

'Done,' he answered. 'Now all I have to do is find a good stone mason who's capable of carrying out all the work necessary. I'll think on it overnight, and have a look online tomorrow. Now I think it's time for bed. It feels like it's been a very long day,' as he yawned.

She smiled as he stood up, and took his proffered hand, preparing to follow him.

'You know, I can't believe you've agreed to be my wife,' he said as he looked at her. 'How lucky can one man get? I didn't realise how much I loved you until I thought you were going to leave me.'

'I think I've loved you for a very long time,' she answered. 'I just didn't realise that's what it was! I nearly broke down in tears when you said you were going to sell Little Bannerman. I thought you wouldn't need me any more and I'd have to find another job. I thought I'd never see you again.'

'No chance of that,' he said, planting a kiss on her forehead. 'I felt the same when I thought you were going to leave. I couldn't face the prospect of never seeing you again.'

Next day, after breakfast, he spoke to the rest of the staff about his plans to sell Little Bannerman and to return here to live.

They were surprised, but it was only Isabelle who spoke up.

'Have you heard from Miss Jayne then? Will she be coming back too?'

'No, I haven't heard anything from her yet. I've advertised frequently for her in the papers, but never had a reply from either her, or anybody who knows her.

The reason I've made my decision is because it's costing too much to run both this and my own home, and I don't want to have to break my promise to you of keeping you all on. This seems to be the most sensible solution.'

'And what about if Miss Jayne returns?' Isabelle pursued.

'It's a big house,' David replied. 'No reason why we couldn't all live here in harmony – but that would be up to her if she ever does return, which I'm beginning to doubt. I have the feeling that she just doesn't want to be found.'

Looks were exchanged between them. They didn't know whether he was right or not, but all their livelihoods depended on him from now on.

Isabelle was the only one with other prospects for the future, but since her enforced and much longer stay with her sister in Anglesey, she was beginning to have doubts as to whether they'd be able to live in the same house together for very long.

The first few days had been fine, but as time wore on, arguments and disagreements had taken place, and over the silliest and most stupid of things: things like teaspoons put in the wrong compartment of the drawer; a pan in the wrong cupboard; sheets not folded correctly; table mats put in the wrong place, and numerous other little things that niggled at them both.

Unfortunately, she didn't have the wherewithal to buy a place of her own, and no pension save for the State one when it finally came time for her to claim it. If he made her redundant now, she wouldn't have anything to pay rent with either.

Cyril, too, was in the same position. He'd had little left after his house had been sold and he'd cleared his debts; including his mortgage. Their wages were paid after taking into account their living accommodation and food costs, so he hadn't been able to save very much towards retirement himself.

Sandra was the only one with a home to go back to, living as she and her husband did in an annexe attached to her father's farmhouse – her husband working the land and the animals together with her father.

David and Anna left them to talk amongst themselves, while Cyril told them Gavin was waiting outside to speak to them.

Donning coats and going outside, they found him sitting on the front door step.

'Morning David,' he said. 'Morning Anna', as he saw she was with him, getting up on hearing the door open behind him. 'I was just wondering how best to store the rose bushes until we can get them re-planted. I think they might be all right put in a big trough of some kind and kept covered and moist until the spring. That new shed of your dad's might be ideal if you don't want to use it for anything else.'

David and Anna exchanged glances, before David turned back to him.

'Forget the roses,' he said, 'we're going to re-instate the fish pond. It'll look much more attractive than the roses ever did, and we can try and get the fountain working as well.'

Gavin was taken aback for the moment, but when he thought about it, that could just be a very good decision. The fountain had always been the main feature of the rather austere house – almost the first thing to be seen on approaching, and had always looked fabulous with the sun's rays sparkling off the water; creating a myriad of different colours shooting off in all directions.

Besides that, he'd taken it on himself to feed the fish every evening after his tea. Once the fountain had been turned off for the night, and dusk was beginning to fall, it was a peaceful place to sit on the stone ledge around the pond and contemplate the day just gone by. It always left him in a state of mind ready for a good night's sleep and time to recuperate from a busy days work.

'Yes, I think that's a very good idea,' he said thoughtfully. 'I always did like feeding the fish and spending some time watching them before going to my bed. That's a very good idea indeed!'

As David and Anna turned away, prepared to go for a good walk out on the moors before turning their hand to anything else, Gavin's voice stopped them.

'What you going to do with all this soil then?'

'I hadn't really thought about it,' David answered. 'I thought we might try and sell it, but if not, we could spread it out around the grounds and get rid of it that way. It'll take a good while to clear it all, but at least it'll be put to some use.'

229

'Leave it with me,' Gavin answered. 'There's always people looking for good top soil, and this is good, I can vouch for that. It's been given a good dressing of manure every year, and its cost you nothing. Farmers are always anxious to get rid of their surplus year on year.'

David and Anna looked at each other and grinned. Waste not, want not had always been the countryside motto, and this would be no exception.

'Just let me know when you're ready and I'll put the word out. I'm sure there'll be plenty of takers,' he called after them as they walked away, surveying the mess he and Morgan would have had to pile back where it had come from. Hopefully, they wouldn't be tasked with moving it again, and he'd be able to leave that to whoever wanted to take it away.

David returned his parting words with a salutary wave of the hand as they began to walk away, enjoying a brisk walk in the weak winter sunshine, and crunching their way over what was still left of the crisp snow. Apart from a few rabbit and badger tracks going in and out of the woods, everything was pristine and untouched; but something Gavin had said had brought another thought to mind. They still had the set of keys his father had kept hidden, and they still hadn't found the place that the small key fitted. That still remained a mystery, but he was sure it must be something to do with the shed – otherwise why have it on the same ring?

After lunch, the sun continued to shine and the path to the shed was completely clear now, as David looked towards it from the kitchen window.

Isabelle had gone to the larder to root round for something for their evening meal, and Cyril had gone off on the quad bike to the local shop to pick up their milk order, and some more meat from the farm.

They'd had a call from the farmer only that morning to say he had a couple of brace of pheasant if they wanted them, knowing the judge had always been partial to them. Isabelle had agreed to buy them and ready them for Sunday lunch, thinking she'd cook them in a red wine sauce which she was sure they'd all enjoy. As it was a fairly dry meat, the sauce would make them more succulent, and she still had some of her home-made cranberry jelly left over from Christmas.

'Anna,' David said, turning to where she was putting dishes away on the old Welsh dresser. 'Do you fancy going to the shed this afternoon to see if we can find where that small key belongs?'

She was surprised, not but averse to the suggestion.

'I didn't see anywhere where it fitted before, but I'm sure another look around wouldn't hurt, and we've nothing more urgent to do, have we?' she asked.

He shook his head.

'We've a bit more clearing out to do, and a few more papers to check, but apart from that, there's nothing urgent. Most of it's for the recycle anyway.'

'Then that's what we'll do,' she answered, rinsing her hands under the tap and wiping them on the towel draped over the bar on the front of the range.

'Ready to go now?' she asked.

'Might as well. Once the sun goes down it'll turn cold again, so we need to get going.'

Fetching their coats from the hall, while David unlocked his father's study and retrieved the key from its hook under the desk, they shrugged into them and let themselves out of the back door, feeling the cold chill immediately the door was open.

Once inside the shed, the sun was moving round and it was dimmer than it had been when they were here last.

'My father always kept a paraffin lamp in the old shed for when there wasn't enough light. I'm sure it'll still be here somewhere,' as he began to look around.

He found it almost immediately, tucked alongside the padded bench, and picked it up, finding a box of matches on the window ledge; but just as he did so, Anna caught her foot on an uneven piece of flooring and pitched forward.

She flailed her arms wildly to stop herself falling; one arm grabbing his, and the other going out towards the table. David, not expecting it, and taken off balance himself, went down with her, both of them ending up in a heap on the floor; his head narrowly missing the shelf at the far end as she sprawled on top of him.

Neither was hurt, but her wildly flailing left arm had grabbed at nothing more substantial than the tablecloth, which she'd pulled completely off the table and which now covered both their legs.

After a moments surprised pause, they began to pull themselves apart, David solicitously asking if she was all right.

'Yes, I'm all right,' she answered, once she managed to get her thoughts together. 'The only thing hurt is my dignity, and at least I had something soft to break the fall. Are **you** all right?'

'I'll live, once the bruises have healed,' he answered, a wry smile on his face, as he tried hard not to show how badly he'd hurt his arm, which was feeling extremely painful.

'What happened?' was his next question, as they both picked themselves up.

'There's a piece of loose board on the floor,' she indicated as they both rose to their feet. 'I caught my toe against it.'

Lighting the lamp, he held it up. The piece of wood flooring near the door had cracked right across, and the end facing the door was sticking up dangerously. No wonder she'd tripped over it.

Going over to it, he stamped down hard on it, but although it went down initially, it popped up again almost as soon as he lifted his foot.

'I'll put the bucket over it for now until we can get around to fixing it,' he said, taking the article out and upturning it over the board.

While he was doing that, Anna picked up the tablecloth, intending to put it back on the table, but stopped in the act.

As she straightened up, she was immediately facing the table, and there, staring her straight in the face, was a drawer underneath the top, and right in the centre of it was a keyhole.

'David,' she said, as he turned back after covering the offending board, 'I think I've found where that little key fits!'

He turned and looked in the direction her eyes were facing, his own lighting up with anticipation as soon as he registered what she was looking at.

'Bingo!' he cried, 'I think you're right!'

Taking the key out, he fitted it into the hole, and immediately heard the mechanism click into place, as he pulled the drawer open.

It wasn't very long, covering only a small area at the centre of the table, and not much deeper than a large jam jar, but it went back to about half the width. As he pulled it open, they both heard something rustling inside it.

He lifted it right out and placed it on top of the table, where they both looked at it in surprise.

Inside were about half a dozen large droppers; each still in its original packaging and each with a squeezable soft top, and a long slender tube. At their side was another pack of antiseptic wet wipes and a couple of small disposable plastic bowls.

They looked at each other, and Anna shrugged her shoulders.

'Any ideas?' she asked.

'Not at the moment,' David answered, 'but there's a notebook at the back. It may give us a clue.'

He reached to the back where there was a small hard cover notebook with a ring binder spine, and moving the drawer to one side he laid it on the table top and opened the front cover.

The first page was blank, but right in the centre of the second page was a woman's name, address, and telephone number, together with a few lines of further information on the facing page. Turning over, subsequent facing pages showed the same sort of information, and every one of the names and addresses were women.

Turning back to the first facing pages, David looked at what was written on them: -

Age:	32
Date:	20th January, 1995
Deposit:	£50 paid
Confirmation:	April
Born:	22nd October 1995
	Boy – 7lbs 6ozs
Balance:	£150. Paid 30th November, 1995

Subsequent pages followed in the same vein, but as they went further on, the amounts of deposit and balances went up, until the final entry was given as June, 2013, with a deposit of £200 and the subsequent balance of £300 paid at the end of March 2014.

After that, all the pages were blank.

There were also some pages with three or four dates given, followed later by the word 'failure - refund', although the refund was only half the amount of the deposit.

David didn't know what to say, and Anna was equally as shocked, before she blurted out, 'David, am I right in thinking your father's been inseminating women with these droppers and charging them a fee! Is that even legal?'

'It looks that way,' he said, feeling complete shock and shame for what it looked as if his father had been doing for many years. If he'd known what he was going to find, he'd never have brought Anna with him. He'd rather have kept such a shocking discovery a secret for his eyes only.

'And is it legal?' she pursued.

'I don't really know!' he answered. 'Insemination is tightly controlled through the official channels, but what happens between consenting adults is never usually made public, and judging by the fees my father was charging, a great deal cheaper.

How many one night stands end in an unwanted pregnancy, with the man walking away and never even knowing he's fathered a child? There's never any control on that unless he can be found and made to pay maintenance.'

Anna, seeing the sense of what he was saying, brooded on her thoughts before venturing, 'These were probably the wives of childless couples, unable to conceive a baby naturally between them. Maybe, judging by the number of successes he's had, there might be some very grateful couples out there, and maybe he was providing them with something they'd never have managed alone. He's probably made a great many women very happy during that time.'

Her words were a little more consoling to David, but he couldn't help thinking about it from his mother's point of view. He wondered if she'd ever known what was happening right under her nose, and if she had, would she have approved or accepted it?

He'd never have been able to tell her, even if she were still alive!

There was also another thought beginning to niggle at him. Had these inseminations been carried out entirely by means of the dropper – or had his father sometimes indulged in the actual sexual act with these women to achieve the same result. That was something he'd never ever be sure hadn't happened with at least some of them.

'Anna,' he said, pushing the drawer back in again, but retaining the notebook, 'please keep this just between the two of us. I don't want anyone to find out about this – least of all my sister if she ever comes back. It would probably upset her badly. I'll go through this notebook and see if there's anyone I may know in here, and then I'll think whether to destroy it for good. If anybody finds it, it wouldn't take too long for them to put two and two together just as we did.'

She touched his arm gently before saying, 'It's been a shock – I can see that. I won't breathe a word to anybody, I promise you.

Now let's get back to the house, it's getting too cold to hang around here any longer.'

Returning the drawer to its place under the table, he locked it and hid it with the tablecloth once more, whilst deciding what to do about the whole place. It was in the back of his mind to burn the shed to the ground and get rid of the somewhat shocking things that must have happened within it, but he put that decision to one side for another day. He'd decided to think long and hard about it before making that decision. It would cause a lot of gossip and speculation amongst the staff if he were to do such a thing!

And, besides that, it was a perfectly serviceable place for storage, and Anna hadn't seemed to think that what his father had been doing was anything too shocking!

CHAPTER 24

When they returned to the house and took a hot drink into the living room, there was already a car at the front of the house, with a man and a teenage lad shovelling soil into an attached trailer.

'Well, it didn't take long for Gavin to spread the word, did it?' he quipped.

A little later that same afternoon, whilst still in the living room, Anna heard a noise outside and got up to look. She grinned and brought David's attention to it, where he was engrossed in his laptop looking for specialist stone masons.

'It'll all be gone soon at this rate, and you won't have had to lift a finger or put your hand in your pocket once,' she said.

David laughed as they both stood watching two men outside, energetically shovelling soil into yet another trailer, together with one very small girl of about eight or nine working assiduously with a plastic bucket and spade trying to help. She seemed to have as much soil clinging to her clothes and body as she did in the bucket.

'Somebody's mother won't be too pleased tonight when they get home and she sees the sight of her daughter,' Anna laughed, looking at the clock and deciding it wouldn't be long before their evening meal was ready.

'I'll just go upstairs and have a lie-down before dinner,' she said, 'I can feel a bit of a headache coming on. Have you any paracetamol?'

'Try the bathroom cabinet,' he said, 'there should be some there,' returning to the laptop once more to continue his search.

She went upstairs, and after finding them, she stripped down to bra and panties before slipping under the duvet, where she fell asleep almost immediately. She hadn't realised she was so tired, but obviously she must have been.

It was almost eight o'clock when she awoke, and realised she must have slept right through dinner.

Hurriedly dressing, she went downstairs, finding David in his father's study, sitting at the desk and leafing through the notebook they'd found in the desk.

'Looks like I missed dinner,' she apologised.

'Don't worry – I realised you must be tired, so I left you to sleep and asked Isabelle to save you something. She'll have gone to her room by now, but I'm sure she'll have left it in plain sight for you.'

Entering the kitchen, she saw the plate on the table immediately; covered over with a glass bowl. There was some mashed potato and gravy, carrots and broccoli, together with slices of roast lamb, which she popped in the microwave to heat up, whilst laying her place and taking the cover off the lemon cheesecake alongside.

It was rather a large portion to what she normally ate, but she thought she'd be able to manage it all. She hadn't eaten since lunchtime, and as the headache had now completely cleared, she felt very hungry.

Finishing off every scrap, she washed up her dishes and made coffee for them both, taking a cup each through to the study.

David was still there; and still avidly looking through the notebook. He had a sheet of paper alongside, and was making notes on things that he obviously thought to be of significance.

'Found anything interesting?' she asked, pulling up a chair alongside him and shutting the floor length curtains to hide the cold, dark night outside. It made the room much cosier.

'Yes, I have,' he answered, breaking off to sip his coffee, 'this lady here,' jabbing his finger at the paper.

Anna looked over and moved the lamp round so that she could see better, nodding her head, 'Julia Leatherbarrow?'

'That's her! She once worked here as a nursemaid, childminder – whatever you want to call her, when we were growing up. She left just before I went to university. Seems she may have been one of the many impregnated by my father, and it says here she had a little boy – but she lived in when she worked here, so I'm sure she wasn't married.'

Anna frowned.

'You don't think there was any hanky panky while she was living here, do you?'

'Who knows? There's nobody left to ask now, and Jayne wouldn't know either. She was only a toddler then.'

She realised sadly that he was still expecting his young sister, Jayne, to return at some time in the future, even though it seemed less and less likely that she ever would. He'd booked a monthly slot in a national newspaper, advertising for her return, or any information about her, and had even had a slot on the radio, but there'd never been any response so far.

'Then there's this one!' as he stabbed his finger at another name on the page, bringing her mind back to the present.

'This lady, Cynthia Lansdowne – she was a friend of my mothers. I remember her name – it's quite distinctive. We called her Auntie Cynthia, and she brought us little presents when she came to see mother. We found her too overpowering though – she always wanted us to sit on her knee, and always talked down to us as if we were babies. I couldn't wait to get away from her once mother said we could go. I must have been round about ten when she stopped coming. I don't know what happened to her after that, and her name was never mentioned again.'

'And might her pregnancy tie in with the time she stopped coming here?' Anna asked.

He glanced at her. Intuitive as ever! Why hadn't he thought of that?

After a quick run through the notes again, and some quick calculations in his head, he said, 'She had the baby when I was eleven, so that does seem to tie in. Good thinking!'

'Any more you know?' she asked.

'There's this lady – Joan Brewer. The name seems familiar, but I can't place where she fits. I seem to remember a tall, thin lady with short dark hair, but apart from that there's nothing.'

'Another friend of your mother's – a member of staff – a teacher maybe?' she tried guessing.

He thought for a moment, then shook his head.

'No, none of those. Maybe it'll come to me later.'

'Any more you recognise?' she asked again.

'I think that's the lot. No other names ring a bell with me. The rest seem to be complete strangers.'

'Let's leave it for now,' she ventured. 'It's getting late and you've been poring over that laptop for ages. I'll go and wash these cups and then we'll go up and have an early night – if you still have the energy left for what I have in mind!'

He grinned.

'Always!' he answered, 'but hurry up with those cups – I'm feeling impatient already – and if you don't, I might just start without you!'

The next day, after lunch, when David was thinking of going back home to prepare some notes for work on Monday, they heard a vehicle pull up to the front and Anna peered out, thinking it was more people come for the soil.

'There's a man and woman outside, and they're coming up to the front door. Do you know them?' she asked.

David joined her and looked out.

'Can't say I do,' he answered, just as the doorbell sounded.

He met Cyril in the hallway going to answer, and told him he'd see to it. Cyril, with a slight incline of the head, turned back towards the kitchen.

As he opened the door, the man, looking more like a prosperous businessman than anything else, looked apologetically at him.

'Forgive this intrusion on a Sunday afternoon, but are you David Bannerman? If so, I wondered if we could have a word with you. It shouldn't take too long.'

David glanced over the pair. They certainly didn't look like desperadoes of any sort, and he and Anna didn't have anything more pressing to do at the moment.

'Yes, I'm David Bannerman. Should I know you?' he asked.

'No. My name is Warren Peters, and this is my wife, Marnie,' the man said. 'My wife has something to say to you, and I doubt I'll get any peace until she does.'

Intrigued and not a little confused, David ushered them into the living room, where Anna had already heard the conversation through the open door.

The man seemed a little abashed at their intrusion on the couple's privacy, and the woman looked as if she was having second thoughts about it too.

'This is my fiancé, Anna,' he said.

Warren inclined his head towards Anna before speaking.

'My wife's car broke down around here at New Year in the snow, and your staff were good enough to put her up for a couple of nights until she managed to get it fixed.'

Cyril had already told David of their unexpected guest, and so he was aware of her presence at New Year – but not the full story!

'Yes, my man did tell me,' he said, eyeing Marnie up.

She looked decidedly uneasy, but he couldn't understand why that should be.

Although Cyril had told him about putting her up overnight, he hadn't mentioned what had gone on between them during her short stay, and Marnie was worried about what would happen if she came face to face with him whilst they were here. She was sure he wouldn't have said anything about it to anyone, but she was still terrified of Warren finding out.

241

Warren had seen David's appeal in the newspaper for information about his sister, and also seen that David was returning to live at Bannerman's. Marnie was still avidly researching her family tree, and still harping on about David being her brother, so he'd decided to make the journey with her and check the story out for the peace of mind of them both.

She'd protested against it at first, but then her curiosity had got the better of her and she'd agreed. She was still very keen to meet the brother she'd never met, although slightly less keen to come face to face with Cyril again.

David indicated for them to sit down, but didn't offer to take their coats. It would be much easier to get rid of them if he didn't like what he was hearing and asked them to leave.

'Thank you,' Warren said, as they sat down on the sofa, Marnie alongside him – Anna perched on the arm of David's chair.

'My wife found out recently when her mother died that she had been adopted,' as Marnie reached in her handbag and handed the letter across to David, waiting while they both read it.

He read it twice before handing it back, an uncomfortable and intuitive feeling creeping over him. The letter said the woman had had sex with someone at a student party, but she was so drunk, she couldn't remember who. Surely Marnie wasn't insinuating that his father had been the man in question. It sounded as if it could have been any one of the lads present, and possibly even more than one. The woman didn't know who he was at the time, so how could his identity have come to light so many years later. It was signed by a Celia West, but David had never heard the name before.

'As a result of this, my wife took a DNA test and started researching her mother online,' Warren continued. 'She found out quite a bit of information about Celia and her parents. It seems they were a middle class family from Cheshire, but we won't bore you with all the details. Then she took a look at possible DNA matches, and came across another woman also researching her own family tree, and the web site showed they were possible matches as first cousins.'

David was beginning to work out what the man was leading up to, and he wasn't feeling very comfortable with it.

'Would you like to continue?' Warren said, turning to Marnie.

Her face was flushed and she too was feeling uncomfortable, seeing the scepticism on David's face, as he sat forward on the sofa, waiting to hear more.

'The woman's name was Gaye Smith. I messaged her through the web site, but she's never replied. Does the name ring a bell with you?'

David said nothing for the moment before slowly nodding his head.

'Yes,' he said, after a short pause. 'She's the daughter of my dad's brother, but I don't have any contact with her now. I haven't seen her in years.'

In fact, he hadn't seen her since her wedding just before he'd been accepted for university, and he'd gone to it under protest. They hadn't seen each other since they'd played together as children on the odd occasions when Randolph's family had visited Bannerman's, but as his father explained, the invitation was for the whole family, and it would seem churlish to refuse.

Marnie was brimming with excitement now, but she mustn't rush things. She must let David reach his own conclusions.

'Your father had two brothers didn't he?' Marnie said, trying to tease him into reaching his own conclusion.

'Yes, he had another brother besides Gaye's father, but blowed if I can remember his name. He went abroad many years ago, before I was born, and I don't think there was any correspondence between them; at least, none that I ever knew about. I don't think we ever had a Christmas card from him either.'

'Do you have a laptop, and I'll show you the family tree,' Marnie said, now that he seemed to be taking an interest.

Reaching down to the side of the chair, David lifted it up and opened it, before handing it to her and waiting for her to log into the web site.

Bringing it up, she handed it back to him to look at, where it showed his father's lineage, and the dates of death of his own three brothers, staying blank under his and Jayne's names; merely showing the colours denoting their sex – blue for male and pink for female.

She couldn't be the daughter of Randolph, as she and Gaye were shown to have partial familial DNA as cousins, so the only other possibility was Jacob. His line showed that he was already deceased, and showed only one descendent, delineated in blue as a male child. However, there was still that faint possibility that she could be Jacob's child, conceived at that same drunken party if he'd also been present, and before he left the country. He couldn't come to any conclusions on this evidence alone.

'I'll concede that this could be right,' he finally said after a quick glance at Anna – her face impassive, 'but what is it you want from me? There's no inheritance here for you to collect. When my father died everything here was willed to my sister Jayne, and I benefited very little from it.'

Marnie recoiled from his harsh words.

'**Is that what you think?**' she cried, '**that I'm just after the family fortune?**'

'Well, what else do you want then?' he answered as Anna put a restraining hand on his arm.

'**I want no money from you, all I wanted was to meet the brother and sister I've never known. It seems I shouldn't have bothered!**'

With that she stood up to leave. Her anger was fast receding and her eyes brimming with tears; which she was finding it hard to hold back.

'Come on Warren, let's go!' she said, walking towards the door; Warren getting up to follow. 'I should have known they wouldn't want to know me. He thinks I'm just after money!'

As she walked towards the door, intent on leaving as fast as she could, Anna stood up and barred her way.

'Marnie,' she said, 'let's not be too hasty. I'm sure David didn't mean to sound cruel. Perhaps we should talk this through a bit more before you leave,' glancing towards David, who'd also risen from his seat.

'I may have been a bit hasty,' he conceded. 'Won't you sit down again and I'll get Isabelle to bring us some tea while we talk it over a bit more?'

Marnie looked from one to the other as she saw Warren nod his head and begin to sit down again. She followed suit and sat down herself, taking out a handkerchief from her bag and blowing her nose.

Anna still stood as David left the room.

'I'm sorry if David was a bit harsh. As he said, his father left almost everything to his sister, and David is putting his own money into keeping the place afloat until she returns. It's quite a strain on him, and he's going to have to sell his own home in order to come and live back here and fund its running costs.'

Warren nodded.

'I understand,' he said, as Marnie tried to compose herself once more. 'I'm in business myself and I know just how hard it can be.'

While they were awaiting David's return Anna asked about his business, and was quite enthralled on hearing of the success Warren had made of it from virtually nothing.

David returned some while later, bearing four mugs of tea, a sugar bowl and a jug of milk on a tray.

'I hope you don't mind it this way, but I didn't want the staff involved in what we were talking about. I'd rather keep them out of it, at least for the time being; although I'm sure Isabelle was anxious to bring it in herself and find out who you are.'

This brought a smile to all their faces as David set the tray on the table, and Anna handed round the mugs – Marnie by this time having had time to compose herself and wipe her eyes – although she'd left smudges of mascara to the sides and beneath them both.

Anna told him about Warren's business in Chester, and David was intrigued. He hadn't yet managed to buy an engagement ring for Anna, and an idea was forming in his mind. Perhaps she'd enjoy having a custom made piece to her own design, and as long as it wasn't too expensive, he could probably afford it – but it would have to wait until his own house was sold. In fact, all the non-essentials would have to suffer the same fate for the time being.

After they'd finished their tea, and Anna had gone back for refills, bringing back with her a plate of Isabelle's home-made biscuits, they found they were all getting on well together, and even David seemed to be taking an interest in whether Marnie might well be his sister.

It was only after they'd gone, over an hour later, that David realised the time.

'I was hoping to be on the way home by now,' he said.

'You said,' she answered, 'but I'm glad we met them. I found them a really nice couple, and I did notice there was a slight facial resemblance between you and Marnie. While you were talking, I was able to study her face.'

David looked at her strangely.

'And just how many other look-alikes do I have out there? he asked. 'After seeing that notebook of my fathers', it looks like there could be many, many more. I hope the rest of them don't find their way to my door in the near future. Let's hope she'll be the last, and I hope she doesn't turn out to be a gold-digger!'

CHAPTER 25

David's week was a busy one and it was the following Saturday before he made his way to the estate agents to put his house on the market, being glad to hear that it was coming up to a favourable time of year for sales.

'People start looking round for properties when the weather starts to improve,' the agent told him, 'although it's coming up to February now, and that's not a good time at all. Still, it'll give you time to finish off any little jobs that need doing before a sale can be made.'

The sooner the better, David thought, as he left the office. His savings were rapidly dwindling, and if he didn't find a buyer very soon, he might have to abandon Bannerman's and let the staff go, awaiting whatever fate might befall it. At the end of the day, it didn't belong to him, and probably never would in his lifetime. The only tie he had to it was if Jayne were to return, but there'd still been no word from her, despite his repeated advertising for information.

A week later, two viewings were booked, and both on the same day. A good thing from both his and Anna's point of view, as it only meant one lot of cleaning and tidying up. Both couples seemed to like the house, but after another week had gone by with only one more viewing, he began to realise they weren't going to hear from either of them again. The third prospective buyer told him that the house was far too rural to be of any use, as they had a young family and they'd have to spend a lot of time ferrying them around.

After that, February came in like the proverbial lion, bringing with it snow, ice, gales and often torrential rain. No more viewings took place during that time, and David was getting more and more worried about his finances. He eventually came to a decision.

'Anna,' he said, as they sat in the cosy living room drinking coffee one Saturday morning, listening to the wind gusting outside and the rain battering on the window. 'I've decided to close up Little Bannerman and move back into Bannerman's itself. I just can't afford the upkeep of both.'

'But what about prospective buyers?' she asked, putting down the book she was reading, and uncurling her legs from beneath her.

'I'll hand the keys to the estate agents and they'll have to send someone out with the viewers. The upkeep of both is draining all my resources. There's nothing else I can do. Nobody's been to view the place for nearly a month now.'

She understood his predicament, but was powerless to help. She liked this house, and didn't really want to leave, but she knew Bannerman's meant a lot to him as his family home and he couldn't sell that either. If Jayne did return, she could claim her inheritance and their financial problems would all be over, but if she didn't, there was nothing he could do until she was officially declared dead.

From her point of view, she felt it would have been better to let the staff of Bannerman's go and hope to find another position, closing up the house and leaving it to its own devices, rather than bankrupt himself in trying to keep it going.

'All right,' she said, trying to sound as if she agreed with his decision. 'When were you thinking of making the move?'

'As soon as possible,' he replied. 'We'll make a start on having a clearout tomorrow if you've nothing else on.'

'So soon?'

'Why not? Seems as good a time as any. There's nothing else to do while the weather's like this,' as a gust of wind battered the rain against the window once more. They both realised from the sound that it wasn't just rain now, but hailstones.

She laughed.

'Okay – but why wait until tomorrow? Why not make a start this afternoon? Is there any reason not to?'

'Not on my part,' he answered. 'I was just planning an afternoon in front of the television. There's nothing better to do!'

'I'll make soup and sandwiches for lunch, and we'll start straight afterwards. There's nothing much in the small bedroom, so we could make a start by checking the other upstairs rooms and putting things in there that aren't really wanted.'

'Fine,' he said. 'Then tomorrow we could make a start on the downstairs. We don't use the dining room very often, so I'll push the table against the wall, and we'll put any junk we find in there.'

Then a thought entered her head.

'What happens if somebody wants to view the house?'

'Don't worry, I'll find a skip company on Monday and get them to drop one off as soon as possible. Once we've got rid of the junk, anything that's too good to throw out, I'll 'phone one of the charity organisations and see if they're interested. If not, I'll arrange a house clearance for anything we don't want to take with us.'

'Good idea,' she said. 'It's almost twelve o'clock, so I'll go and make those sandwiches and then we can get started.'

By four o'clock they were both tired, dirty, and in need of a rest.

Not knowing what he wanted to keep, and what not, she'd decided to work alongside him and ask his opinion when she wasn't sure if he wanted a certain item kept or not. Slowly but surely, the small bedroom was beginning to fill up with non-essentials.

'A lot of this furniture can go as well,' he said, when they'd finally decided to call it a day. 'There's plenty of furniture at Bannerman's, so we don't need half of this.'

249

'Aren't you burning your boats?' she asked, putting her hands on her hips and stretching her aching back. 'What if Jayne returns and decides she doesn't want you living there? Or worse still, if she decides to sell the place?'

'I don't think she'd turn me out,' he said. 'Jayne and I always got on well together. She always loved me and looked up to me as her big brother. Besides that, the house is plenty big enough to divide off into separate living and sleeping accommodation. We can live there without interfering with each other. I'm sure she'd agree to that.'

Never having met Jayne, she couldn't venture an opinion, but she hoped he was right. If his sister did decide to sell up, not only would he have to find them another place to live, but he'd have to fork out for all new furniture as well.

She could see all prospects for their own wedding day fading into the far distant future!

Within a fortnight they were ready to make the move, but there'd still been no more viewings of Little Bannerman, and both of them were beginning to get worried.

'Early days yet,' the estate agent assured them, 'and it only takes one. The very next viewing could just be that one. It's far too early to worry yet, and the peak viewing season will be starting soon. Spring's always a good time for sales.'

David had already advised the staff that they'd be moving into Bannerman's next weekend, and they'd all been busy cleaning and getting the place ready.

With Anna's agreement, he'd decided to move them into his parents' old bedroom. It was by far the biggest of the bedrooms, and still contained their big old four-poster bed. It also commanded the best view over the open moorland, with far reaching views toward the distant mountains.

The estate agent had informed them that the house would be far better with the furniture left in it, as viewers could picture their own furniture in situ if there were already some there from which to gauge. Anna had agreed wholeheartedly, worried that they may have to move back again, and with no furniture, with which David agreed in the end.

The staff all met them at the door, and Cyril helped carry their bags up to the big room, where Anna was delighted to find a vase of flowers sitting on the window ledge.

This could only be Cyril, she thought. Who else would have thought of such a welcome, and with such a homely touch! She must remember to thank him when they'd finished unpacking.

Isabelle too had done them proud! Lunch was served with roast lamb, mint sauce, roast potatoes, and three different veggies, followed by sherry trifle.

'That was much appreciated,' David told her when they'd finished eating, 'and just to thank you, you can all take the rest of the day off while Anna and I settle in. We won't need much this evening after that huge lunch, so we'll just make ourselves a sandwich and put our feet up later.'

After the effort they'd all put in getting the place ready for occupation once again, they were appreciative of the time to put their feet up; Isabelle electing for a few hours sleep during the afternoon. She wasn't getting any younger, and preparing the homecoming meal had taken more out of her than she cared to think.

With that in mind, she took a couple of pork pies from the larder and made up small lunch boxes for herself and Cyril – which also contained some crackers, a piece of cheese, and a banana. They already had a kettle, and all the necessaries for making drinks in their own rooms, so they needn't venture downstairs until the next morning.

Sandra had already left and gone home to her own family after the lunch dishes had been cleared, so David and Anna virtually had the whole of the house to themselves for the rest of the day.

CHAPTER 26

Next morning, David decided it was time to take a look around the property, and see if there was anything needed doing in the grounds.

Anna must have been tired after the move yesterday, and she was still asleep after he'd eaten his breakfast; resisting Isabelle's endearments to bacon, eggs, sausages and tomatoes, and eating just a couple of rounds of wholemeal toast and marmalade.

'You'll have me fat as a pig at this rate,' he chastised good naturedly. 'I'm still full after that lunch you provided yesterday. All we ate later was a bowl of cornflakes before going to bed.'

She smiled. Even though she'd slept for nearly two hours the previous afternoon, she'd still slept right through the night afterwards, barring the frequent visits to the toilet she made every night, which were increasing in frequency as she grew older. It made her morning a lot easier if she didn't have to provide cooked breakfasts every day for them, and would give her that extra few minutes in bed.

'Anna won't want anything much either,' he said, as he shrugged into a waterproof jacket and wellingtons hung on a rack alongside the back door. 'She only ever eats cereal or toast in a morning, and she's usually up well before this. She must be tired after the move yesterday. I've left her to sleep a bit longer.'

Outside the back door, he stopped to look around. Everything was as it had always been, and nothing seemed to have changed much during his long absence.

The morning was bright, and a weak watery sun was shining, but there was no warmth in it, as there was a cool breeze blowing.

The raucous cries of the jackdaws and crows sounded high in the treetops at the back of the house, as they always had during his boyhood.

As his eyes travelled upwards towards the sounds, he espied the roof of the new shed, his attention caught by the waving tree branches around it, and wondered if it had suffered any damage during the winter storms.

It looked intact when he checked, and seemed to have suffered no apparent damage. He hadn't brought the key to check inside, but as they'd already taken the notebook back to the house, there seemed little reason to go inside again.

It was then that he thought about the fountain at the front of the house. Soil was already being taken from it last time they'd been here, and he wondered if it might have been cleared completely by now. They'd driven past it yesterday, and his car was still parked between it and the house, but with all the palaver of the move, he hadn't really noticed it.

Striding back down to the house again, he walked round the side nearest the woods, checking for damage there as he passed – but then he didn't really need to bother with that again. It no longer belonged to him. All the papers for the transfer of ownership to Gavin had already been signed, and the deal completed. It was in Gavin's own interests to keep the whole area in shipshape fashion from now on, and the nearest trees were too far from the house to cause any damage, even in the fiercest of storms.

Reaching the fountain, he looked over the rim and into the base of the former fish pond, seeing that almost half the soil had been removed.

'Soon all be cleared now t'weather's improving,' he heard a voice from behind him say. 'It's bin too wet during t'last month, but there's a lot of folk interested – should all be gone soon.'

David turned to find Gavin striding towards him from the track leading to what was now his own cottage.

It was quite some time since he'd last seen him, and he grinned, holding out his hand to shake the other man's.

'Long time no see,' he said. 'It's good to be back again and to see all the old familiar faces once more. Even though I've lived at Little Bannerman for so long, I still think of this place as my real home.'

Gavin's face turned grim.

'It's a shame you 'ad that terrible row with your father,' he said, 'otherwise he'd prob'bly 'ave left this place to yew and not to Jayne, an' then yew'd 'ave the money to run it and pay wages as well.'

He was treading carefully now, trying to find out a reason for the row, but he should have known better than to think David would give him one. He was, after all, a barrister, and well used to keeping things up his sleeve.

'All water under the bridge,' David said noncommittally, staring into the interior of the large circular area, where he hoped to have fish swimming around again soon – that's if he could offload Little Bannerman in the not too distant future. It would be nice to see it up and running during the coming summer months. He longed to show it to Anna in all its former glory, with the sun playing on the water as it jetted high into the air from the centre of the sculpted shell; the droplets shining with a myriad of colours as they fell back onto the sparkling surface of the water.

Then, changing the subject completely, he turned and sat down on the edge of the rim.

'How are you finding it owning your own home, and running your own piece of land these days?'

Gavin moved towards him and sat down a few feet away, still keeping a respectful distance from David; still treating him as his employer, and not as his equal.

'Owning t'cottage 'asn't made much difference to us, but not 'aving to pay rent on it any more, 'as. Woodland 'as made a difference though. We've 'ad a lot of damage during the winter storms, and me and Morgan 'ave been chopping up and selling fallen branches for firewood, and it's been quite a good little earner – although I've also filled up the wood shed for yewr use as well. I'll do that for yew while you're 'ere.'

'Thank you, but there's no need to do that. I'll pay you for it from now on.'

Gavin looked at him and grinned.

'No need,' he said. 'It wasn't all from owr woodland – there was plenty of it in yewr own grounds as well, and most of what's in the shed is from yewr own land anyway. You still pay my wages, so collecting it is all part of my job.'

Before David could say anything more, they both spotted Anna coming round the side of the house.

'There you are,' she said. 'Isabelle said you went out of the back door, so I've been looking for you round there.'

'Come and join us,' David called. 'We're only having a chat.'

'I was hoping to go for a bit of a walk,' she said, coming over. 'It's a nice day, and it'd be nice to enjoy a moor land walk.'

'Suits me,' David replied, standing up and turning towards Gavin. 'We'll catch up again later.'

Gavin inclined his head.

'I've plenty to get on with,' he said, standing and turning towards the pond. 'There's somebody else coming to take some soil in about 'alf an hour, so I'll just sweep up some of the fallen leaves and branches from arownd the 'ouse while I'm waiting.'

'Okay, see you later,' David said, as he and Anna started out on their walk, turning first towards the path through the woods.

It was almost three hours later before they returned.

The sun had become warmer as the day progressed, and the temperature had gone up – but both knew that it was still early in the year, and it would soon go cold when the sun began to go down.

They'd rambled some of the pathways David remembered from his youth, and he'd found a long forgotten one down to a little stream. He remembered it as somewhere he used to jump across, and then straddle, whilst he lifted Jayne across. She was only a toddler, and could never have managed to get across on her own, as he looked back on those days with fond memories.

Now, it was no longer a little stream. He'd never been here since returning from university, and during the intervening years, it had become much wider – the water flowing faster and more ferociously.

Whilst they stood watching it, he told Anna about him and Jayne jumping across and she laughed.

'Well, there's no way I'm chancing it now. You can if you like – I'll watch! I can have a good laugh when you fall in!'

He gave her a wry look.

'You would too, wouldn't you?'

Giving a little laugh she skittered back away from the waters' edge and out of arms' reach, where he turned and chased her back up to the path they'd just left.

'Well, that's enough of that for today,' he laughed as he caught her and pulled her into his arms, 'I'm not getting any younger, and that's certainly made me feel my age.'

'Let's sit down on those rocks over there and get our breath back,' she said, pulling away from him and taking his hand as she led him towards them, 'then I think we should be heading back.'

'Tell me some more of your relationship with your family, and the things you did together,' she said, as she sat down close to him.

'There's not much to tell about what we did as a family. When I was little and I had my brothers around me, mother often brought us out for rambles and picnics, but she became less interested in those sorts of activities when they all began to die one after the other. She changed completely and became more introverted. Then things changed again when Jayne came along. It was as if a spark had come back into her life – as if she'd been given something to live for once more; but by then, I was older and less inclined to want to join in with anything like that. I had my own friends, and although I did bring Jayne out here to get her away from the house for a bit, it wasn't very often.'

'And what about your father? You haven't mentioned him. Did he never join in?' she asked.

'Nah, he never showed any interest in joining us. I always thought it was because of the busy life he led, but now I'm not so sure after finding that notebook. I'm beginning to wonder exactly what he was doing while we were all away from home.'

After a brief pause he continued.

'He did show more of an interest in Jayne when she came along though. It was as if he'd been waiting for a girl child all along, and he was always lifting her onto his knee and cuddling her.'

He seemed to be worried by his thoughts now, and Anna said nothing for a few moments, before jumping up and pulling him to his feet as well. Maybe he was worried by his troubled past and was regretting things that had happened between him and his father. Things couldn't be changed now though, there was only the future to look forward to.

'Come on, it's time we were getting back. Isabelle will already have a meal on and I'm beginning to feel hungry.'

He stood and she linked her arm through his, trying to take his mind off anything that he might be brooding on. Whatever it was, there was no going back and it would be as well to try and help him put it all behind him and forget his father's disinterest and apparent aggressive attitude towards him.

On the walk back, she tried to bring him out of his mood by talking about other things, and what they'd do in the future now that they were living at Bannerman's. He seemed to be interested in her plans for the future, but she could still feel that little pang of regret for his father's attitude towards him. Her own father had always been a caring and loving parent, seeming to live for nothing more than to see his family happy and enjoying life.

They retraced the route by which they'd come, and it was just after they'd left the woodland behind and were coming in sight of the house that they noticed activity around the front entrance, which seemed to be centred around the fish pond.

There were two police cars parked at the front – one at the end of the driveway – its uniformed driver standing at its side and barring access to any unauthorised entry – and the other parked closer to the central structure, where several people were milling around.

Right next to the broken down wall was parked a 4x4, its trailer backed close up to the opening. It was already part filled with soil, and a spade was propped against the side of the stone rim.

Standing talking to someone wearing a suit, topped with a fur collared jacket, was Gavin, seeming distraught. Another uniformed officer stood on the doorstep, talking to Cyril – Isabelle joining them just at that same moment.

Even as they watched, a van came up the driveway, and the uniformed officer stood to one side to let it pass, where it stopped some distance from the fish pond.

The couple had been mesmerised at the sight before them, but the arrival of the van seemed to spur David into action. Without a word he began to hurry forward towards the house, all thought of Anna seeming to go from his head.

She followed at a quick pace, but didn't run, knowing whatever had happened, it was something David needed to help with, not her.

Gavin noticed his approach over the shoulder of the man in front of him and after a few quick words, moved forward to intercept his employer – the other man saying nothing, but also turning to see who it was approaching.

'What's happened?' David said breathlessly as he and Gavin met.

'David, I'm sorry, but there's bin a discovery in fishpond.'

Then turning towards the other man, he said, 'This is my employer, David Bannerman, an' he's just returned to live 'ere this weekend. Can yew give me a few moments to explain things to 'im?'

258

The man nodded his head, but stayed within earshot, as several people climbed from the van and opened the back, beginning to don white coveralls and boots.

Gavin ushered David out of their way, the other man following but keeping his distance.

'Do yew remember when you left I told yew someone was coming to pick up some topsoil?'

David nodded just as Anna arrived and stood by his side.

'Yes, I remember. Is that him?' nodding towards the 4x4 and the man still sitting in the driving seat.

'Yeh,' Gavin replied. 'I 'ad intended to give 'im an 'and, but he'd started before I go' my spade. When I go' back, 'e wuz standin' lookin' puzzled, an' when I asked him what was up, 'e showed me the end of a rolled up carpet sticking out of the soil. 'e asked me why somebody would have pur it in there, bu' I knew nothin' about it. I don't ever remember seein' tha' carpet before.'

'Okay, get to the point,' David said almost angrily. 'Why call the police?'

By this time, David was beginning to have horrible suspicions about what he was going to disclose next.

'I uncovered more of the carpet to see if I reco'nised where it had come from, bu' when I did, part of the end unrolled itself, and there was somethin' inside.'

'What?'

David was now getting really anxious, as Gavin seemed more and more anxious himself as to what he was about to reveal.

Suddenly, after a large intake of breath, Gavin decided not to beat about the bush any more, and came straight out with it.

'There was an 'uman foot inside it, an' part of a leg. I think there might 'ave been an 'ole body inside as well, but we both stopped and just stared at it. We didn't know what to do, before we decided we needed to call the police. 'oever it was couldn' 'ave buried themselves; so somebody else must 'ave done it.'

David wasn't as shocked as he might have been. His thoughts had been leading him down that path ever since the moment

259

Gavin told him about discovering the buried carpet. Why would somebody have buried an old carpet under a mound of soil unless there was some reason to hide it? Whoever it was who'd buried it there was disposing of a body and not just a carpet!

As David hurried past Gavin to take a look for himself, the other man followed; eager to see his reaction when he saw the remains buried there.

David looked over the rim and stared into the bottom of the stone structure, his eyes taking in the unfurled end of carpet, and the partly mummified foot and lower leg. The carpet had been placed right on the base of the pond, and covered over with soil later.

'Do you recognise the carpet?' a voice said from one side of him.

After a few minutes hesitation, he looked round. It was the man with the fur collared jacket, and he was waiting for an answer.

'And you are?' David asked, knowing without doubt that he must be a police officer.

'I'm Inspector McDonald, and I'm investigating this case,' taking out his identification and holding it in front of David, before pocketing it once more. 'Do you recognise anything here?'

The foot and leg were without any form of clothing to identify its gender, but David had immediately recognised the carpet from where it had become unrolled.

'The carpet came out of my father's old shed,' he said. 'We used to sit on it when we sneaked in there for a crafty cigarette or to drink some cheap cider when we were kids.'

'And where is this shed?' was the next question.

'Long gone! There's a new one in its place now, and all the junk that lived in the old one is long gone too. I have the key to the new one if you want to look inside.'

'I'll collect that later if you'll have it ready. Do you know when it was replaced?'

'I've no idea. My father and I fell out years ago and I left home for good. I haven't been back since then until I heard of my fathers' death. You do know who he was, don't you?'

The Inspector answered in the affirmative, wondering if David was asking for preferential treatment just because of who his father was. The old trick of trying to pull rank! Not that he'd let that prevent him from doing his job!

'Do you know whether the body's male or female yet?' David asked.

'Not yet,' was the slightly acerbic reply. 'As you should know,' the Inspector insinuated, letting him know he knew he was a barrister, 'we won't touch anything until the pathologist has had a good look at the body and it's been removed for post mortem. Then the SOCO's have to photograph and preserve any evidence there may be. It'll probably be a couple of days before we have any more information to give you. In the meantime, would you mind going back into the house while the SOCO's get to work and I'll come and find you later for a statement.'

David had almost forgotten about Anna until he felt her touch his arm.

'Come into the house,' she said, 'there's nothing more we can do here, and the police need to get on with their work.'

He allowed her to guide him back through the front door, where Cyril was ready to take his coat and boots back to the kitchen.

'It's been a terrible shock to all of us,' he said. 'Do you have any idea who it might be?'

David said nothing for the moment as he shook his head and walked over to the living room in his stocking feet, sitting down in an armchair and staring into space.

Anna and Cyril looked at each other.

'Get Isabelle to make him some tea would you – he's had an awful shock. I'll sit with him for a while.'

Cyril nodded and went back to the kitchen, while Anna perched on the arm of David's chair, putting her arm round his shoulders and trying to give him some comfort. She didn't speak and they

261

both sat like that until Cyril arrived back with two mugs of tea for them.

'Thought you could do with one too,' he said, putting David's down on a little side table next to his chair, and handing Anna hers.

It was only after Cyril had been gone for a few minutes that Anna said, 'Drink your tea David. It'll help.'

He still sat, saying nothing, and she reached over for his mug and handed it to him, giving him no alternative but to take it from her.

It was only after he'd drunk almost half the mugful that he seemed to rouse his senses, and he looked up at her with soulful eyes.

'You don't think its Jayne, do you?' he finally said in a small voice.

That very same thought had been playing around in her head, although she would never have voiced that thought if he hadn't.

'I've no idea,' she said, after a pause. 'Let's not speculate for the moment. The police investigation will soon tell us if it is or not.'

CHAPTER 27

Gaye Smith was in a quandary.

She'd had yet another message from Marnie Peters via the website asking if she'd received her previous message about their being cousins, and requesting more information from her.

It wasn't the first message she'd had from people claiming to be related, and unless she had more information to make sure they were definitely genuine, she made it a rule never to reply. This woman, however, could give her no such information. All she had to go on was a DNA match, and although she'd checked out Marnie's own family tree, there seemed to be no tie-in with her own.

Marnie's mother was called Celia West, and Gaye had never heard that name mentioned in her family before, so she'd more or less forgotten the previous message she'd received when the next one arrived.

This one said she'd been in contact with David Bannerman, and he'd accepted her as a genuine relation, but her quandary stemmed from an article she'd just read in Royston's morning paper.

She needed to contact her cousin David to make sure Marnie wasn't telling her porkie pies, and to check out what she was saying was true; although she could think of no reason why she should want to do that. What could she possibly hope to gain by it?

The article in that mornings' paper had come as a complete shock to her. It showed that a body had just been found at Bannerman's. The family must be in turmoil at this moment in time, so there was no way she could bring this trivial matter to his attention right now.

'You've been staring at that screen for ages now. What's the problem?' Royston's voice broke in on her thoughts.

'Mmm. . .?' her train of thought broken. 'Oh, it's this woman online. She's taken a DNA test and she claims to be related to me.'

'Well, what's the problem?' he asked. 'She either is or she isn't! Do you know her?'

'No, I've never heard her name before.'

'Is there anyone you can check with?'

'Yes, there is. She seems to think my cousin David is her step brother, and he's accepted that after she went to visit him, but I can't get in touch with him now after what's happened at Bannerman's, can I?'

Having read the article himself that morning, and brought it to her attention, he knew just what she was alluding to.

'No. I doubt he'd be pleased if you bother him with that now! Leave it for the time being. You can always go back to it later if you decide to. It's hardly anything of importance at this very moment, is it?'

She agreed and closed down the website, deciding there were other more important things to think about now – such as checking the pie she'd left in the oven. She could already smell it, and hurried to the kitchen before it decided to burn to a crisp.

Several hours later, just after they'd finished their evening meal and settled down to watch some television, the 'phone began to ring.

Royston, thinking it was probably for him, as it usually was, got up to answer.

Being the manager of a country hotel could be a bind at times, even though he enjoyed the work. There were always problems cropping up; and 'phone calls, even when he was off duty, often interrupted his home life.

He dealt with the call – as usual, something and nothing, but just as he walked away from it, it began to ring again.

What now? Surely not somebody else with a trivial problem so soon after he'd dealt with the first!

Heaving a sigh, he turned back to answer; but this time it wasn't from the hotel. The voice on the other end turned out to be Gaye's mother, Rose.

'Is Gaye there?' she asked.

'Hang on a minute. I'll just get her,' he said, and put the receiver down while he went to fetch her.

'It's your mother,' he said, flopping back into the armchair he'd just vacated.

Always pleased to hear her voice, Gaye hurried into the hallway to speak to her.

Her mother and father owned the hotel where Royston worked, and they lived in their own suite of rooms on the top floor, although, now partially retired, they left most of the day to day running to her and Royston, where she ran the reception and the housekeeping side of things.

'Hello mother,' she said guardedly; not knowing whether a problem might have cropped up at the hotel that she needed help with.

'Hello Gaye,' her mother answered. 'Your dad and I were out most of today and we didn't see you before you left this evening. Everything okay at work?'

'Yes. For once things went smoothly all day and there were no complications. Did you enjoy your day out?'

'Yes, we went to visit friends for lunch, and we didn't get away until after six o'clock. You remember them don't you, Rita and Mark, live in the old manor house near Broxton? She breeds bull mastiffs in the stable block at the back? She's got ten of them now.'

Gaye did remember, and said so, although she hadn't seen them for several years now.

'Well, I was just checking in to make sure everything went all right today, so I won't keep you. I believe you took a booking today for a diplomat and his wife from America.'

'Yes, I did, but they're only staying two nights before going down to London.'

'I hope you gave them the best room, did you?'

'Not just a room mother, they took the Magnum Suite. It hasn't been occupied for a while; it's too expensive for most people, but the price didn't seem to bother him, and he agreed immediately to take it.'

'Good. We could do with a few more bookings like that to bring in the extra cash. Make sure he has everything he needs and he may pass the word around when he gets back to America. More like him are what we always need.'

'Don't worry, mother. I'm already on it. I've arranged a team to go over it first thing tomorrow and make sure everything's spick and span for them. I know the importance of a booking like this. People like that don't come along very often with cash to splash.'

'Yes, I know you'll make sure everything's just right. When your grandfather first bought the hotel and had it done up, he insisted on having two suites like that. He said, even though they wouldn't be occupied that often, they'd be money spinners when they were.'

It was at the mention of her grandfather and of past happenings that brought her mind back to the messages she'd had from Marnie.

'Mother,' she said, 'you don't happen to know a Marnie Peters do you?'

'No, who is she?' Rose's answer was almost instantaneous.

'She's contacted me a couple of times online just recently. She claims to be a daughter of dad's brother, Hector.'

'Hector? She can't be. Hector had four boys, three of them dead now. There's only the one girl, and she's called Jayne, not Marnie.'

266

'That's what I thought,' Gaye sighed.

'What makes her think Hector's her father?' Rose queried.

'She's taken a DNA test and it's shown she's related to me as a first cousin.'

'Mmm...!' Rose sighed contemplatively. 'Come and see me tomorrow when you have time for a quick coffee. I'll be home all day. Your father's out tomorrow so I want to get on with the new curtains I'm making for our bedroom.'

'Will do,' Gaye replied and replaced the receiver.

Rose stood thinking for a few moments after the call ended; the receiver still in her hand.

Hector had always been a randy old dog, every since she'd first met him. Her husband, Randolph, had often told her tales of Hector's exploits whilst at university, and how many metaphorical notches he had on his bedpost.

It would be no surprise if this Marnie did indeed turn out to be his daughter – and maybe there'd be more than one illegitimacy of his coming to the surface after news of his death began to circulate. There'd always be someone looking to share a piece of the pie, and they all knew he'd been an extremely rich man.

After a while, the alarm made by the 'phone alerted her to the fact that she was still holding it, and brought her back to reality – at first wondering why it was still in her hand. Laughing to herself at her own stupidity, she put it down just as Randolph entered the room.

'Been on the 'phone?' he asked.

'Yes, I just gave Gaye a ring to make sure everything was okay while we were out today.'

'And was it?'

She nodded.

'It went really well. That American diplomat who rang last week has booked the Magnum Suite – but it's only for two nights. He's leaving for London after that.'

He looked suitably impressed.

'Maybe he'll stay over again when he comes back. With any luck, we may get another couple of nights out of him.'

She smiled as she sat down and picked up her sewing again. The curtains were turning out to be a bigger job than she'd expected, and tacking the hems in position before stitching them on the sewing machine was turning into an arduous task.

The next afternoon, Gaye found herself with some time on her hands after the lunchtime servings had all been finished and the tables prepared for the evening meals.

Ringing the extension to her mother's apartment, she was answered almost immediately.

'You free for that coffee now? I've got an hour before I'm likely to be needed again.'

'Yes, come on up. I'll get the percolator on.'

Her parents' apartment was up on the fourth floor, but instead of using the lift, she used the stairs instead. Even though she was on her feet nearly all day, she felt the exercise did her good.

The door was already standing open when she reached it.

'It's only me,' she called as she went inside.

'Come right in. I'm in the kitchen,' the familiar voice called back.

Shutting the door behind her, she made her way across the spacious living room looking out over the manicured lawns and shrubs on the south side of the property, and entered through the open door into the kitchen.

This room faced south west, and the sun was just beginning to stream in through the two long windows facing onto the shrubbery and the woodland walk.

The shrubbery, containing rhododendrons, choysia, and amalenchier, had all been the choice of her husband and provided a mass of flowers in the springtime, followed by numerous summer flowering plants in the rear garden; but the woodland beyond was by courtesy of their neighbour. It was entered via a gate at the back of the shrubbery with his prior agreement, and covered an area of almost three acres. The hotel guests could stroll through there when the weather was too hot to sit out around the open lawn; the tranquillity of the native British trees offering cooling shade, where they often saw Fallow, or Pere David Deer within their confines, which their neighbour kept as part of a breeding programme.

'Sit down, dear. Coffee's ready,' Rose said, putting two steaming cups on the table while she fetched some shortbread biscuits from the cupboard.

'These are homemade – courtesy of Rita. I think she intended them for afternoon coffee, but there was so much lunch, we couldn't eat more than one each, so she gave me some to bring home.'

Gaye herself had only just finished her own lunch, but she took one just to be sociable.

'Nice,' she said, licking her fingers, 'but I'm afraid I can't manage any more. Chef had some pheasant left over after service was finished, so I had that with a couple of roasties and veg., and all done with a rich wine sauce. I'm really stuffed.'

'You should have told us. We could have helped out,' Rose laughed. 'We just had sardines on toast. Anyway, enough about food – you wanted to talk about this woman who's been messaging you.'

'Yes,' Gaye said, putting down her cup. 'As I told you, she claims to be Uncle Hector's daughter.'

'And do you think she could be?'

Gaye looked a little shocked as her mother continued.

'How old is she?'

'I didn't ask. She says she didn't know she was adopted until after her mother died. She found a letter written by a Celia West, claiming to be her birth mother . . . .'

She tailed off as she saw the look on her mothers' face.

'What is it?' she asked.

Her mothers' face had gone pale, as she sat down again, almost dropping the box of biscuits she was about to put back in the cupboard.

'Did you know her?'

This time there was a nod and a short pause before she spoke.

'Yes, I knew Celia. We were at school together. We were in the same class and we were friends for a while.'

Taken aback, Gaye sat for a moment without saying anything.

'And did she have an illegitimate baby?' she asked, her voice quiet.

'Yes, she did,' Rose replied. 'And I remember the terrible time she had with her parents. She wanted to keep the child – a little girl, but they wouldn't hear of it, especially her father. An illegitimate child was considered a sin in those days, and he was adamant that she had to have it adopted, although I think her mother would have relented given time.'

Another pause before Gaye tried to persuade her to finish the story.

'And what happened then?' she cajoled.

'I never knew. She dropped out of university, and she didn't contact me for some time. The next time I saw her, she didn't have the baby any more and she refused to talk about it when I asked. I never knew what happened to it, or what sex it was, so this Marnie Peters could very well be her. She'd have to be around fifty years old by now if she is Celia's baby.'

'And was it the same university that Hector was at?'

Her mother nodded.

'Yes, I think it was, although I don't know whether they ever knew each other. Life rather got in the way after that, and we didn't see much of Hector or his family very often. My grandfather died and mum and dad took over the hotel. I was in my early twenties at the time, and I came to work with them and help out. That's where I met your father. He'd already been the manager of another hotel that closed down, and he was taken on as manager here about a year later.

'And what happened to Celia. Did you remain friends?'

'No, we completely lost touch after that. I never heard from her again.'

This information, although she was interested to learn about her mothers' past, was rather digressing from what she'd really come to talk about. She didn't have much time left, so she needed to steer the conversation back to Marnie Peters.

'So do you think I ought to correspond with this woman or not?'

'I don't know what harm it can do, but try and get more info from her without telling her anything about yourself. Let her tell her story and then, when things calm down at Bannerman's, you can check your story with that she's given to David.'

Gaye thought for a moment before accepting what her mother had said. What harm could it do? The more information she could wheedle out of Marnie the better; then she could check the story with David at a later date – and perhaps find out more information about the body that had been found on his property as well!

CHAPTER 28

The police asked David to have the house vacated for the next couple of days while investigations were carried out.

He and Anna went to a local farm, which provided bed and breakfast accommodation, but Gavin and Megan offered to put Cyril and Isabelle up for the time being.

David was pleased at not having to pay for rooms for them both, and Gavin refused to take any money for their impromptu stopover.

'Yew've been very good to me, David,' he said when his employer offered to pay for their keep. 'I's the least I can do for yew by way of recompense. Some of t'rent money I would have still been payin' yew will well cover their keep for the next coup'la days.'

Morgan relinquished his bed to Isabelle and made use of an old camp bed they still had tucked away in a lean-to they'd put up at the side of the main house, whilst Cyril slept on the sofa. It wasn't the best of accommodation for either man, but it only turned out to be for two nights, and they were able to manage reasonably well for that short period of time.

Turmoil had raged for days at Bannerman's with civilian and police personnel coming and going day after day, and even after they were allowed to move back in, numerous questions kept being asked. Each person who came along seemed not to have had the required information from those who'd come before them, and they were asked to go over and over their stories time after time.

Ultimately, there was nothing much any of them could add to the previous information they'd already given, and finally, when their stories tallied almost completely, and when there was nothing more to elicit from them, the police finally went away and left them alone for the time being.

The post mortem showed that her date of death more or less tallied with the time the alterations were done on the house, and Isabelle, Cyril and Sandra all told the same story. The judge had let them have time off while they were being carried out, during which time the fish pond had been filled in and was already full of soil when they returned – their stories all being corroborated by others who'd seen them or been with them while they were absent.

David and Anna also managed to account for most of their movements at the time; David having been present as counsel at the trial of a prolific burglar for almost the whole period in question. Anna's story was sketchier, as she, in her capacity as housekeeper, spent a lot of her time alone at Little Bannerman, but David confirmed that she was always there when he returned either at lunchtime, or in the evening with a meal ready and waiting. There were also receipts from shops in Denbigh which she had frequented during the time in question, and had meticulously documented for David's accounts system.

She too, even though there was the possibility of her having had the time and the opportunity to bury the body during that time, was ruled out of their list of suspects almost immediately.

They already knew just where the woman had met her death from forensic evidence, and were aware of how noisy that death probably would have been.

Even the burial itself would have been in full view at the front of the house, where the judge's bedroom overlooked the whole area.

If she did have the strength to haul a body, wrapped in a heavy piece of carpet over the stone parapet and dump it in the base; that still left her having to cover it with enough soil to hide it completely. Hector would surely have heard something if it was happening right under his window and in the dead of night.

The workmen would also have been in attendance during daytime, and they must have wondered how some of the soil had come to be loaded into the pond overnight. It would have taken some time to complete a task like that!

The only person left who could have had the opportunity to do all that overnight, and with no interruption, was Hector himself!

Pathology reports were now in, and they needed to speak to David and let him know their findings! He needed to know how the person had died, and perhaps he might be able to provide the why, once he found out the identity.

'Mr. Bannerman, this is Inspector McDonald,' the voice on the 'phone said. 'We now have some results from all the evidence taken and I need to come and see you. When would that be possible?'

'I can be here tomorrow if that suits,' David said, anxious to hear what he had to say. At least he wasn't going to be arrested; otherwise there wouldn't have been any warning. They'd just have turned up on his doorstep and marched him away.

The Inspector and a uniformed officer turned up just after eleven the next morning, and David was surprised to see the other man was the officer who'd informed him of his fathers' death, now learning that his name was Robbie Richards. David felt he knew him from somewhere, had done on their previous meeting, but couldn't remember from where.

Showing them into the living room, he called Anna downstairs to join them, where she'd just been making their bed.

'Please, do sit down,' he instructed as he joined the two men.

The Inspector inclined his head and did as instructed, whilst the uniformed officer remained standing, slightly to one side and to the rear of his superior.

David took a seat opposite and looked guardedly towards the Inspector, as Anna entered the room and perched on the arm of his chair, one arm laid across the back proprietarily. She was worried what his reaction would be if he found out that the body was that of his much loved little sister Jayne; which she'd been thinking for some time could be the case, and knew that it was also in the forefront of David's mind as well, although he'd never voiced that thought.

Once they were all settled, the Inspector brought out the clipboard he'd been carrying, and peeled back the top flap.

When he began to speak, his voice seemed loud in the quiet air of expectation that had settled over the room.

'First of all,' he said, 'let me put your mind at rest that the body we found was not that of your sister, Jayne Bannerman.'

Even though she wasn't actually touching David, Anna felt the breath he'd been holding leave his body, and felt him begin to relax perceptibly.

After a moments' pause, whilst letting David gather his thoughts together, the Inspector continued.

'We have, however, ascertained that the woman was a Noreen Wilkins. Do you know her by any chance?' lowering the clipboard and looking across at David, who thought for a moment. The name seemed familiar but he couldn't place her, or where he knew her from.

'The name seems familiar. Did she live around here?'

'She lived near Denbigh. She was the wife of a butcher running a farm shop from his home, where he sold his own lamb and pre-packed oven-ready chickens.'

Now David could place the name.

His father had often bought meat from her husband, and Cyril had been the one sent to fetch it from there. Although David had heard her name before, he'd never actually met her.

'Yes, now I know who she is,' going on to explain about his father buying meat from there, before continuing, 'Cyril may know more about them than me though. He was always the one who went to collect the order.'

'We'll speak to him later,' the Inspector continued, before referring to his clipboard once again.

Anxious to know more, David pursued with his own questions.

'Do you know why she was here, and how she came to die? Was she murdered?'

His previous anxiety had returned, as he realised the onus for her demise may inevitably fall upon his father.

The Inspector, however, wasn't to be hurried, as he held up a staying hand and continued to read through his notes.

Anna put a restraining hand on David's shoulder, feeling the tension building once again in his body. No matter how much they might have argued and been apart for so many years, the family bond was still strong. She knew he was worried that his father would turn out to be a murderer. Even if he was no longer around to stand trial, the stigmata would forever be on David's shoulders. People didn't forget things like that very easily! He might forever be known as the son of a murderer, which didn't bode well for an up and coming barrister!

With a slight clearing of the throat, the Inspector began speaking again.

'It seems most likely that her death occurred on the lower staircase, as our forensic results confirm. There are scuff marks on the wood at the sides, and on the slate flags at the bottom, where her body would have come to rest. There are also traces of blood on the flags, which somebody has attempted to clean up; and there is also a splinter of wood in the heel of her shoe which matches with a chip from a banister near the bottom.'

He stopped here, waiting for David to take it all in, whilst scrutinising his reactions; seeing nothing but puzzlement.

'She had a broken neck, and it seems highly likely that she fell from top to bottom of that flight. Do you have any idea why she might have been upstairs in your father's house?'

'I've already told you,' David sounded aggrieved, if not a little annoyed. 'I hadn't seen my father in years, and I've never been back to this house since the time we rowed and I left.'

'And what was that row about?'

'Nothing to do with anything that concerns this inquiry – it bears no relevance to your inquiries!'

'And if it bears no relevance, would you mind telling me just what it was about?'

The Inspector didn't seem inclined to let things drop. He seemed intent on finding out all he could, but David had vowed never to let anyone know what the row had been about.

'No, I'm not going to enlighten you about that. It was years before Noreen Wilkins' death, and can bear no relevance on this case.' He was determined to stand his ground.

'I see,' the Inspector answered, seeing that David was adamant.

David was a professional barrister, and it would do him no good to try and pursue that line of questioning once the man had made up his mind it had no bearing, which he knew he probably wouldn't divulge even under rigorous questioning. There was absolutely no proof that it may have played any part in Noreen's death.

He put his papers away, before getting ready to leave. As David had said, the row could bring nothing further to bear on the case in question. It seemed clear that whether it might have been an accidental fall, or she'd been pushed down the stairs, nobody would ever know.

There'd been no evidence of any sort of trauma to the body, and no signs of a struggle or a fight at the top of the stairs or in the judge's bedroom, which was almost adjacent. The pathologist was adamant that the death had been caused entirely by the broken neck and the subsequent rupture of the spinal column.

Why she'd been upstairs in the house could only be pure speculation, but in his mind, there must have been something going on between her and the judge. No normal visitor would have needed to go upstairs in the house, especially as there was a cloakroom with a toilet downstairs.

There was only one more piece of information that he needed to impart to David, something that he hoped might bring about a reaction.

'By the way,' he said, as David opened the front door for him, 'the woman was also pregnant – about four months gone. DNA tests have proved that the baby was your fathers'. Do you think that might have been the reason why he found it necessary to bury her body?'

Stunned, David stopped and looked at him, before exchanging glances with Anna; which didn't go unnoticed. She merely shrugged her shoulders, as if she weren't at all surprised.

'You've seen that notebook of my fathers',' was David's only reply, as he turned to look at Inspector McDonald again. 'I think you can draw your own conclusions from that! There's nothing more I can add to that!'

The Inspector and the constable, Robbie Richards, arrived at the Wilkins' farm that afternoon, having stopped at the local shop to buy pies, which Robbie had assured him were very tasty, and made locally.

He wasn't wrong, and they'd both enjoyed them before carrying on to see James Wilkins, whom they found in the shop alongside the house. He'd just finished serving a customer and welcomed the newcomer with a smile, not seeing the uniformed officer standing outside the door ready to turn away any intrusion whilst the Inspector spoke to him.

'What can I do for you? I've some lamb steaks, or perhaps some nice chicken drumsticks might suit better,' he said, smiling genially and expecting to make another sale when the man entered.

'Sorry, I'm not here for that,' Angus announced, producing his warrant card and holding it up. 'I'm here to ask you a few questions.'

'About my wife?' the man said, the smile dying on his face. He'd already been informed of her death, and the manner in which she'd met it. He'd been expecting this call wouldn't be long in coming.

'You'd better come through to the house,' he said, going to the shop door to close it; Angus forestalling him and asking Robbie to come inside and accompany them. James closed it after him; at the same time turning over a sign that read: Please ring for attention, before leading them both through a door at the side of the counter.

They found themselves in a small room which contained four plastic chairs arranged around a table under the solitary window, and a rather ancient looking sofa along the wall opposite. Another wall next to the shop contained a sink and a shelf alongside, on which sat a tray containing four mugs and a kettle, as well as all the ingredients for making tea and coffee.

Closing the door to the shop, he indicated for them to sit on the sofa, whilst he himself pulled out a plastic chair from the table and sat down.

'What is it you want to ask me?' he said with a resigned look on his face, and a heavy sigh. 'I suppose you're wondering why I don't look more upset at hearing about her death.'

They had been wondering! Most men would have been very distraught under the same circumstances, but James Wilkins was showing no such signs.

'Let me first explain our living arrangements,' he continued before either could speak. 'My wife and I have been living under the same roof as a matter of convenience for many years now, and we haven't really had anything to do with each others' lives during that time. She goes – went – her way, and I went mine. The house has been practically split in two, and we each kept to our own half. I'm afraid I won't be able to tell you much about

279

how she lived her life. I work on the farm or in the butchery department all day and didn't see anything much of her. I knew she had a job, as she wasn't usually around during the day, but I know nothing about it or where it was.'

It didn't often happen that either man was taken aback with so many years experience of other peoples' lives and the way they led them, but neither knew what to say at that moment following his blunt statement about their living arrangements.

There was a pause before Robbie pulled himself together and was the first to speak.

'What about children?' he asked. 'Are there any? And are they still at home?'

'There are no children,' James answered rather curtly. 'We never had any. Noreen always wanted them, and we did try when we were first married, but it just didn't happen. None came along and she never got pregnant. For my own part, I never wanted any anyway, and her childless state suited me down to the ground.'

Robbie and his Inspector looked at each other, before Angus, his equilibrium now recovered, brought himself back to the task in hand.

'Would it surprise you to know that your wife was pregnant when she died? She was about four months gone,' he asked, hoping to provoke a reaction.

The man merely shrugged, although there was a slight hesitation beforehand; possibly because he was thinking now that he could have been the cause of her infertility and not her. Had he always thought of it as her fault and blamed her all along. Not many men liked to think that it was them that could be infertile, and usually didn't like to face up to the fact that it could be them to blame.

'As I've said, what she did was her own business, not mine. It worked both ways!' he continued, after a slight clearing of the throat.

'Aren't you interested to know whose baby it was?' the Inspector pursued.

'Not really,' he replied. 'As I've already said, what she did with her life was no business of mine. We were married in name only. We lived under the same roof as she was joint owner of the farm, and the arrangement was convenient for both of us.'

Angus looked at Robbie. The man obviously had no interest whatsoever in his deceased wife, and there was no use pursuing the matter any further, but as he picked up his clipboard ready to leave, Robbie put forward a question of his own.

'And didn't you wonder where she was when you didn't see her around for the last few months?'

James Wilkins seemed to notice him for the first time as he scrutinised him before replying.

'Can't say I did! As I've already told you, we lived completely separate lives and our paths didn't cross very often. We never spoke unless it was absolutely necessary, which wasn't very often either.'

'What about the household bills?' Robbie persisted, determined to get some sort of a rise out of the man.

'We had a holding account at the bank. We both had direct debits going from our own personal accounts into that to cover the household bills, and all payments were made from that by direct debit. Neither of us knew how much were in each others' personal accounts.'

As they re-entered the shop and James Wilkins went to open the door for them, his parting shot was, 'I'm sorry not to be able to help any further, but my girlfriend will be delighted to hear that she can move in here with me now. She was my wife's sister and she didn't want her to find out about our affair, so we can get married and she can leave her job at the pub now if she wants to.'

'It takes all sorts, doesn't it?' Angus said, as they walked back to the car. 'How the other half lives!! They've obviously been married a good few years. What a horrible way to exist – after all, you can't call it living, can you? It's no wonder she turned to somebody else, after she'd been married to such a callous man! The judge was years older than her, but maybe he'd been more like a father figure to her, and he **was** able to give her the baby she wanted. Maybe she and the judge had been planning to live together with a baby on the way – she had plenty of grounds for divorce. Maybe they might even have been planning to marry when it came through, but nobody will ever know now!'

'And have you ever thought that James Wilkins may just be the reason why the judge buried her body? A man like that would only be too happy to sully the judge's reputation by making known the fact that she'd fallen down the stairs from right outside his bedroom door, and that she was expecting his baby!' Robbie said, making a rueful face at his superior. 'Most people would reach the same conclusion that you and I have – that they were having an affair and she'd just been leaving his bedroom!'

CHAPTER 29

Marnie Peters was surprised when she opened her laptop and fired it up after their evening meal a couple of weeks later.

Her usual routine was to look through the e-mails first to see if there was anything interesting in them before checking out her Facebook page. There were the usual cajoling advertisements to place another order from them; some offering cash inducements if she bought before a certain date, and yet others asking for reviews on the products she'd already bought.

Most of these she deleted immediately, but one of those near the bottom informed her that there was a message for her on the genealogy website.

Quickly closing down the e-mails, she logged in to her own account and clicked on the icon for 'new messages', where she finally found the message she'd been hoping for. It was from Gaye Smith – it read:

I'm sorry not to have answered you sooner, but I've been making inquiries as to how we come to be related, and I think it's about time we met. Can you come to the Traveller's Hotel on Sunday afternoon next at around 4pm.'

The last few lines were taken up with directions and sat nav information. She'd already told the woman in previous messages roughly where she lived – after all, Gaye Smith could have lived the other end of the country as far as she was aware.

She found that the Traveller's Hotel was less than ten miles from her own home. Just to think, Gaye Smith must live close enough to her own location to even contemplate meeting there. Perhaps they could have been living close to each other for years and never known of each others' existence.

She was excited and wanted to tell Warren immediately, but as she got up to tell him, she remembered he was trying to complete the repair on a necklace which the customer was calling to collect next day. He'd been trying to get it finished all that day, but the shop had been busy and their assistant hadn't turned in, ringing in with the excuse of a stomach upset, so he'd spent most of that day helping in the shop. Her news would have to wait 'til he'd finished!

In the meantime, she looked for the website for the Travellers Hotel, finding it an old sandstone manor house in a small village off the main A41 just south of Chester.

It shouldn't take her long to reach it, and she decided she must go. She wasn't aware they were doing anything on Sunday, so she couldn't see any reason not to confirm the arrangement.

The message had come in that morning, so she replied straight away in the affirmative, hoping that Warren hadn't arranged anything in the meantime.

Just as she pressed the 'send' button, she heard Warren's voice behind her.

'I've finished it, but I'm tired. Whatsay we have some supper and an early night? It's been a busy day, and the takings look all the better for it.'

She smiled, and swivelling round in her chair she told him of the message from Gaye Smith.

'We haven't anything on on Sunday, have we? I didn't think we had, so I've already agreed to meet her.'

'Nothing as far as I'm concerned,' he said, 'but do you think it's wise to go on your own. Want me to come with you?'

'No, I'll be fine. I've looked the hotel up online and it looks like a nice place. Besides that, you'd be bored to tears listening to us talk about families. I know you're not as interested as I am.'

He put on a pained expression.

'I know when I'm not wanted,' he said, chuckling. 'Now, how about that supper? Any of that chocolate fudge cake left?'

'You shouldn't eat that sort of thing before you go to bed,' she chastised. 'It'll give you indigestion.'

'Bugger the indigestion! I'll face that when it comes. Now, is there any left or not?'

Sunday was a nice day, but there was a cool breeze blowing as Marnie turned into the Travellers Hotel car park, which was almost empty; three cars departing just as she arrived.

She'd chosen to wear a pair of black trousers and a dark blue polo neck jumper with a sequined butterfly on one shoulder. It didn't look too formal, but seemed just right for afternoon wear.

When she inquired for Gaye Smith at the desk, the receptionist seemed to be expecting her, and took her straight through the lounge and into a small booth situated in a bay window at the far end. It was slightly away from the other seating areas in the room, and provided a more intimate area where they could talk without being overheard.

'I'll just get her for you,' she said, turning on her heel and going back the way they'd come.

Within less than five minutes Gaye arrived, a welcoming smile on her face.

She was shorter than Marnie had expected, and she, at her five foot nine, seemed to tower over her. It never occurred to her at the time that she herself was taller than most women.

She was wearing a black pencil slim skirt and a red tailored jacket with a black blouse beneath.

'So nice to meet you,' she said as she slid into the window seat on the opposite side to her guest. The waitress will bring us some coffee in a moment – you do drink coffee, don't you?'

Marnie agreed that she did, and Gaye proceeded to open a folder that she carried with her, lifting out several sheets of paper and arranging them on the table in front of Marnie.

'I've printed off my family tree from the website to make it easier to check out the people named and the relationships, although I'm afraid there's no mention of your mother on it.'

'I didn't expect there to be,' Marnie said. 'I know my real mother was at university with your uncle, but the name of my father doesn't appear on my birth certificate either. That space was left blank. Until all this came to light, I'd never even heard the names Celia West or Hector Bannerman in my entire life, and I didn't even know I was adopted until my supposed mother died.'

'I'll leave you for a few moments to look through things while I go and see where that coffee's got to,' Gaye said, pushing the folder across to her while she left the table and headed for the door.

She was back almost immediately, followed closely by a man bearing a tray with two cups, a silver coffee pot, sugar, milk, and a plate of mixed types of biscuits.

Gaye slid back into her seat and the man put the tray on the table, before looking across at her, where Marnie saw him give a slight inquiring inclination of the head; returned by a nod from Gaye. He turned and smiled towards Marnie before leaving the room. Somehow, Marnie was aware that the two had known each other before today, but she said nothing about it, as Gaye began to fill the cups.

'Milk and sugar?' she inquired politely, as Marnie replied, 'Dash of milk and one sugar please.'

'Look,' Marnie said as she took a sip of the extremely hot coffee and replaced the cup on its saucer. 'We both know that this family tree means absolutely nothing to me. We both know

286

that I was the result of a binge drinking session at university, and that not even Celia herself knew for sure who my father was. What I'm really interested in is whether you can tell me anything about him, and whether you ever knew Celia.'

Gaye had already gone through the type of questions that might crop up in her mind, and knew she had to be very careful with the answers she gave. She didn't yet know what Marnie hoped to gain by her quest for knowledge of her parents, but as Hector had been an extremely wealthy man, she had to be very careful what knowledge she imparted.

'I'm afraid our families weren't really close and we didn't see very much of each other once we children began to grow up. Dad and uncle Hector led very different lives. When their parents died, Hector was the eldest and he inherited Bannerman's. My dad and Uncle Jacob received generous bequests, with which my father bought his present home. What Jacob did with his I never knew, as he was already living in Australia, and I'm afraid there's very little else I can add to that.'

During this discourse, neither had touched their coffee, and both reached for their cups at the same moment; smiling at each other as they recognised the similarity in their behaviour.

'And what about Celia? Did anybody in the family ever know her, or hear anything about her?' Marnie persisted.

'My mother knew her when they were at school, but they lost touch when Celia went to university. She did hear she was pregnant and that her parents had made her give the baby up, but she never knew anything more and she never had any further contact with her after that.'

Again it seemed to be a dead end. Nobody seemed to know anything further about her mother – but then, was there a great deal more to know? It had only been a few years later that Celia had died. Nobody seemed to know anything more about her, or what had happened to her after her baby was adopted in the intervening few years she had left. There seemed little to gain from pursuing the matter any further, but it would have been nice if the family had accepted her as one of their own. It would be comforting to know she had a brother and a sister to welcome her into the family, but who could blame them for not wanting to know her and the way in which she'd been conceived.

They drank some more coffee and she desultorily ate a couple of the biscuits just to be sociable, but all in all, the afternoon had been a big disappointment, and after a short chat about little in particular she took her leave of her so-called cousin. There really was nothing left to say to each other. It was time to go home and forget the whole episode.

Whatever she hoped to gain by it had not been forthcoming. Gaye had been friendly, but not over-enthusiastic at welcoming her into the family, and certainly had never been aware of her existence.

David had shown the same friendliness when she'd visited there too, but again, hadn't treated her as a long-lost sibling – step sibling – as she must now think of herself. Unwanted, and unaccepted as a member of the family was probably all that she'd remain.

She was totally unaware of how many other children there were around who'd been fathered by Hector Bannerman, and David and Anna were only too anxious to keep that knowledge a deep, dark secret; only hoping it wouldn't come to light as a result of the police investigations into Noreen Wilkins' death.

CHAPTER 30

As the spring arrived with a glorious beginning to the month of May, David was becoming more and more concerned about his finances, and the beautiful warm sunny weather could do nothing to allay his fears of impending doom.

Little Bannerman remained unsold, even though the agents kept assuring him that it would do very soon now that the weather was improving and more people were beginning to look around. They told him sales were increasing week on week.

The previous month, one of the national newspapers had taken an interest in his constant advertising for the return of his sister, and had written an article about his quest. He'd said nothing about the fact that she'd inherited her father's estate, and not himself, as everybody was bound to surmise. He merely informed them that he was concerned about her welfare and whether she'd come to any harm, but, without his prior knowledge they'd published an aerial picture of the house and the estate, something he hadn't envisaged them doing

The property wasn't named, but she was, and anybody who cared to look her up couldn't fail to find that she was the daughter of Judge Hector Bannerman, and that the estate was called Bannerman's.

The newspaper was inundated by people claiming to know where she was, none of which turned out to be of much use. One crank even rang on several occasions to say he'd seen her being abducted by men who bundled her into a spaceship and took her away to another planet.

All the letters received were passed on to David, as well as some of the e-mails that seemed remotely feasible, but at the end of the day, after the endless reading through of them by both he and Anna, none of them turned out to be of much use. They were back at the same place from where they'd started, and still with no positive news of where she might be.

It was at the end of that first week in May that David received the news he'd been dreading.

It was from his bank – telling him they'd noticed large amounts of money being taken from his account over the last few months, and wanting to check whether those amounts were legitimate or not.

Sadly, he had to admit that they were. He'd been paying not only the overheads for both Bannerman's and Little Bannerman ever since Christmas, but he'd been covering the wages of the staff as well, and even the £50,000 a year his father had left him was being swallowed up in the increased amount of money being paid out.

Adding to his worries, the end of the letter culminated with the bank offering to let him have overdraft facilities at what he considered an exorbitant rate of interest as a temporary measure.

He took the letter out to Anna, who had taken a lounger outside and was sitting on the lawn at the side of the fish pond, which still held neither soil nor water: the side of the parapet still not having been repaired. Finances wouldn't allow for that at the present time.

'Anna,' he said, as he waved the letter in front of her and sat down on the grass alongside. 'I've just had this letter from the bank.'

She took it from him and read through it before handing it back and looking at him seriously.

'I've been expecting this,' she said. 'I didn't know how much you were spending, and I didn't know just how much you had in the bank, but I realised how much the upkeep of this place and the staff wages must be costing you. What do you intend doing about it?'

He thought for a moment before she cut into his thoughts once more.

'As far as I can see, there's only one thing you can do, and I think you already know what that is!'

He looked at her, hoping she might have some sort of way of getting him out of his predicament without having to make the decision himself.

'You're going to have to let the staff go and walk away from Bannerman's. Close up the house and leave it to its own devices in the hope that Jayne comes back one day. We still have Little Bannerman to go back to, and we've always been happy there before. I can't see any other way out of this, and there's every possibility that Jayne may not still be alive after all this time,' her voice falling to no more than a hushed whisper as she made the suggestion. She knew it must obviously have been in the back of his mind as well. 'You've certainly made every effort to find her. If she has seen it, she probably doesn't realise the house has been left to her, and she may never come back.'

He knew she was right. It had been in the back of his mind too, but he hadn't wanted to voice his thoughts out loud.

The house had been in his family for three generations now, and held many memories for him through his childhood. He was reluctant to let it go, but he ultimately had to face that prospect. Without the money his father had left, the income from his investments, and the sale of Little Bannerman, there was no way he could go on paying the bills for much longer.

He hated to think what he was going to say to the staff who'd been here for so many years. All of them were getting on in years, and although Isabelle had the prospect of going to live with her sister, even if she didn't know whether she'd be able to stomach it for very long, Cyril had nowhere else to go, and didn't seem to have any friends or relatives he could rely on to give him a home. They'd possibly be able to take him back to Little Bannerman with them, if he wanted to go, which seemed highly likely. There were always plenty of jobs for a handyman.

Sandra had a husband and a family with whom she had a home. She'd probably find another job locally given time, and Morgan and Gavin would be alright. They had the cottage and the woodland. Gavin could probably make a living from selling the timber for the time being, and he was resourceful enough to find another way of living from the land as well.

Ultimately, he had to admit that Anna was right. He'd come to the end of the road. He had to call it a day; give the staff their notice and close up the house for good.

He couldn't bear the thought of telling them all but it would have to be done. He was heading for bankruptcy if he didn't, and that would do nobody any good. The end result was always going to be the same whichever way he looked at it, and it was no use trying to go on without the finances to do so.

He sat on the grass alongside Anna for a while as he thought things through, until he heard the 'phone ringing in the hall and jumped up to answer it.

Cyril was just about to pick up the receiver when David walked in through the open front door.

'I'll get that thanks Cyril,' he said, as he reached out for it; Cyril nodding his head in acknowledgment and returning to the kitchen.

'David Bannerman,' he announced as he picked up the receiver.

'Hello, David. Long time no speak. This is your cousin, Gaye – Gaye Bannerman as was,' the voice on the other end said, with a slight trace of familiarity in her voice.

'Hello, Gaye,' he said. 'It is a long time, isn't it? To what do I owe the honour?'

As children they'd always got on well together, and he remembered how much of a tomboy she'd been, seeming to enjoy climbing trees as much as any boy ever did. He didn't ever remember seeing her with a doll in the entire time he'd known her.

'David,' her voice had become more serious now, 'I've had a meeting with a Marnie Peters just recently, and I believe she's been to see you too, is that right?'

He paused for a moment.

'Yes, she has paid us a visit.'

'And do you believe her claim to be related to us? Do you think your father could possibly be hers too?'

'She certainly seemed to have the evidence to back it up,' he answered, knowing there was a lot about his family, and his father's activities, that Gaye wasn't aware of.

'I think we need to get together and talk about this,' Gaye said, 'don't you? I'm worried she's after some of your fathers' money.'

David couldn't help but laugh.

'After fathers' money – fat chance of that!' he said.

'Look, I know you're a barrister, and you must know all the ins and outs of inheritance laws far better than me, but do you think she could have any claim on his estate? She definitely seems to be your step-sister as far as I can see.'

'I've no doubt she is – but she's only one of many!'

His words seemed cryptic, and Gaye had no idea what he was talking about.

'How do you work that one out?' she queried. 'You mean he was putting it about a bit?'

David laughed again.

'I'd say it was a bit more than that!'

'How so?'

'Look Gaye, there's far too much to tell you over the 'phone. I need to show you some things here before you'll understand everything. Why don't you and your husband – Brian – wasn't it, come over one weekend and I can explain everything. I'm living here with my fiancé, Anna, for the time being.'

'Well, well, finally been pinned down, have you?'

It was Gaye's turn to laugh now, but then her tone turned more serious.

'I know you were at my wedding to Brian, but I'm married to Royston now. Brian was killed in an accident only three years after our marriage. He was a surveyor and he fell from a ladder whilst inspecting buildings on a new housing estate. He hit his head on the corner of a pile of bricks and was killed outright.'

David was instantly concerned.

'I'm so sorry,' he said. 'I had no idea. We should really have kept in touch more often.'

'It's as much my fault as yours that we haven't kept in touch, but I do think it's about time we met each others' better half's, don't you? And we do have a lot to discuss.'

'Of course,' he answered, then impulsively, 'look, why don't you and Royston come over next Saturday and spend the weekend with us. We've plenty of room here for you, and there's lots to catch up on.'

Her answer was slow in coming, and a little tenuous.

'Royston came to us as the new manager of mum and dad's hotel – that's how we met, and I'm the housekeeper now. I'll have to see if we can both be spared next weekend. If we can, I'd only be too glad to take you up on the offer. I wouldn't mind looking round Bannerman's again and visiting the places I remember, and it'll be good to catch up with you and meet your wife to be.'

The following weekend, having been assured that her mother and father would overlook things at the hotel, Gaye and Royston arrived at Bannerman's just before twelve o'clock, to be greeted animatedly by both David and Anna.

'Lovely to meet you both,' Anna smiled, 'and we're glad to welcome you to Bannerman's. I hope you'll enjoy your stay.'

Gaye smiled. It was exactly the sort of thing she was used to saying to a newly arrived hotel guest. She wondered if Anna had ever been in the hospitality trade herself.

Isabelle had done them proud with a roast and all the trimmings, as they all sat down to lunch together in the newly opened dining room in their honour.

'Wow,' Gaye said when she'd finished eating, and she and her husband sat back, stuffed to the gills. 'That was as good as anything our own cordon bleu chef could have produced at the hotel – if not better,' watching Isabelle swell with pride at her words. 'My compliments to you,' she continued, watching the woman's cheeks flush deep red.

'She can excel herself any time she needs to,' David said, 'although Anna and I eat more sparsely these days. We couldn't eat that sort of thing every day. We'd soon look like the telly tubbies if we did!' culminating in more laughter round the table, and a huge belch from Royston, for which Gaye chastised him.

Not at all perturbed by it, he said, 'That's supposed to be a sign of appreciation in some Arab countries – so you could say I'm just showing my appreciation!'

'Well, not when you're with me, you don't,' Gaye said with mock severity.

Laughter rippled round and the conversation flowed as Sandra entered and offered coffee all around, whilst Cyril cleared away the plates.

After lunch, when Gaye and Royston had unpacked their things in the newly aired and cleaned room they'd been allocated, and admired the view from the window – Royston seeing its magnificence for the first time, he turned to her and said, 'This is some place, isn't it. I'd hate to have to pay the bills for its upkeep though. The old man must have been well minted!'

'Probably was. Father always said he was a whizz at making the right investments over the years, and he would have been earning plenty as a judge.'

'Well, I'm glad you've brought me to see it. How the other half lives eh!' as he stretched out on the bed and relaxed while she put their clothes away.

A few minutes later there was a knock on the door and Gaye opened it, to find David standing in the doorway.

'It's a nice day. Thought you might like to take a quick walk and look round everywhere – help to settle that enormous lunch.'

'Thanks,' she answered. 'We'll be down in about quarter of an hour when I've finished putting things away and changed. I thought you might want to walk round the grounds and visit some of our old haunts, so I've brought outdoor things as well.'

When he'd gone, Royston looked at her with a quizzical expression on his face.

'Do you really want to go tramping around? I'd far rather have a snooze for the next couple of hours and sleep that lunch off.'

'Lazybones,' she laughed, picking up a pillow and throwing it at him. 'The walk will do you much more good and I can show you the places where we used to play when we were kids.'

Disgruntled, he got up off the bed.

'Okay, where are my things?' he asked. 'Have you brought my walking boots? I don't fancy getting wet feet in that long grass out there,' pulling a face as he glanced through the window.

''Course I did!' she answered. 'You didn't think I'd bring mine without bringing yours as well, did you?'

'Oh well, it was worth a try,' he answered ruefully, hauling himself resignedly off the bed and taking the waterproof trousers and the boots she handed him.

'Turn your back woman, to spare my modesty,' he joked, as he noticed her watching him unzip his trousers.

'Well, perhaps David wouldn't mind if we were a little later than anticipated . . .' she said, lying down on the bed and holding out a hand towards him.

He needed no second invitation! They didn't very often have time during their busy working days to indulge in a little extra marital excess, so whatever time they could make for that sort of thing was always acceptable

David and Anna were ready and waiting in the hallway when they finally came down the stairs, glancing at each other as they saw the flushed face of Gaye as she apologised for keeping them waiting, but Anna was quick to gloss over their lateness.

'No rush,' she said brightly to hide Gaye's embarrassment. 'We have the rest of the day, and Isabelle's leaving something cold for tonight, so it doesn't matter how long we're out for. Is there anywhere you'd like to go in particular?'

Gaye thought for a while.

'Perhaps a wander through the woods and down to the stream would be nice,' looking at David. 'I remember us all splashing about in the water when we were younger, and the time when Jayne fell in. She was so upset when she thought your mother would be annoyed with her for getting so wet. It'd be nice to see it again.'

'I'm afraid it's no longer a stream any more, more like a river these days, but we'll go there anyway and you can see it for yourself,' David said, opening the door to lead the way.

Within a short distance, the two couples had paired off with each other's partners, Anna engaging Royston in conversation, as she knew David and Gaye had things they needed to talk about.

'Now, what's this you were telling me about your father?' Gaye stated bluntly as they trailed behind the others, knowing they perhaps didn't have much time to talk alone. 'You hinted he'd been putting himself about a bit? Is Marnie Peters going to turn out to be one of his extra maritals?'

'Probably,' David said, 'but she isn't the only one by a long way.'

'How do you mean? Have others come forward since you inherited Bannerman's?' Are they all claiming a slice of the pie?'

'Firstly,' David said, 'you need to be aware that I didn't inherit Bannerman's. My father left the house, the estate, and the main bulk of his wealth all to Jayne. That's why I've been trying so hard to find her.'

'And did he leave you nothing?' She stopped and looked at him in surprise.

'Yes, he left me a good sum of money payable annually for the next ten years, Gavin's cottage, and the woodland, but that's all. I've since given the cottage and the woodland to Gavin and his family. Even if I don't own the house and the grounds, I have my own home not far from Denbigh, so I really have no use for the cottage. Gavin's served this family well over the years and he deserves it.'

'Then why are you living here now?' she asked as they started walking on again.

'I'm holding it for Jayne and trying to make sure she has somewhere to live when she comes back – and to be really truthful, I'm hoping she'll be agreeable to Anna and I living in part of the house as well, but it's taking so long to find her, the upkeep is beginning to cripple me. I've put my own house on the market, but I'm coming to the end of the road. It hasn't sold yet, and I don't think it's going to be too long before I have to close up Bannerman's and let the staff go.'

Gaye was looking thoughtful.

'And has there been no word from her yet?'

David shook his head.

'I'm facing the possibility that she may no longer be alive – and Anna thinks the same way, but until I can officially have her declared dead, I can't touch any of fathers' money, and that could be years ahead. I'll be lucky if I can afford to keep on its upkeep for the next month or so.'

She said nothing as they trudged on, until she stopped once more and turned to him.

'Do you think there's a possibility that she's living somewhere so remote she hasn't even seen your advertising?'

It was a strange thing to say, but not a possibility he'd faced yet.

'I've had it in all the nationals regularly for months, and its even been covered by one of the local news programmes on the

298

television, so surely she'd have seen or heard something about it by now.'

'Not necessarily. Even if she has seen it, you've mentioned nothing about an inheritance. Maybe she doesn't even know she's inherited your fathers' estate. It would be only natural for her to think it would all revert to you.'

'I had thought about that, but when she knows I'm so desperate to find her, why wouldn't she have contacted me?'

Gaye shrugged her shoulders.

'I've no idea, but maybe she has her own reasons. Maybe there's something she's trying to hide from you.'

It was David's turn to stop now.

'What do you mean? Have you seen or spoken to her?'

'No,' Gaye said. 'I was just thinking of all the possibilities. Look, the others have stopped. They're waiting for us. Isn't that the path that leads down to the stream?'

They walked on then, catching up with the others.

'This is the right path, isn't it?' Anna said, searching David's face for some signs of having had an agreeable discussion with Gaye, but his face was unreadable. He seemed to be deep in thought about something.

'Eh? ... Oh yes, it's just a few yards further on,' he said, taking over the lead. 'Be careful you don't slip. It can be a bit muddy near the bottom.'

As Royston followed on behind him, Anna found herself alongside Gaye.

'Did you have time to talk properly?' she asked.

Gaye glanced at her and smiled, realising she'd been keeping Royston occupied so that she and David could talk alone.

'For the moment, yes, but I think we may have more to say yet. I need a bit of time to think first.'

Then, changing the subject, she said, 'What's this about his father having more illegitimate kids floating around?'

David and Royston had reached the stream now and begun walking the bank. It was quiet now as the weather had been fine for some time and the banks were much drier than the last time they'd been here.

Anna sat down on a rock, indicating for Gaye to sit alongside as they rested and watched the sparkling water cascading over the rocks in its path.

'We found a journal in the shed at the back. Didn't David tell you about it?'

'He did mention something about his father having been up to no good with other women, but he didn't elaborate on it.'

'He'll probably show it to you tomorrow. I know he intends to. It seems he'd been impregnating women – probably previously infertile women – for many years. The first notebook we found showed it to have started in 1972, but the one in the shed starts in 1992, which seems to be the period when he was most active, up until about 2013, when the entries stop completely. I think it's best if David shows you for himself. As you can see, there are probably many more of what could be considered his illegitimate children out there somewhere.'

Gaye was amazed. She'd never thought of Uncle Hector in this light. He'd always been a very staid and plodding man in her eyes, mostly disinterested in his children – apart from Jayne. He'd seemed to come alive after she was born, and as a child herself, although much older than Jayne, she'd never found his interest unnatural – but maybe there might have been something more sinister in his attitude towards his daughter when she thought about it now. He'd never shown much interest in any of his boys during the times she'd been there, and he'd never accompanied them when the two families had picnicked or walked around the grounds together.

David and Royston were now coming back, and after a quick conversation between the four of them, they decided to take a circuitous route back and through the woods, where Gaye remembered happy hours playing on a rope swing which Gavin had put up for them, but she didn't mention it. She remembered his brother had died when playing on that swing.

'You said you'd given the cottage to Gavin and his family, so I presume he's still here. Is Morgan still with them – or is he married and moved away by now?'

'No, he's still with them, but I believe he's seeing someone, and he intends to marry her,' David replied.

'About time too!' she laughed. 'It's not before time, is it? He was always a handsome looking lad, and I know I had a crush on him for a long time.'

Royston gave a pretend pout.

'You never told me anything about that!'

'Why should I? I'd forgotten about it myself until now. Don't tell me you never had a crush on other girls before you met me!'

Laughter broke out, and they were still talking happily and reminiscing about old times when they reached the house again, Anna and Royston joining in the banter, learning about the happy childhood times spent by both at Bannerman's during hot summers long since past.

Isabelle made them all coffee and biscuits when they arrived back, which they drank in the lounge, and the conversation flowed easily until she called them for their evening meal.

All elected for an early night after the full day they'd spent together, and it was as David emerged from the shower, dressed only in a bath towel draped around his waist, that he noticed Anna looking up at him from the book she'd been reading in bed.

'What?' he queried, looking down to see if he'd left anything poking out.

She laughed and put the book down across her lap.

'I've been thinking,' she said. 'Hearing you and Jayne talk today about happy memories of this place, I know you don't want to leave here, any more than I want to fly to the moon. Is there no way you can think of to forestall closing the place down? Jayne's been missing for many years now. Surely it can be considered by now that she won't be coming back. Is there possibly some legal way you can have her declared dead – and then your fathers' estate can be turned over to you?'

301

'I'd have to see if that could be made possible,' he said, thinking about it. 'I'll have to talk to somebody who has some knowledge of that sort of thing – it's not in my area of expertise.'

Next day, David took Gaye over to the shed and showed her the contents of the drawer hidden under the table.

She was amazed.

'To think what the old devil was doing right under everyone's noses. Do you think your mother knew anything about it?'

'I have no idea,' he replied. 'I certainly hadn't, and I'm sure Jayne wouldn't either. I think she'd have been as surprised as I was – and probably appalled by it as well. Don't forget, she was only 15 when I left. She wasn't even a proper adult by then.'

Gaye looked at him, a strange light in her eyes.

'You mean he and she were alone here together after your mother died? Do you think that was very wise, knowing the way he was always fawning over her!'

David suddenly realised the direction in which Gaye's thoughts were heading.

'I didn't know my mother had died until after my father was killed, and I didn't even know Jayne had left either.'

'Well, I'd think about it if I were you. That could be part of the reason why she doesn't want to be found.'

The look that crossed David's face made her think she might inadvertently have said too much, as she tried to turn the subject round to his fathers' activities by picking up the notebook and looking through it.

'There are lots of names in this book. Have you ever counted them?' she said, putting it down hastily when she realised what might have been on Hector's hands during previous times he'd handled it.

'I think Anna did. I think she said it was over 40.'

'Wow! All those little step-Bannerman's running round out there! Let's hope they don't all find their way to your door claiming a slice of the inheritance.'

After lunch that afternoon, they sat round talking for a while before Gaye decided it was time to get packed and be on their way home.

'Hotel work starts early in a morning, and we have to be up about 6.30 ready for breakfast service – me in particular – but lazybones here doesn't always appear on the scene before nine o'clock.

They'd all enjoyed the weekend, and agreed they must do it again sometime – if David did manage to find a way of staying on at Bannerman's, but it was a very quiet Gaye who sat brooding in the passenger seat as they drove home.

Royston realised there was something pressing on her mind, but drove on in silence, knowing she'd tell him when she was ready. She always did!

CHAPTER 31

Two days later, after a great deal of consideration, Gaye made a 'phone call. It wasn't something she undertook lightly, as she'd been instructed only to use the number in an emergency.

The 'phone rang for a long time before it was answered, and when it was, the voice didn't sound like that of Jayne. It sounded much younger than she would have expected Jayne to sound.

'Is that you, Jayne?' she asked, surprised.

'No, she's not here,' the voice replied, 'but I can take a message.'

'Yes, my name is Gaye Smith, and I'm her cousin. We haven't spoken in a long time, but I have something urgent to tell her. Will you ask her to ring me back as soon as possible.'

'I'll do that,' the voice said. 'I'll take the number you're calling from off the 'phone.'

'Thank you,' Gaye said, 'and may I know who I'm talking to?' but the 'phone had already gone dead in her hand.

She brooded for a while after it ended and wondered whether she'd made the right decision. She had no idea who she'd been speaking to, or where she was, but she had to trust she'd pass the message on.

In the end, she decided to trust Royston and tell him everything. Two heads could be better than one in a time of crisis, and she felt that this was just one of those times.

'Roy,' she said, using her familiar term of endearment for him, 'can you spare some time for a chat? I need to tell you something and to ask your advice.'

He was just about to sit down and put his feet up with the morning paper before returning to work.

'It's about my cousin, David Bannerman.'

'What about him?'

'You know he's struggling to keep the house afloat until he manages to find his sister Jayne, don't you?'

He nodded. They had discussed it, and at some length after their return from the previous weekends' stay.

'Well, I don't know where Jayne is any more than he does, but I do have a mobile number for her.'

He looked at her in surprise.

'Everyone seems to think she's probably dead. Why didn't you tell him at the weekend?'

'I was wondering whether to or not, but I decided to try calling the number first. It's several years since she gave it to me, and I'd no idea whether it would still be connected or not, but it is. She still has the same number, and a young woman answered. She said she'd pass a message on to Jayne for me, so she must still be alive.'

'And what did you tell her?'

'Nothing. I just asked her to get Jayne to call me.'

'That's all you could have done under the circumstances. That was probably the right decision.'

'There seems to be some sort of secrecy connected to her disappearance Roy, but I don't know what that is. I have no idea where she's living now, but I could hear sounds in the background. It sounded like waves breaking on a seashore – and there was the sound of seabirds as well.'

By this time, Royston had given up all idea of reading his paper, as he put it down and prepared to listen.

'Spill,' he said, when she didn't say anything more. 'You obviously have something else to say.'

She looked at him, before deciding to tell him everything she knew.

'When Jayne left Bannerman's, she contacted me. She said she needed to get away and that I was the only one she knew who might help her. She never explained why she needed to get away, but as she sounded so desperate, I told her to come to the hotel, where she stayed with us for some time. She was very upset and tearful when she arrived, but she still wouldn't say why she needed to leave. I thought she probably would in her own time, but meanwhile, I didn't push her for answers.

She lived in staff accommodation, and, as she had little money of her own, mum offered her a job as one of the maids.

She'd never had to clean anywhere before, but she was a quick learner and the other maids soon had her in a routine. She never complained about the work, and seemed happy to have something to do and some money in her pocket.'

Here she paused, and Royston, now intrigued, probed for more information.

'Then what happened?'

'We had a man came to say with us from over in Yorkshire. He was attending a shoot on an estate somewhere nearby – I don't remember the details now, and he brought his estate manager with him.

Jayne was the maid assigned to their rooms, and she and the estate manager took a shine to each other straight away. When he was around, she was never very far away. They stayed for almost two weeks, but when they left, it was obvious that Jayne was upset by his leaving. Two weeks later, she didn't turn up for work one morning, and when we checked her room, she'd gone – and so had all her belongings.

She left a note of apology in the room, but no forwarding address, and no indication of where she'd gone, but I always thought it had something to do with that man.'

'Then how did you get her number?'

'It was about two months later. Her conscience must have been getting the better of her and she rang to apologise once more, telling me not to worry about her - that she was making a new life for herself, and that she was very happy. She also said that I could use the number she was calling from only in an emergency, as she wanted to disassociate herself from all her previous life and connections – particularly her father.

She wouldn't explain what she meant by that – only that she'd rather I didn't ask, as she wasn't prepared to tell me anything more.'

'And did she never contact you again?'

'No, never! That's the last I ever heard from her – until I decided to 'phone her today, and even then I never found out where she is.'

'Seems to be the best you can do. Best leave it for now and see whether she rings. There's nothing else you can do. It's no use telling David anything until you hear from her.'

He was right of course. She couldn't get David's hopes up. There was always the possibility that her 'phone had been stolen or passed on to somebody else, and they were just fobbing her off with promises of passing the message on.

Two weeks went by and with no word from Jayne, until one morning when she'd just stopped for a break, her 'phone began to ring.

She was delighted to see the name 'Jayne' appear on the screen.

'Jayne, I'm so pleased to hear from you,' she said enthusiastically.'

'I haven't got long!' the voice replied.

Jayne's voice was weak and breathy, and Gaye worried immediately that something was wrong.

'Is something the matter?' she asked.

'I'll be fine,' the voice said. 'You wanted to speak to me? '

'Yes, but can you hold on a minute while I make sure there's nobody listening in? I'm at work at the moment,' going to the door and making sure there was nobody in the passageway before shutting it.

Returning to the 'phone, she picked it up to hear the tail end of a coughing session. It was obvious that Jayne was far from well.

'What is it Jayne? You don't sound very well!'

'I've been in hospital with this wretched cough, but I'm out now and I'll soon be on the mend,' the same small voice said.

Maybe she thought that way, but the sound of her voice and the coughing sessions were telling a very different story.

'I'll be as quick as I can, but I'm very worried about you,' Gaye persisted.

There was silence from the other end, but she could hear the sound of Jayne's wheezy breathing. She decided to get on with it, in case Jayne decided to end the call prematurely.

'Are you aware that your father died some months ago?'

There was hesitation on the other end before there was the breathy and almost inaudible sound of a 'no'.

'He had an accident on his motorbike – a hit and run – and he died at the scene. When the Will was read, it seems he'd left almost everything to you – including Bannerman's.'

'But what about my brother David? He's much older than me – he should have inherited!'

Concern and consternation were evident in her voice.

'I have no idea why, but David has been living in the property and trying to keep it in good order until you return. He's even kept the staff on and been paying them out of his own pocket.'

She heard a sharp intake of breath at the other end causing her to cough again.

'Did my father leave him no money either?'

'Some, yes, but it's not enough to keep paying out for the upkeep of the house and the staff wages. He also inherited Gavin's cottage and the woodland; which he's given to him in return for his loyal service over the years. He's mostly been financing everything from his own pocket whilst he's been trying to find you, but he's running out of money rapidly, and he can't even sell the place to help out. He needs desperately to speak to you and find out what you want to do about the situation. If I give you his number, will you ring him?'

'I'll try!' Jayne said, any further level of conversation seeming to fail her. To Gaye's mind she seemed desperately ill.

Gaye rattled off David's number, having to repeat it several times before Jayne read the correct number back to her. Her cognitive perception seemed to be no better than her physical condition, and Gaye only hoped she'd respond quickly to David and resolve the matter with him.

She'd done all she could to bring the pair together again, and it wasn't up to her to interfere any further. She needed to step back into the shadows and hope she hadn't left things too late.

Another coughing session followed before the conversation ended, and she waited until it had finished before saying anything further.

'Sorry,' Jayne said when managed at last to speak. 'I'll ring you again when I'm feeling a little better. I've only been out of hospital a couple of days,' and, without saying anything more, she cut the connection.

CHAPTER 32

David had had a particularly galling day in court, the judge having called for a recess shortly after lunch, when he asked for a clarification of some evidence to be made clear. The prosecuting barrister didn't have that to hand, so proceedings had been brought to a halt for the day until he was able to obtain whatever was needed.

It was a disgruntled David who finally drove into the driveway at Bannerman's. He'd been hoping the trial would be concluded by Thursday afternoon and he could have Friday and Monday off, giving him a day either side of the weekend before he was needed at another proceeding on Tuesday.

He really needed those days off to get his thoughts in order. He'd just had a final demand from the water company for Bannerman's, which seemed exorbitant to him, considering the few people living there, and when he was no longer paying those for Gavin's cottage either.

Anna had found herself a little job too, working a few hours each day in the local shop. It seemed the woman's daughter had run off with her boyfriend when she'd found herself pregnant by him, and was no longer on hand to help out. It was only for the morning until midday, but the little she earned was enough to cover most of their food bills at least – David still being left with the rest of the overheads to find.

He was surprised to find a strange car sitting alongside the front door, but just as he parked his own and climbed out of the driving seat, a man carrying a clipboard came round the corner of the house.

David had never seen him before and had no idea who he was, but he seemed to be making himself quite at home as he stopped and peered in through the living room window.

'Can I help you?' he said, rather authoritatively, wondering just why the man was wandering round the house, seemingly without permission.

The man looked round and surveyed him from top to bottom, leaving David feeling rather annoyed at his condescending attitude.

'And who am I speaking to?' the man replied, dropping the clipboard down at his side.

'I'm David Bannerman, and I live here! I might just ask you the same question!'

David's voice was clipped and terse, feeling angry with the man's obvious lack of knowledge.

'Then you must be the sitting tenant,' the man said.

David was well and truly riled by the man's arrogant attitude, as he went into true barrister mode.

'Did you not notice the name of this property when you entered? It says Bannerman's on the gate, and that is also the name I've just given you. Now, can I ask what your business is here, before I ask you to leave?'

The man's attitude seemed to wilt a little under David's penetrating glare, as he fished in his pocket for something.

'Allow me to introduce myself,' he said. 'My name is Anthony Bartholomew – and I am the owner of Bartholomew's Estate Agency,' as he handed his card to David. 'I have been asked to value the property by Mr. Donald McFarlane, with a view to putting it on the market.'

David was taken aback, before recollecting his composure.

'Donald McFarlane! I've never even heard of him. This house and the surrounding land all belong to my sister Jayne – Jayne

Bannerman, and I'm living here and holding it in trust for her return.'

The estate agent didn't seem to know what to say for the moment before collecting his thoughts together and regaining his composure.

'I know nothing about that!' he finally said. 'All I've been told is that I'm acting on behalf of Mr. McFarlane, and he's asked to value the property with a view to marketing it. Perhaps you should take it up with him. If you let me have your number I'll ask him to call you.'

David fished in his pocket and produced a card, handing it over before saying, 'Perhaps, if you've finished, you'd like to leave now until I've spoken to the man. I consider this an intrusion on my privacy until then.'

The estate agent gave a slight inclination of his head and walked over to his own car, climbing inside and driving away without saying anything further.

Now all David could do was wait for that call to find out what it was all about, but he didn't have long to wait. It came on Saturday morning just after he'd been taking a look round the shed again to see if there was anything there they'd missed, and with a view to putting it to another use.

'Mr. Bannerman – David?' the voice said. 'This is Donald McFarlane.'

David's hackles rose immediately.

'I've been waiting for your call. What's this about bringing in an estate agent and trying to sell Bannerman's out from under me?'

'I'm sorry about that,' the voice said. It was slightly Scottish in accent, but not very pronounced. 'I didn't know how to get hold of you, but now that I have, I owe you an explanation.'

'I should think you do! What's going on?'

'Let me tell you first that your sister Jayne and I have been married for several years now, and that we live in Scotland, just south of Oban. I'm the manager on an estate and when we

312

married she came to live with me in my cottage down by the seashore.'

'So she's Jayne McFarlane now, and not Jayne Bannerman. No wonder nobody ever contacted me with any information about her.'

The man's voice sounded rueful as he continued.

'I'm very sorry to have to tell you that Jayne passed away last week,' waiting for a reaction before continuing.

'Jayne passed away! How did that happen? She couldn't even have been 30 yet!'

He felt completely stunned by the news.

'Yes, that's right, but I'm afraid she was diagnosed with a tumour close to her brain at the end of last year. They took her straight into hospital and operated, but they weren't able to get it all out – it was too close to her brain stem. The consultant told us before she was discharged that she probably didn't have much longer to live – possibly a year if she were lucky, but more likely just a few months. As it was, she managed just under six months, but during that time she was only a shadow of her former self, and was often rather muddled in both her speech and her thoughts.'

He waited for David to say something, but the only thing he heard was a strangled sob, accompanied by a hardly perceptible voice saying, 'Why did nobody let me know? I'd have wanted to see her for one last time at least.'

'I never knew anything about you. When I met your sister, she was working at her cousin's hotel as a room maid, and I stayed there with his lordship to attend a shoot. At the time, I was going through a divorce with my former wife, and when I returned to Scotland, I kept in contact with Jayne. I soon realised I didn't want to be without her – and she seemed to feel the same way.

Luckily, one of the house maids up at the hall had just left, and so I persuaded his lordship into employing Jayne, which he was only too happy to do, as it saved him having to look round for somebody else, and he'd already met her during our stay.

When my divorce was finalised, Jayne and I married, and she moved in here with me. She never talked about her family or where she came from. That part of her life was a closed book as far as she was concerned. As you can see, that's why I didn't know anything about you.'

David didn't know what to say for the moment. This news was all completely new to him, and as he said nothing, Donald continued speaking.

'Her funeral will be at the end of next week if you're able to attend. There's no room here for you, but there's an excellent pub in the village which has rooms.'

'Did she manage to make a Will? Has everything been left to you then?'

Donald agreed that everything would come to him under the terms of the Will she'd made after being diagnosed with the tumour. It seemed that she too had been made aware of her imminent demise.

David could now see any future plans for Bannerman's – his childhood home – evaporating in front of his eyes. If Jayne had made no proviso for it, it was obvious Donald had no intention of keeping it on, and every intention of selling it to the highest bidder.

He wasn't feeling mercenary towards his sister, just angry that he'd poured everything he had into the upkeep of Bannerman's awaiting her return, and there'd never been any chance that she ever would. He'd almost bankrupted himself for it, just so that the brother-in-law he never even knew he had could snatch it away from him and pocket the proceeds.

And as for the loyal staff – they were about to be put out on the streets with no recompense after all their years of service. He and Anna still had Little Bannerman to go back to, and he still had his £50,000 a year to help him get back on his feet, as well as his regular earnings – but the staff had to rely on a complete stranger for the time being. David doubted he would keep them on under the circumstances, and they could expect nothing from him.

'Please text me the time and the location, as well as the number for the pub,' he said, 'and I'll see if I can manage to get there.'

There seemed little else he could say under the circumstances, and he couldn't help feeling some hostility towards the man.

That afternoon he talked things over with Anna after they'd eaten lunch. He'd already told her about the estate agent, and now related all that he'd learned from Donald McFarlane. She seemed just as shocked by it all as he did, but they both decided he had to tell the staff straight away what was happening, and make them aware that they would soon be losing their jobs.

When he finished telling them all, which included Gavin and his family, as their property would now adjoin that of their new neighbour and might affect them as well, their faces showed more surprise than consternation.

'Miss Jayne's dead? But she was only young!' was Isabelle's first reaction. 'I can't believe it!'

David could only shrug. There was nothing more he could say. He still hadn't managed to completely come to terms with the news himself yet.

'And what's going to happen to the house and all of us?' was Cyril's first reaction.

This was the moment David had been dreading.

'I'm afraid Anna and I will be packing up and leaving right away. Little Bannerman hasn't been sold yet, so we'll be moving back there and taking it off the market. It's no use me paying any more upkeep towards this house now that it belongs to my brother-in-law,' finding the words uncomfortable to say. 'I'll pay your wages up to the end of next week. We'll be moving back to Little Bannerman this weekend.'

They looked stunned, but David knew that it was all he could do now. It might take ages for such a large house to find a buyer, but then again, he had done his best towards its upkeep, and it was in reasonably good condition, so maybe it might find one sooner rather than later. Maybe whoever bought it might take them back on if it were a family, but, given their ages, probably not, and it might be a good while before it did sell.

The trial David was attending from Tuesday onwards the following week turned out to be a non-event, as the defendant tested positive for the dreaded Covid 19 disease which was by then sweeping the country, and moving ever more rapidly from one part of the British Isles to the other.

As a result of this, David and Anna, who'd already made the move back into Little Bannerman, were also able to attend Jayne's funeral. For once, even though he wouldn't be earning his anticipated fee for the time being, he was glad of the chance to arrange everything and get them moved back into their former home.

He'd asked Anna to go with him to the funeral, and as it was the beginning of summer and the weather was forecast to be good, they booked into the pub for a full week. Even though the funeral would be a sad affair, particularly for David, and for her husband, they could look forward to a short break afterwards. Neither had ever been to Scotland, and looked forward to exploring its very different countryside.

They arrived at their destination late on Thursday afternoon, telephoning Donald to say they'd arrived, and were surprised when he turned up at the pub shortly after they'd eaten their evening meal.

Both were also surprised by his age when he arrived and introduced himself. Jayne wouldn't yet have reached her 30th birthday, and Donald must be around 40 years of age at least.

The lounge was almost empty, and they were able to find a quiet corner away from anyone else who might come in and interrupt their conversation.

'I felt I had to come and greet you after the short chat we had on the 'phone,' he began, as two frothing pints were placed in front of them, and a glass of red wine for Anna.

'I know you must have a lot of questions to ask, and I have some of my own too. Perhaps we could get some of them out of the way while you're here.'

David wasn't too sure what he meant by that, but he was an adept listener.

'What sort of questions?' he asked, as Anna prepared to sit back and listen. She knew little about Jayne, and little about David's family life apart from what he'd been willing to tell her. There was still some mystery around his angry row with his father and his subsequent leaving of his home, as well as his refusal to contact his family again. There was also Jayne's sudden disappearance after her mother died, which both hoped might come out into the open as a result of their discussion.

Somehow, everything seemed to weave around his father, and she was anxious to know what that may be. Maybe David might be more willing to talk about it all now that he was the only survivor of the once quite large family.

'When I first met Jayne, she wouldn't tell me why she left her home, and why she never wanted to contact her father again. Was it for the same reason that you left – whatever that was?'

David realised he was fishing for information, and wasn't sure whether to tell him anything or not – after all, this was their first meeting, even if he was, or had been, Jayne's husband.

Anna saw his hesitation, but she too was anxious to learn the truth about all the secrecy as well, and couldn't help but give him a push into revealing the truth.

'What does it matter now?' she said. 'They're both dead, as well as your mother, so it can't harm anyone now to let the truth be known.'

He still seemed hesitant, as he took another few sips of his beer, whilst seeming to make up his mind whether he ought to say anything, and if so, how much to say.

'I can't speak for Jayne, and she's not here to tell you her side, but for my part, the row I had with him was about his treatment of others around him, and his incessant controlling of my sister,' he eventually began, still holding back a little as he started, but then, as he got into his stride, he began to elaborate more widely. It was as if the floodgates were opening and he was now anxious to get it all off his chest.

'He wouldn't allow her out of his sight very often, and when she was around, he seemed to want to control everything she did, and who she mixed with.

Gavin, my father's gardener, who also managed the woodland, had a son called Morgan. He was six years older than Jayne, and when father thought she was spending too much time with him, he forbade her to speak to him, or to have anything to do with him.

They'd known each other since they were kids, and Morgan has since told me that they'd been quite serious about one another at the time, even though she was only 15. It was probably just a teenage crush and would have soon been over if left to run its course, but he couldn't see it that way.

I tried to speak up on their behalf and make father see sense, but he wouldn't listen. He told me it was none of my business, and if I didn't like the way he treated his family, it was time I got out.

He was beginning to stifle Jayne, and I found her in tears many times when he'd forbidden her to go anywhere with her friends, or to even have them round to the house.

Shortly after that, I came in late one night, and saw him coming out of Jayne's bedroom. When I knocked and asked her what he'd wanted, I found her in tears, but she wouldn't tell me why.

I felt his obsession with her was becoming unhealthy, but she would never tell me if he was paying any untoward attention to her.

Eventually, after another blazing row with him, I decided it was time to leave and I asked Jayne to go with me. I intended to look after her and pay for her upkeep myself until she was old enough to get a job. I think she was rather frightened by the prospect and said she'd think about it first, but when the arranged time came for us to leave, she didn't turn up.

I thought she'd be safe enough with mother still around, but then, without my ever knowing, she died. If I'd known Jayne was all alone in the house with my father, I'd have gone back there and made sure she came away with me. I realise now that even if she had decided to leave after mother died, she had no idea where I was, and she couldn't have got in touch with me even if she'd wanted to.'

Here he stopped and Anna could see tears sparkling in his eyes as he picked up his glass and drank from it, trying to hide his distress, but Donald's face was an inscrutable mask, his lips firm as if he was angry about something.

Now he seemed ready to say something himself, as he downed the rest of his beer and made for the bar, bringing back another two pints, although Anna declined any more wine.

When he sat down again he seemed more composed and ready to tell his side of things.

'When I first met Jayne at the hotel, we hit it off straight away, and I knew, even after just such a short stay, that I wanted her to come back to Scotland and marry me when my divorce was finalised. As I told you, I managed to get her a job with my own employer as a housemaid, but when I gave her the news, she was very quiet. It was then that she told me she was four months pregnant, but that she wasn't able to tell the father or to marry him.'

David's thoughts flew back to Morgan's revelation about his relationship with Jayne, as he looked at Donald in surprise. Morgan said it had only happened once, but might he have been glossing over the facts? Might he have been having a full-blown relationship with Jayne while she was still underage? He must see him when he got back and try to get to the bottom of things, but he was already feeling very angry about the situation if that turned out to be the case.

'But you said she took the job with your employer! What happened about the baby? Did she have it?' Anna couldn't help but chip in; her own curiosity getting the better of her.

'Oh yes, she had the baby. Her Ladyship was only too glad to have more help around the house, so she put her on fairly light duties, mostly dusting and polishing, until after the child was born. It was a little boy, and everybody tried to persuade her to have him adopted.'

'And did she?' David asked.

'No. She found a family who'd look after him while she was working during the day, and she picked him up after she'd finished in the afternoon.'

'So what's going to happen to him now she's dead?' David said anxiously.

His family were all gone now apart from him, and he felt worried about the young boy. If anything, he must be sure he was being looked after properly, and that he was safe and well. If not, that responsibility would fall on his shoulders from now on, although he didn't know how Anna would feel about that.

Donald suddenly stood up without saying anything further on the matter. The whole conversation seemed to have upset him badly, and they could see he was anxious to get away.

'I'll see you at the funeral tomorrow, and then you must both come back to the cottage for some refreshments. We'll continue this conversation then,' and with just a slight inclination of his head, he was gone.

CHAPTER 33

Next day they awoke to gloomy skies. A gloomy day for a gloomy task Anna thought, as she pulled back the curtains. She thought there was every chance that David would be very upset during the burial of his sister; blaming himself for never having helped her out of her previous living conditions – all alone with a possessive father as her only companion and never allowed to live her own life. It must have been very tedious for her, but at least she had managed to get away, and what little was left of her life seemed to have been happy enough. Maybe she'd be able to pacify him with that thought.

He'd been very quiet after Donald's departure, even though they'd gone through to the bar and been included in the banter with the locals. Seeing his reticence to join in, she'd suggested an early night, and they'd turned in just after ten o'clock.

There were black and purple threatening clouds over the distant mountains this morning, although luckily, when she looked out again after washing and dressing, they seemed to be receding and not coming towards them. If his already tormented mind had to cope with torrential rain as well, she didn't know whether he'd be able to stay calm and get through it without breaking down completely.

David had risen before her, saying he needed a walk, and didn't arrive back until she was just going down to breakfast, although when they sat down, he didn't eat more than a couple of slices of toast and marmalade.

'My stomach's churning,' he told her when she queried his not wanting anything else. 'I can't eat. I'm dreading today. I don't know how I'll stand up to it. I feel so guilty that I didn't get her out of there sooner. Things might have turned out very differently if I had.'

'David,' she said, putting a hand on his arm. 'Nothing would have been any different if you had taken her away, and at least she found happiness with a new husband and a child of her own for a few good years. You couldn't have stopped her getting a brain tumour – there's no way you could have foreseen that!'

He smiled a wan smile, but still didn't seem any more comforted, and was still the same when Donald arrived to pick them up; even though the black clouds had rolled away and the sun had come out.

She linked arms with him as they walked into the little Kirk, which contained only a small congregation of people, none of whom they knew; but the smiles they received showed that most of the people were aware of who they were.

They sat next to Donald, who had a girl of about sixteen alongside him, whom he quietly introduced as his daughter, Maura. She'd already been there, sitting in a pew at the front and waiting for them. She gave a shy smile before looking down at hands clasped in her lap and without speaking.

The service was conducted by a small, rotund minister, who had a very pronounced Scottish accent, and was sometimes hard to understand, but he led the congregation with a strong and powerful baritone voice when it came to the hymn singing.

Donald didn't elect to speak, and neither did David. They both seemed not to want to share their grief publicly, and were both extremely overcome when the coffin was lowered into the ground, as was young Maura. Anna herself, even though she hadn't known Jayne in life, felt a sense of grief at her passing, and the tragic waste of such a young life. She left the graveside with tears trickling down her own cheeks, but knew she must try and stay strong for the sake of both men.

As they walked out of the churchyard, Donald gave Anna the keys to the car and asked them to wait for him there; he just needed to thank the minister and speak to a few people before he joined them. David, feeling that he ought to do likewise, tried to pull himself together and join him in his thanking of them, but after just a few short words, their kindness and words of comfort overwhelmed him. Anna eventually had to lead him away and back to the car, where he managed to calm himself, sitting and staring out across the graveyard and on towards the mountains beyond.

It was beautiful scenery, but he seemed to see nothing of it as he stared stoically into the distance and tried to compose himself, before Donald climbed into the drivers' seat, where she'd left the keys on the dashboard.

Most people had drifted away by this time, but there were still the odd few walking away who lifted an arm in farewell.

'They seem a friendly lot of people,' Anna commented, trying to smile and lifting a hand in return. 'Are they all friends of yours?'

'Most of them live locally in the small hamlet we passed through on our way here, but a lot of them are staff from the Hall. They all knew Jayne while she was working and living there, and she got on well with everybody too. Did you see the big wreath that was on top of the coffin?'

'Yes, there was one enormous one I noticed. I thought it must have been yours,' Anna commented.

'No, it wasn't mine, although mine was alongside it – it was from his Lordship – he was in the congregation as well, but he didn't come to the graveside and left at the end of the service. I did manage to speak to him and thank him for coming, and I intended to introduce him to you both, but you'd already taken David back to the car. His Lordship said not to bother you now. He'd try to speak to you both sometime before you left.'

'Isn't that rather unusual for somebody of that high a standing to be so familiar with their staff?' David asked, coming out of his state of torpor at last.

Donald smiled.

'I should have explained before,' he said. 'He's not just my employer – he's my uncle as well. He married my mother's sister. That's how I came to get this job. I'm not originally from the west of Scotland, my parents live just south of Edinburgh on the east coast. They didn't attend the funeral because my mother has dementia and my father can't, or should I say won't, leave her.'

Anna and David looked at each other with a sense of surprise, before they felt the car turn off the road and into a narrow lane – just wide enough for one vehicle at a time.

To either side of them was rough open moorland, and as they continued on further, the smell of the sea became stronger; the moorland soon giving way to sand dunes and tufts of rough marram grass, interspersed presently by outcrops of tough and weathered granite.

Gradually, the track began to go downhill, and presently the sea came into view as they found themselves looking towards the horizon. The vista soon opened out into a wide sandy bay, surrounded on either side by craggy cliffs, plumes of spray breaking against the rocks at their bases.

Suddenly, the Jeep lurched to the right, and Anna and David felt their seat belts pull tight.

'What the ...?' David said, as the vehicle lurched to a halt.

'Sorry about that!' Donald said; a chuckle in his voice. 'Often happens round here,' as Anna found herself face to face with a shaggy goat peering in through her window. 'His Lordship is partial to a bit of goat meat, and my aunt only drinks goat's milk, so I get the job of managing the unruly creatures. They get everywhere on the estate, and I'm the one who has to find them and bring them down from the tops of the wildest of crags, with the aid of about half a dozen others. It can often take days to get them all down, and it's no easy task to keep them all penned until we can let them go again.'

The car started up once more as the last of the goats passed by, and continued its turn to the right, where a long, low, whitewashed cottage came into view on their right.

It stood about fifteen feet or so above the highest part of the beach, which shelved steeply down to the waters' edge. It was a wild and beautiful place, and they hadn't seen a soul since leaving the church. Had Jayne enjoyed living in such a remote place? That question, when put to Donald, was answered in the affirmative.

'Oh yes, she loved it, and she never complained about its remoteness. She seemed to revel in it, and that's why you've just had the company of the goats – she used to feed them outside the front door when there wasn't much food in the winter. She took to it like a duck to water, and she had a cry all of her own that used to bring them down from the hillsides for food. Even though they couldn't be seen anywhere around, they always appeared within minutes of her call.'

David, thinking of her upbringing, and the remoteness of their own home, began to understand Jayne's apparent love of these surroundings. She'd always been used to the remoteness of the area where she lived, but now she'd had a loving family around her, with her as the matriarch sharing her own love with them, and not being stifled by an overbearing father who ruled everything she did. She'd at last been free to express her own personality, even if it was only for such a short time.

'There's food in the house if you'd like to come inside,' Donald said, getting out of the car.

'Can we go down to the beach?' Anna said spontaneously. 'It's a beautiful day and I'd love to feel the sand and the water between my toes.'

'Of course we can,' Donald said, coming round and opening the door for her, 'but I'm afraid you won't find the water as warm as it is round the coast further south. This water rolls in from the

Atlantic, and it's never very warm at this time of the year, in fact, never at any time of the year!'

She never often wore tights, but on this more formal occasion, she'd chosen to wear a skirt, and bare legs wouldn't have been appropriate.

Stripping them off behind the privacy of the open door and stuffing them inside her high heeled shoes, she followed the men down to the shoreline barefooted, where they were sitting on a rock near the waterline.

'Better take your dip now,' Donald urged. 'Tides coming in; and it comes in fast here as the beach shelves so steeply. It won't be long before this rock's under water as well.'

Laughing, she lifted up her skirt and waded out almost knee deep, relishing in the feel of the water around her legs; but she wasn't there for long. As Donald had said, it was extremely cold, and when she waded back out, her legs had turned red from the increased circulation in them as her body tried to compensate for the freezing water.

'Told you,' Donald said, as both he and David laughed, and she sat down alongside them, stretching out her legs to warm them in the sun.

They'd been sitting there for perhaps five minutes or so, when Anna spotted two figures coming towards them from the far end of the beach. They were a long way off, but they seemed to be a girl with a young boy trailing behind her.

'There's somebody coming along the beach,' she said. 'I thought you said it was always very quiet here.'

Donald looked up.

'Oh, that'll be my daughter. I thought she'd be in the house waiting for us. She must have taken Fergus out. He loves the beach.'

Donald said nothing; sitting in silence until the pair drew nearer, when the boy began to hold back shyly, sheltering behind the girl as he noticed the presence of strangers.

'David, this is my daughter Fiona. Fiona, this is Jayne's brother David and his fiancée Anna.'

Fiona, a girl of around 18, smiled and inclined her head towards them in greeting, stepping to one side so that they could see the boy.

'And this is Fergus,' Donald said, as the boy was revealed to them. Holding out his hand, encouraging the child to step forward, he said to him, 'Come and meet the lady and gentleman Fergus. He's your new uncle – mummy's brother.'

Seeming reluctant, the boy stepped forward and politely held out his hand towards David, his face flushed pink.

David, with a look of amazement on his face didn't at first take hold of it, but Anna nudged his arm, and seeming to return to the present, he took the limp little hand and shook it.

Seeing how shy the boy seemed, Fiona interjected and took his hand.

'Come on Fergus, we'll go and finish getting the food ready and put the kettle on for a cup of tea.'

David couldn't take his eyes off the boy as they walked away, turning his head and watching them make their way to the house. When they disappeared from sight, he turned back again, and Anna saw a look of incredulity and disbelief on his face.

'What is it?' she asked. 'Surely you guessed Jayne's son would still be living here with his new family!'

He said nothing, but Donald was the one to speak as soon as he saw that look.

'Jayne said there was something familiar about the boy that you might notice, that's why she didn't want to make contact with you again.'

'Do you know who his father is?' David asked quietly.

Donald inclined his head.

'Yes, she told me just before she died.'

'Who?' David asked, a presentiment stealing over him.

'Can't you guess?'

There was a single streak of white hair curling over the boy's forehead, made more evident by the darkness of the rest of his hair – the same single streak as his own father had. There was a picture in the hallway at Bannerman's of him as a boy, together with his brothers, and the likeness to him was remarkable.

'I can, but I'm hoping I'm wrong.'

'No, you're not. The boy's father is your own father, Hector Bannerman.'

David said nothing, his face blanching. He'd always wanted to believe he was wrong and that his father wasn't making inappropriate advances towards Jayne, but now he knew he wasn't.

Why, oh why, hadn't he made her go away with him when he'd wanted her to? None of this might ever have happened if he'd made sure she did.

FIVE YEARS LATER

'Anna, they've got it! Permission's been granted!'

Anna was unloading washing from the machine as David entered the kitchen. She dropped the box of pegs she'd been carrying at the sudden sound of his voice.

'What are you talking about?' she said, as she surveyed the sea of plastic pegs surrounding her.

'Bannerman's! That developer who bought it – I told you he'd applied for planning permission to turn it into five apartments – it's just been granted!'

'I thought there'd been a lot of objection to it! How come he's managed to get it passed?'

'The objections came mainly from the locals. They didn't want more traffic going past their homes in the future, but it seems that the Council have had plans of their own in the pipeline as well. There's going to be a road built on the other side of Bannerman's, and they need some of its land to make that happen. Provided they can use that land, and the developer uses the access to the homes from that new road, they've no objection to his plans. The original access is to be permanently blocked off as a condition of the permission being granted.'

He seemed gleeful as she looked into his face.

'I didn't think you'd be pleased by it. I thought you'd have been one of the objectors when it's been in your family for so long.'

'Me? Why should I? If my father's watching, he'd turn in his grave. It serves the old bastard right – I have no love left for him or the house after what he did to my sister, and he'd have been really angry that Jayne's husband inherited the whole place. He's made a killing out of it. As far as I'm concerned my father can rot in hell! He's got exactly what he deserved!'

She'd never seen him like this before – it was a side she'd never even known existed.

'Please David, watch what you say. Young ears may be listening,' looking round to make sure they weren't close at hand.

'He was busy on his X-box last time I saw him,' David said. 'We're going to have to regulate the time he spends on that, you know. He should be spending more time playing outdoors or reading some of the books he's been set for his coursework.'

'Oh, I'm watching that all right,' she said, as she bent over, starting to pick up the pegs, and wincing with the effort.

Seeing the look on her face, he said, 'Here let me do that. You've only a few weeks before you drop the sprog. You should be taking things a bit easier.'

'I know,' she answered, 'but it's not easy when there's three of us to look after at the moment, and I'll need more help from you when the baby comes. You'll need to get off you ar...,' stopping in mid sentence as a young boy came into the kitchen.

'I know what you were going to say,' he said, grinning, 'and Uncle David tells me off for saying that, so you shouldn't say it either.'

She and David exchanged wry grins before she said, 'You're quite right Fergus. I'll mind what I say in the future.'

'And don't worry about help when the baby comes. I'll help you with her, and I'll make sure uncle David gets off his arse to help too before I go back to Scotland after the holidays. She will be born before then, won't she?'

'I hope so,' she answered, looking towards David, 'but you'll see her at Christmas anyway. We've been invited to spend Christmas with Donald and your step-sisters – then everybody will have to get off their arses and help!'